the forbidden note

REDWOOD KINGS BOOK 4

NELIA ALARCON

Copyright © 2023 by Nelia Alarcon

All rights reserved.

No part of this publication may be reproduced, distributed, or transmitted in any form or by any means, including photocopying, recording, or other electronic or mechanical methods, without the prior written permission of the publisher, except as permitted by U.S. copyright law. For permission requests, contact the author at neliaalarcon.com.

The story, all names, characters, and incidents portrayed in this production are fictitious. No identification with actual persons (living or deceased), places, buildings, and products is intended or should be inferred.

Book Cover by GetCovers

First edition 2023

Chapter One

GRACE 'GREY' JAMIESON

Six Months Ago

The card slips from my hand and falls into the bartender's. His eyes regard me with pity as he fixes my drink and returns with it.

It must be all over my face.

The pain.

The sorrow.

It won't be there for long. I plan on blowing the last of my savings to get hammered.

Tonight marks the end.

Or more like the beginning of the end.

I take a sip and people-watch.

A couple on the opposite end of the bar whisper to each other.

The woman giggles.

The guy smirks.

A moment later, they get up and leave.

I slide a chipped fingernail around the rim of my cup as a wound in my chest throbs.

What would it feel like to look at someone like that? To love someone like that? What would it feel like if every minute of every day wasn't tainted in blood?

I tilt my drink back.

It's bitter at first, but warm as it slides down my throat.

The music in the bar is loud and invasive.

Can't they turn it down?

No, Grey. You don't come to a bar and ask the manager to turn down the music.

I'm such an idiot.

For pulling on this short, barely-there dress.

For slipping into these stupidly high heels.

For thinking I could do this without her.

I don't belong here.

She was the brave one. The one who flashed fake IDs at the bartender and didn't bat an eyelash. Dragged me to the dance floor. Made complete fools of ourselves as we flailed to the music.

'Damn, you take everything so seriously, Grey. Loosen up!'

Sometimes, it feels like everyone in the world is living in 'normal' mode. I'm the only one in Bizzaro land.

She was the person who made me human.

"A beautiful woman like you shouldn't be frowning like that," says a man to my right.

The chair had been empty a second ago. I hadn't noticed when it became occupied.

I tighten my fingers around the cup and look at him. "Excuse me?"

"You need another drink." He snaps his fingers at the bartender. "Yo! Another round for the lady."

The bartender, busy with other customers, doesn't even glance up.

I'd do the same.

"Geez, can I get some service around here?" He slams his hands on the counter, drawing more eyes and making me squirm in second-hand embarrassment.

"I don't want another drink." I ease off the bar stool. Grab my purse. Scramble to get away from him.

"Don't be like that. Look." He flashes cash in my face. "I've got money. I'll pay for it."

Wow.

"I'm fine," I say tightly.

The stranger glances at my chest that's bursting out of my low-cut dress. A slow, lecherous grin crosses his mouth. "Sweetheart, you didn't come here tonight looking like that, expecting to leave alone, did you?"

My skin bristles.

Yet another strike in the *'should have stayed home'* column.

"You here with someone?" He leans forward, getting in my face. The overpowering scent of his cologne makes me nauseous.

"I'm not interested," I say, trying to wave the bartender over so I can get my card and leave.

He chuckles and grabs my arm. "Baby, that's not what I asked."

I freeze, my heartbeat accelerating. Everything inside me wants to throw my drink in his face and run, but I can't move.

Do I make a scene or just keep quiet?

My heart burns.

My eyes drop to the floor.

It's easier to keep my mouth shut.

It's what I've done all my life.

You're only one person. You can't change anything. You can't make a difference.

But that was the old me.

I have a mission, a new job.

I'm moving back to that despicable city... to make a change.

I'm done being quiet.

As I open my mouth, a dark voice slices the air behind me.

"Does she look like your 'baby'?"

Shocked, I glance up. All I can see is the back of a black T-shirt stretching over wide shoulders as a man brushes past me. He stands guard in front of my chair, fingers loose, legs firm. In his back pocket are a pair of worn drumsticks.

The jerk flings to his feet. "Who the hell are you?"

"None of your business." There's venom in that tone. A hint of gravel. Like an otherworldly beast in a classic Greek tale.

I see the jerk's shifty eyes pinballing between me and the stranger.

Why don't you give him a show?

The thought sounds like her.

It makes me smile. Makes me feel like she's still here.

I want to chase that feeling, chase it all the way off a cliff if I have to.

Angling my body toward the stranger, I smile. "Why are you so late?"

Shocking blue eyes, like pieces ripped out of the sky, beam down on me. It's my first time getting a good look at his face and it makes my heart slam against my ribs.

This guy is *stunning*.

A little younger than I'd expect—there's a rebellious glint in his eyes and a tilt to his chin that says the world hasn't beaten the fight out of him yet—but those broad shoulders and that deep voice compile into an enticing package.

"Sorry, tiger," he says. The way his eyes dip to my lips makes my knees weak. "Traffic."

"You're kidding me," the jerk grunts. "You're not together. I saw you sitting in the corner a few minutes ago."

Shoot. We've been had.

"Are you messing with me?" The jerk grabs the stranger's collar and hauls him forward until they're nose-to-nose.

A chair topples.

The bartender glances over in alarm.

"I suggest you remove your hands."

"Or *what*, punk? You think I can't take you?"

A shiver of fear runs down my spine. Both men are around the same height, but the jerk has a bit more girth to him. It's a toss-up who'll win this fight.

Suddenly, two men approach us. They flank the stranger on either side, saying nothing and yet amping up the tension.

I glance between the newcomers. They're both tall and broad-shouldered. One is blonde. The other has silky black hair and almond-shaped eyes.

The energy in the bar shifts when the three stand together. Darkness wafts around them. An intimidating, radioactive *something* that could set off fire alarms.

The jerk looks nervous. For a second, he hesitates, shoulders ramping up, chin trembling.

One.

Two.

The face-off doesn't get to three seconds.

Scowling, the jerk drops his grip and stumbles to the exits, muttering '*she's not worth it*' under his breath.

The three strangers watch him leave with hawk-like stares.

"Thank you," I say, easing my purse over my shoulder.

The newcomer with the beautiful almond-shaped eyes stalks off, looking annoyed. The blond guy taps my rescuer on the shoulder. They exchange a loaded nod before he walks off too, blending into the darkness.

"You okay?" the stranger asks.

I nod.

There are so many words in the English language. With all the books I've read, you'd think I'd have a better grasp of them. But I'm drawing a blank.

The bartender arrives with my card.

I take it and slip it in my purse.

"Are you leaving?" The stranger looks at me.

I chew on my bottom lip. The smart thing to do is go home to my empty apartment. I have a flight tomorrow. I have my new job on Monday.

Something deep in my chest stops me.

Tonight, we're being more like her. We're being brave, remember?

I reclaim my seat. "I could use another drink."

Chapter Two

GREY

His eyes slide over me and the smile he aims my way is dangerous. "I was hoping you'd say that."

A hundred butterflies start bashing around in my stomach.

I set my card on the counter. "This round is on me."

"No way." He slides the card in my direction.

"The least I can do is buy you and your friends a drink."

"Put your card back, tiger. That's not going to happen."

"Tiger?"

He nods to my dress.

I glance down. "This is cheetah print."

"Looks like a tiger to me." His eyes stay locked on mine. He leans closer to be heard above the music. "Graceful. Sly. Pounces when the time is right. I think tiger fits you better."

A whiff of darkness, like a plume of smoke, rises inside me.

Mischievous.

A little insidious.

I swivel toward him.

Our thighs are touching, but he doesn't move away.

Neither do I.

I motion to the drumsticks. "You're a musician?"

"Struggling."

"No shame in that."

He tilts his head. "You think so?"

"It's hard to make a living. Might as well pursue what you love when you're young."

One corner of his lips arches up again. The sight of it burns me alive.

"Why are you talking like you're older than me?"

"Aren't I?"

"What?"

I take a sip. "Older than you."

"How old are you?"

"Don't you know you should never ask a woman her age?"

He squints at me. "Can I guess?"

"Be very careful." The words sound seductive. Now, I know I'm tipsy.

His eyes linger on my curly hair and move down to my lips. I feel his study like a caress on my skin.

"Twenty-four."

My brows hike.

"Am I right?"

"No." I glance away.

His lips curl up higher. "You can't lie, tiger. That's cute."

"Cute?"

"I have other adjectives, but I'm trying to be a gentleman."

My skin sizzles with every second that passes. It's been *so* long since I've felt this attracted to someone.

"What if you weren't?"

"What?"

"A gentleman?"

"Is that a challenge?"

"Just curiosity." Heart slamming against my ribs, I motion for another drink.

I've had more than three bottles tonight.

Smart Grey says slow down.

But Reckless Grey is in the driver's seat.

He extends a hand. "Nice to meet you."

I slide my hand against his palm. Warm, rough fingers close around mine. I feel the callouses on the inside of his knuckles, probably from years of playing the drums. I imagine what those rough hands would feel like on my skin, skating over my shoulders, slipping up my legs.

Embarrassed, I drop his hand and reach for my drink. It's empty.

He motions to his and I take it, knocking it back.

My best friend was better at this. Flirting. Talking to guys. They gravitated to her. Maybe that's why things ended up the way they did.

No.

That's not why.

She was innocent. The people who hurt her deserve all the blame.

"Are you okay?"

I let out a deep breath. "Fine."

"I'll buy that." He studies me. "But if you want to talk..."

"You'll be a gentleman and listen?"

"I didn't say that."

"That you'll listen?"

"That I'll be a gentleman."

I can feel the alcohol sloshing through my veins. Liquid courage. It unravels my inhibitions.

Have fun, Grey. You're going back to hell. Might as well let a hot, mysterious stranger take you to heaven first.

I reach for another drink.

He pulls it back.

I shoot him a playful look. "Can't keep up?"

"Can I at least know why we're getting wasted tonight?"

I purse my lips.

"Post breakup? Relationship drama?" A possessive glint in his eyes, he growls, "You're not taken, are you?"

"No."

"Good."

"Good?"

"You looked upset when you walked in tonight," he says. "I thought I'd have to pummel someone on your behalf."

"You saw me when I got here?"

"You were the only thing I could see."

"Me or the cheetah print?"

He laughs. It's a low, booming sound. Like the instrument he plays. "I take it you're not really an animal print person."

"Tonight, I'm an animal print person."

He leans in, his mouth brushing my ear. "And tomorrow?"

He's flirting.

I usually can't tell, but I can see it clear as day.

His body is still leaning toward mine, sheltering me. He smells so good. Like leather and spice.

I want it.

I want him.

Is it really okay for me to have him? To have this one thing? To make this one potentially stupid decision?

"Let's not worry about tomorrow," I whisper.

"Do you mean that?"

"Yes," I say breathlessly.

His voice an easy, over-confident purr, he says, "You want to leave with me?"

I blink in shock.

"Careful, tiger." His voice holds a hint of a warning. "Because the moment I have you alone, I'm not going to take my hands off until every inch of you belongs to me."

Anticipation zips up my spine.

"I don't..." I lick my lips. "I don't usually do this."

"Do what?"

I gesture between the two of us, heart in my throat even as excitement skitters through me.

"Can I tell you a secret?"

I nod.

He puts his lips against my ear. "I like you."

"Already?"

"Already."

"Why?"

He purses his lips. "Your tits."

I roll my eyes.

He smiles. "I liked you the moment I laid eyes on you. I couldn't help myself. And I don't screw women I like, tiger. It's a personal rule."

My body sways forward. I curl my fingers over his shoulder—to steady myself. To keep him close.

"Is there a but?"

"There shouldn't be."

"But..."

"But," he breathes in, eyes closed, and it feels like he's inhaling me, "I'll make you the exception."

"The exception. That's a nice line. Very original."

He smiles again. Impossibly long lashes splay over tan cheeks.

I notice that I'm moving my hands over his defined shoulder muscles. It's a bold move. I'm not a bold woman, and yet I don't stop.

"My flight leaves tomorrow morning," I whisper.

He looks up with those smoldering blue eyes. "Then we better make tonight count."

Chapter Three

GREY

His fingers are warm and rough against mine as he pulls me through the lobby, parting the crowd with his long-legged stride and dark charisma.

My limbs are all liquid.

Every inch of me is pounding with frantic heat.

This isn't me.

And yet, here I am, diving headfirst into the thrill of a passionate night with a stranger.

We stop in front of the elevator and he punches the button too many times. How high is his suite?

The thought disintegrates when he pulls me into the elevator. The doors barely close before he's on me, hands around my waist and pushing me against the wall.

Sea-blue eyes swirling with gold flecks, his lips a breath away from mine. Calloused hands slide into the back of my hair, gripping my curls. His other hand sinks under my skirt.

I whimper, already feeling the throbbing build of satisfaction when his hands sweep my inner thigh. It's been so long since I've burned. Since I've moaned. Since I've thrummed with pleasure. The parts of me that long to be teased, sucked and licked are crying out in need.

"You have no right to look that gorgeous wearing a freaking animal," he growls, fingers skating over my quivering flesh.

"Will you finally admit it's cheetah?"

"Will you finally give me a name?"

"No names." I suck in a breath.

"Let me guess. You're a spy out to steal my heart?"

I chuckle.

He brings his finger to my lips and traces my mouth. A breath skitters out as he teases the inner lining. "You have a beautiful smile."

"You have beautiful eyes," I whisper. "But I bet you've heard that before."

"Not from someone who says it like you do."

He makes it sound like I'm important. Like I'm special. Different from anyone he's slept with before.

It's probably just a line, one he uses to get women to fall for him.

But I give myself permission to believe it.

At least until the morning.

Come on, Grey. Do something. When will you get a chance like this again?

In a streak of courage, I slide my hands down his chest and to his pants. His breath catches and I feel a surge of confidence.

He's powerful and masculine.

Everything about him sets my body on fire. His deep voice. His cocky smirk. His roaming hands.

And for tonight, he's mine.

All six-foot plus of him.

"Bad girl," he teases. His lips coast over my throat as his fingers trace a slow, seductive line under my skirt. "Did you lie when you said this was your first time?"

I'm trembling, aching with need as he grinds his hips on me. "Maybe you're the one who makes me bold."

My skin tingles as he closes his mouth over my shoulder and nips it with his teeth. Breathing hard, he whispers, "Be as bold as you like, tiger. As *wicked* as you like. Tonight, I'll show you what it means to come to the dark side."

We stare at each other.

A look of understanding.

Of danger.

I know instinctively that I'm about to step off a cliff.

It's going to hurt when I slam to the bottom, but on the way down...

The view is going to be amazing.

Desire.

Lust.

Passion.

It swirls in the air between us.

The sound of our ragged breathing is so loud that I barely hear the elevator ding.

He takes my hand again.

Each step to the hotel room builds the anticipation.

The way he carries himself is already a teasing promise. Every inch of him drips with seductive strength and skill. I can't wait to feel him. To have my hands full of him. To breathe in his pleasure as I breathe out my own.

He slams his keycard against the door.

It lights up green.

A moment later, I'm being yanked inside and he slams the door shut with his foot.

There's no formality.

No shyness.

Just a driving force that demands I touch him everywhere and anywhere and all at once.

Inside the dark room, we claw at each other. Our bodies collide like rolling thunder. The pure chaos of reaching hands, discarded clothes, low moans and the heat of his mouth on my chest.

I wrestle him out of his T-shirt just so I can run my hands down his shoulders, arms and back. He teases me with his tongue and I groan, barely able to see clearly as he walks me backwards and tips me on the bed.

He climbs over me.

Limbs trembling, I run my hands over his shoulders and then press them into the small of his back, driving us together. His weight crushes me into the mattress.

Black hair falling over his forehead and screaming blue eyes wild with hunger, he growls, "You are so freaking tempting."

"So are you." I wrap an arm around his neck, rocking our hips together.

I have no idea who this sultry, seductive Grey is, but I like her.

His lips curl up in a wicked smile. Eyes locked on mine, he drops a kiss on my throat. Then lower, on my stomach.

Grabbing both my legs, he drags me to the edge of the bed and kneels in front of me. In mere seconds, he has me writhing, squirming, screaming in a way I never have before.

His mouth and fingers are greedy for as much as he can

get, devouring me until my voice goes hoarse and I devolve into breathless pants.

I'm begging for more by the time he works his way back up my body, but he doesn't rush. Instead, he slides his hands over me, tracing every line, every curve, every scar and making me feel like a priceless work of art.

"So beautiful," he murmurs, kissing my shoulders, behind my neck, the back of my legs. "So, so beautiful."

I reach for him, desperate to be put out of my misery.

He stops to grab protection and then he's back on me.

His invasion is sharp.

Swift.

A painful twinge rips my stomach.

I wonder if I signed myself up for more than I could handle.

It's too much.

And yet not enough.

"You okay?"

I exhale. Nod.

"Just breathe." He sets his forehead on mine, eyes on me and watching for every muscle twitch in my face. "I got you, tiger."

It truly sounds like he cares.

My heart flips over.

A strange sensation fills me. A softening of my heart. Like a thread of solid gold slithering through a pitch-black night.

For a moment, everything is still. Suspended in time. A perfect rhapsody of sensations and smells. The slick heat of our skin. The ridges of his muscular chest. The way our bodies connect, heat sinking into heat.

And then he moves.

A thick friction that sends me bursting into flames.

I claw at his back.

Gasp in shock.

Pull him closer.

My body snaps apart with a furious need and I understand keenly that he meant what he said in the bar.

I won't stop until every inch of you belongs to me.

The bed creaks.

Our moans fill the room.

I'm being torn apart from the inside and put back together with his name stained into every part of me.

He keeps going, not stopping until I'm on the edge again. I lose all sense of time, of everything except his body on mine, faster, deeper, harder.

Just as the world shatters and lights explode behind my eyes, I feel him lean down and kiss me passionately. He relishes my lips, drinking from them as if he'll never get enough.

My fingers dig into his side and I kiss him back for all I'm worth.

When he catches his breath, he braces his elbows on either side of my head and looks down at me. There's a hint of surprise in his gaze. "It's not..."

"Usually like that?" I laugh and slide my hands down his side.

His hair is rumpled from my fingers and he looks deliciously sexy. My heart flips again.

"You're bad for me, tiger."

"Why?"

"When I'm with you, I want to break all my rules."

Our gazes lock and hold.

His phone starts ringing in the distance.

I start to get up.

He pushes me back down.

"Shouldn't you get that?" I point out, smiling as he grabs my waist again. "It could be your friends from the bar."

"Uh-uh." His voice a low grumble, he flips me over. "I told you I'd make tonight count." Mouth descending on my back, he growls, "The night's not over yet."

* * *

My eyes burst open in alarm—crap! The sun is way too high in the sky.

I spring upright, hissing when I see the time on my phone.

Shoot. Shoot. Shoot.

I search frantically for my clothes and glance back at the slumbering stranger who made me scream in about five different languages.

His back is filled with scratch marks, evidence of the way I clawed at his skin in passion. It was all I could do to contain myself when it felt like he was literally splitting me apart.

The stranger was right.

He's no gentleman.

The way he devoured my lips…

He was brutal. Rough. As wild as his love-making.

Heat climbs up my chest.

How could a man totally destroy my body while making it feel so good?

He's a beast.

An animal unrestrained.

Barely human.

And I lapped up every second of it.

My fingers tremble at the memory of his delectable mouth groaning low in my ear as he plowed me into the mattress.

What. The actual. Hell.

I swallow hard and push off the bed.

The night is gone.

The woman I was last night is gone too.

I ended this era with a bang. Literally.

It's time to step into my new life.

I dress gingerly, feeling the soreness in my muscles and hoping the strong, latching kisses he left on my neck don't turn into bruises. My light brown skin can hide blushes, but it can't hide love bites from ridiculously sexy strangers.

My shoes clop together as I balance them on the edge of my fingers.

This is my first walk of shame.

Might as well make it memorable.

I take one more look at the stranger and feel a slight zip of unease. He seems younger in the morning light with his eyes closed and his hair a mess of violet-black strands. Not quite a man, but definitely not a boy.

I withhold a groan.

I can't believe I had a one-night-stand with a college student.

Without the gripping hand of alcohol around my neck, I'm starting to wonder if I made a mistake.

It doesn't matter.

Even if it was a mistake, I'm leaving it behind too.

The door closes softly behind me and I rush to make my flight.

In a plane high over the clouds, I whisper goodbye to my past.

At least I think I do.

But the past swaggers into my classroom one month later.

Wearing a Redwood Prep uniform.

And calling me Miss Jamieson.

Chapter Four

GREY

Present Day

Eerie silence fills the room. It's dark except for the one, lone light hanging from the ceiling.

The air stinks of bleach and the unmistakeable scent of death.

I'm standing in a circle.

To my left, Zane is leaning against the wall, arms folded over his chest.

To my right, Cadence is holding her little sister.

We're all staring at the woman on the metal roll-out. Eyes closed. Lips blue. Fingers flat on a sterile metal sheet.

The dead body is... well... dead.

And it surprises me how relieved most of the people in this room are to see that.

My teeth slide between my bottom lip as I glance at

Cadence, waiting for the opportune moment to offer support.

That moment never comes.

Maybe it never will.

For one thing, she has Dutch, Zane and Finn here to comfort her.

For another, I don't think she's grieving.

I could be wrong. Everyone expresses sorrow in their own way, but I've seen grief before. The way it crushes you. Twists you in a vice grip. It's like having your heart ripped out of your chest and tossed into the ocean.

I've tasted darkness. Hopelessness. Loss.

And I don't get that vibe from Cadence.

She looks resigned rather than mournful.

Or maybe she's just so shocked she's gone numb.

"I'll give you a moment," I say, sensing that this is a private gathering.

"You can stay, Miss Jamieson," Cadence says bleakly. Her solemn brown eyes move to me. "And thank you."

"It's..." I choke on the words 'my pleasure'.

It's not that it was a hassle.

I just don't think responding to a call from the police about a student's mother being found in the back of an alley is something I should attach the words 'my pleasure' to.

"Are you sure?" Viola, Cadence's little sister, cries out. The two girls look alike, but Viola seems more fragile than her sister. "Are you sure she's dead this time?"

This time?

Cadence walks right up to the dead body and pokes it.

My jaw drops.

Dutch snorts.

Zane shuffles his feet and coughs into his hand.

Finn narrows his eyes in disgust.

"I'm sure," Cadence says flatly.

My eyes travel from her dull expression to the body and back again. The light above us flickers and it feels like I'm in a classic horror novel. *Frankenstein. Dr. Jekyll and Mr. Hyde. Dracula.*

I may not be a guidance counsellor, but I don't think these kids are okay.

Viola covers her face with her hands. Her dark hair flails against shoulders that shake with her sobs.

My heart aches for her.

Whatever Cadence's complicated relationship with her mother, it's clear that Viola had a much different experience.

"Sorry, Vi," Dutch Cross says. His tall form casts a shadow over the cadaver.

He doesn't look sorry.

More like annoyed.

Cadence just stares at her mother's body, unmoving from her place at the head of the metal slab.

Viola cries louder.

Zane gives her a hug. He's much bigger than her. Covered in tattoos. A bad boy in a groomsman tux. But, when he brushes his fingers over the little girl's face, he's gentle.

Viola turns into him and hugs his waist.

Touching Cadence's shoulder, I say, "I'll wait outside."

Zane catches my eye as I slip past him to get to the door. I pretend not to see and stop in the lobby just outside the morgue.

The air is cleaner here. Not as cloying. Not as much bleach.

I press my hand against the wall and place a fist to my chest.

Memories of another dead body fill my head.

Except her body wasn't in one piece.

Don't think about it.

I cover my stomach with one hand and try not to hyperventilate.

The sound of heels clicking prompts me to turn around.

Cadence, Viola and the Cross brothers are walking out of the morgue. Cadence's fingers are tight in the skirt of her fluffy white dress. Her little sister is under her arm, still crying. The sound of her stifled sobs make my stomach turn.

A nurse enters the room.

She glances at Dutch first, gaze lingering on his face and then moves to Finn before landing on Zane. She bounces around the three of them, her eyes widening in shock after every rotation.

Not surprising.

The Cross brothers paint a terrifyingly beautiful picture. Today, they're all standing in three-piece suits and tuxes, their hair carefully styled. Each one of them is intimidating in their own right, but together? They own every room they enter, just like they own Redwood Prep.

Zane doesn't shy away from the nurse's ogling. He crosses his arms over his chest, his hot, menacing slash of a mouth curling up. Like his twin, Zane is over six feet but his eyes are sapphire blue rather than whiskey-amber and his hair is an almost purple-black.

The nurse blushes harder.

I feel a stab of annoyance.

"Did you need something?" I ask, prompting her.

"Ah yes." She manages to rip her eyes from Zane. Her

words are aimed at Cadence. "The police would like to speak with you."

Viola stiffens and grabs her sister's arm.

It feels like I'm missing something, but I'm not sure I want to know what *it* is.

"Dutch," Cadence says.

He nods. "I know."

"Vi, go with—"

"Finn, can you watch Viola?" Dutch speaks at the same time.

Cadence's eyebrows tighten. "I meant for you to—"

"I know what you meant," he answers gruffly. "And if you think for a freaking minute that I'll leave you to handle the cops alone, you don't know me at all."

The two glare at each other.

I watch them both.

The teenagers make an unusual pair.

Cadence Cooper is a gifted piano prodigy. At the start of the school year, she was recruited by my friend Henry Mulliez—the previous music teacher at Redwood.

Henry asked me to look out for her when he left, but I would have done it anyway. Cadence and I have a lot in common.

We're both scholarship kids.

We both come from broken homes.

We both have a Cross-sized target on our backs.

Unfortunately for her, she couldn't outrun Dutch.

I have no plans of following a similar path with Zane.

Even if I *wanted* to—which I don't—it wouldn't be possible.

For many reasons.

Finn escorts Viola out of the room while Cadence and Dutch leave with the nurse to speak to the police.

My duty as a teacher is done.

Besides, the last thing I want to be is alone with Zane Cross.

I make a break for it.

Zane's answering footsteps pound through the hallway.

I hasten my stride and make it all the way outside when he decides to end the chase. In three giant footsteps, he's in front of me.

"Hold up, tiger."

I stiffen at the name. My eyes dart around the parking lot.

It's relatively empty this early in the day, but that doesn't mean people aren't watching. Listening.

"I told you not to speak to me," I hiss.

One side of his lips curl up in that devil-may-care smirk. He draws closer. "Is there some law against me talking to my step-sister?"

My stomach churns at the term.

Zane Cross does not look at me like I'm his step-sister.

And the things he's done to me...

Damn.

I put myself in an awkward position by accidentally sleeping with a student, but Zane Cross being my brother?

That's all mom.

I have no idea why she showed up married to Jarod Cross of all people. She explained it a hundred times and it still doesn't make sense.

Why would Jarod Cross, a living, breathing musical legend fall for a random waitress at a truckstop diner? Why would he get married to her after only a few weeks?

Zane narrows his eyes, turning serious. "We need to talk."

"About what?"

"Have you noticed anyone following you?" He glances at my car. "Or felt like you were being tailed?"

"No."

His jaw muscles work.

"Why are you asking that?"

"I have a bad feeling about this."

"About Cadence's mother being dead?"

"About who might be behind it."

The accusation behind his words give me pause. "What does that mean?"

He doesn't answer.

"They say it was an overdose," I remind him.

The serious look disappears, instantly replaced by his signature smirk. "Just to be safe, why don't you move out of dad's house and move into mine? Nowhere is safer than in my bed."

Of course, he's messing with me.

I scoff. "Now that we're here, I want to speak to you about something too."

He tilts his head.

"It's about what you did that day."

"What day?" He leans down. His warm breath fans my lips. "You have to be more specific."

I feel a shudder run down my spine, but I steel myself against it. "When we're at school, I am your teacher. If you ever," I step closer to him and poke a finger in his chest, "pick me up and throw me over your shoulder like that again—"

"You'll what?" He moves into me, his nose practically on top of mine.

My heartbeat pounds.

"Put me on time out?" Zane taunts. "*Spank* me?" His voice is deep and rumbles through me, scratching at the parts of me that have never forgotten his touch. "What's my punishment, Miss Jamieson?"

My nostrils flare. I step back. "Rule number one, don't speak to me unless you have to. Rule number two, don't touch me. Rule number three, always return to rules one and two."

He licks his lips, a flash of a pink tongue over full lips. "Sorry." He shrugs. "I'm not the type to follow rules."

"Zane," I growl.

He smirks, sticks his hands into his pockets and walks away.

I glare daggers into his strong back.

Zane Cross is a tall, tattooed menace. He has an air of danger around him that's only gotten stronger since our first meeting. It doesn't help that he has a bomb that could explode all over my career and ruin my mission at Redwood Prep.

I wish with all my heart that I'd never laid eyes on him.

He turns back, sees me still watching and winks.

Disgusted, I yank my car door open and climb in.

I don't know what's worse—having a one-night stand with a student or having a one-night stand with my stepbrother.

Either way, I'm ruined if anyone finds out.

My phone buzzes.

I glance at the screen as a hum careens through my veins.

I've got a new message.

From Jinx.

* * *

Unknown Number: You've been a very naughty girl, Miss Jamieson. Are you holding out on me? Trade a secret for a secret. What's going on between you and Snare King?

Unknown Number: By the way, save this number. And I suggest you spill fast before I find out for myself. Something tells me, Redwood Prep isn't ready for its first Snare Queen.

Chapter Five

ZANE

"They say it's bad luck to have a funeral after a wedding." I wrap my fingers around the soda can, but I don't drink. It doesn't have the same kick as a strong, cold beer.

"Who's 'they'?" Finn asks, lounging in the pool chair with a book in his hand.

"And why the hell should we care what *they* think," Dutch adds.

"You know, I actually haven't heard that." I lean back on my elbows. My legs, up to mid-thigh, are in the pool. "But it should be a thing. A wedding and a funeral on the same day feels like bad freaking luck to me."

"We actually haven't had the funeral yet," Finn points out, flipping a page of his book. "We just identified the body."

"Still bad luck."

"I don't believe in luck. I believe in Cadey," Dutch says. "I believe in us."

Finn makes a face.

I splash water in my twin's direction. "You're despicable." I point a finger at the man who, hours ago, went from single to husband in a hot New York minute.

I swear, there was a point I thought Dutch wouldn't ever get it together. Or maybe that he *shouldn't* get it together.

But the impossible happened.

Dutch and Cadey are like oil and water yet, somehow, they figured it out.

My situation is different.

Vastly more complicated.

A spectacular crapstorm of 'Do Not Enter' signs.

Damn, but I do like trespassing in places I don't belong.

"What's wrong with what I said?" Dutch frowns.

"You're being sentimental."

"No, I'm not."

"You like Cadence—"

"I *love* Cadence."

I spray more water at him. "Get this married man away from me. He's turned into a sap."

Dutch jumps back to avoid getting splashed and scowls in my direction. "I can still break your neck."

"You want to see more dead bodies today?" I fire back.

Dutch thinks about it and grunts, backing off.

Love should have softened him, but it hasn't. At least, not towards us.

To Cadey?

Guy's a doormat.

To everyone else, he's just as snarly and gruff as ever. Maybe even more so now that he has the weight of a family to protect.

I know he takes that crap seriously—being a husband. Maybe even a father someday... hopefully soon.

Of the three of us, Dutch is the most ready for that kind of life.

"How's Cadey holding up?" Finn asks.

"She's insisting she's fine and wants to do everything by herself."

"That why you're here drinking with us instead of at her apartment helping her pack?"

Dutch scowls. "She told me to come home. Said I'm breathing down her neck."

"For the record, women never push me away when I'm breathing down their neck."

"Is that why I saw Miss Jamieson ripping you a new one in the parking lot?" Dutch spits back.

Touché, brother.

I take a swig rather than admit defeat.

Dutch stares straight ahead. "Cadey wants to go through her mother's things on her own. I agreed to give her a few hours."

"Marriage is about compromise," Finn says wisely.

Dutch's wedding ring glints in the light as he lifts his beer. "I'll let her pack on her own. I'll even let her decide where we live. But I'm hiring a funeral parlor so she doesn't have to think about all those details. She's got enough on her plate."

"She'll still have to direct the funeral people. Tell them what she wants," Finn says.

I glance at my brother. "How do you know that?"

"That's common-sense."

"I'd rather she didn't mess with this funeral at all. It was bad enough she had to lie to the police and falsely identify a dead body last year. This year, she's doing it all over again. Except she has Viola's grief to handle on top of her own. She shouldn't have to go through the motions of a memorial service twice."

I twirl my drumstick around my fingers. "I'll do it."

Both Finn and Dutch stare at me.

"You'll do what?" Dutch blinks slowly.

"I'll plan the funeral."

"Like hell you will," my twin grunts.

"What's wrong with me planning it?"

"You?" Dutch's eyebrows fly to the top of his head. "Between you and Sol, I don't know who skips class the most. You barely show up to gigs sober and you want to plan a funeral for my wife?"

"Ugh." I groan. "You're going to throw that phrase in as often as possible, aren't you?"

"She *is* my wife."

I shudder dramatically again.

"Let him be," Finn says, turning the page. "The funeral is cutting into his honeymoon. Plus we have school on Monday. Things are going to get a lot less romantic. He might as well experience *some* benefit of being married."

"Makes sense. Having to identify your mother-in-law's dead body can put a damper in the bedroom."

Dutch scowls harder and takes another sip.

I fall into the beach chair beside my twin. "Come on. Let me plan it. It'll be fun."

"The fact that you put fun and funeral in the same sentence is already a bad sign," Finn says dryly, eyes never leaving his book.

"Not helping, Finny."

Finn looks up at me with a hard stare. "Don't call me that."

THE FORBIDDEN NOTE

I grin.

The one thing I love most in the world—more than beautiful girls getting on their knees for me, more than a sweet drum solo with sweat rolling down my back, more than Miss Jamieson shooting fire from her eyes and telling me to back the hell off...

Okay, not that last one.

Miss Jamieson raining hellfire on me, those plump lips mashing together, just begging for me to plunder them is the *only* thing I love more than messing with my brothers.

"Fine." Dutch glowers at me. "But nothing crazy."

"Would you define strippers bursting out of a casket as 'crazy'?"

"Zane," Dutch growls.

I smirk. "Got it. Keep it tasteful."

"Respectful," Dutch snaps. "Viola's having a hard time. I don't want her to be in even more pain after the service is over."

"Look at him being a dad." I point a proud finger in Dutch's direction.

Finn just rolls his eyes.

My phone rings.

"Damn," I hiss under my breath.

"What?" Dutch arches a brow.

"It's Sol." I show them the phone. "I told him we're back in town, and he's coming over."

Finn sits straight up, a worried look crossing his face.

I stare at Dutch next. It was his idea to leave Sol out of the wedding. There's something weird going on between those two. And since Sol is like a brother to us, the only thing that could cause friction is Cadey.

Should have figured this would happen when I saw

how obsessed my twin was with both 'Redhead' and Cadence Cooper.

I love my brother.

But I know he'd plunge a knife in our backs for Cadey's sake.

He'd find a way to bring us back from the dead—even if it meant going down to hell himself. But he'd still shove the knife in.

"He's going to be pissed," I mutter.

Finn rubs the back of his neck.

"Let him," Dutch says casually.

I scowl in response. "We don't do this, Dutch. We don't fight over girls."

"She's not a girl. She's *my wife*."

"So you've said." My eyebrows crash together. I didn't like the thought of leaving Sol out of the loop. Now that the moment of reckoning is upon us, it feels like an even worse decision.

Sol has been through a lot this year.

Most of it is our fault.

I might be a heartless bastard most of the time, but I own my damage.

"Screw this. I need a beer." I hop off the chair and stalk into the house.

On the way back, I overhear Finn and Dutch talking.

"You think dad has something to do with it too?"

"I'm seriously considering if I should hire a protection team for Cadey."

"She'll hate that."

"Yeah, but it's better than something bad happening to her."

I step onto the pool deck. "Dad being involved in this crap? Yeah, I had the same thought."

Dutch and Finn stare at me.

"What?" I sink into the chair, my eyebrows tightening. "I'm not an idiot."

"No one said you were," Finn says calmly.

"Someone helped Cadence's mom fake her death in the first place. Now, she conveniently overdosed and died right after we find out about the inheritance. Something's off."

"I don't want to think dad is a killer," Dutch says. "He's a twisted, manipulative, psychotic bastard. But murderer is next level."

"Who's a murderer?"

We all jump at the voice.

Sol stands in the sliding glass doorway, his eyes on Dutch. He's been our best friend since we were kids. Practically a Cross by association.

"Sit down," Dutch says gravely.

Sol gives him a wary look.

"We need to talk," I add.

"About what?" Sol asks.

"About everything."

* * *

Sol takes it well, although I'm not sure how any sane person is supposed to respond when he finds out that...

A: Dutch got married to Cadence—partly because of an inheritance our grandmother left us which states we need to be married and have a son to qualify.

B: Our dad sent Cadence out of the country to keep her from Dutch, got Dutch arrested and he might also be responsible for murdering Cadence's mother.

And C: Dutch will now actively and intentionally proceed to get Cadence pregnant.

"You good?" Finn clasps a hand over Sol's shoulder.

He blinks slowly.

I think we broke him for real this time.

Dutch's phone goes off.

From the way he shoots to his feet, I know it's Cadence calling.

"Gotta go," he says gruffly. Picking his way past the scattered beer cans, he hustles out the door.

Finn checks his watch and snaps his book closed. "I'm heading off too."

I don't ask where he's going. Not like he'd tell us anyway.

Finn is like a magic mirror. He only reveals what he wants and if he doesn't want to show anything—screw you.

I lean back on my elbow and twirl my drumsticks.

Sol turns to face me. "Why the hell did all that happen and you didn't tell me a thing?"

"Ask Dutch."

Sol's voice is sharp enough to cut. "Like I'm doing that."

I ease up and stare at the man I consider a brother.

"What?" Sol takes a sip of the beer. The sun is setting and the moon is already out, reflecting on the blue of the pool.

"Do you really have feelings for her?"

Sol's shoulders stiffen, but that's the only indication that he's affected by my question.

He says nothing for a long time.

I wait, already sensing what the answer is.

"She's like me." He squints into the distance, fingers tightening around his beer can. "It feels like we're made of the same stuff. Like we beat with the same heart."

"Sounds like love to me."

"It's deeper than that. I want to protect her like I couldn't protect myself."

That is deep.

I let the comment sit because I can't think of a joke to lighten the tension.

Somewhere in the distance, a dog barks.

As darkness sets in fully, I struggle with what to say. I feel Sol's desolateness. It's like a person sitting between us, sipping a beer. Like a living breathing *thing* that's got a leash on him.

I face my best friend. "Have you been going to therapy?"

"Screw off, Zane."

"I'm just asking."

"No, you're asking a whole lot behind that." He gets up, crushes the beer can and tosses it. "My folks locked me up in the loony bin for months, so excuse me if I'm not a fan of doctors."

"Is that a no?"

"I've got my own form of therapy."

"Which is what?"

He stops and throws a look over his shoulder. "You don't need to worry about it."

Damn. That makes me even more worried.

Sol disappears and I'm left with the silence of my house.

It's usually like this. My brothers and I converge for a bit and then we go off to do our own things.

Alone, I default to two options—bang my heart out on the drums or bang a chick into next year. Usually, one or the other soothes my restless soul.

Tonight, I'm not feeling like going off on the drums. Music takes something out of me. It chomps at my flesh, pierces a hole in my heart and oozes out all my energy. I'm always spent after a good drum session. Just like I am after a good hookup.

I open my phone and scroll through my contacts. It would take all of two seconds to have a girl under me, groaning my name while I make her see stars.

But my night's shot after meeting Miss Jamieson.

No matter who's under me, all I'll be able to see is her face. The way her lipstick smeared over her mouth from my kisses. The way her curls got big and frizzy when I grabbed her head. The way her chest heaved, hot points piercing my sweaty skin.

No girl compares to her. Her heat. Her taste. Her groans in my ear.

The way she responded to every touch made me wonder if it was her first time. Or maybe it was just her first time being lapped up like the feast that she is.

An uncomfortable throbbing starts in my pants.

It sucks that I won't be able to find satisfaction tonight.

I sigh and pick up another soda.

The urge to drink gets stronger, like a craving that I can't control.

Fighting it back, I set the soda can down and pick myself off the lawn chair. I need to do something to keep busy.

Guess it's time to plan a funeral.

* * *

Jinx: Three kings left Redwood Prep in a cloud of mystery. Three kings returned in a blaze of glory. One came back with a ring on his finger. One came back with a book in his hand. One came back with a scandal that could rock the halls of Redwood Prep forever.

Guess which king is which?

Until the next post, keep your enemies close and your secrets even closer.

- Jinx

Chapter Six

GREY

"Good morning, Miss Jamieson."

The greetings float back and forth as I glide down the hallway.

It's a familiar phrase. One I hear almost every day after parking in Redwood Prep's fancy lot.

The hallway is crowded with students in sharp uniforms. Fancy sweaters. Pleated skirts. Knee-high socks. All the same, yet different because they customise their outfits. Accessorize with designer brands. Limited edition shoes. Expensive purses and wallets.

Perfect and privileged.

Kids like this were once my terrors and now, I'm their teacher. Strangely, it doesn't feel like I've managed to climb above the ranks. It still feels like I'm serving the rich at Redwood. I just traded a mop for a textbook.

Whispers blaze like a fire as I pass by.

I'm painfully aware of the attention, but I can't escape it.

Accusing eyes peer at me from all directions.

Seeking.

Prodding.

Curious.

What's going on between you and Snare King?

Jinx's text echoes in my mind.

For a brief moment, there's panic.

A sharp, unhinging nausea.

I breathe deeply and slide my hand over my pencil skirt.

It's been almost a year of teaching and it still happens. That discomfort. Like the first downward spiral of a rollercoaster. The way your stomach flops and jumps to your throat. The way you grip the bar for dear life. The way you scream as your heart is torn out of your chest.

But I can't scream.

I can only smile. Polite. Put-together.

I can only step through the giant doors every day and enter this world of shadows and money with as much class as I can.

No one knows what I did with Zane Cross in that hotel room.

And no one knows why I'm really here.

As long as I keep pretending that I have it all together, maybe it will start to feel that way.

Smile fixed, I spot one of my students.

"Vanya," I stop her as she's rummaging in her locker, "remember to turn in your essay before four p.m. today. I'm not offering another extension."

"Yes, Miss Jamieson."

As gently as I can, I remind her, "I understand that

you're busy with the cheer team, but you can't neglect your studies."

She nods, studying her sneakers.

The boy beside her—I'm assuming he's her boyfriend—stares at me with a sleazy gleam in his eyes. His cataloguing sweep ends with a slow lick of his lips.

"Mr. Hall," I say curtly. My tone demands that his eyes return to my face. Immediately.

"Miss J." Lifting a hand, he runs his fingers through his brown hair and the fancy watch on his wrist glitters. His Tesla key fob is hanging carelessly from a fisted hand. "I heard you denied my transfer again."

My smile disappears. Woodenly, I say, "I'm pleased by your... *enthusiasm* to join my class, but I have a select number of seats. Maybe try again next semester."

"You said that last semester."

"And it still applies. If you'll excuse me—"

He pushes off the locker. "Why are you playing hard to get?"

I freeze, my heels skating against the ground and turning into wooden pillars.

"Next year, I'll be a senior. It'll be my last chance. Your last chance."

"Mr. Hall," I struggle to keep my tone even, "I don't understand what you mean."

"You act all high and mighty with me, but you let Zane Cross bag a seat." Voice low, he whispers, "Do you two have some other arrangement?"

I tense.

The students around me hold their breath.

Hall prolongs the silence, throwing down a challenge that I can't back away from.

Prickles of irritation zip down my spine. "Perhaps,

rather than worrying about others, you should learn to write your own essays. I'm sure your tutor is tired of doing your homework for you."

Mottled red stains his cheeks.

I shove the knife in deeper. "Until you can form a cohesive sentence without assistance, it's best you keep your mouth shut rather than spouting off nonsense. It only makes you look more foolish."

A chorus of 'oohs' pepper around us.

Hall's face is hard as he stares me down, but he has no comeback.

I maintain eye contact, letting the humiliation soak in.

There's only one thing stronger than money here in Redwood and that's the truth. When it's on my side, I'm not afraid to wield it.

Satisfied that my point has been made, I continue on my way, clasping my books for dear life.

Stupid, Zane.

Stupid, stupid, stupid.

I pass a private classroom with a card slot.

It's The King's practice studio.

If anyone needs evidence that Zane and his brothers run the school, it's the fact that they have their own dedicated space and permission to play music *during* class time.

Snots like Theodore Hall understood the hierarchy.

Even if they didn't like it.

But after Zane threw me over his shoulder last week, he broke the delicate balance. One impulsive move totally destroyed the boundaries I've tried to preserve with my male students.

This is his fault.

But ultimately, it's mine.

Guys like Hall were a menace before and I, obviously, haven't done a good job at controlling them.

This is Redwood.

A place where the most affluent, powerful, and entitled children are thrown into one extravagant building. Here, rules are foisted upon them that they don't have to obey out in the real world.

And even inside Redwood Prep, there are some rules that can be broken for the right price.

It's a scary, sinister game.

I learned very quickly not to show any signs of weakness. In that sense, Redwood has already changed me. Who's to say if it's for the worse or the better?

Musical chimes ring out.

I inhale deeply, enjoying the shift in energy as students make a frantic dash for the classrooms.

In a moment, the crowd is gone.

I take my time as I stroll, not ready to go to class yet. As a teacher, that's my only privilege.

Redwood is particularly stunning today. Sunshine splashes over gleaming wooden statues. The hint of furniture cleaner and a light lemony fragrance fills the air, dragging my memories back to the days when I was more acquainted with the janitor's closet than any other room.

I can appreciate the school for its beauty—now that I'm not the one preserving that grand display. Giant arched ceilings tower overhead. Delicate windows let in tons of sunlight. I look through them and see the elegantly maintained lawn.

Money. Pretention. Secrets.

It flows through this building's veins.

Lockers mounted against the wall and the students in uniforms are the only indication Redwood serves a higher purpose. Everything about the architecture feels distant, like a cold cathedral.

I almost laugh. Redwood Prep may have the face of an ancient church, but the acts committed within these walls are far from holy.

My classroom is up ahead. I screech to a stop when I see Zane sitting in the back row. His blue eyes lock on mine, piercing me through the glass.

Unholy secrets.

I have a few of my own to toss on the Redwood Prep altar.

Heels clicking against the ground, I saunter into the classroom and set my purse on the desk.

"Good morning." Carefully looking away from Zane, I face my students. "*Romeo and Juliet*. Did anyone read the assigned chapters this weekend?"

Every hand shoots up.

I'm not surprised.

I run a tight ship. The students sitting in these chairs have *earned* the right to be there. They care about school, about college, about their futures.

My eyes slide past the raised arms until I get to Zane. He's slouched in the back, the only one without his arm up.

I've done everything I can to try and kick him out of my class, but he's still here, skating by and giving the least amount of effort.

My voice quivers. "Good. Let's begin."

As I turn and write on the board, I feel Zane's perusal.

His heavy gaze is a relentless reminder of that night.

That mistake.

That pleasure.

I turn back around, my palms sweaty.

Zane's still watching.

Taunting me with those sea blue eyes.

Distracting me with those full lips.

Making me feel like an awful human being for noticing those things about a student.

"Any questions about the chapter you read?" I ask.

A hand shoots up. "Not a question so much as a rant."

"Go ahead, Maisy."

"I read *Romeo and Juliet* and I still don't understand. Why make life so complicated? If you know you *shouldn't* be with someone, then don't. I'm tired of the drawn-out, forbidden love story. Shakespeare should write something else."

I lick my lips. "That's an interesting stance. But I'd like to point out two things. One—Shakespeare wrote many different types of plays. Two—*Romeo and Juliet* is a tragedy not a love story."

"I disagree."

My pulse begins to hum and I look up with the rest of the class to the Redwood prince lounging in his chair.

Unlike the other students who at least *try* to adhere to the school rules, Zane doesn't bother. He's a walking dress code violation from his tight-black T-shirt to his scrunched up jacket sleeves, jeans and military boots.

Tendrils of his violet-black hair skate lazily over his eyes.

I fold my arms over my chest, heat skittering down my spine. "And what do you disagree with, Mr. Cross?"

"A tragedy. A love story." He moves his drumstick back and forth. "It doesn't have to be one or the other. It can be both."

"Love stories should end in happily ever afters." Maisy is my best student and she's also competitive.

Her face mashes into a frown. "This play ends with the two main characters dying."

"But they die *because* of being crazily in love. You can't have the tragedy without the romance. That's like a one-night stand without the sex." A wicked glint in his eyes, he adds casually, "Romeo and Juliet were banging when they weren't supposed to. They knew what could happen, but they did it anyway. Even if you don't call it love, you gotta admit it's something close."

Hot pockets of sweat roll down my back.

My nostrils flare.

Zane stares me down. "Right, Miss Jamieson?"

My chest heaves.

I curl my fingers into fists.

Maisy turns to look at me.

So does the rest of the class.

I offer a wooden smile. "I think this is exactly why *Romeo and Juliet* is still relevant today. There's a lot to be discussed. Now, if we'll move on to chapter—"

"Cop out."

My eyes meet Zane's sky-blue ones, and I swear, as light as they are, I see shadows gathering like a storm to crowd his gaze.

My back stiffens. "Mr. Cross?"

"You didn't answer the question."

I narrow my eyes in response. "And what exactly was your question?"

"Falling for someone you can't have. Losing everything in the end." His eyes caress me. "Love story or tragedy?"

The rest of the class falls silent, watching our exchange keenly.

I walk behind my desk and lift my tablet. "Romeo and Juliet are teenagers in the original poem. They made the choices they did because they were young and foolish. When you're older, when you have more experience, you realize there is no love that's worth losing everything."

Maisy pushes her glasses up her nose. "I agree. If it hurts, if it's difficult, if it makes you want to die, then that's not love."

Heads bob in agreement.

"Who says?" Zane twirls his drumsticks. "What if the pain makes the pleasure even sweeter? What if denying yourself is worse than death?"

I can't help the way my breath catches and my hands shake.

Blinking rapidly, I lift my tablet to cover the way my heart thunders. "Everyone, open your books. Maisy, please start from page 56."

I finish the lecture with Zane's stare drilling into me the entire time.

The musical bells chime.

"Your assignments will be in the school app," I say. "And Mr. Cross..."

Everyone freezes when I call Zane's name.

"Can I see you for a moment?"

The way I end the question makes it sound like a demand, not a request.

Zane observes me thoughtfully, eyes stripping me apart. I glare back, unable to slip under a guise of professionalism.

Students file past, giving us curious looks.

"Later, Miss Jamieson." Maisy waves.

I nod.

As the students leave, Zane saunters behind them.

"Where do you think you're going?" My voice is sharp.

Zane's shoulder muscles go tense, but he doesn't stop

THE FORBIDDEN NOTE

walking. I'm shocked when he closes the door, locks it and lowers the blinds on the glass pane.

My heart thunders. "Keep the door open."

Zane turns. A flash of frustration filters through his gaze before he covers it with a practiced smirk. "I'd rather you yell at me in private."

"We can't do anything in private," I snap. "Open the door."

"No."

"Zane."

"You have no idea how often I've imagined this. You... asking to see me after class." He prowls toward my desk, moving like a predator on his prey. "You're getting me excited, tiger."

I stiffen. "Don't call me that."

Zane stalks closer. With that violet-black hair and black T-shirt, every step he takes seems to gather the shadows. His military boots thump the ground. He's a brutally gorgeous commander, except his army is the darkness hidden within the human heart.

The cruel twist of his lips makes me jumpy.

Between the brothers, Zane is the one more likely to smile and joke around, but he's no less dangerous. No less powerful.

I've seen the way other teachers cower before him. I've heard the whispers in the lounge. They say that Jarod Cross brought this school back to life after the shameful scandal that nearly tore Redwood apart.

They say his sons, by extension, hold all the power in this new era.

I don't care.

Zane crossed the line for the last time.

I lean in with fire in my voice. "What the hell is wrong with you?"

His lips curl up. Unruffled, as always. "What do you mean?"

A red haze settles on me. I want to punch him in the face so badly that my fingers twitch.

I shouldn't let him get to me.

And I shouldn't be holding him back after class when there are so many rumors about us.

But why the hell not?

I'll never get anywhere if he keeps this up. The only way to reclaim my respect is to fight for it.

"You know what I mean. Your little speech in class!"

"I was defending my position." He shoves both drumsticks in his back pocket. "Do you have a problem with that?"

"I told you to never mention *that incident*."

"What incident?" He arches a brow, his smile getting wider and more wicked.

I glare at him, chest heaving. Refusing to say it.

"You mean our night together." He circles me like a shark. "The night you let me touch you the way no student should touch a teacher?"

At the mere mention, the ache between my thighs burns with a desperate adrenaline.

"Do you think this is a joke?" I snap.

"You want me to cry then?"

"I want you to grow the hell up," I growl. "You're acting like a child."

His expression shifts in an instant. From careless and cocky to a smoldering wolf. He prowls toward me, all six foot plus of him crowding my space.

My eyes dart fearfully to the hallway. The door is locked, but that doesn't mean people aren't listening.

I back up. "Zane."

He stops an inch away, those painfully blue eyes boring into mine. "Miss Jamieson," Zane reaches between us and touches one of my curls with his rough, giant hands, "we both know that I am not a child."

My breathing is coming in harsh pants, and even though I despise my body for turning on me, I can't deny the effect he has.

The tension between us thickens.

Dark.

Forbidden.

But unmistakable.

I dig my fingers into the edge of the desk. "If this is how you'll be, don't come back to my class."

He laughs.

The freaking monster *laughs*.

My heart slams against my ribs and I realize that I'm in way over my head.

No wonder the other teachers duck when Zane and his brothers stalk through the hallway. No wonder crowds part to let them pass. No wonder they're denied nothing—from the principal going down to the lunch ladies.

I forgot.

Or maybe they allowed me to pretend I was different.

Zane was softer with me.

Almost kind.

But there's no kindness in his eyes now. No hint of affection.

It's just pure darkness and twisted depravity.

"This little game of ours is getting old." He narrows his eyes, a frightening chill beneath his words.

"Game? You think disrespecting me at every turn is *fun?*"

His eyebrows tighten. I feel his heat, his shattered restraint.

Every instinct tells me I should stop pushing, but I can't. A part of me wants to fight, to scold him, to do everything I can to hide the way my body still aches for him. Still longs to be shattered to pieces again. To spin out in hot, lashes of pleasure like we did that night.

Ridiculous.

Despicable.

I hate him.

I can't have him.

Damn. I shouldn't even *want* him.

"I'm not playing games with you, Zane." Our harsh breaths mingling, I spit out. "I'm your teach—"

He surges forward, pinning me against the wall and grinding his jeans into my aching core. I flutter my hands over my mouth and push back a moan.

The friction of his big body against mine sends pleasure tearing through me like a storm.

Zane bends to my ear. Too dangerous. Too dark. "I haven't been treating you like a teacher, Miss Jamieson. Not even close. But now, I think I'll give you what you're asking for."

I should move. Shove him off.

But every instinct is being shoved down by a throbbing, visceral heat.

"You do what *I* say from now on." His commanding fingers brush down my hip and tease a circle against the bone. "That's how I treat my teachers at Redwood." He slides his hands lower. "Especially the ones who forget their place."

"Get off—"

His mouth rocks toward mine.

I brace myself for a rough, angry kiss, but he stops just short of meeting my lips. Eyes glittering like a crazed animal, he smirks.

"If you don't listen like a good little girl," his warm breath teases my cheek, "I'll tell everyone I've seen what's hiding under that tight pencil skirt." His fingers brush my inner thigh. "Not only that." He bends down to whisper in my ear. "I've *tasted* what's under that skirt. And if you really don't behave," his lips tug on my ear and I feel the quick flicker of his tongue, "I'm going to taste it again."

A moan escapes my lips that I can't hold back, no matter how badly I want to. The ache between my legs is about to split me apart.

I glare up into his stormy blue eyes. My voice is breathless. "Are you... threatening me?"

The musical chimes go off.

Without warning, Zane drops his hands and steps back. He sticks one of those long, wicked fingers into his mouth and licks it. "You're still sweet, tiger."

The smirk on his face is *infuriating*, but I can't do anything because my legs are jelly and I'm barely standing up.

"Make time for me tonight. I'll send you an address," he says calmly.

I glare at him, unable to stop the riptide of hatred and anger.

Damn him.

Damn him to death.

He arches a brow. "I expect you to be on time. You don't want to know what'll happen if you're late."

Zane smiles, punctuating the steel in his voice.

Without warning, he throws the door open and leaves.

I stumble back.

My legs buckle.

Shakily, I press a hand to the whiteboard, curling my fingers against the smooth, cool surface.

I thought Zane was horrible before, but I was wrong. There's more beast than man inside him. And I think I just unlocked the monster.

* * *

Jinx: Snare King got a royal dressing down from Sexy Teach after class. Does it have anything to do with last week's epic shoulder-throw?

Battle lines are being drawn, but what is Snare King really fighting for? Is this a war to conquer and destroy a rebel or has our dark prince set his sights on a new, forbidden concubine?

One thing's for sure, Sexy Teach better brace herself. I have a feeling she's not done getting thrown around.

Until the next post, keep your enemies close and your secrets even closer.

- Jinx

Chapter Seven

GREY

Mom sticks a hand in front of my face, waving around until my eyes catch on the obnoxious gemstone glued to her knuckle.

"Gracie, I need you to pay attention. It feels like I'm shopping alone."

"Sorry, mom." I swallow hard and force myself to focus. "That looks good."

"Doesn't it?" She giggles and cups her face so the gem catches the light. It's bright enough to blind someone.

"You wear it beautifully, ma'am." The clerk arrives with a tray held between gloved fingers. With practiced ease, she doles out steaming cups of tea.

"Oh thank you." Mom grins as if she's never been paid a compliment before.

The clerk folds her hands together, almost drooling. "Will you be taking that one home?"

"Yes, please." Mom shoos her away. "Send it to my

address, darling. And pay with this." She hands over a black card.

"Yes, right away, Mrs. Cross."

Once the clerk is gone, eyes probably rolling like slot machines with dollar signs, I lean toward my mother.

"Isn't this too much?"

"Too much? Darling, there's no such thing." Mom sips daintily from the cup. The moment the liquid touches her tongue, she curses. "Ow, that's hot."

Her grimace is exaggerated. Almost cartoonish.

In an instant, her genteel act fades away.

I see the woman who spent every day waiting tables at a rundown diner, ketchup stains on her obnoxiously pink uniform, hair frizzy and unkept, wrinkles carving into dark brown skin that looked far more weathered than it should have.

That struggling single mother is gone. Hidden, really, beneath hair that's fried to a straight crisp, professionally applied makeup and an outfit chosen by the best stylist in the city.

But the harried waitress lives on.

No amount of Jarod Cross's money can erase her.

I chew on my bottom lip. "I just think—"

"That's your problem, Gracie. You think too much. You'd have a much more enjoyable life if you slowed down and smelled the roses."

"These roses are worth," I lift one of the price tags on the jewels beautifully arranged before us, "ten thousand dollars."

The words are too outrageous to be said aloud.

I finish in a whisper, "I'd rather not."

Mom laughs and blows on the cup before she drinks the

tea again. This time, she takes a dainty sip, pinky out and eyebrows arched, looking like she was born for this world.

That's the thing about her. Mom never finished high school, but she learns fast. It doesn't surprise me that she's managed to mimic the rich after being a wealthy person for less than a year.

Mom sets the cup back down and it makes a clinking sound. Turning to me, she flutters a hand down her tweed jacket. "You know what you need?"

I groan because I already suspect where this conversation is going.

"A man." Mom wiggles her eyebrows.

I close my eyes. At once, a pair of dangerous blue orbs pierce the darkness.

"A handsome one," mom adds.

I see a body molded like a priceless sculpture.

"One who makes your heart thump."

The desire I try so hard to keep at bay seeps into every vein.

Zane freaking Cross.

I can still feel him on me, powerful, corded muscles flexing against my arms. Tattooed fingers kneading against the soft flesh of my hip. Blue eyes darkening with lust even as he scoffed at my attempt to put distance between us.

I hate him.

And yet, I'm thinking about him in front of my *mother*.

"You need a strong, capable man. Preferably a lawyer or a doctor," mom says.

In my mind, I see Zane's calloused hands gripping his drumsticks and twirling it around.

"Someone older than you. Obviously. That's the only way your interests will align."

I see Zane grinning over me, tall and imposing. Aggravatingly charming even with a smile tinged in danger.

Mom gives me a teasing nudge in the side. "Lord knows, you're an old soul. No one your age will think reading books on a Friday night instead of going dancing is fun." She rolls her eyes. "So you need a nice older man who isn't about that fast life."

Everything mom is saying is the opposite of Zane.

He's not the man I should be looking for.

Thinking about.

Locking classroom doors with.

I *know* this.

The problem is I had to shuffle around school, giving lectures in discomfort while ruing the fact that I don't carry spare panties in my purse.

Which is something I should probably do if Zane corners me again.

Not that he will.

Not that I'll allow it.

"You should be focusing on your own marriage. Not trying to arrange mine," I mumble, picking up my cup. My skin is a light brown and it's not possible for me to blush, but I feel uneasy anyway. As if mom can see the thoughts I'm having about my step-brother.

"You're too picky," mom says, pretending not to have heard me. "That boy with the sports car? What was his name again? He was so nice."

"Harry Winston the Third?" I roll my eyes.

The pretentious corporate heir picked me up from school a few months ago, driving a loud, obnoxious convertible.

I pasted a smile on my face and hopped in the car for my mother's sake, but the date did not get better after that dramatic entrance. He had no personality outside of being rich and I was bored to death.

"What happened to him?"

"He liked the sound of his own voice a little too much," I murmur.

"Your standards are too high, Gracie. You need to lower them a little."

The clerk returns, saving me from mom's lecture. She hands the card back to my mother. "Here you go, ma'am."

"Thank you." Mom rises gracefully and slips a hundred dollar bill from her purse. She hands it to the clerk. "That's for being so helpful."

The woman grins. "Thank you."

We're about to leave when a trio of ladies enter the VIP section.

The one in the middle is slim and has blonde hair teased into an elaborate bee-hive. Her face has the look of someone who overindulges in Botox. Unnaturally plump lips. Stiff cheekbones. A forehead that can't scrunch even if she sneezes.

"Cynthia!" Mom cries in a warm welcome.

Cynthia does not return her greeting. Her eyes narrow in distaste. "Yes?"

"It's me." Mom seems a little taken aback. She taps her chest. "Jarod Cross's wife."

My eyes shift to my mother, sharpening. I've noticed that she never introduces herself by name anymore. Every time we're out, she calls herself 'Mrs. Cross' or 'Jarod Cross's wife'.

"Oh, yes." Cynthia's voice is dry. She does *not* look impressed.

Mom waits expectantly. Whatever she was waiting for

doesn't happen because Cynthia walks away without another word.

"Are you shopping?" Mom follows them. Her voice borders on desperate. "You should have told me. I would have joined you." Breezy laughter escapes her lips. "It's more fun to shop together. Maybe we can come here together next time."

Cynthia stops in her tracks and sends a frigid look over her shoulder. "Thank you for the offer, but I'm afraid our *tastes*," her eyes drip over mom, "don't align."

My eyebrows furrow as Cynthia and her minions strut away.

Hurt crystals over mom's face, but she shakes it away with a smile. "Gracie, why don't we get some ice cream before going home?"

"Mom."

"I'm feeling parched. I think that tea was too hot," mom says, walking ahead of me.

"Mom."

"Let's go all out today. A chocolate sundae with sprinkles."

I grab her arm. "Mom."

She veers to a stop.

"Why did you let her talk to you that way?"

"Oh, that's just how Cynthia is."

Irritation burns in my heart. I don't always agree with mom's decisions—this sudden marriage to Jarod Cross being a great example—but she doesn't deserve to be treated like dirt.

Having people look down on her was an expected part of her waitressing job, but I think she was *more* respected back then.

At the very least, it seemed she respected herself more.

"You should have told her off," I hiss.

"They're Jarod's friends."

I frown. "You're doing all this for Jarod?"

"No, I just..." She squeezes the band of her purse. "Gracie, let's not talk about this anymore."

I stay where I am, staring into mom's back.

She stops and glances over her shoulder. "Coming?"

"Mom, are you happy?"

She blinks in shock. "Of course I'm happy—"

"Are you happy with him?"

She snaps her mouth shut.

"We live in that big house all alone. Jarod Cross is barely home and even when he is, he barely talks to either of us."

"Jarod is a busy man, darling. I knew that before I agreed to marry him."

"But mom—"

"Relax." She rubs her hand down my shoulder. "Gracie, I know you're worried about me, but you don't have to be. Everything isn't some grand conspiracy. You have to learn to live in the moment."

I stiffen, seeing the flash of pity in her eyes. "What does that mean?"

"I know you're upset about what happened to Sloane—"

"Don't." I pull away from her. "Don't go there, mom."

"Darling, all I'm saying is that you've been stuck in the past for too long. I remember Sloane being a bright, happy young lady. She was the type who'd grab life by the horns. She wouldn't want you to carry this burden all the time."

"You don't know what Sloane would have wanted," I spit.

"Maybe I don't." Mom arches a brow. "But do you?"

I grit my teeth, my heart flaying in pain. It feels like someone's prying at my ribs with a crowbar.

Glancing down, I murmur, "I forgot I have an appointment. I'll see you at home, mom."

"Where are you going?"

Fighting back the stinging tears, I run to the bathroom and crash into a stall.

My breath comes in hard, fast spurts.

The room starts spinning.

I hang my head and catch my breath.

In the silence, I feel my phone buzz.

My entire body stiffens when I read the message.

Jinx: Horses, footmen and beautiful dresses turn to ash at midnight. I wonder what will burn when your time runs out? Tick-tock, Miss J. Trade a secret for a secret.

Chapter Eight

ZANE

I lean against the wall facing the parking lot, eyes on the street. Dusk is settling on the city and the moon is bright, yet it's drowned out by the lights from nearby skyscrapers.

My fingers expertly flip around my drumstick, causing it to spin like a pinwheel.

Two girls saunter past, their hair flying in the breeze. They do a double-take when they see me and giggle, whispering to each other.

Uninterested, I take out my phone.

Two minutes.

I sent Miss Jamieson the location an hour ago. She didn't respond, but that doesn't bother me. After the turn things took in the classroom today, I don't expect her to be cheerful and cooperative.

But I do expect her to be here.

I wasn't joking when I told her I was tired of this game we're playing.

She's been running around in my head since the night we spent together. Because of that, I've been holding back.

And where did that lead me?

She called me a freaking child.

Big mistake.

I'm tired of fawning over her.

If she wants to be treated like every other woman I've screwed, so be it.

We'll do it her way.

"Excuse me. You seem so familiar."

I look up and see the girls from before. One is a cute brunette. She's wearing a tube top that looks like a bra with hooks at the front. My eyes linger on her tits before moving up to her face.

Hand sliding into her back pocket, she thrusts her chest forward and gives me a flirty smile. "Are you... the lead singer of that band?"

"What band?" I play dumb.

"The Kings."

Her friend elbows her in the side. "He's not the lead. He's the drummer." She juts her chin at my stick. "Obviously."

"Oh." Eyebrows hiking, the brunette flushes. "I'm sorry. You guys look so much alike."

"We're twins," I say.

It doesn't bother me that people mistake me for Dutch. I have dark hair and blue eyes compared to his blonde hair and hazel eyes, but that's about the only difference between us.

Back in the day, I used to change my hair and wear contacts just to mess with the girls my twin was hooking up with. I stopped right before he met Cadence.

A good thing.

I've never seen Dutch more possessive over a girl.

"Can we take a picture with you?"

I nod and stoop a little so I'm in the shot. Anything for the fans.

"And an autograph?" The friend shoves a marker at me.

I accept it and scribble on the paper.

Distractedly, I check my phone again.

Miss Jamieson is late.

Damn it.

Does she really want to mess with me?

"Can I have one too?" the brunette asks.

"Sure," I grumble.

"Here." She pushes her shirt up and points to the underside of her tits. Eyes dripping with invitation, she says, "You can write your number too."

I accept the marker from her.

Just then, I hear the familiar rumble of an engine.

My attention snaps away.

Miss Jamieson's rusty car speeds into a parking spot, wheels burning rubber. She's going so fast, she almost rams into the yellow parking block.

A grin spreads on my face. Carelessly, I toss the pen over my shoulder. I was aiming for the brunette's hand, but it hits the ground instead, clattering loudly.

"Hey!" the girls protest.

I ignore them and start moving, eating the distance between me and Miss Jamieson's vehicle.

The door pops open.

One sexy red stiletto is joined by another. I slide my gaze up her pasted-on jeans and simple flowery blouse.

Damn.

It annoys me that my skin gets hotter watching Miss

Jamieson fully clothed than it did when that brunette lifted her shirt to flash me.

"I'm here," she growls. Her eyes spit flames hotter than Hades, and my body goes hard instantly.

Hell, I must be out of my freaking mind.

Forget the fact that we're step-siblings, I'm not the kind of guy who goes for a challenge. Not like Dutch.

I like easy.

Which those girls were.

The brunette, especially, seemed down to suck, lick, and swallow anything I dished out. On the other hand, Miss Jamieson goes out of her way to draw the line between us.

Yet here I am, fighting a wild, dangerous tension with the only woman I can't have. The only woman who'd rather jump off a cliff than admit she wants me back.

Dammit.

I curl my fingers into fists, forcing a crap-eating grin.

For now, this is *my* game.

I won't let her take over.

"You're late," I say, leaning an elbow against her door.

"You're lucky I came at all," she snaps. Her hair is bigger than usual, the curls expanding all around her face and down her shoulders. The breeze throws soft black coils in front of her cheeks, teasing me with a coconut fragrance.

Miss Jamieson's hair is one of the things that makes her so freaking irresistible. The curls seem to have their own damn personality—weighed down and shiny against her scalp on some days and big, textured and gravity-defying on others.

I remember sinking my fingers into that mane and yanking her head back while I pounded into her from behind. The memory is visceral. As clear as day. My heart beats so fast I feel dizzy.

"You better have a good reason for dragging me down here, Zane," she hisses. "Or else..." Her eyes catch on the door of the shop and she makes a startled sound. "Is that a funeral parlor?"

I grin and slam her door closed. "This way."

We get inside and the funeral director greets us with an enthusiastic smile. For someone who's in the business of death, he seems rather cheerful.

"Dutch and Cadey Cross?" He points.

"Zane, actually." I gesture to Miss Jamison. "We're here in their place."

"Ah." His eyes glitter. "You're a couple?"

Miss Jamieson stiffens.

I briefly consider saying yes, but I decide not to for her sake. "Family friends."

Relief loosens the tense line of her shoulders.

The director nods. "I'm sorry for your loss."

I almost snort. Tina Cooper dying is many things but a 'loss' is not one of them. From what I've observed, the only good thing she did was give birth to two healthy babies. Everything from that point on is a ledger of red.

"Come on, let me show you our best," he says.

Miss Jamieson leans toward me. "What are we doing here?"

"Dutch didn't trust me to plan the funeral alone."

"Why not?"

"I suggested strippers."

She says nothing. Just spears me with two accusing pinpricks for eyes.

The funeral director leads us into another room. This one has coffins in all shapes, sizes and stains.

"Walnut is the most popular." He shows it off. "But it's also the most common. For your loved one, I'm thinking we go with polished hazelnut." He slides a finger over a gold-plated handle.

I point to the giant, gleaming white caskets in the front. "What are those?"

"These are our top-of-the-line caskets. Softest lining in the world."

That's a weird flex.

"Your loved one will rest in peace with memory foam linings and fragrance pockets." He gestures proudly. "Patent pending."

"How comfortable is it?" Miss Jamieson asks.

The director smiles. "Test it and see."

She curls back, looking disgusted.

"How about you, sir?"

I push my hand into the coffin. "It is soft."

"This is our deluxe casket for obese adults. It's our fastest growing line." He sees our intrigued faces and adds, "You can lie in it if you'd like."

I grimace. It's one thing to be here, planning a funeral.

It's another to climb into a casket while I'm alive and kicking.

Miss Jamieson sees my resistance and a mischievous grin teases her full mouth. "I would love to see you in a coffin, Zane."

"You first."

She shrugs and faces the funeral director. "He's a coward, so I don't think he'll do it."

I scoff.

"That's okay. You don't have to get in." The director laughs.

"Screw it." I climb the table and step into the casket. The lining is surprisingly plush. "It's not that bad if you don't think about it."

The director's phone rings.

"Excuse me," he says, walking out of the show room.

I motion to Miss Jamieson. "Your turn."

"Absolutely not."

"Come on." I spread my arm out on either side of the coffin, getting comfortable. "Let's see if you're a coward or not."

She arches an eyebrow.

I lean forward, sliding my arms over the locked bottom half. "Scared?"

Annoyance glitters in her eyes. "Scoot over."

Grinning, I roll across and extend a hand.

She doesn't take it and climbs in on her own.

Her bottom lip trembles. She sinks one leg in the coffin like a swimmer testing the temperature of the pool.

"Just get in," I grumble.

Miss Jamieson ignores me, holding onto both sides of the coffin and lowering herself slowly.

My eyes swing behind her and I gasp. "Is that a ghost?"

"Ah!" She screams, flinging herself down. Her flailing hands dismantle the stand holding the casket open. The lid thuds shut as she crashes into my chest.

We're thrown into darkness.

I wrap an arm around her instinctively, absorbing her fall. My head slams into the back of the coffin, knocking against the metal flooring. A pained grunt fills my throat and shoots past my lips.

Miss Jamieson is panting hard, her head buried in the hollow between my neck and shoulder. Her body is soft and supple. My pulse picks up, muscles tensing as the urge to hold her takes over.

Before I can really enjoy having her sprawled on top of

me, she shoots her arms out on either side and scrambles to sit up.

The sound of her head thumping against the top of the casket rings out.

"Ow!"

I peer at her through the darkness. "You okay?"

"I..." Thumps sound. I can't see what she's doing, but I can see the faint outline of her arms.

She's still sitting on top of me, temporarily distracted by whatever she's doing. The way she's squirming over my hips whips my blood to a hot boil. I want to thrust up, easing into the friction.

"Zane," her worried voice snaps me out of my lust-filled haze, "I can't open it."

"What?"

Her breath hits my chest in panicked spurts and she whimpers, "I think the coffin's locked."

Chapter Nine

GREY

Panicked, I struggle to shove the lid off. Pushing with my arms and bumping into it with my shoulder. Nothing works.

The coffin is locked.

"No, no, no," I whimper.

There's no way out.

No way...

The darkness is chewing at my fingers, my toes, nibbling at my skin and tearing at my flesh.

The box is getting smaller.

Smaller.

Smaller.

My fingers claw at the top of the casket as desperation consumes me.

"Is anyone there!" I pound on the casket lid. "We're locked in here!"

My nails rake the plush lining.

I slash through cotton and silk.

I open my mouth to yell again, but my throat closes up like someone pulling a corset tight. My brain seizes, drowning in a river of fear. Why can't I scream? Why can't I breathe? It's a stab of helplessness, like I'm not even in my own body.

My eyes steer to the side and I see her.

Sloane.

Blond hair limp. Face dirty. Body crumpled.

Is this how she felt when we buried her? Is this the panic, the terror that roared through her soul?

Tears spring to my eyes.

"I can't breathe," I wheeze, fingers scraping down my throat.

"Hey, hey." The gentle voice is matched by two heavy arms around my waist. The moment Zane touches me, the image of Sloane disappears.

He curls me against his chest. "Sh." He smooths a hand down my hair. "You're going to be okay. You're going to be okay."

I squirm, fighting him.

Frantic sobs tear out of my mouth.

The guilt and panic mingle, forming a new monster. One hell-bent on burning me to ashes.

Zane holds firm, battling the monster with every breath he exhales.

"I'm here. I'm here."

He keeps muttering tenderly in my ear and rubbing my hair, my back, my side until the panic shrinks to the size of my palm.

"Come on, tiger. Come back to me."

His tenderness pierces the fog and I slide back to reality in a slow descent.

For a moment, I hold him, anchoring myself in the hardness of his body. Reacquainting myself with reality through the parts of him I can feel, touch and smell.

His skin is hot.

His heartbeat is a steady rhythm.

His unique smell of leather and sandalwood fills my nose.

Warm hands round over my shoulders and down my back. "You okay now?"

"Y-yeah," I mutter. My breathing evens out and I blink rapidly, stripped raw by a moment I wish he hadn't witnessed.

It's impossible to see his face in the casket. There are no openings to allow light, and yet I can feel his energy radiating in my direction. It's different than his usual arrogance. Softer. Concerned.

"I..." I lick my lips, unsure of what to say. "I don't like small spaces."

"I can see that." There's a hint of laughter. An ease that makes my shoulders relax.

"How are you not freaking out?" I croak, my heart still beating fast. "We... we could be buried alive."

His chuckle vibrates through his body and mine.

"You think this is funny?"

"I think you almost gave me a heart attack." He pushes my hair away from my face.

I'm not sure how he did that so effortlessly in the dark.

"That's weird." There's a note of thoughtfulness in his voice.

"What?"

"You always seem so strong."

"Everyone looks strong from a distance."

He's quiet. "What do I look like from a distance?"

Like a bad decision.

Like an anxious dream.

Like a wall that I can't ever break down.

"Like a student," I say finally.

He scoffs, but it's not as angry as usual.

"You better now?"

I nod and try to ease away from him. "You can let me go."

There's a beat where he doesn't move and I wonder if he'll keep holding me. I wonder if I'll have the strength to push him away.

It's safe in his arms. Warm.

But Zane releases me without a fight.

I roll to the bottom of the coffin, lying next to him. Awkwardness teases the air between us. The silence stretches on.

"Get Dutch on the phone. Ask him to call the funeral home and get someone to help us."

"Good idea." Zane takes out his cell phone. The moment he turns it on, I flinch. The light from the screen is extremely bright. My eyes adjust and I can see what I couldn't before. Creepy white lining. A glossy wooden coffin.

We're two dead bodies about to be buried.

My stomach roils.

I hear my breath escaping quicker and quicker.

Just as I'm about to fall into panic again, a hand descends over my eyes, blocking out the light. Callouses scrape my cheek and a hard palm grazes my sensitive lips.

Thrown into darkness, I angle toward Zane. "What are you doing?"

His voice is low, rough, but in a comforting sort of way.

The heat threaded within traces like expensive velvet across my heart. "Don't look if it scares you."

I nod.

"Close your eyes, tiger."

My heart flips in my chest.

"Are they closed?"

I squeeze my eyes shut and nod again.

He removes his hand. Zane's cell phone beeps as he dials the number.

A moment later, I hear his twin pick up.

"Dutch," Zane grunts, "call the funeral parlor. Tell them to send someone to the show room." His voice rumbles close to my ear. "No, I'm not going to tell you why. Just call the freaking parlor and tell them to look for us."

He hangs up.

"What did Dutch say?" I ask.

"He'll call them."

"Good."

I feel Zane turn his head. The length of his arm is pressed against mine, which makes it easy to sense when he's moving.

"Do you have any other phobias?" he asks.

"Why do you care?"

"Because I'm curious about you." A moment later, I feel the muscular planes of his chest. His hot, hard body is flush against mine. He must have turned over on his side to face me.

My heart pounds harder and lodges in my throat.

I exhale to calm down. "Don't be."

His silence is sharp.

"We're never going to be friends, Zane. You and I are just—"

"Say teacher and student. I dare you." His voice bristles with a threat.

I tilt my chin up tensely. "Step-siblings."

He barks out an ironic laugh.

It's not funny.

None of this is.

Zane and I should never have crossed paths and yet here we are, tangled together in a ridiculous web of circumstances and buried under a mountain of scandal.

"I put my phone away. You can open your eyes now," Zane whispers.

My eyelashes flicker as I slowly adjust to the pitch-black coffin.

Sheepishly, I rub my throat. "My eyes are sensitive to light."

"Or maybe you prefer darkness."

"Don't say it like that."

"You ashamed?"

I can't see him, but I can *feel* the smirk he's tossing in my direction.

"The kind of darkness you're referring to is bad."

"Bad. Good. It's all relative."

I snort. "That's something only people with a corrupt moral compass would say."

"Darkness is where you find out who you really are." His voice is mellow and yet his words are dangerous as hell. "It's where all your true desires come out to play. Everything you deny yourself in the light," he eases closer, "you can indulge in when it's dark."

His finger slide confidently down my face to my mouth. He traces my parted lips and I shiver.

"What would you do if you knew it would never come to the light, tiger?" he coaxes.

I breathe out. "That's a pointless exercise."

"Because you're scared?"

"Because it's not for me. Even if it hurts, I want to live in the light."

His finger goes still.

I'm held captive by the tension between us, the many truths spilling in the quiet of the coffin.

I can't be with you.

I won't be with you.

I will never let the darkness overtake me.

Zane withdraws his hand and rolls away. I ache for the loss of his warmth.

"They're going to get us out of here soon," he says stiffly.

"How do you know..."

There's a rustle of fabric and the coffin lid creaks.

At that moment, the top opens. The funeral director peers over us, his face tight with horror.

"Oh my. I'm so sorry." He extends a hand to me. "Are you okay?"

"We're fine." I accept his hand and step out of the coffin.

It feels like we're walking out of a nightmare.

My feet land on the ground and I start sinking. My legs fell asleep in the coffin and now a million ants are biting up my shin.

Zane wraps his fingers around my upper arms, steadying me.

I shake him off, feeling self-conscious and foolish now that the crisis is over.

"That has never happened before. Truly. Are you sure you two are okay?" He peers intently at me. I guess I look as haggard and weary as I feel.

"Yeah." I clear my throat. "We should, uh, discuss the funeral arrangement now."

"No," Zane says stiffly.

I glance at him in shock.

He narrows his eyes at me. "You will."

I remain in place, totally confused.

He juts his chin at the door. "I have things to do. Text me the details."

"Are you kidding? You're just leaving?"

Zane smiles, but it's one of the cruel smirks. A villainous twist of his lips that makes me clench my fists.

My eyes darken in response.

"Let me remind you, tiger. We're playing my game now." He advances on me, blue eyes glittering. "You want to be treated like a teacher at Redwood. This is what that means."

"Screw you," I hiss.

His eyes are flat. His tone, cold. "You already did."

I stiffen.

We're locked in a challenging stare.

Two bulls clashing in the middle of a colosseum.

I remember his threat.

Do you want them to find out I touched you the way no student should touch a teacher?

He arches an eyebrow.

Jaw clenched, I glance at the funeral director. "I'll take over from here."

Zane stalks off without a word.

I glare in his direction. Zane Cross is the most dangerous of his brothers. He hides that wicked streak under warm charisma and a pretty smile. He lures you into feeling like a friend before he stabs you in the back.

I lick my lips, struggling to tune in to what the director is saying.

Like an idiot, I believed for a moment that Zane wasn't half as bad a guy as he pretends to be. The way he cradled my face, calmed me down, and talked me out of my panic attack felt sincere.

But it was all a lie.

The feelings he stirred up will stay buried in that coffin.

And they'll never see the light of day.

Chapter Ten

ZANE

I slam my drumsticks against the snare, listening to the deep ricochet. My sticks rattle over the worn centre, bouncing up and back down again with every flick of my wrists.

I'm sweating. Drenched to the freaking skin.

My wife beater sticks to my chest and I stop for only a second to pluck it away before I dive in again.

My music is chaos.

Just like my freaking head.

The noise bounces around the garage. Perfectly clamoring.

Drumming isn't that complicated.

That's why I love it.

The music pours out of me without the need for chords or fingers mashing against brutal nylon strings stretched to the point of snapping. With one boom, I set the rhythm, the pace, form the pulse of any song.

I don't want darkness.

Miss Jamieson's voice is still in my head, no matter how much noise I make.

Even if it hurts, I want to live in the light.

The freaking light.

It's my freaking nightmare.

I heard exactly what she was saying. No matter how hard I try, no matter how drawn we are to each other, the two of us can never exist outside of the darkness.

So what?

Where the hell does that leave me?

The only choice I have is to move on, but I can't do that. I've tried so many times and I keep coming back to her. She's ingrained in my skin. An itch I can't scratch. A craving that suspends into infinity.

It pisses me off.

So naturally, I want to piss her off too.

My fingers tighten around my sticks and I lean over the drums, beating out a staccato rhythm.

Trapped in the coffin, she clung to me and this inescapable feeling settled over my chest. Like she was a puzzle piece snapping in place. Like maybe she was destined to be in my life and tear it up—for better or worse.

Grace Freaking Jamieson.

Tiger.

My teacher.

My step-sister.

My freaking obsession.

I wish we'd never met.

And I wish she was better at hiding her feelings.

She doesn't hate me.

Damn, I wish she did.

That would make this a little easier.

She says one thing with her mouth, but those pretty eyes beg for me to bend her over the teacher's desk and show her what inappropriate behaviour really is.

It's impossible to move on when she pushes and pulls like that.

My calves are burning. Slamming my foot against the pedal, I crash my sticks into the cymbals. The gold plates vibrate and suspend the sound.

Two shadows slip into the garage.

I stop, both sticks raised in mid-air. My foot leaves the pedal and I quickly clip the cymbals between my thumb and forefinger, killing the metallic resonance.

Dutch drags his guitar over his head with practiced ease. His eyes—hazel mirrors of mine—flash on me. "Keep going like that and you're going to need a new snare."

"The music store keeps extra just for him," Finn says.

I stare at my brothers. "What are you doing here?"

"We heard your cry for help from across town." Dutch nods at my drum set.

I frown at him.

He strums his guitar. A throaty C chord rings through the amp. "I wanted to get an update on the funeral arrangements. Cadey kept asking me."

"You haven't told her I'm the one planning it?"

Dutch glowers.

I scoff and run a hand through my wet hair. Sweat droplets fling all over my set. "Am I that freaking unreliable?"

My brother is wise enough not to answer that.

Finn eyes me. "You been drinking?"

"No," I snap.

Dutch plays an intricate melody on the low notes. Neck

craned toward his guitar, he asks casually. "Who did you take to the funeral parlor today?"

I stiffen.

"On the phone, you said 'us'. Meaning there was more than just you."

I glance away.

Finn notices. "You were with Miss Jamieson."

I flip him off.

A wrinkle forms between Dutch's eyes. "I thought she was still dodging you. How did you get her to go?"

"I asked."

"Please and thank you?"

"Something along those lines."

"Huh." Finn looks intrigued.

"Are we practicing or gossiping here?" I point a stick at Dutch. "Don't you have to hurry back to your wife?"

"Cadey's spending the night at Breeze's."

"She's been kidnapped," Finn says dryly.

"Breeze is the best friend who hates you, right?" I smirk at Dutch. "How did she react when she heard you and Cadey got married?"

Dutch glares into the distance.

By that expression, I'm guessing Breeze didn't take it well. The blond is loud and feisty where Cadence is quiet and stubborn. I bet she raked both Dutch and Cadey through the coals.

"We're talking about you, not me," Dutch growls. "Don't change the subject. This thing with Miss Jamieson is important."

"He's right," Finn says. "You're on Jinx's radar now."

I roll my eyes. "I'll pay her off."

"And if that doesn't work?" Finn asks.

"If she had solid evidence, she would have posted more details."

"It's enough that she's hinting at it," Finn says. "People are going to talk. It might end up badly for her."

"I'm more concerned about dad using this as ammunition," Dutch adds. He grips the neck of the guitar and gestures toward me. "Now that I'm so close to qualifying for the inheritance, there's no telling what he'll do."

A silent chill fills the air.

I'm still convinced dad had something to do with Cadence's mother being dead. After my stint in the coffin, the thought of murder is ten times more unsettling.

"Honestly..." Dutch hesitates.

"What?"

"I'm concerned about whether this city is safe for Cadence and Vi."

I go deadly sober.

Finn whips his bass over his head and grips it in a tight fist.

"Are you saying... that you'll move?" I croak.

My twin rubs his chin. "I'm just thinking."

Finn roughly drops his bass in the stand.

I shoot to my feet. "You gotta be freaking kidding me."

Dutch slips out of his guitar strap and sets the electric away. "Don't overreact. Like I said. It's just a thought." He takes out his phone. "I have to pick up Vi from her afterschool class. Text me the details for the funeral. I'll let Cadey know."

I grit my teeth, saying nothing.

Dutch stalks out of the garage.

In the silence, I glance at Finn. He stares me down with those dark brown eyes that seem to see everything. I swear, my brother is creepily stoic. It's near impossible to tell what he's thinking in a given moment.

"Am I the only one who thinks that Dutch leaving means dad wins?" I say.

Finn folds his arms over his chest. "He's got a valid point. There's no way to keep Cadey and Vi safe if he stays."

"And you think dad can't hurt them if they're overseas?" I scoff. "He's safer with us."

"That decision is up to Dutch."

My eyebrows tighten like angry slashes over my eyes. "Now is not the time to be such a freaking *Finn*. Dutch just talked about moving away from our city. Did you hear that? If he goes, everything changes. Our band. Our lives. Us."

He juts his chin at me. "Maybe some change will be good for us all."

I watch my brother leave the garage, as emotionless and cold as a freaking pillar.

Emotions bubble in my chest.

I can't contain them. Not like Finn.

Stomping over to the fridge, I rip the door open and yank out a beer. Cracking the lid, I guzzle the contents and grab for another.

My world is descending into havoc and I have no control, no way to stop it.

I need to get out of my head tonight.

Grabbing my phone, I dial a number and a girl's purring voice picks up.

I grab my motorcycle keys, growling, "Meet me at the ridge. Make sure your clothes are off when I get there."

* * *

Jinx: Mirror, Mirror, on the wall, who's the deadliest of them all?

Snare King was spotted outside a funeral parlor after school today. Check out the photo his fans uploaded online. Inquiring minds want to know, is he buying his own coffin or someone else's?

Until the next post, keep your enemies close and your secrets even closer.

- Jinx

Chapter Eleven

ZANE

The motorcycle almost topples over from my powerful thrusts. Tonight's distraction is noisy. Which I typically like. Yet, in the moment, I find her annoying.

She grips the handlebars, holding on for dear life and screaming loud enough to scare a flock of birds. The sound of beating wings rolls over the wilderness, but it's drowned out by the chaos of skin slapping skin.

My grunts and her moans mingle together. A crude, animalistic song rolling across a vast expanse that seems to go on forever.

The wind picks up as if my lashing hips can control the weather and I'm whipping up a storm.

The shadows are thicker than cream out here. When the sun is high, the mountains chop up the sky with ragged cliffs and sharp peaks. Tonight, the darkness swallows them whole, turning the hills into stark, ghostly outlines.

I increase the pace, closing my eyes and wishing I didn't see *that* face behind my eyelids.

But she's freaking there.

Brown skin. Pert nose. Full lips.

The bane of my existence.

In my head, I'm holding her.

Touching her.

Sinking deep into her.

It's enough to send me right over the edge.

My partner twists her neck and smiles, thinking she's the one responsible for that.

Dammit.

I step back, feeling annoyed more than satisfied.

"Zane, that was amazing."

"Yeah," I mutter, zipping up. I've been messing with this chick off and on. She doesn't expect anything more than a good time and that's pretty freaking hard to find in a girl at Redwood Prep.

"We should," her fingers slide down my chest, "do this more often. Can I call you when I'm the one who needs to let off some steam?"

I smile, not giving her an answer.

Her phone rings.

She rolls her eyes and shares even though I didn't ask, "It's Vanya having another identity crisis. I swear it's so stressful being cheer captain." She pulls her skirt back up. "After Dutch de-throned Paris, the team fell into my lap and now—"

"Baby," I cut her off because I really don't care, "I gotta head back. Band practice."

Her eyelashes flutter.

She looks pleased.

Poor thing has no idea that 'baby' is just a placeholder

since I sometimes mix up the names of the girls I'm with. Nothing cuts a good time short like looking down at the girl I'm riding and saying the wrong name.

Lipstick smeared and eyes glinting, she leans forward to kiss me.

I push her back. "You know the drill."

Sighing, she folds her arms over her chest and pouts. "You never let me kiss you."

"I gave you plenty more than kissing." I grab my helmet and nod at her. "Sweet dreams."

"Night, Zane."

I send her a backward wave, wait until I see her get safely in her car and then head home.

The motorcycle rumbles between my legs, a powerful thrum that roars down the road. The wind batters my face and makes my eyes sting.

In the past, I wouldn't go out of my way to screw a chick in the wilderness, but since our lives have become the spotlight of Jinx's app, I'm more conscious of where and who I'm hooking up with.

The last time I got clumsy, my bare butt was plastered all over the app.

The motorcycle rumbles.

I push faster.

The mountains blur and the road morphs into one, long stroke of asphalt.

My chest aches even though my body's spent.

I got what I set out to get tonight, so why doesn't it feel like I made any progress?

Dutch might still move away.

Miss Jamieson is still untouchable.

Dad is still...

Here?

I'm a couple meters away from home when I see dad's sleek black town car.

I get closer and notice Ron is waiting outside.

Ron is dad's muscle. The fact that dad refers to him as his assistant means absolutely nothing because anyone with eyes can see that dunce is no executive.

Ron's fitted black suit strains against his giant body and does jack squat to lessen the edge of violence steeped in his expression. The guy has eggs for brains, but I guess that makes him easier to control.

I don't see dad's right-hand man Lucien around. Lucien is thinner and more conniving. Less muscle and more evil villain support.

Between Lucien and Ron, I prefer the latter.

Lucien always gives me the creeps.

Fingers turning clammy, I ride up to the driveway.

The moment I get close, dad winds his window down.

To the world, Jarod Cross is a deity. People line up in droves to attend his concerts. They tattoo his name and song lyrics on their bodies, making him a permanent part of their lives, baking him into their skin.

They worship him.

If only they knew...

Or maybe it wouldn't matter if they knew.

No, I don't think it would.

Devout worshippers don't ever say their god is flawed.

I stare at him in the twilight, cold and closed-off. The shaggy hair. The long neck. The fingers bearing too many silver rings. He looks like he's posing for *Elle* magazine, not coming to visit his sons.

Dad originally wanted to move in with us. We barely stopped him by calling mom to our aid. Now, he lives in the hills, just outside the city, but it's like he's on Mars.

"What do you want?" I growl.

Dad twists his head and hits me with a frigid stare. "Get in."

I contemplate ignoring the instruction. The last thing I need after the day I've had is a round alone with dad. I'm exhausted and restless. I was looking forward to crashing in bed and maybe playing a few video games before signing off for the night.

But Ron cracks his knuckles.

The sound of bones snapping sends anger swirling through my stomach.

The hell?

Is this what we've come to, dad?

Annoyance mounts inside me, but I don't let it show. That's my superpower.

I don't scowl and grumble like Dutch.

I don't keep my thoughts hidden like Finn.

I… laugh.

"Your bones are a little tense, Ron. You should consider yoga." I grin. "Really loosen that up for you."

Stark silence meets my quip.

Ron isn't amused.

"What is this about, dad?" I tilt my head to the side. My smile is as sour as vinegar. "Wait… is this the apology tour? I heard you haven't said sorry for throwing Dutch in jail yet."

"I'm not going to ask twice," dad growls.

A low buzzing starts in the base of my skull and drops to my toes. I swing off my bike, kick the stand and lean it on the side.

The wind goes dead as I stomp to the car.

Clouds thicken the star-lit sky, choking out the moon.

Even the night knows it's better to hide from dad than to face him.

I wrench the door open and throw my bulk into the backseat. The leather is slick. My knees almost slam the back of the chair as I slide down the seat.

Grabbing the headrest, I hoist myself up. "There are nicer ways of saying you miss me."

He scoffs.

Dad's relationship with us is as varied as we are.

Dutch is the golden-boy. Literally and figuratively. My twin thinks fast on his feet and always has a solution. He's sharp and decisive. It's why he's the leader of our band and the one we defer to when we make any big decisions.

To control him, dad had to jump through crazy hoops. Setting Dutch up to look like a drug dealer. Manipulating Cadey. Sending Dutch to jail. He put in vast amounts of effort because he sees Dutch as the brother most likely to squirm out of loopholes.

Finn, on the other hand, is harder to pin down, which is why dad seems the most nervous around him. It's uncanny the way he shuts down when Finn enters the room.

Finn might be the kid dad adopted when he needed a PR boost but, in an ironic twist, I think he and Finn are the most alike. Both are quiet. Calculative. Sly. You never really see what their end game is until it's too late.

With me...

It's different.

Dad doesn't fear me the way he fears Dutch.

He doesn't respect me the way he respects Finn.

To dad, I'm a joke.

Easily pinned under his thumb.

While he made complicated plans to subdue my twin

and didn't even bother trying to put shackles on Finn, he only did one thing for me.

One massive thing.

And it freaking worked.

"Is it just me you want to talk to?" I ask sarcastically. "I can grab Dutch if you need to plant drugs on him and call the cops again. Or am I the one you want to falsely accuse this time? What will it be, dad? Coke? Pills? Or something more creative?"

Dad doesn't even blink. The lamppost sprays the side of his face in silver, making him look like a robot.

It suits him.

Unfeeling. Frigidly objective. Programmed to take over the world.

"I want an update," dad says calmly.

My shoulders stiffen. "On what?"

"The Cooper girl." His voice is soft but threaded in iron. "Is she pregnant?"

A puff of air escapes my lips. I should be surprised, but I'm not.

"You think I'm just going to tell you that?"

Dad turns slowly. I meet his eyes. They look obsidian, as cold as the night sky devoid of stars. The way he watches me isn't like a father. It never was. He's all cold businessman, any familial loyalty washed away by his thirst for power.

After his long, calculating stare, dad lets out a chilly breath. "She isn't."

"I didn't say that."

"You're a little too anxious. If she was pregnant, you would have been smug." Dad takes out his cell phone, reads a message and sighs. "Get out. I have things to do."

The buzz in my veins makes me feel like I'm sitting on

top of a hill of explosives. One little match and everything goes boom.

Dad sees I'm not moving and looks back with an impatient glare. As a child, I would have mourned this twisted, manipulative father-son dynamic. There were many times I cried alone, wondering why it felt like my dad didn't love me. I never told Finn or Dutch. Neither of them seemed as impacted by dad's callousness as I was.

Now, at eighteen, I don't feel sorrow.

I feel lashing, poignant *fury*.

"I almost want to ask if you're not ashamed of yourself. But that would be a waste of breath. Because you're not, are you, dad? You don't feel shame. You don't feel anything because you're dead inside."

One corner of his lips curls up.

I grit my teeth. "Don't even *think* about coming after Dutch again. I will make it my personal mission to see that you never touch my brothers. I'll make sure you never win."

There's nothing more to say.

I twist around and grab the door handle.

Dad's voice crawls behind me like black goo. "How?"

My jaw clenches and the handle snaps back into place.

"What will you do to me, Zane? No, a better question is what *can* you do to me?"

I face him, my whole body burning.

"Drum on my car? Sleep with my wife?" He scratches his chin. "Because that stick in your pants seems to be your only weapon."

For a brief moment, I consider grabbing one of my drumsticks and beating it over his face.

Dad leans forward, eyes glinting black. "This is why you will never be a threat to me, Zane. This is why you will never amount to anything."

My nostrils flare.

"You explode with emotions. You can't control yourself, which makes it so easy to see your self-destruct button."

His words are like poison, coiling around me and choking me with a smoky, cloying insistence.

He reaches for something at his feet. A moment later, he throws a box at me.

"A gift," dad says.

The bottom of my stomach drops out.

Condoms.

"Don't misunderstand. It's not because of the inheritance." I can practically hear him hissing, like the snake inside is coming out to play. "This is for your own good. I don't want you to ruin some girl's life the way you so easily ruin your own."

My chest pumps up and down.

The box of condoms remain in my lap, singeing through my jeans to my skin.

"You can never have what you want, Zane," dad whispers. "Those little girls at Redwood might be blinded by your looks and talent, but a sensible woman will see right through to what you are—irresponsible and unreliable." He juts a finger, calloused from years of playing lead guitar, at the box. "So you're better off trying to minimize the consequences of your reckless actions."

Crazed laughter rams into my chest, fighting to pour from my mouth. It feels like an invisible hand is grabbing my heart and pinching *hard*.

I blink away the angry tears stinging my eyes. Dad will misinterpret it. He'll think I'm crying because I'm hurt when, in reality, I'm crying because the other option is to choke him.

Dad winds the window down. "Ron."

The giant stomps around to my side of the car and opens the door. He gives me a pointed look that says '*are you going to get out or do I need to escort you out?*'

I storm out of the car and the condoms drop to the ground.

Ron picks it up and hands it to me.

I grab the box and hurl it inside the car. Silver-wrapped packets pop from the lid and explode over dad's head like confetti.

Dad's eyes widen in shock and he bats the latex down in rough, frantic movements.

It's satisfying to watch.

So satisfying that I know I want more.

More of that shock in his eyes.

More of that feeling of victory.

My lips curl up in a show of dark confidence and I lean against the car to speak through the window. "You're right, dad. I'm the son who flies off the handle without caring about the consequences."

Dad sneers at me.

I smile at him. "I'll show you what it feels like when I lose it."

I walk inside with a new determination.

Dad thinks I'm a screw-up.

So freaking what?

Everyone likes an underdog.

It's time I show dad the hell someone like me can rain on his kingdom.

Chapter Twelve

GREY

I hate funerals.
    They remind me of her.
    Of Sloane.
    The way her mother wailed, refusing to let the cemetery workers lower her casket into the ground.
    The way her sisters cried, silent tears rolling down their faces.
    The way no one came.
    She died alone.
    Rejected.
    Forgotten.
    And no one gave a damn.
    No one except the reporters.
    News vans. Cameras. Journalists who had to be held back with police tape and 'do not cross' signs. Jackals feasting on our pain. Vultures with a carcass. Exploiting her even in death.

I look out over the grassy knoll where Cadence's mother is being laid to rest. Before me is a meticulously well-maintained lawn, lavish tombstones and a garden where mourning family members can find a moment of solace among colorful blooms.

Sloane's final resting place is nothing like this. Her body's stuffed in a government plot with tombstones cracked and chipped away. Some even have graffiti on them. Surrounding her are impoverished shacks, signs of illegal squatting. Drugs run rampant. Daily murders feed a direct line to the graveyard.

There's no peace there.

No garden.

Only weeds that grow rampant, feasting on the decaying bones that feed the soil.

Bile rises in my throat and the anger that lay dormant, the fury that simmers just beneath my skin, comes to a boil.

What happened to Sloane is unforgivable.

The one responsible was caught and is in jail now, but the blame belongs to more than just the man who wielded the knife. There are people walking around whose hands are stained in blood. People who have yet to receive their punishment.

I should be further along on my mission by now. The stalled investigation is my fault. I've gotten too immersed in my role as a teacher at Redwood Prep. I've started to care about the students.

Some of the kids are entitled jerks, as to be expected in a place as exclusive as Redwood. But there are many who, like Sloane, are just trying to find their way.

The scholarship kids, especially, have a place in my heart.

I want them to succeed.

THE FORBIDDEN NOTE

I want them to soar.

I want to be the wall between them and the ugly truths that Sloane and I were forced to face at Redwood.

Between the chaos with Cadence and Mulliez, investigating the perp behind the fire, dodging my feelings for Zane—I've been busy.

With the wrong things.

All distractions.

Today's funeral cracks the ice, peels back the layer of confusion and makes everything clear.

I'm not just a teacher at Redwood Prep.

My purpose goes much deeper.

Sloane is waiting for me to find the truth.

I clasp my hands together as the minister says a few words about heaven and resting in peace.

Viola, Cadence's sister, lets out a little sob. The thirteen-year-old is wearing a black dress with a fluffy skirt and black heels. Cadence is wearing something a little more formal—an A-line black velvet dress and a small veil in front of her face.

Dutch, Zane, and Finn are all in matching suits.

It's funny. A few days ago, they were wearing suits for Cadence and Dutch's wedding.

Now, they're in suits for her mother's funeral.

After all the crazy things they've done, I can't help feeling sorry for this group of friends. Losing a loved one—even if it's someone who made plenty of mistakes—can rip your heart apart.

The minister drones on. *"And I know Tina's watching us from heaven, smiling and wishing she could give you a hug."*

Heaven?

Is Sloane there too?

I don't think so. Sometimes, I feel like I can see her

staring at me. Waiting for me to do what needs to be done before she can go home.

The minister closes his book. *"May God have mercy on her soul."*

I almost laugh.

The God I know is not a God of mercy. If so, why allow Sloane to suffer? Why let the people responsible for her death flourish and move on without justice? Why leave me behind to live with the guilt and pain?

Soft murmurs reach my ears. I see the minister moving down the line of funeral attendants and shaking hands.

A blonde girl has her arm around Cadence's waist and is saying something to her. On Cadence's other side, Dutch is holding her hand and giving it a squeeze.

Behind them, Sol and Serena are standing a distance away. They both seem uncomfortable.

Zane and Finn look appropriately grim.

I sweep a curl behind my ear, studying Zane from the safety of the trees. It's hard to see his eyes from this distance, but I know they must be glittering in the sun. A mixture of green, blue, and a snap of gold.

The jet-black suit along with his midnight-violet hair gives him an aura of danger. Knife-like. Sharp and cutting. It doesn't help that his hair is pasted back, bringing my attention to high cheekbones and a jaw that could slice someone in half.

I hear leaves crunching behind me.

Stiffening, I turn and gasp in shock.

"Mr. Cross?"

"Miss Jamieson." The superstar's voice has a deep, husky quality.

The moment I hear it, I think of Zane. They both have

similar timbres, but Zane's is like a rough caress while Jarod Cross is like honey, smooth and seductive.

"Why are you hiding in the trees?" Jarod Cross asks.

My eyes dart from side to side. "Oh..."

"Shouldn't you be down there?" He points past the secluded tree line to the funeral.

My mouth goes dry.

I intentionally stayed a distance away. This is my first funeral since Sloane, and I feared that the burial would stir up painful memories. I also didn't want to be around Zane after that tense moment at the funeral parlor. The more walls I can put between us, the better.

"I didn't want to interrupt," I say finally.

"Mm." Jarod Cross tilts his chin up, inhaling a breath.

I watch the way the light hits his face, a little fascinated by the shimmer to his appearance. Do all celebrities glow like that or is it just him?

Plus he's one of the most handsome men I've ever seen. His hair is thick, his nose straight and his chin sharp and slightly roguish. Ink crowds every inch of the skin I can see.

His sex appeal is no surprise. In no time at all, he got mom to fall in love with him. And he's the father to three of the most handsome seniors at Redwood Prep.

The three shiny apples don't fall far from the shiny tree.

Jarod's eyes catch on mine, two shadows that make the forest feel a little darker than it did before.

Unnerved, I glance away.

I don't know much about the rockstar.

And I've always suspected that's intentional.

He strikes me as a man who knows exactly what to show people at any given moment. In fairness, I'd be cautious too if I was a mega-star living under a microscope and being dissected by the public for years.

On the other hand, he could be hiding something.

If the reason is more insidious, I can't tell.

And I wish I could.

His movements don't make sense to me.

But I *want* to like him.

I want to believe the fairytale. That he saw my mother at a diner after playing a late concert. That he fell madly in love. That he couldn't be without her and asked her to marry him.

Mom deserves to be a Cinderella for once.

I just wish this love didn't feel like a delicate glass slipper, easily shattered at any moment.

More leaves crunch as Jarod Cross comes to stand beside me. He smells like the forest—fresh pine, sunshine, and something earthy. I bet I wouldn't be able to find his cologne in a store. He strikes me as the type who'd have even his underwear custom-made.

"Did you know her?"

It takes me a second to realize he's referring to Cadence's mom.

"Uh, no." I face the gravesite again.

Dutch has his arm looped around both Cadence and Viola now. The younger sister is leaning heavily into his side and shuffling as if it hurts to walk. Zane, Finn, Sol, Serena and the blonde girl trail behind in a grim procession.

"She was the mother of one of my students, so I figured I should pay my respects."

He glances around. "No other teacher attended?"

"No." Redwood Prep doesn't have a track record of caring about scholarship students. I'm not surprised that I'm the only member of faculty that turned up.

Jarod surprises me by speaking again. His tone is carefully conversational.

Weird.

He's never seemed like the friendly, chatty type.

"I've only been teaching at Redwood for a few weeks now, but it's a hard job. I don't think teachers get the credit they deserve these days."

My lips curl up in a sad smile. "The kids have it hard too."

"How so?"

"Kids these days have to grow up too fast. Their world is supposed to be safe, but it always falls apart before they're ready."

"The world does that often, doesn't it?"

"What?" I glance at him.

"Fall apart." He cocks a brow at me. "It's a never-ending cycle of shattering and coming back together. Over and over again. Until you learn whatever lesson you're supposed to learn or achieve whatever you're supposed to achieve."

"Like a fairytale," I muse, my eyes sliding to Zane without any conscious thought. "The more you run, the bigger the dragon becomes."

"Kids at Redwood would say you're the dragon."

"Do they?"

"Talk in the teacher's lounge is that you're hard on them."

"I heard you're the same."

He shrugs. "Metal can only be bent when it's beaten."

"We're long past the days when you could beat kids in classrooms, Mr. Cross."

He chuckles.

I smile.

"I heard you don't engage in school politics either," he says.

"I'm trying to be the administration's dragon. Wait until I start breathing fire." I'm only half-joking.

But he laughs. It's a rough, chalky sound.

"I should go." He checks his watch. "I've taken a hiatus from my classes at Redwood to prepare for a tour. It's sad that I won't be able to see you in the hallway for the time being, Miss Jamieson. But at least I can see you for dinner."

My smile is brittle. Those words are meaningless. I can count on one hand the times he's been home to eat with mom.

The reminder of his neglect towards her brings me back to earth.

There's something about Jarod Cross that makes you want to trust him. To earn his approval. To be his friend.

It makes it so easy to forget everything else.

But I don't want to forget.

He turns to leave and I ask, "What were *you* doing here?"

He freezes.

"You never told me."

For a moment, his face hardens. It's so quick that, by the time I blink, the expression is gone.

"Same as you. I came to pay my respects."

"From a distance?"

"I only have a couple minutes to spare. It would be rude of me to show my face for a short time only to disappear." He smiles and there's something a little sinister about it. As if we're playing a game where he's the only one who knows the rules. "Are you suspecting me of something, Grace?"

"Just asking."

He checks his watch. "Tell your mother I'll be home late."

Tell her yourself.

The words are on the tip of my tongue, but they don't spring free. "Sure."

He hesitates. "Grace, I hope you won't feel this awkward with me for long. You can call me any time. I might not be your father by blood, but I consider you a daughter just the same."

I dip my head.

Jarod Cross leaves and my gaze wanders to the crew piling dirt on top of the casket.

An idea lights up my brain.

Whirling around, I dash after the rockstar.

"Jarod, wait!"

I find him just about to get into his town car.

Two mean-looking guys glower at me. One moves forward as if to keep me back.

With a slight wave from Jarod, the guy backs off.

"Actually, I do have a favor," I say.

He waits.

"I need information about a Redwood Prep student who was brutally murdered six years ago. Do you know someone who can help me?"

Chapter Thirteen

ZANE

For some odd reason, I keep looking at the tree line surrounding the cemetery. It feels like someone's watching but, whenever I look in that direction, all I can see are thick pines and stillness.

Damn.

Is someone there or not?

Maybe I'm losing it.

"You coming?" Finn asks.

I nod and trot behind my brothers.

My suit is itchy. I'm more of a jeans, T-shirt and leather jacket kind of guy but, out of respect for Cadence and Dutch, I dressed up.

Cadence approaches me when I'm ripping off my jacket by the car.

"Hey, Zane."

"Cadey."

"I wanted to thank you for today. I heard Dutch *wasn't*

the one who planned today's funeral."

My eyes swerve to Dutch.

My twin scowls, leaning on the hood of his car, ankles crossed in front of him.

Chuckling, I rub my chin. "I guess I couldn't get that one past you."

"Dutch didn't even know what hymns we were singing," Cadence says. She touches my arm. "Thank you, Zane. It was really sweet of you to do that."

"It was nothing. But if you *really* want to thank me, you can give me a nice big hug. Your husband is currently glaring at the hand you have on my arm and I think that would really piss him off."

Cadence giggles like a woman after my own heart and throws her arms around my waist. I squeeze her to me, dipping my head in her shoulder.

Dutch is on us like lightning. "What the hell do you need to hug for?"

I release Cadence just enough that she can move out of the hug, but I drape an arm over her shoulder. "I can hug my sister-in-law if I want to."

Hazel eyes glittering with annoyance, Dutch growls, "Keep talking smack and we'll have two funerals today instead of one."

"Can you two *not* for one freaking minute," Finn groans. Always caught in the middle.

Sol smirks and walks up to us. "Don't stop them. It's kind of refreshing. Lightens up the mood."

I meet my best friend's eyes. Sol is drumming up a tight smile, but there's something off about it. Like it's hiding a world of pain. When we told him the funeral details, I was half-hoping that he wouldn't show.

"Thank you all for coming," Cadey says. "You too,

Breeze." She reaches out to her blonde friend who takes her hand. "And Serena." Cadey extends her other hand and a brunette wearing bright red lipstick, fishnets and a leather jacket joins her.

I've seen Cadey hanging out with the goth chick at school. She's always seemed a little weird to me. Quiet. Studious. Kind of like a female version of Finn.

I wink at the ladies. "We're having the after-party at our place. You ladies are free to come."

"After-party?" Breeze scrunches her nose.

"Don't you mean repast?" Finn corrects me like the smart aleck he is.

"Whatever. It's the part of the funeral where you eat, drink, and play music. Sounds like a party to me."

Serena licks her lips nervously. "I'll, uh, bow out. I've got plans."

"What about you?" I arch a brow at Cadey's friend. "In the mood to party?"

She rolls her eyes. "My best friend made the ridiculous decision to marry the lead singer of a rock band at eighteen. I don't have a choice but to tag along."

"Nice." I ease over her. "I get to corrupt you for the night."

"You get to do no such thing." Cadey drags Breeze behind her. "Back off, Zane. She's untouchable."

I laugh at Cadey's protective stance.

Viola joins us, her steps slow and draggy.

Everyone immediately sobers.

"You okay, Vi?" I ask, touching her back.

"Yeah, I said my goodbyes to mom." She sniffs, shoulders slumping. "Can we go home now?"

I pat her shoulder, not sure how to console a thirteen year old girl. It's always been me and my brothers. We don't really get emotional. When we do, our form of commiseration is to jam together at the highest volume and then drink until we pass out.

Unfortunately, Viola is more into makeup than music.

And Cadey will kill me if I give her baby sister alcohol.

We separate into our own trucks.

Dutch takes Cadey, Vi, and Breeze in his car while Finn gets behind the wheel of his electric convertible. Sol is in the backseat while I take shot gun.

I lift one leg on the dashboard. "I've been thinking..."

"Ugh..." Sol groans, eyes going dark. "Those three words never mean anything good coming from you."

"Get your feet off my dash," Finn orders.

I drop my leg, take out a drumstick, and twirl it. "I think we should do something for Cadence and Dutch's wedding."

"Didn't we already?" Finn mumbles, flicking the indicator.

"We only *watched* them get married. And it doesn't count because Sol wasn't there. Right?" I meet his eyes in the rearview mirror.

He shrugs.

It's not an enthusiastic response, but I'll take it.

"Plus they didn't get to have a reception because Tina, you know," I slide a finger across my neck, "at a very inconvenient time."

"Don't let Viola hear you say that," Finn warns.

"What do you propose?" Sol says.

"A party."

Finn rolls his eyes again. The punk says so much without saying anything at all.

"Think about it. It'll brighten up the vibes, clear the air

after the funeral. Give them a proper beginning. What do you think?"

"Do whatever you want, Zane. You've never let us stop you before," Finn mumbles.

I smirk all the way home.

In the driveway, Dutch moves toward us.

"Where did the girls go?" Sol asks.

"They went to change out of their funeral clothes," Dutch answers.

"Cadey looks like she's holding it together," I note.

"It's just a front. She's torn up about this, but she doesn't want to be."

Sol nods as if he gets it.

I'm glad to see Dutch and Sol talking politely again. There's still some unresolved tension, but at least it doesn't feel like they're on the edge of duking it out.

My eyes slide to the driveway where dad was parked last night.

"Guys, there's something I need to tell you," I say.

Finn, Dutch, and Sol were already starting to head inside, but they stop when they hear the serious note in my voice.

"Dad came to visit me last night."

Finn's eyes widen.

Sol stiffens.

Dutch glares at me. "What did he say?"

I give them a quick summary.

Dutch runs a hand through his hair. "If dad is sniffing around Cadey, trying to figure out if she's pregnant..." He sighs. "What will he do if the answer is yes? He was crazy enough to throw me in jail to get his hands on this inheritance."

"I'm starting to think moving away is a better idea," Finn says.

I shake my head. "Before you buy your plane ticket, I have a plan."

"What plan?" Sol asks.

"To stop dad."

"And how do we do that?" Dutch growls.

I smirk. "We ruin his marriage."

Dutch narrows his eyes. "I'm not staking Cadey's life on a joke, Zane."

"It's not a joke." I look each of my brothers in the eye. "Dad only cares about the inheritance because he qualifies. And he only qualifies because he's married. So how do we knock him out of the race where it hurts?"

"We destroy his ticket in," Finn whispers.

Dutch looks thoughtful.

"It's crazy," Sol says with a shake of his head.

"Crazy enough to work."

Finn studies me with those sharp eyes. "Convincing Miss Jamieson's mother to let go of dad won't be easy. She loves him."

"Love doesn't last forever."

Sol snorts.

"You might have to get dirty," Finn warns.

"I've never been afraid of getting dirty."

"You attack her mom, Miss Jamieson will never forgive you," Dutch points out.

The words thud to the ground.

I don't have a response.

My brothers stare at me, an unspoken warning in the air. *You can never turn back if you take this road.*

"Miss Jamieson and I aren't like you and Cadey. She

made it clear that she wants nothing to do with me and I'm not the type to chase someone who doesn't want to be caught."

"Like I said, it's crazy." Sol stares at me. "But I think you can do it."

"It's the most solid plan we've had in a long time," Finn agrees.

We all turn to look at Dutch.

He frowns. "Even if you win, even if you protect us and ruin dad, you lose something. There's no way you walk out of this unscathed."

"Just tell me if you're in or not."

"Fine. I'm in," Dutch says.

I nod.

Convincing my brothers was the first step of my plan.

I did it.

But now that I'm thinking of what needs to happen next, it doesn't feel like a victory.

* * *

Jinx: What dies, comes back to life and then dies again?

Scandals and secrets.

Today, Redwood's princes buried a secret in the Lakeshore Cemetery. A secret that left our new Cinderella heartbroken. At least it should have. But New Girl seemed a little too eager to grab that shovel and hide her dirty sins from the light.

Can the darkness stay buried this time? Only time will tell.

Here's a warning to the girls who plan on becoming the new queens of these royals: our resident kings have a little too many sins to hide.

You're going to need a bigger shovel.

Until the next post, keep your enemies close and your secrets even closer.

- Jinx

Chapter Fourteen

GREY

"Are you sure you have enough time?"

"This is important." Jarod Cross gives me a cursory scan and motions to the chairs across from his desk.

Gingerly, I sink into a chair.

This is my first time in a recording studio. The office is well-decorated with a thick rug, frames of Jarod Cross's best-selling albums, Billboard Charts topping awards, and a host of other trophies.

"Hand me the folder," Jarod says, a hint of authority in his tone.

My fingers, instinctively, tighten on the document.

After I asked for his help, Jarod wanted to get started right away. He offered to look over the materials I'd gathered and promised to send it to his private investigator friend.

Everything fell into place so perfectly.

THE FORBIDDEN NOTE

And yet, there's something deep inside that tells me not to release these files into his hands.

"Grace?" Jarod arches a brow.

My throat bobs as I swallow. "We really don't have to do this now." Jarod turns those dark eyes on me, clearly seeing through my B.S. "I mean... you said you had a sound check." I glance at the time on my watch. "I didn't mean for you to set your schedule aside."

He aims a tight smile at me, but there's something sharp about it. Calculative. It's like a severe and disapproving frown is hiding right behind those perfect white teeth.

"You're the one who asked for help, Grace. Isn't that because you have nowhere else to turn?"

He's right. Every avenue I've taken has led to a dead end. The security guards from six years ago have all been fired, their information wiped from the Redwood Prep files. The teachers who were working at Redwood six years ago clam up when I try to bring up Sloane's murder.

It's like chasing smoke.

Every time I think I'm close to the truth, it disappears without a trace.

As a last resort, I reached out to Jinx. The blackmailer wasn't around when Sloane and I attended Redwood, but I figured she had access to a network of information. Maybe there was *something* that could help me.

Unfortunately, Jinx isn't just a blackmailer.

She's a trader of secrets.

For access to her information, I need to give up some of my own. But confessing my connection to Zane could ruin my career and any chances of working undercover at Redwood.

Jarod Cross is my last shot.

The silence stretches as the rockstar waits. The longer I hold out, the more he looks at me like I'm a misbehaving child who took the cookie without asking. Thinking fast, I slip my thumb in the crook of the folder and offer it to him. At the last second, I drop my thumb and the folder splatters to the ground.

"Oh no." I gasp.

Jarod rises staunchly.

"I got it," I say, holding a hand out to him and kneeling next to the mess.

He remains standing for a long beat, eyes narrowing. Slowly, hesitantly, he sits back down.

Hunkering close to the desk, I sweep the files up while laughing. "I'm so clumsy. Every day, I spill books just walking down the hallway. It's ridiculous."

Quickly, I tuck my personal notes into my bra.

"Here," I say, shoving the messy folder over the table.

Jarod Cross turns his dark eyes over to mine and assesses me. It's an awful feeling to be under that pointed stare, and I shiver.

"Can I use the bathroom?" I ask.

One corner of his lips etches up. It's a smile that promises he's running out of patience with me. "Sure."

I hurry to the bathroom with the papers I stashed chaffing against my skin. The moment I'm alone, I hunker over the sink and grip the edges tight. My brown knuckles turn red as I squeeze.

What was that? Why do I keep getting weird vibes from him?

The folder I left on Jarod's desk is filled with newspaper clippings and online articles—things anyone could glean with a deep Google search. They won't do him as much good as the janitor interviews and police reports currently stuck to my breast.

Hands trembling, I tuck the papers more securely in my bra and wash my hands. Wetting my curls to give them a little refresh, I re-do my lipstick and smile.

There.

I look like a confident woman and not the nervous wreck I am inside.

I return to the office and Jarod Cross is waiting.

He nods at me. "You okay?"

"Yes, I'm fine," I stammer.

As I return to my seat, I notice him eyeing my blouse as if he can see the papers through the fabric. It takes everything in me not to squirm and check that the documents are out of sight. I *know* I hid them well. Looking down now would just give away the fact that I hid something.

"Is something wrong?" I prod, holding his stare.

He breaks eye contact first and slips a pair of glasses over his nose. Nodding to the folder, he says, "This isn't much to go on."

"It's all I have so far."

He arches an eyebrow. "That's not true."

My blood runs cold.

Heart racing, I run my tongue over my lip. "What do you mean?"

He juts his chin at me and leans back in his chair. "You."

"W-what?"

"You were there when this student was attending Redwood. Even if she didn't personally tell you anything, you would have heard the gossip."

My nostrils flare. I choose my words carefully. "I have my suspicions, but I don't know if they're warranted or not. Ultimately, I'd like closure for Sloane and her family."

"Were you friends?" He temples his fingers.

"Yes."

He nods slowly and I wonder what kind of conclusion he's arrived at. "I'll forward this to the PI and call you when he has an update."

I hear the dismissal. "Thank you."

Rising, I push my chair back in toward his desk and walk to the door.

"Miss Jamieson."

I freeze.

His eyes are hot on me, two lasers drilling into my face. "If you remember anything else or have any information you'd like to add, let me know."

My throat closes up. Why does that sound like a threat more than an offer to help?

I slip out of the room.

And then I run.

I don't stop until I'm home.

There, I lock my bedroom door, checking twice.

My hands press flat against the wall as I wilt and catch my breath.

I'm being ridiculous.

Jarod Cross is my mom's husband.

My step-father.

A member of my family.

But beyond that, he's also a household name, a worldwide legend and a public figure.

There's no way he's a bad guy... right?

Chapter Fifteen

ZANE

I roll my suitcase into the kitchen that looks big enough to feature on TLC.

"Zane!" My dad's new wife throws her arms around me. She smells like cocoa butter and some kind of warm savory spice.

"You're early." Marian steps back. Brown eyes glistening, she gives Finn the same warm welcome.

My brother's eyes nearly pop out of his face.

"Were you cooking?" I ask.

"I got up early this morning and started frying up some cornbread." She points to the counter that's filled with pancakes, waffles, cornbread, bacon and sausages.

"You made all this?" I point.

"That's right."

"Your... self?" I clarify.

Finn clears his throat. "I think he meant to say you didn't have to go to all that trouble."

"Oh, I like keeping my hands busy, and I wanted to welcome you boys." She grins wide, revealing all her teeth.

Watching Miss Jamieson's mother, I feel a twinge of guilt. When dad first announced that he was getting married again, I assumed she'd be just like all the other young, brainless, copycat social media models he cheated on mom with.

I was wrong.

For one thing, Marian isn't that young. She's younger than mom, for sure, but there are wrinkles bracketing her dark brown skin and she dresses conservatively, no plunging necklines, tats or piercings.

She's also much warmer than dad's other girlfriends.

Which is new.

There's something appealing about her sunny personality. She's guileless. Upfront. The 'what you see is what you get' type.

I have to question any woman who falls for dad—since he's a walking scumbag in leather, but at least she seems honest. In our world, sincerity is hard to come by.

"Why are you staring at me like that?" Marian asks, picking up a spatula. Suddenly, her smile falls. "Ya'll aren't the type that don't eat breakfast, are you? Oh no. And I made so much food."

"I'm hungry," Finn says, taking a seat.

"Me too."

Marian smiles and throws her arms around me again.

I stumble back, shocked. Our family isn't the affectionate type. Growing up, we spent more time with nannies than with mom and dad, and there was always a certain distance kept by the help. Love isn't something we express out in the open.

That's not to say mom doesn't love us.

She does.

In her own way.

But she doesn't dole out hugs like coupons at the local supermarket.

"Sorry." Marian eases back. "I've just… always wanted a full house. And when Jarod told me he had three sons, well, I instantly imagined us all living under one roof and being a big happy family."

My eyes connect with Finn's. Big, happy family is a phrase that could never describe the Cross dynamic.

"I'm so glad you guys decided to move in."

"Thanks for having us," I say since Finn is being moodily silent.

Marian glances past us to the door. "Is Dutch coming?"

"Not today."

"Oh." Her lips curl down in disappointment.

Dutch is bringing Cadey and Viola to live with him. To say he had to drag Cadey there is putting it lightly. She complained that the villa was too big for three people, but when Dutch pointed out that the three of us lived there without complaint, she gave in.

The last we saw of the newlyweds, they were scowling at each other and then, a minute later, Dutch was carting her off to his room, where we heard loud moans rattling the walls. I have no idea how those two find butting heads so appealing. Just watching them toss insults back and forth exhausts me.

At least, Viola seemed oblivious.

'I can't believe I get a bathroom to myself!' she shrieked as I brought her bags in from the car. She was setting up her makeup when we left, but there's no guarantee she'll always be that distracted.

I make a mental note to tell Dutch to either be quieter or soundproof his walls.

Seeing my twin with his family today made it all seem pretty freaking clear to me.

Dutch is moving on with his life.

He's still here.

He's still a part of us.

But things are different.

And I don't know how I feel about that.

"Alright, that's enough yapping from me." Marian claps her hands. "Finn, what will you have? I didn't know what ya'll liked so I made a bit of everything."

While Finn starts filling his plate, I point upstairs. "I'll put these bags away."

"Of course, of course." Marian waves me up. "You can have your pick of the rooms. This house is too big anyway. I begged Gracie to move in with me, so it'll be the four of us. And Jarod when he's not on tour."

"Gracie?" Finn hikes a brow.

I freeze.

Marian's brown eyes alight on me and then move to Finn. "Yes, my daughter."

A full-body shiver takes hold of me and I have to bite my lip to keep from smiling wickedly.

"Didn't you know she lives with us?" Marian clears her throat. "That's not going to be a problem, is it? I know Gracie's your teacher at Redwood. I wouldn't want any of you getting in trouble."

"Trouble has a way of finding us," Finn says, glaring at me.

My heart starts beating fast.

Finn gives me a pointed look and juts his chin at the hallway.

THE FORBIDDEN NOTE

"Zane, should I fix you a plate for when you come back?"

"I'd appreciate that." I give Marian a charming smile.

Finn is scarily silent as he stomps to the corridor. I slip my drumstick out and twirl it as I trail my brother out of the kitchen.

The moment we're a distance away he whirls on me.

"What the hell, Zane?"

"What did I do?"

Finn gives me a loaded stare. "Did you know about this?"

I shake my head. "I swear I didn't."

"If all that talk after the funeral was just a way for you to sneak into Miss Jamieson's bed again—"

"The hell? I told you it wasn't. I meant it when I said I'm done chasing her."

Finn's eyes narrow to slits. My brother's the scariest when he's scowling like that.

"Her living here is not going to be a problem."

"We'll see," he says stiffly.

I watch my brother stomp back to the kitchen. Finn volunteered to move in with me, but I think he and Dutch just wanted me to have a babysitter.

Guess they made the right move.

Miss Jamieson just became a bigger part of this twisted game.

I sweep my gaze toward the stairs.

It's time I go hunting for my prey.

* * *

Jinx: Is the band breaking up?

Snare King's hot selfie this morning had more than just a

perfect row of abs on display. Did I spot suitcases in the background? Are the Kings going on a secret tour or is the war on the horizon a family battle?

Until the next post, keep your enemies close and your secrets even closer,

-Jinx

Chapter Sixteen

ZANE

I head up the stairs, adrenaline rushing through me. There's something utterly depraved about seeking out the room where my step-sister sleeps.

But I revel in the feeling.

Which one of these is hers?

It's hard to tell. None of the rooms I peek in look lived-in.

I get to the end of the hall and hear a shower running.

"Mom!" Grace calls. "Is that you?"

I freeze.

"I forgot my towel again. Can you bring one?"

My breath catches as a full-blown image of her naked and wet fills my mind.

"Mom?"

I see a half-open closet door up ahead. Stalking over, I nab one of the fluffy white towels on the shelf and push the door of the bathroom.

It creaks when I enter.

The heat from the shower smothers me like a hand on my chest.

Immediately, my eyes snap to the frosted glass.

Grace makes the sexiest little humming sound, as if she knows I'm watching. As if she knows I'm about to lose my damn mind.

This moment is too perfect.

The way she's exposed but hidden.

The way she's vulnerable but confident.

It's like a burlesque show all for me.

She twists to the side, showing off more of her body. I get an eyeful of her delectable, feminine curves. That tempting silhouette sends a bolt of lightning straight to my pants.

Mischief and desire propel me.

I walk forward.

Something tells me I shouldn't mess with her.

But I've never listened to that voice.

"Thanks, mom," Miss Jamieson yells to be heard over the shower. "Can you hand it to me?"

I push the glass door a little.

A slim arm, dripping wet, reaches out.

"Here," I say.

Brown fingers with white nail polish tangle in the towel, but they go lax when she hears my voice.

"M-mom?"

I pause. Let the moment stretch out.

I can feel the tension building.

I can practically hear her thoughts.

I must be dreaming. It isn't him. Zane isn't in the bathroom with me.

My lips curl up cruelly. "It's me."

Grace screams and releases the towel, arms windmilling backward.

Through the frosted glass, I see her lose her balance.

My eyes widen. Tossing the towel, I move on instinct. I step into the shower and grab her by the waist. My hand makes a slapping sound as it collides with her soft, wet skin.

Grace grabs my shoulders, hoisting her body against mine in a frantic effort to keep upright. One limp curl sticks against her puffing cheeks. Her chest pierces my T-shirt, ramming into my abs like pinpricks of soft, tempting delight.

This close, I can see *all* of her.

She's a perfect chocolate brown. Skin unbroken. Unblemished. Like a sculptor poured a vat of melted Hershey's over his prized statue and painstakingly waited for it to cool. Her skin is soft and tight. Water drips down the curve of her spine to a pert and perfectly grabbable—

"Ah!" She squeezes her eyes shut and I see soap gathering under the arch of her brow.

Grazing my thumb over her eyes, I blow on it.

Her thick eyelashes flutter and I doubt it's helping. She rubs her eyes over and over again.

"Stop. Your hand is full of soap. That won't help."

"Shut up," she growls.

I laugh a little, wrapping her tighter in my arms and feeling the pressure build inside me.

She's like a wet dream come to life.

Soft. Sweet. Open.

I hold her there.

Warm water batters the top of my head and falls into my eyes. I lean closer, inhaling the scent of her sweetly perfumed skin.

"If you wanted us to shower together, you could have just asked," I whisper in her ear.

Her eyes are red from irritation and anger. I see a glint of outrage behind her scowl. It shouldn't excite me as much as it does.

Brown hands flail as she shoves me.

I hold firm.

Now that I've got her in my arms, there's no way in hell I'm letting her go. My gaze flicks down her delectable curves again, retracing the places my fingers beg to touch.

"Get your hands off me!" she snaps. Her nostrils flare with anger.

I lift a dark brow, tilting my head so the water runs down the side of my face instead of right in front of me.

"Do you really want me to do that?" I challenge.

She struggles to keep her face angry, but it doesn't work.

Her fingers tighten around my neck.

Her mouth parts.

She's saying one thing, but her body's telling a whole different story.

"Do you really want me to let you go?" I growl, walking her backward. My sneakers slosh into the wet puddles on the ground. My shirt sticks to my skin, showing off the outline of my abs.

Her eyes dip there and she licks her lips.

A sick, twisted smile unfurls.

I keep going until her back smacks against the wall. A wet, *schlopping* sound mingles with the patter of the shower. The ricochet sends her body jolting against me. Our hips brush and she lets out a little cry that whips a blaze in my blood.

"Tell me what you want, tiger. I'll listen."

She swallows hard. "I want..."

"What?" I swoop in, hovering my lips over hers.

Her eyes slide to half-mast and she tilts her chin up.

A dark chuckle vibrates through my chest.

"What you really want," I bracket my hands on either side of her head so she knows I'm not the one keeping her here, so she knows that she's here on her own, "is for me to make you beg the way you did that night."

She moans softly, a sound that penetrates straight through my skin to my heart. The bathroom is hotter than before, and it has nothing to do with the steam from the shower.

"You say you want the light," I lick at the drops of water on her shoulder, my voice dropping to a depraved whisper, "but why do I always find you in the dark next to me?"

Her skin is sweet on my tongue and I lick my way up to her ear.

The words, "I hate you" pass between her trembling brown lips.

"Say it again," I whisper.

Her eyes glow with anger and desire. A strange mixture that glints like gold in her soft brown eyes. "I. Hate. You."

"You hate me." I slide my fingers down her jaw and wrap them around her throat. "You hate me... *so much*, that it kills you, doesn't it?"

The steaming shower gets even hotter.

"Gracie!" Marian's voice shatters the tension. "Are you finished showering? Come meet your brothers."

Miss Jamieson's face tightens. She wrenches my arms off her and skates out of the shower.

When she dips to pick up the towel, I get an eyeful of her glorious peach. She quickly wraps it away in the towel.

"I don't care what you're doing here. I don't care what you want. Get out of my house while I'm asking nicely."

I give her a cocky grin. "Sorry, *sis*. This is our home now. I'll be seeing you every morning." I push my hair back with a hand and drape both arms on the open shower door. "Every evening. And every…" I slip my eyes down the towel, "night."

She gives me a scathing look and stomps out of the bathroom.

I flip the shower off.

My body's aching like crazy.

"Zane? The food's getting cold," Marian yells from downstairs.

I adjust myself as best as I can and leave the bathroom.

Burning hot flames lick at my feet with every step. The heat I'd expected to feel with that girl in the desert is here now. Throbbing. Roaring. Demanding release.

The words I told Finn downstairs come back to haunt me.

I'm done chasing Miss Jamieson.

But I'm not done wanting her.

Those two things can be true at the same time.

And here's another truth for the hell of it—she's not done wanting me either.

Chapter Seventeen

GREY

"Let me take that for you." Zane wraps his long, wicked fingers around my mother's coffee mug and pushes back from the table.

"Thank you, Zane. Aren't you just a sweetheart?" Mom beams at him, falling under his spell.

She has no idea how evil he is.

How depraved.

How despicable.

If she did, would she be throwing heart eyes in his direction? Would she be patting his back like he's a good boy?

"What about you, Miss Jamieson?" Zane's eyes burn into me, and I can tell he's thinking about the shower. "Is there anything you want?"

"No," I grind out.

His gaze drops to my lips, his hot stare as heavy as his

hands around my throat. The memory is thick, visceral. And it makes me tremble with a desperate, aching need.

It's filthy.

Probably unlawful.

And yet it's persistent.

I can't help how much I want him.

How much I hate him.

How much the two blend in a sharp swirl of pain.

If I didn't have Sloane's case binding me here, I'd probably run. Far from this city. Far from Redwood Prep. Far from Zane freaking Cross.

Not because I lack self-control.

Because he's showing me that I'm as much of a monster as those behind Sloane's murder. An unscrupulous authority figure. One who indulges in her own passions. Tramples on laws. Dances over the grave of propriety.

The night we met, I genuinely had no idea he was only eighteen and a student in high school. But what's my excuse for trembling under his touch and pressing my naked body to his now?

I hate who I'm becoming.

And yet, I can't stop the transformation as much as a werewolf during full moon.

The only defense I had against Zane was distance.

And now...

Now my biggest temptation—

The boy with the sky-blue eyes who can undo everything that matters to me—

Is sleeping down the hall.

"Gracie, are you alright?" Mom asks.

"Huh?" I glance up distractedly.

"You usually tear into chocolate chip pancakes." Mom

THE FORBIDDEN NOTE

tilts her chin and says proudly to Zane and Finn, "She eats like a horse. Don't let that slim frame fool you."

"Mom." I groan.

"I didn't know that," Zane says.

"No?"

"Miss Jamieson never eats with us at lunch."

"Gracie, why don't you eat with your brothers?"

I cringe. Why does she keep calling them my brothers? "Teachers don't eat with students, mom."

"Yes, they do." Zane arches a brow.

"You should eat with them on occasion," Mom says. "Family bonding is good."

"Yes, it'll be good to *bond*."

My eyes zip to Zane and narrow. We don't need any more 'bonding'. Especially not the naked kind.

Soul bonds? Those are a different thing. I've heard that every time someone has sex, their soul bonds with their partner. If so, Zane probably has a million different souls attached to his.

I'm just one of many.

I drag my gaze back to the eggs.

"Here you go. Strong coffee. Two creams. Two sugars." Zane sets the cup on the table.

His biceps flex as he bends over mom and gives her a charming smile. The tips of his hair are slightly damp from the shower and the way it hangs over his face makes my fingers itch to brush them back.

"You sweet thing." Mom pinches his cheeks.

It's so weird seeing her coo to Zane like he's a baby. I'm surprised that he's allowing her. The Cross brothers are menaces at Redwood Prep. They part crowds and send freshmen skittering into hiding places. With their tats, muscular chests and dark personas, they don't seem like the type who'd appreciate mom's form of coddling.

But Zane smiles at mom.

And Finn seems amused by her coddling.

Zane takes the seat right across from me, looking smug.

I bristle in discomfort. He's all the way across the table and yet he's all over me. I can still feel the cool tile at my back, the heat of the shower, his tongue on my neck, his rough fingers grazing my face.

Zane's eyes linger on me and the tension begins to creep around the table.

I clear my throat and glance away. My gaze catches on Finn. The adopted Cross brother is watching everything closely. His true thoughts are hidden behind his ice-cold expression.

I've noticed that he doesn't speak much. That's more frightening than I care to admit.

Has Zane told him about us?

I've always suspected, but now I get the feeling that the brothers have definitely talked about me. At length.

The thought is horrifying.

Mom pinches Zane's sleeve. "Young man, I still don't understand how you got your uniform all wet. It's like you ran through the rain."

"I checked out the water pressure in the bathroom," Zane says, eyes sliding over me. "And then things got a little... wet."

My mouth flattens into a hard, thin line.

I press my palms on the table. "Thanks for the food, mom. We should get going or we'll be late for school."

"Oh, sit down and finish your plate, Gracie. You still have time."

"Yeah, *Gracie*, stay."

THE FORBIDDEN NOTE

"Do not call me that," I snap.

"Her friends call her Grey," mom informs him. "She hates when anyone calls her Gracie, but it was a childhood nickname, so I can't let it go."

"Grey, huh?" Zane's eyes glint in my direction.

"Sit, sit." Mom waits until I claim my seat again.

"This food is amazing, Ms. Marian. Best I've ever had," Zane says.

"Thank you."

"Isn't that right, Finn?" Zane elbows him.

Finn nods.

"Forgive him," Zane chats easily. "He's a bassist. Has to keep things mysterious."

Mom gasps in excitement. "Oh, that's right! You three have a band, don't you?"

"It's four of us actually," Zane says, staking his fork into pancakes. "We're called The Kings."

"I'd love to hear you play."

"We have a set next month," Zane says.

"You know..." Mom wiggles her eyebrows. "I used to do a little singing in my day."

I roll my eyes. "Mom."

"What? It's true? I thought I'd be a singer-songwriter. Had big dreams of heading to a big city and changing the game. And then I had Gracie." She smiles softly at me. "Now, I only sing in the shower and while I'm working around the house."

"You should sing in one of our sets," Zane offers.

My eyes widen in surprise.

Mom looks touched. "Seriously?"

He shrugs. "Why not?"

Suspicious, I stare at him. Why is he being so nice to my mom?

"I've never performed in front of an audience before. What if I don't do well?"

"Dutch's wi—girlfriend," Zane corrects himself, "has severe stage fright, but he got her on stage and she managed to play with us. We'll take care of you."

Finn grunts in agreement.

Mom giggles. "I've got to break out my boa and practice my runs."

"You know they play rock, right, mom?" I say a little snottily. "It's a totally different sound."

"So?" Zane tilts his chin up in challenge. "Aretha Franklin is the queen of soul and she did plenty of rock covers. Music is a language that everybody can understand, no matter the colour of their skin..." his eyes pierce mine, "or their age."

"That's right. Listen to that boy, Gracie. He can teach you a thing or two."

Zane chomps on a strip of bacon. "Don't worry. I already have."

"Mom, how long are the boys staying for?"

"Until they move to college." Mom blinks. "Why?"

Dread pooling in my veins, I shoot to my feet again. "I'm heading to school."

"I'm—" Zane starts to get up.

Finn grabs his shoulder and drives him back down in his seat.

I take that opportunity to flee.

Grabbing my purse, I shoot out the door and hoof it to the nearest bus station.

My car is in the shop. Mom offered to buy me a new one, but I don't want to. Not having a car actually helps me out when I want to do after-hours sleuthing at Redwood. Nothing screams 'Miss Jamieson is here' like my rusty car parked in the lot late at night. It's better when I don't take it.

I walk a distance to catch a bus since there are none in this fancy, gated community.

By the time I get on, I'm sweating.

I check my phone.

There are no new messages from Jarod Cross.

Quickly, I type:

Any news from your friend?

There's no response.

The bus stops close to Redwood and I get off. Sunshine hits the top of my head and I fan my face to cool down.

Kids in the Redwood Prep uniforms swarm the lawn and huddle in groups on the front steps.

"Good morning," I say, throwing a welcoming nod at a set of cheerleaders.

I'm met with dark scowls. Youthful eyes cut sharply into me as if they want to slice my skin from my bones.

I blink once. Twice.

Weird.

"Good morning," I say to a group of guys this time.

They, too, give me weird looks, their eyes sliding down to my skirt.

My fingers tighten around my satchel.

I enter through the double doors and, the moment I step into the hallway, the entire corridor goes quiet. It's the first time I've ever heard such a sharp silence in the halls of Redwood.

No one moves.

No one speaks.

It feels like no one is even breathing.

I take a step.

Another.

Another.

The unholy hush sweeps down the corridor as far as the eyes can see. Students back away from me, cell phones clutched in their hands and eyes tracking my every move.

My chest tightens.

My breathing turns shaky.

What is going on?

Feeling like there's something on my clothes, I hurry to the bathroom and check my outfit. I'm wearing a simple blue button-down blouse tucked into a thigh-length pencil skirt. I paired that with my usual black pumps.

There are no rips in my blouse, no missing buttons in my shirt, my panties aren't showing.

So why is everyone staring?

Fearfully, I navigate to Jinx's app.

Is there something about me there?

I refresh the page.

There's nothing. Only a few posts about Dutch and Cadence, another post about Redwood's masquerade ball, and an exposé about two cheerleaders found stoned under the bleachers.

Jinx hasn't written a post about me.

So what could it be?

I merge back into the hallway, fighting to ignore all the stares.

Maybe it's all in my head?

Or maybe I won an award for something?

A familiar face walks past me.

"Vanya," I blurt.

"Miss Jamieson?" She jumps, nearly splattering her papers.

"Can I see your cell phone?"

"Um..." She curls her fingers around the device.

"Please," I beg.

Slowly, she offers the phone to me. Expertly, I navigate to the previous tab.

That's when I see it.

A private article.

Three words jump out at me.

Redwood's Newest Romance.

And below... is a picture of me and Zane.

Chapter Eighteen

GREY

I exhale, my eyes sweeping closed and my fingers tightening around the cell phone.

No, this can't be happening.

This *isn't* happening.

But when I open my eyes again, the picture is there in full color. The photographer captured me and Zane walking into the funeral parlor together. His hand is at the small of my back and I'm hunkered close beside him.

The picture itself is pretty tame, but the insinuation is devastating.

"Uh, Miss Jamieson, can I have my phone back?"

An ache springs in my head. It feels like someone's taken a sledgehammer to my skull.

"Miss Jamieson."

"Huh?'

"My phone."

I hand the phone over, setting it in her manicured hands.

Vanya peers closely at me. "Is it... true?"

My mouth parts.

At that moment, the front doors explode open.

Dutch, Finn, Zane and Sol stalk into Redwood. They're all huge. And I don't just mean their height. Their presence fills the entire corridor, pushing everyone out. All incredibly gorgeous and charismatic, they always draw their own riptide of appreciative stares and curious gazes.

But today is different.

Because, while The Kings always command every eye in the room, a few of those eyes swing to me.

Vanya turns too. "Zane is here."

The way she says his name, with a hint of awe and hero worship, sends a dark feeling through me. It's so unexpected that I internally flinch. Why do I care that someone is fawning over Zane when my world is literally imploding?

Jocks swagger up to Zane and pat him on the back. Words like 'right on' and 'good for you' echo through the hallway.

Zane looks confused. His dark gaze wanders the hallway and briefly flicks to mine. My heart surges to my throat, and I feel this sharp, piercing prick in my chest.

Zane quirks one of those thick, black brows at me.

I whirl around, darting out of the hallway and into the teacher's lounge. I can't stand to look at him right now.

The placard on my table reads 'Grace Jamieson, AP English'. I wrap my hands around the wooden stick and squeeze, trying to calm down.

I need to figure a way out of this mess.

The other teachers in the lounge glance at me, but no

one says anything. I get the feeling that they don't know about the picture. If they did, they'd be more glib about it.

None of the teachers here at Redwood Prep like me.

There are many reasons for that. I'm younger than most of them and, arguably, closer with the students. I also have a small, but passionate group of male students who routinely carry my books, bring me snacks and leave notes and gifts on my desk.

I'm also the only teacher at Redwood who's immune to the scorching power of The Kings.

Or at least I was.

Before Zane started blackmailing me.

Is this his work? Did he sneak into the bathroom, move into my house, and charm my mother—just to stab me in the back like this?

Anger surges anew. I feel like tearing through the hallway, stomping right over to the obnoxious four and slamming a punch into each of their faces.

I rub my temple and contemplate what I should do next when the door bursts open. All the air gets sucked out of the room when I glance up and see Zane. He didn't bother with a Redwood Prep jacket—it's probably still drying at home. Instead, his stark-white shirt is unbuttoned at the top and tucked into a pair of dark trousers. The sleeves are folded up and tattoos snake over the pale skin from his wrist to his fingers.

Blue eyes slice through the room, landing on me with a thud.

I stiffen, form fists, and prepare for anything.

Zane stops in front of my desk. "We need to talk."

"I'm sorry, Mr. Cross. I have to prepare for class," I say professionally. "You need to leave."

The teacher's lounge has gone deathly silent. Everyone is staring at us and they're not bothering to hide it.

Zane's intense energy rockets up to a near nuclear blaze. I've never seen him this angry.

"I wasn't asking," he snarls.

I lift my head and glare at him. "Neither was I."

"Grey."

I stiffen at the nickname.

He taps his fingers on the table.

I look up.

Zane jerks his head to the door, insistent.

I stubbornly look down again, taking out a red pen and writing notes over a student's essay. I'm pretty sure I'm writing gibberish, but I'm desperate to look busy.

The shadow over me gets smaller. I don't check, but I feel Zane's domineering presence withdraw from my desk. His military boots thump the ground and I think he's going to leave.

For a second, relief washes over my body.

I let out a sigh.

Until I hear his voice lifting in the quiet lounge.

"You heard her. She said to leave," Zane growls.

A confused hush settles on the room.

I whip my head up.

Stunned, I see that Zane is glaring at the other teachers.

At once, grown adults shuffle their papers into folders, replace their comfortable shoes with pumps and shiny leather oxfords, and slink out of the room.

In less than five seconds flat, the room is empty.

Just like that.

He commanded every teacher at Redwood Prep.

One word.

One snap of his fingers.

I'm shaking so badly, I'm sure Zane can notice.

His dark gaze moves over me. He slams the door closed and locks it angrily.

I shoot to my feet. "What the hell do you think you're doing?"

He stalks across the room, scowling.

"You can't just do that." I throw an arm at the door. "You can't just chase out your teachers and lock doors and act like you own this place. Because you don't. You don't own Redwood and you don't own me. So get the hell out of my face."

He remains standing by my desk, staring at me with those stormy blue eyes.

My entire world seems to shrink to this moment, to this anger, to this desperation.

I lash out, a tornado of pain, anger and guilt. "What? What do you want, Zane?" I drop my voice to a harsh whisper. "You think I'll let you screw me again if I get fired? Is that why you did this?"

"I didn't."

"I don't believe you."

"Liar." He presses his palms against my table, on either side of my plaque, and leans in. "You believe me, Grey. You just want to take your anger out on someone. It's fine if that person is me, but at least have the guts to admit it."

The emotions welling in my chest reach a breaking point.

I swing at him.

He grabs my arm. Rough fingers wrap around my wrist.

"Let me go, Zane."

"It wasn't me."

My other hand whips through the air to smack his face.

He grabs that wrist too. My hips press painfully into the

desk as he pulls me forward so we meet in the middle. The world falls away until it's just his burning blue-flame eyes and the steady hit of his minty breath on my face.

I go still, my anger cracking under that deep, soul-melting gaze of his. The tension between us unfurls like a whip, snapping painfully against all my defenses and bringing the undeniable connection between us to life.

"I didn't do this." His words escape in staccato beats. Short, punchy truths. "I need you to know that. It's important that you know that."

"I..." I start, but there's a knock on the door and I mash my lips shut, confining the storm of words pressing into my throat, desperate to spring free.

I want to believe you. I do believe you, but this is not okay. We can't be alone in the same room like this. It wasn't safe before and it's definitely not okay now. I don't know what to do. I only know that I can't have you. What we did, what we are is wrong.

"Excuse me? I forgot something," a teacher's feeble voice rings from behind the locked door.

"Get it later!" Zane yells.

Everything goes silent.

I stifle a groan of frustration and shake out of his hold. It's barely eight o'clock and today has already been a massive crap-fest. I almost cracked my head open in the shower, my step-brother licked my neck and I enjoyed it, my reputation is being smeared all over campus, and I still feel *something* toward a person I shouldn't feel *anything* for.

Now, I've got to worry about losing my job at Redwood Prep.

"Give me time to figure this out," Zane says, running a hand through his hair.

"No," I snap. "You don't do anything. *I'll* figure this out."

Zane stares at me with those screaming blue eyes.

My phone rings.

I dive into my purse for it and wrench it to my ear. "What?"

"Miss Jamieson? This is the principal's office."

The color drains from my face, and I feel the room spin.

"Principal Harris would like to see you."

* * *

Jinx: A Picture's Worth A Thousand Words But Can Those Words Be Trusted?

Just like real beef and vegan beef look the same and taste different, manufactured scandals don't have the same whiff. Bring me gold and I'll sell it. Bring me a rock spray-painted yellow and I'll throw it out.

Stay safe out there.

Until the next post, keep your enemies close and your secrets even closer.

- Jinx

Chapter Nineteen

GREY

Principal Harris is waiting, fingers templed and arms bunched in front of his ill-fitting grey suit.

Harris is a small, unassuming man whose head barely tops his massive chair. The light bounces against his balding scalp, always with a sheen of sweat like his body knows he's guilty and needs a way to express it.

"Have a seat, Miss Jamieson." He points a crooked finger.

I fold myself into the chair and grip the handles. The room is unfamiliar to me. The walls are black and gold. Expensive artwork hang together in a sickening mash-up. Almost like the buyer chose by price tag rather than cohesion.

My eyes return to Harris and I shift in my seat. I'm uneasy. Uncomfortable. It's one thing to see Harris at school events or during teachers' meetings, but I've done my best to never end up alone in his office.

It's not because I want to stay out of trouble.

It's because seeing his face makes me think of Sloane.

The night she went missing, she got a phone call.

From Harris.

She took the call outside. I never heard what she said.

I only know she never came back.

Thinking of Sloane makes my heart scream in pain.

I close my eyes.

For a moment, I descend into the darkness.

Into sadness.

Regret.

Rage.

My fingers form tight fists and it takes a load of restraint to keep them at my sides.

Harris smiles at me. "This is our first one-on-one since your hiring interview, correct?"

I dip my chin.

"It feels like just yesterday you shuffled through those doors, slid your resume in front of our hiring committee and told us you wanted to give back to the school that changed your life."

I bite down on my lip, hard.

"As you know, you're the youngest teacher at Redwood Prep. Only a few years older than our seniors. Some would say, the age difference isn't much at all."

"Who would say that?" I interrupt him.

His lips curl up even more, edges hiking so high over his face he looks like the Joker.

I stare expectantly at him.

"The general public," Harris says slowly.

I tilt my head. "Is the 'general public' the reason you called me into your office?"

Harris pauses, taking stock of me. I've tried my hardest

not to be aggressive with him. In nearly a year at Redwood, I haven't spoken in meetings or disagreed with any of his policies. When Cadence and Serena were in trouble, I fought him at every turn, while still remaining as docile and unassuming as possible.

He licks his lips, shifting in a way that reveals his displeasure. "Are you upset, Miss Jamieson?"

"Just trying to figure out why I'm here."

"Relax. This is a friendly chat." He flashes those big teeth at me. "No need to be nervous."

I almost snort.

"Would you like some tea? Coffee?"

I would like you to get to the point. "No."

He lifts his gaze carefully from me to the awards framing his walls. "How do you like it here at Redwood?"

"It's fine."

"For an English teacher, you don't seem to use descriptive language."

"I like the cafeteria food."

He laughs and it makes my ears bleed.

"I'm curious. Why did you want to become a teacher?"

I pinch my fingers together. "I told you at my interview."

"Tell me again." Harris swivels his chair toward me and smiles. "Please."

My breath escapes on an exhale. "Reading was my escape from a reality that was less than appealing. I fell in love with words and wanted to share that love with others."

"Mm." He bobs his head. "That passion must be contagious. I heard students are begging to join your class, almost as if they can't get enough of your curriculum. Or perhaps, they can't get enough of you."

"What exactly are you insinuating, Mr. Harris?"

"Just trying to figure you out."

"You picked an inconvenient time to do so. I have a class to teach."

His eyes narrow, a flash of annoyance.

We stare at each other.

Principal Harris backs off first. "Miss Jamieson, it feels like there's something you'd like to say to me."

"What could I possibly have to say?"

"I don't know. Why don't you tell me?"

He's talking in circles and, maybe if things weren't so dire, I'd go on that ride with him.

Today, I don't have the patience.

"You've obviously heard something unflattering about me."

"I wouldn't call it unflattering."

"I wish you'd call it *something*."

His upper lip goes stiff. "It's more like an observation."

"You observed that my age and popularity amongst the students are a concern. Maybe even a weakness. Did I misunderstand?"

Harris folds his arms over his chest. "Here at Redwood Prep, we value honesty, excellence and propriety above all else."

I almost laugh. What propriety? The kind that allowed him to call out a sixteen-year-old girl ten o'clock at night?

"You're young, beautiful," Harris gestures to my pencil skirt. "It might be confusing for students to look up from their textbooks and see someone who could so easily be their friend, perhaps even their lover—"

"Principal Harris."

He flashes his teeth again. "Sorry. I misspoke. I meant to say their crush."

My entire body bristles with annoyance. "I can't control what the students feel. I can only control my own behaviour."

"Have you, Miss Jamieson?" His voice is quiet, sneakily prying at my skin.

"Have I what?"

"Been controlling yourself."

I inhale sharply as visions from that night at the hotel fill my head. Zane's hands in my hair. His moans against my lips. His tongue between my legs. My fingers scraping over the heat of his jeans.

"Yes." My voice is dark, sharp, slicing.

Harris bends his head in an accommodating nod.

"It doesn't matter how close I am in age with the students, my capacity here at Redwood is as a teacher. I've done my job well and professionally."

His high-pitched, almost cartoony laugh gives me chills.

Harris emits a harmless, bumbling fool vibe. It's so easy to overlook him. To count him out. To convince yourself he wouldn't possibly do anything as disgusting as he has.

Every muscle inside me coils as he rises, rounds his desk and leans against it. His new position puts him right in front of me. I smell the disgustingly thick scent of his aftershave.

He lifts a phone to my face.

On the screen is the picture of me and Zane walking into the funeral parlor.

Harris's lips curl up and I can tell he's enjoying this. It makes me wonder if we were both hiding our disdain for each other all these months. Maybe he feels as good letting it out as I do.

"You want to explain this, Miss Jamieson?"

"A student asked for help planning a family member's funeral." I slip my fingers together and tilt my chin up. "That's all it is."

"You met a student after school."

"Yes."

"Alone."

My heart thumps. "Yes."

"You meet Zane Cross often?"

I go stonily silent.

He smirks. "Let me ask it another way. Is this the first time you have met Zane Cross after-hours?"

"Is there a rule that I cannot meet students outside of Redwood?" I glare at him.

There isn't such a rule, and if there was, he broke it long before I did.

"Perhaps not, but there is a rule about inappropriate conduct."

"What is inappropriate about this?"

"I would say there's no reason for his hand to be on your back..." Harris baits me. He zooms in on where Zane's hand is possessively pressing into my shirt. "Does this look appropriate to you, Miss Jamieson?"

"Zane Cross," I lick my lips, "was being a gentleman."

I almost choke on the word. 'Zane Cross' and 'gentleman' don't belong in the same sentence.

"I believe you, Miss Jamieson. I do, but you can see how easily these things can be misconstrued."

"I'm not following."

"Rumors are... such a dangerous thing." Harris pockets the phone and smiles, a dark show of teeth that sends alarm bells ringing in my head. "We're a high profile school. We teach high profile students. Sons and daughters of congressmen, millionaires, celebrities. The public eye is constantly turning toward us, looking for their next story. Hungry for someone to fall off their pedestal."

He forces a laugh. "I don't want to see anyone knocked to the ground. Especially from our staff. You see, in these cases, students aren't the ones who have to pay. It's the teachers who lose everything. Pretty, young teachers like you fall the hardest." He lifts a pen and lets it clatter on the table. "So easily shattered."

For a moment, there's silence.

I stare at the pen, watching it roll back and forth.

Finally, I ask, "Have you ever stacked dominos, Principal Harris?" I lean forward. "When one domino falls, the others go crashing down too. And the last to crash? That one falls harder than the rest."

His lips twitch into a scowl.

I stare him down. "I don't mind falling first, but I guarantee you that when one falls, there's no stopping the rest."

He laughs again. I can't stand the braying, obnoxious sound of it.

"Why do I feel like that's a threat, Miss Jamieson?" The smile is still on his face, but his voice is hard. He flexes a wrinkled fist around the rim of the desk.

"I'm just making an observation."

Harris thumbs a finger over his nose and returns behind his desk as if he needs to sit in his fancy chair to feel powerful.

I get up. "Are we done here?"

It's not a question as much as it is an announcement that *I'm* done.

My feet carry me to the door.

"You've been asking about what happened six years ago," he says abruptly.

Inside, shock careens through me, but I arrange my face

into a blank stare before turning around. I expected my investigation to get back to Harris. It would have been naive of me to think I could question Redwood Prep personnel without alerting the principal.

Harris frowns, his voice a cold whisper. "Let it rest."

"And if I don't?"

He waves the cell phone around. "I'll have no choice but to investigate this matter *fully*." A slow, victorious smile crosses his face. "And expose the results of that investigation to the school board and to the law."

His tricks are the same.

It's funny how he hasn't changed.

"Go ahead," I coo, and Harris looks at me like I'm crazy. He opens his mouth to spit another veiled threat when I lift a hand. "Let's see if the board has a problem with me spending time with my step-brother."

"Step-brother?"

The door suddenly bursts open.

Zane prowls into the room, a vicious look on his face and his eyes locked on Harris. Moving quickly, I slip an arm around his waist, partly to reinforce what I just revealed and partly to hold him back.

"Zane, you're just in time."

A hot thrill snaps down my body as he rakes his gaze over me. His eyes land on my smile and then drop to the arm I have around him. Blue and gold flecks start burning.

"Principal Harris wasn't aware that our parents had gotten married." I face the old man and smile tightly. "Zane, Dutch and Finn are my family. We're very close."

Harris blinks in an exaggerated fashion.

"Does that clear things up for you? Or do you have more questions?"

A frown takes over his mouth and he slides both palms on the desk. "No more questions."

The musical chimes ring.

I unwind my arms from Zane. "I have a class now. If you'll excuse me..."

Both men stare at me, but I don't care. In fact, I feel numb. Winning that match didn't bring me any satisfaction. The war isn't over yet. Revealing Zane as my stepbrother got me off the hook this time, but it's a band-aid on a bullet wound.

The claws are out now.

Harris knows what I'm after.

And all bets are off.

I need to make progress on Sloane's case *fast* before Harris finds a way to kick me out of Redwood and keep my mouth permanently shut.

* * *

Jinx: And The Plot Thickens...

With rumors of Snare King and Sexy Teach being a pair, all eyes are on them. Including the dukes and lords who run this kingdom. And let's just say... the powers that be aren't pleased.

The royal brothers have their fair share of enemies, but it looks like Sexy Teach just earned one of her own.

This twisted Cinderella story isn't what you expect.

Be careful, Sexy Teach. Forbidden love... bites.

Until the next post, keep your enemies close and your secrets even closer.

- Jinx

Chapter Twenty

ZANE

Grey is shining like a freaking angel. Eyes on fire. Brown skin glowing hotter than a supernova. Energy radiating like she has a piece of the sun inside her.

I swear that woman is supernatural.

She glides off in a cloud of sweet perfume, leaving me in Harris's office. Her absence drains all the light from the room and leaves me in a space that reeks of stale coffee and perspiration.

Harris falls back in his chair. The furniture creaks, accepting his weight. I see him mouthing 'step-brother' with a look of annoyance on his face.

I feel a similar confusion.

Grey made my world tilt with that one word.

I can't believe she let the truth rip. Our family connection is now out in the open. Harris might not say a word, but his receptionist heard everything. The woman with the long nails and perpetually sour expression is a blabbermouth.

Once, I banged a chick in Harris's office on a dare. The receptionist walked in on us and nearly busted a lung, screaming louder than the chick who was getting her back blown. By the end of the school day, everyone knew about it.

I bet that dare was the first and last time his desk saw any action. Harris walks around like a dork from the sixties, head always bent to the ground, muttering politely, and being practically invisible. Guys like that don't exactly have girls falling at their feet.

I stuff my hands into my pockets, ready to go. With Grey gone, I no longer have a reason to be in Harris's office.

"Zane," he calls.

I face him.

His eyes have this weird sheen, almost like a cornered animal. "You know this isn't the end, right? It'll only get worse from here. There's no way this gets better."

"What are you talking about?"

"No." He shakes his head. Dull eyes dart back and forth in a face as pale as paper. "This can't get out."

My jaw works in irritation. What the hell?

Suddenly, Harris's eyes clear and snap to mine. "I don't care what she is to you—sister, lover, long-lost egg donor. Just keep her in line."

His words make my shoulders tense. I smile, but it's not a pretty sight and I see when he flinches.

"Do you even know why she's here at Redwood? Do you know the implications?" He grabs a napkin and sops the sweat on his face.

"Of course I know." I lie, standing straight up.

"No, you don't." He laughs and it sounds unhinged. "Freaking hell. We're screwed."

I roll my eyes, tired of watching this pathetic, sniveling mess. But I only get one step toward the door before I turn back.

"Harris."

He glances up.

"Today's incident was a one-off. This is the first and last time you try and get rid of her. Do you understand?"

He trembles. "What is that woman to you?"

"Exactly what she said. She's family." I slip my drumstick out and point it at him. "So think twice before you come for our girl."

Two red stains creep over Harris's cheeks.

I pass the wide-eyed receptionist, my mind buzzing. There was a strange tension between Grey and Harris earlier. The way he was looking at her—like he couldn't stand that she was breathing air—it made all the hair on the back of my neck stand.

Tiger, what the hell are you mixed up in?

Harris isn't the scary type. He's usually smiling, cracking bad jokes, and looking totally overwhelmed. Every time he takes the mike at a rally, he has to yell 'silence' several times before anyone pays attention to him.

He's a figurehead.

A puppet.

Dangling on the strings of those more powerful than him.

And there are many more powerful than him.

Dad being one of them.

Miller, the chairman of the board, is another.

I've never seen Harris as a threat, but I can't shake the feeling that there's bad blood between him and Grey.

THE FORBIDDEN NOTE

I'm curious as hell now.

"About time," a familiar voice says.

I glance up, stopping right outside the door.

Dutch, Sol and Finn are waiting for me in the hallway.

My twin is leaning against the lockers, face dark and features hard. Sol has his eyes trained on me. Finn looks impatient.

"What are you guys doing?" I ask. "Weren't you in the practice room?"

"We thought you might need backup," Dutch says.

Sol frowns. "That was rude of you."

My eyebrows hike.

"Going after Harris without me," he finishes.

I stalk down the hallway.

The three of them follow.

Finn catches up to me first. "What was that about?"

"Honestly? I'm still trying to figure it out."

"You ditched practice and ran at a breakneck speed to confront Harris for the hell of it?" Dutch scowls.

"That's not what I meant," I snap.

"He had a reason," Sol says.

"Of course he had a reason. I'm asking if he was successful or not."

"Grey took care of her own business."

Finn looks at me. "So they didn't fire her?"

"No."

Dutch purses his lips.

Sol smiles.

Finn just looks bored.

"But that's not for lack of trying. She had to pull the step-brother card."

Sol whistles low.

Dutch quirks a brow, impressed.

Finn slips a hand in his pocket. "She must have been desperate."

"Or angry." I recall the way her eyes singed me when she stormed past.

"It's over now," Dutch says. "She explained herself. Everything's good. That should be the end of that."

Given Harris's foreboding words, I don't think it is.

"Do any of you know why Grey started working at Redwood?" I ask absently.

Dutch gives me a strange look.

Sol shakes his head.

Finn points out, "You could ask her."

"I'm sure she'll tell me. Right after she admits she's in love with me."

Sol snorts.

I take out my drumsticks, twirling it around my fingers. It usually helps me think, but this time, it's not doing anything but making me feel more restless.

Dutch jerks his head at the practice room. "Let's finish our set."

"Later." I glance at my watch. "I'm late for class."

Dutch stops me with a hand on my chest. "You sure that's a good idea?"

"Why the hell not?" I grunt.

Finn smirks.

Sol tilts his head to the side. "Not being there just confirms you're guilty."

I glance at Finn. "What do you think?"

"It's up to you." He shrugs. "Of the three of us, you know her the best."

I glance longingly at Miss Jamieson's classroom and then turn in the opposite direction.

"I'm in the mood for a beer," I mumble.

Dutch makes a disbelieving sound.

Finn sighs.

Sol pats me on the back. "Our little boy is growing up."

I flip him off.

The three of them laugh.

For a moment, it feels like old times.

Before Dutch got himself a wife.

Before Sol tried to off himself.

Before dad went full psycho.

I wish I could stay here, in this moment, laughing with my brothers for an eternity. Or at least for a few more minutes.

But that's a pipe dream.

Because Harris was right.

Things are about to get so much worse.

Chapter Twenty-One

ZANE

That morning, I keep my distance from Grey, which is freaking hard to do when the questions keep piling up in my head.

The more I think about it, the more unsettling it all seems.

Why did Grey look so angry when she got that call from Harris's office?

Why did she expose our parents' marriage when she seemed so determined to keep it under wraps since the beginning?

And what the hell did Harris mean when he said she could destroy Redwood?

How?

She's the most popular teacher, sure.

And it's freaking aggravating how the lust-crazed dirtbags at Redwood drool over her.

But that's nothing that could cause the very foundations of Redwood Prep to crumble.

Harris is out of his mind.

I should just forget about it.

But there's this sneaking suspicion in my gut that I'm missing something.

Looking back, it's a little strange that Grey didn't quit Redwood after she found out who I was. Even if she couldn't leave right away because of a contract or something, she'd have booked it eventually. The fact that she's holding on, that she's insistent on staying, lands different now that I'm seeing it from a new perspective.

What exactly does she want from Redwood?

"You okay, Zane?" Dutch asks, peering at me as the musical bells chime.

I nod, stepping away from my drums. "Just thinking."

"That's rare," Finn mumbles, setting his bass in the stand.

I flip him off.

Sol rolls his eyes from where he's lounging in the sofa.

"I gotta pick up Cadey." Dutch's amber gaze drills into me. "You want to come?"

"Why? You think I'm going to sneak off and see Grey if you're not watching me?"

"It was just an offer, Zane. But thanks. Now I know what you really want to do."

"Let's go." I slap Sol on the leg. "If he's on the move, we're all on the move."

Sol groans, but he gets up and follows us without complaint.

It's second period and students are pouring out of classrooms. The moment they see us coming, they step aside, leaving a clear path for us.

Cadence is hanging out by her locker with her friend Serena. The brunette in the leather jacket gives Finn a quick glance before smiling at me.

"Hey," I say, lifting my chin.

A nervous grin flits over her face.

While her friend looks uncomfortable, Cadey doesn't. She walks boldly toward Dutch. My brother moves into her as if they've been apart for years rather than just first period.

I notice Sol hanging back, looking moodier than usual.

"Had a good class, babe?" Dutch asks, slipping an arm around Cadence's waist and giving her a kiss.

"Yeah, you'd know if you'd *attend* for once."

"I'll steal your notes."

"To do what? I never see you take any tests." She holds the side of his face, her giant wedding ring sparkling bright enough to blind someone.

Everyone passing by stares at them. Most of the guys are staring at Dutch in confusion. Most of the girls are staring at Cadence's ring, which Dutch made sure could be spotted from the moon.

I wonder when Jinx will break the news of their marriage to the masses. Dutch paid her off and told her to keep her virtual mouth shut, but there's no hiding how much he loves Cadey. Everyone knows something's up and that ring is just confirmation. I heard several girls weeping after finding out my twin was off the market for good.

I wish he wasn't.

Now that Dutch is settled down, Jinx seems more obsessed with me. I've noticed my name ramping up in her app. If I wasn't paired with Miss Jamieson, I wouldn't really give a damn, but things are getting complicated. Having more and more eyes on us won't spell anything but trouble.

"Let me hold your purse," Dutch says, reaching for Cadence's bag.

I scoff as my brother swings the purse over his head and walks with one arm over Cadey's shoulders.

Those two are freaking obnoxious.

We take off beside them, heading for Cadey's next class.

At that moment, three jocks stalk into the hallway. They're tall and bulky, walking squares in puffy letterman jackets. One carries a football under his arm. It's obvious to me, from the moment they spot us, that they're looking for a fight.

"Heads up," I mumble, tapping Sol on the shoulder.

Dutch pushes Cadey behind him.

Finn pauses to bookmark his e-book before pocketing the phone.

The jocks come closer, crap-eating grins on their faces.

My fingers coil. The rivalry between the music and the sports department is legendary. Since dad is practically the ambassador of Redwood, music has gotten most of the financial support and media buzz.

The jocks have always resented us for stealing their thunder.

I don't feel sorry for them.

Maybe if they didn't suck so much, they would get more acknowledgement.

"Yo," the meathead at the front says, swaggering over to us, "which one of you is the lucky bastard who bagged Jamieson?"

Immediately, the hallway goes quiet.

Fights are rare at Redwood.

Here, it's more convenient to throw money than fists.

Money's cleaner. Quicker. And there's no need to get your hands dirty.

My hands are begging for this guy's blood though.

I take a step forward.

Finn moves slightly in front of me.

"Come on. Who was it? I just want to shake your hand." The idiot grins. "Preferably, the one that was inside her."

My entire body jolts forward.

Sol steps in front of me this time.

I'm being blocked by the two of them and it still isn't enough.

Dutch unleashes a scowl. "Walk away. Now."

The jock sizes Dutch up. "Or what?"

"Or I'll bash your skull into your freaking tail bone," I snap, lunging.

Sol grabs my shoulder.

Finn stretches his arms over my chest, barring me.

"Why so uptight after hitting a babe like Jamieson? Don't tell me you couldn't handle her?" He laughs. "Tell Miss J to come my way if she wants a real man." He grabs his crotch. "I'll make eighteen feel like thirty-seven."

"Have some freaking respect," Cadence snaps, stalking up to the guy even though she's pint-sized and can do zero damage. "You're disgusting."

Dutch pulls his wife all the way behind him. Cadence struggles to be free, looking ready to beat the crap out of everyone.

No wonder Dutch fell head over heels.

His girl's a dynamite.

"Don't be so selfish, *kings*. At least tell us if she tastes as good as she looks." The jock grins, showing off teeth just begging to be smashed in. "Is it just one of you who got to smash?" Eyes glinting, he whispers, "Or do all of you share—"

THE FORBIDDEN NOTE

I break out of Sol and Finn's human barricade and lash my drumstick across the bastard's face. He lets out a scream that rattles through the hallway. Bending down, he grabs his head.

His two friends rush me, lips twisted darkly. Sol and Finn launch at them.

Sol throws a dirty right hook.

Finn does a round-house kick and the other guy crumples like a potato sack.

The fight is over before it even begins.

We form a straight line, staring at the jocks.

They pick themselves off the floor, skin flaming in embarrassment. The one at the front has a large, drumstick sized welt on his cheekbones.

"Stop now unless you want your face rearranged," I warn them.

The jocks curse and rush at us, roaring.

Just then, the football coach enters the hallway.

"What the hell is going on here?"

"They threw the first punch, coach. Wasn't us."

The meathead bawls and sets a hand on his face which is already starting to swell. "I think he blinded me, coach. I can't see."

The little prick.

My stick was nowhere near his eyes.

A vein pops in the coach's face. "You. You. You. And You." He stabs a finger in our direction. "Principal's office."

I glare at the coach.

Dutch folds his arms over his chest.

Finn doesn't move.

The coach sees our resistance and goes red. "I don't care who your father is, we do not allow fighting at Redwood. If my star QB is benched, I swear, I'll take this straight to the school district board. Principal's office. *Now.*"

Dutch drops his arms.

Finn looks annoyed.

The jock preens at me, sticking out his tongue.

I want to rip his spine out by the throat.

"Let's go." The coach motions for us to walk in front of him.

Under his breath, Sol lets out a spew of colorful curses in Spanish. I don't need a translation to hear that he's not in the mood for this crap.

Dutch grabs Cadence's shoulders. "I'll be right back."

She nods.

Dutch, Finn, and Sol trail me down the hallway.

Everyone watches our procession with solemn eyes. We've done our share of crap here at Redwood, but this is the first time we've started a fistfight in broad daylight.

You're reckless. Emotional. Irresponsible.

Dad's words echo in my head.

Now, as I walk beside my brothers, watching the heaviness on their faces, I wonder if he was right.

* * *

Jinx: Do Kings Fight For Their Concubines?

They say music is a weapon and Snare King showed he's just as dangerous as Prince Charming when he uses those sticks on something other than drums.

With rumors swirling about who's been occupying the Snare King's bed, tempers reached a boiling point. The battle ended swiftly and there was a clear winner, but why didn't it feel like a victory?

Perhaps, Snare King and his royal brothers should have kept their dirty deeds from the light. Because now that the world is watching, there won't be anywhere for their secrets to hide.

Until the next post, keep your enemies close and your secrets even closer.

- Jinx

Chapter Twenty-Two

GREY

I arrange my books, level them out by tapping them twice on the table and set them down neatly.

Musical chimes ring through the classroom, signaling the beginning of class.

Students file in through the doors, more excited than usual. A low buzz fills the air, gathering to the ceiling like an invisible storm of anticipation.

"Settle down," I say. "Class is about to start."

No one pays me any attention.

My eyebrows tighten. Things were awkward in my AP English class, but I'd expected that. Thankfully, none of my students asked me any inappropriate questions.

This class is Literature 101, a very different demographic. What little respect these students had for me is eclipsed by whatever happened before they walked in here. I hope it has nothing to do with this morning's leaked photo. If I'm lucky, they're doing normal teenaged things like getting ready for the masquerade ball.

When Redwood throws a school dance, they hire high-end caterers, fly in professional DJs, and work with world renown event planners. Redwood dances are engineered for the students to take pictures and flaunt their wealth all over social media.

Motioning to someone in the front row, I ask, "What's going on?"

"The Kings fought the football team in the hallway. Coach caught them and took them to the principal's office."

"What?" My eyes bug.

A stark silence falls on the crowd.

All the students turn to look at me.

Clutching at the front of my shirt, I chew on my bottom lip. "Uh, everyone, I understand that there was an... *incident* in the hallway, but there will be a quiz today, so I need you to focus on the lesson."

No one responds.

"Understand?" I prod.

"Yes, Miss Jamieson."

They speak in unison.

I crack my book open and guide them through the lecture, but I'm far too distracted by thoughts of Zane. Did Harris punish him severely? As far as I remember, Redwood has a zero-violence policy. Throwing hands on campus equals an immediate expulsion.

I don't get it. Why would he start a fight in the hallway?

After class, I walk to the cafeteria. Whispers follow me everywhere. The students watch me differently. Laughter cackles when I leave the lunch line. Male students ogle my body in an obvious show of desire.

The sentiment is clear: *now that Zane Cross had her, she's free game.*

I thought I'd at least have *someone* on my side, but no one seems to believe I'm innocent. At this point, I don't know if admitting I'm Zane's step-sister would make a difference.

In that sense, Redwood is the same now as it was then. Having so much money, the rich have to manufacture their own drama to keep themselves entertained.

In Rome, they threw the poor into a colosseum to fight.

Today, they feed on other people's pain, near bloodthirsty for scandal. Lapping at the downfall of those they deem unworthy. Anything to feed their little egos.

The musical chimes ring.

I'm more relieved than the students.

Quickly stuffing my books into my bag, I hurry to my next class and pass Harris's office on the way. If I *happen* to run into Zane and check on him, there's no harm done.

Right?

I'm halfway to Harris's office when someone blocks my path.

"Mr. Hall." I jump back in surprise.

He takes a step forward, his shoes kissing my pumps. "Miss J, where are you off to in a hurry?"

"My next class." I glance behind him. "Excuse me."

"Your next class is that way." He points in the opposite direction.

I freeze, my fingers tightening over my books.

He smirks at me. "Want me to walk you there?"

I shoot a longing glance at the principal's office and paste a smile on my face. "It's fine. I'll walk by myself."

Turning abruptly, I shuffle in the direction of the classroom. Theodore Hall's eyes linger on me and, when I turn around, he smiles.

A shudder wracks through me.

I have a bad feeling about that kid.

* * *

In third period, my concentration is shot.

Screw it.

I need to find out what happened to Zane.

As soon as class is over, I text Cadence.

I heard about the fight. Are the boys okay?

She answers back immediately.

Cadence: They got sent home for the day.

I type back.

Since when do the boys get punished?

Cadence: They started a fight in the hallway in plain view of everyone. There were too many witnesses. Harris had to give them something.

I chew on my bottom lip, debating whether I should text Zane.

In the end, I choose against it.

Better not to confuse things by reaching out.

My scandal has spread to the teachers now. The lounge goes silent when I walk in. My co-workers break out of huddles and stare at me. I remain frozen in the doorway, my stomach churning with nerves. After a few deep breaths, I walk in and take my seat around the desk.

It's fine.

I can live like this.

I'm here for Sloane, not to make friends.

Everything is going to be okay.

At the end of the day, I get a text from Jarod Cross.

My contact hasn't found anything yet. As soon as he does, I'll get back to you.

I read and re-read the message.

There's something so... distant about it. Jarod Cross jumped at the chance to help me. He was the one who pushed to meet me immediately after the funeral.

Now, that energy is missing.

My head is pounding.

Something tells me I need to make progress on my investigation before things get worse.

I linger in the teacher's lounge until everyone has gone home. When the hallways are clear, I tiptoe to the basement. In the bowels of Redwood Prep are dusty sports equipment, broken chairs, and a ton of boxes with old files. I've been methodically going through them since my first day here. So far, I haven't found any information about Sloane's case—not that I thought it would be so easy. However, I've taken pictures of everything dated six years ago.

I might not have the answers I need now, but I'm hoping it's only a matter of time before I stumble on the key behind her murder.

The steps creak eerily when I tiptoe down the stairs. Once I get to the door that leads to the basement, I push confidently.

Chains rattle.

The door doesn't budge.

Stunned, I shine my light down and notice that the broken lock's been replaced. There's a new gleaming, silver deadbolt.

I grit my teeth.

Harris.

He must have changed the locks after our argument.

THE FORBIDDEN NOTE

I open my phone, maneuver to YouTube and choose a lock picking video. Sliding bobby pins out of my hair, I follow the steps on the screen. The person in the video makes it look so easy, but my hands tremble too much and I can't get the bobby pin to twist right.

"Dammit!" I yell, sending the bobby pin flying into the wall.

I toss a frustrated look at the door.

On the bright side, Harris reinforcing this room means there really *is* something incriminating down here.

The bad news is... he'll know if I tamper with the lock.

Sighing heavily, I give up for the day and tiptoe to the main floor. Next time, I'll come back with a solution. For now, I'm exhausted. All I want is some of mom's homemade cobbler, a bubble bath and an audiobook drifting me off to sleep.

Wearily, I drag myself back to the teacher's lounge, collect my purse, and head through the exits.

Redwood after dark is far more sinister than it is during the day. Black light oozes through the stained glass windows. Shadows sweep over the floor.

I quicken my pace, heading for the rear entrance since the front doors are locked. The rear of the school is isolated. Trees claw toward the ground, branches heavy with leaves.

Across the lawn, I see lights on in the sports centre. A loud whistle tells me the football team is practicing. It's late. I guess the coach is punishing the team for their leader's mistake.

I make my way down the stairs and check my phone, considering whether or not to spring for a taxi instead of catching the bus.

"Miss J?" Someone peers at me from across the parking

lot. He's wearing a loose pair of basketball shorts and an arm band around his forehead.

It's Theodore Hall.

Great.

Hall hurries over, grinning like I'm a Christmas present delivered early.

"Mr. Hall, what are you still doing here?"

"I could ask you the same thing."

I notice he's breathing hard and the front of his shirt is stained with sweat. The disgusting stench of body odor wafts to my nose.

"I was just about to head home." Brushing past him, I hurry down the stairs.

Hall follows me, his expensive sneakers thumping the steps. "Since we ran into each other, we should grab a bite."

"No thank you."

"Come on. I know a great place."

"I said *no*."

"Don't be like that." He smirks and grabs my hand.

I shake him off. "Mr. Hall, this is not appropriate."

"Since when do you care about being appropriate?" He pulls me close.

I try to tear away, but his hands are sweaty clamps.

My heart jackhammers against my ribs. "Let go!"

"Come on, Miss J." Dark shadows play over the planes of his face. His teeth flash like a wolf's. "I bet you didn't give Zane this much trouble." He starts yanking me down the stairs. "How much did he pay you to screw? I'll give you double."

The acrid taste of panic surges up my throat.

He's too strong.

I can't break away from him.

"Those rumors aren't true."

THE FORBIDDEN NOTE

"Yeah right." Hall glances back at me with a sardonic grin. "You act so high and mighty. Like you're so much better than us. Like you can't be bought. But in the end, you're just like everyone else. That picture was proof. You'll do anything for money."

Using all my strength, I rip his hands off me. Hall lunges forward, but I'm ready for him. Hurling my purse full of books, I smack him across the face.

He roars, arms lifting to protect himself.

Desperately, I dash down the rest of the steps.

He pursues me. I feel his clammy fingers close around my elbow and dig into my flesh.

He wrenches me around.

I open my mouth to scream, but he clamps his hand on my lips.

I gag. He tastes like sweat and sand.

Holding my breath, I bite down on his hand.

Hard.

He shrieks in pain. Anger glittering in his eyes, he comes at me like a whirlwind. I brace myself, prepared to be slammed into the ground.

A hand suddenly grabs Hall's shoulder and wrenches him off me. Before his body even hits the stone, he's being slammed in the face.

His body drops like a sack of sand.

My eyes widen and I peer through the darkness. A tall boy in a hoodie climbs on top of Hall and punches him.

Over and over again.

After the third punch, Hall stops responding.

But the attacker doesn't quit.

I hear the sickening crunch of bones splitting.

That's when I move.

Grabbing a hoodie-clad arm, I yell, "Enough!"

Slowly, the boy turns to look at me. The side of his face is splattered in blood. The stark red is a brutal contrast against blue eyes swimming in the darkness of dusk.

"Zane?" I gasp.

He lifts those blood spattered hands to my face. He's breathing hard, but the fingers that cup my cheeks are tender.

"Are you okay?" he growls.

I meet those sky blue eyes and realise that I am not okay. Not even remotely.

Because in this moment, my student...

My step-brother...

My biggest danger...

Made my heart skip a beat.

Chapter Twenty-Three

ZANE

I would have killed Theodore Hall if she hadn't wrenched me off him.

He would be dead at my feet.

I'd be a murderer.

And I wouldn't even be sorry.

Because he hurt her.

He put his hands on her.

So why the hell should he be breathing air?

It's scary.

Not my thoughts.

How calm I am with them.

How accepting.

She's turned me into a monster. Or maybe I already was and she just makes that monster bold and unafraid of the light.

"You're getting blood on your steering wheel," she says.

"It's Finn's car," I mumble.

Her chocolate eyes land on me. "Even worse."

My jaw flexes.

She sighs. "Should we have just left him there?"

"As opposed to what? Taking him for coffee?"

"The stones are uncomfortable."

I grunt. "He attacked you and you're worried about his freaking comfort?"

"He might need to go to the hospital."

"Screw that. Let him bleed out like the animal he is."

Her teeth dig into her bottom lip.

My eyes drop there. Her lipstick is smudged and it streaks a little at the corner. The collar of her shirt is stretched out. Curls expand all over her head, frizzier than normal.

Holy crap.

Looking at the damage Hall inflicted makes me want to turn the car around and beat him to a pulp again until his brains splatter out of his skull.

I'm sinking into darker and darker thoughts and I don't realize my fingers are tightening over the steering wheel until I feel a soft sensation on my knuckles.

Grey's feather-light touch descends on my bloody hands. "You should probably go to a hospital too."

"I'm fine."

"Are you sure all this blood is his?" Her eyebrows quirk.

My stomach tightens in the strangest way. "I've been beating my drums instead of people for a long time. This isn't anything I can't handle."

Those soft brown eyes meet mine. "Why did you come back to school? I heard you'd been suspended."

I suck in a sharp breath.

She stares through the windshield. Light from the lampposts spray gold and silver all over us.

Her voice is bleak and withdrawn. "Did the fight in the hallway today have anything to do with me?"

Rather than answer that question, I turn down the air conditioning.

"Zane."

"Your mom said your car was in the shop. She was worried about you catching the bus so late at night."

"She's always worried."

"Yeah, I'm seeing that."

"You didn't have to come."

I laugh, but it sounds brittle. Even I can hear it. "I didn't. I was on my way to a party. I just happened to pass by."

"You wear *that* to parties?" She eyes my hoodie.

"What am I supposed to wear?"

She shrugs.

"We're not like *your* generation. No one dresses up to go to parties. Everything's chill."

"My generation?" There's laughter in her voice.

That's good. Real good. If she kept frowning worriedly like that, I would have lost my mind and turned this car around, just so I could see if Hall was still lying where I left him.

And then I would have run him over with my car.

"My generation was definitely the superior one," she muses.

"Did you even have internet back when the dinosaurs were roaming?"

She scrunches her nose. "Very funny."

I flick the indicator and take a left. The smell of Hall's sweat and the copper scent of his blood still clings to me. The first thing I'm going to do when I get home is burn this hoodie.

"Zane," Grey says, going serious again.

"What?"

She backs off. "Nothing."

"I hate when people do that." I flick her an annoyed glance. "Drives me crazy."

"To be fair, you seem to live on the edge of crazy. So it doesn't surprise me that such a little thing would set you off."

I chuckle. "Miss Jamieson, did you just insult me?"

"I'm calling it like I see it." When she turns her face to the window, she's smiling.

I grin too.

Suddenly, she sits straight up. "Zane, this isn't the way home."

Her words startle me and I glance around. The houses are familiar. The driveways. The gated yards.

A growing awareness fills my chest.

I brought her to the place I used to share with my brothers.

This villa has always been home.

And it still feels that way even though I changed addresses.

I start to turn the car around. "My bad."

"Don't." She stops me.

I freeze.

"My mom can't see you like this." Her eyes slide over my blood-stained hoodie and knuckles rubbed raw from the fight. "It's better this way. You can shower and change here."

I agree and drive into the garage.

Viola greets me with a hug when I walk through the door. I see her eyeing the blood on my hoodie, but she doesn't ask any questions. Given the rough neighborhood she grew up in, she must have learned to keep her mouth shut the hard way.

"Hey, kid." I ruffle her hair.

She smacks my hand away. "I'm not a kid. I'm almost fourteen."

"Exactly. You're practically a baby."

She sticks out her tongue. "*You're* a baby."

I press both hands over my heart and stagger back. "Ow."

Grey chuckles, her eyes sparkling in a way that makes my chest tighten.

Viola smiles at her. "Oh, you're pretty. Can I do your makeup? Wait, I don't think I have a foundation that would match your complexion. If you bring your own foundation, I could totally rock a soft glam."

"Um..."

"Forgive her. She barely talks English."

"I talk English," Vi says.

"You talk makeup."

"Makeup is not a language." She rolls her eyes and then presses insistently against Grey, inspecting her like a designer with a model. "You have such thick eyelashes. I wouldn't even have to use my lash set."

"Rein it in, Vi." I give her a little nudge. "Grey is tired."

"I'd love for you to do my makeup another time," Grey says, being way too nice as always.

"Where's your sister?" I cross the room to grab a bottle of water for Grey.

"She and Dutch went to buy groceries."

"Really?" I arch a brow.

Dutch has never bought groceries in his life. I can't imagine my giant, scowling brother browsing the vegetable aisle, picking out the freshest cucumbers and haggling over salmon.

Love really has changed him.

"Zane, how about I do your makeup, huh?" Viola wiggles her eyebrows.

"Sorry, kiddo." I crack the water bottle open and hand it to Grey. "We're not staying long."

Viola doesn't miss a beat. "How about another collab with me on my makeup channel?"

"That depends."

The kid sighs heavily. "I've been practicing."

"Is that why you haven't sent in your homework for three days?"

She scrunches her nose. "Why do I have to practice every day?"

"Because that's the only way you'll get better. Even if you pretend you're beating your worst enemy, you still gotta do it."

"Fine." She sighs like I asked her to swim with sharks.

I look up and find Grey watching me with a weird look. "What are you two talking about?"

"I'm teaching her the drums."

Her eyes soften for a second before she quickly masks it with a dry, "Oh."

"I'm not that good," Viola says.

I shrug. "She's getting there."

Grey smiles. "I'm sure you're great." She sticks out a hand. "I don't think we've been formally introduced. I'm Miss Jamieson, but my friends call me Grey."

"I know who you are," Vi says, casually accepting the handshake. "You're Cadey's teacher."

"That's right."

"Are you Zane's teacher too?" Her smart brown eyes

dart between us. "Why are you here? Is this, like, a private study session for The Kings? That is *so* cool."

Grey's eyes jump to me and wander back down to Viola. She laughs nervously.

The guilt is all over her face. It's like a shadow on her features. Tightening her lips. Chasing the light from her eyes. It's almost suffocating to watch.

Damn.

I clear my throat and back away. "I'm gonna take a shower."

Maybe that'll clear my head.

Chapter Twenty-Four

GREY

I sit in the middle of the lavish living room, noticing the pictures of Cadence and Dutch together, as well as pictures of Dutch and all his brothers.

The frames sit neatly over the mantle, a tiny window into the world of the dazzling Cross brothers and their unshakeable bond.

Viola sees where my eyes have landed. "Cadey put those up. There was not even *one* picture in this entire house when the boys were living here."

Curious, I snoop around. There's a photograph of Zane, Dutch, Finn and Sol at a beach. The boys have sunny expressions on their faces. It's hard to imagine that they were once so young and innocent. Sometimes, it feels like they came out of the womb dangerous, scowling and inked.

I pick up another frame. This one is of The Kings during a concert. Pink and yellow lights beam on the stage, drowning them all in an otherworldly glow. Dutch has his head bent toward his guitar. Finn has his head tilted back as if he's seeing another world. Zane is the only one whose gaze is on the camera. He's drenched in sweat, hair falling over glittering eyes, a devilishly enticing grin on his face.

"Is it true that all the teachers at Redwood are scared of The Kings?"

"Huh?" I whip my eyes up to her curious and excited brown ones. Viola is practically leaning into my face, scanning me.

"And is it true that everyone runs and hides when The Kings pass by?"

"Um..."

"And is it true that girls are so crazy about Zane that they stuff his locker with bras?"

My eyes widen. I ignore the strike of jealousy that hits me. "I don't know much about Zane."

Viola pushes her lips out at the picture where I was, very obviously, staring at the drummer. "Then why were you looking at him like that?"

I swallow hard and put the frame back.

Undeterred, Viola follows me. "Do you know about Jinx? Is the school trying to find out who she is?"

"I think a lot of people want to know who Jinx is."

Viola laughs. "Honestly, I think all the boys want to know her real identity. Especially Finn. He has a crush on her without even knowing what she looks like. Isn't that funny?"

"Mm-hm."

"By the way, do you know who Sexy Teach could be? Like... who's the sexiest female teacher at Redwood?"

I start fidgeting with the ring around my finger. No wonder Zane is always flipping his drumsticks. I need something to keep my hands steady. "I-I really don't know."

Her gaze turns a little more intense and she studies me again. "How old are you, Miss Jamieson?"

"Uh..."

"Do you have a boyfriend?"

"Well..."

Suddenly, her eyes widen. "Oh my go—are you 'Sexy Teach'?"

Horror tears through my veins.

Viola looks me over. "You're her, right? The one Jinx has been writing about. The girl Snare King is obsessed with."

It feels so crass hearing this thirteen year old who's never been to Redwood discussing the highly toxic and extremely dangerous situation I've been caught in like it's the latest plot twist in a Disney Channel show.

Popping to my feet, I smile shakily. "Is it okay if I look around the house?"

"Sure. I can give you a tour and you can tell me all about how you and Zane met."

"How about you show me what Zane's taught you on the drums?"

Her expression falls. "I'm really not that good."

"It's okay. However you play, you'll be better than me."

I breathe a sigh of relief when she drops the subject of Jinx and 'Sexy Teach'. That stupid moniker. Could the secrets trader *not* have been more creative?

Viola leads me to a separate garage—it's insane that rich people need *two* garages in the first place—and climbs behind a shiny drum set. She looks so slim and frail behind those giant instruments. I almost want to scoop her out of there and rescue her.

"Um…" She beats one of the drums nervously. "He taught me a song, but I forgot."

"Someone hasn't been practicing." Zane's deep voice curls around us. I whirl around and spot him watching me, tatted arms folded over his chest.

He looks freshly showered. The blood-stained hoodie is gone. So are the blood spatters on his knuckles. The black undershirt he's wearing exposes all the ink on his arms. Grey sweatpants hug his muscular legs and hang low over his hips. The gold chain dangling from his neck makes the edges of my fingers tingle.

Viola shoots to her feet. "I practiced. I swear."

"Go ahead then. Play," Zane challenges.

"Just… give me a minute."

While Viola flits around, I glance at Zane.

Our eyes meet and linger.

Even his gaze is dangerous. He refuses to let me breathe.

There's a half-hearted *tap* behind me and then a noisy crash of the cymbals. I look over my shoulder and notice Viola's confused expression.

"Uh… I just remembered I have homework. Gotta go," Viola squeaks. In a flash, she darts from behind the drums and disappears.

Zane smirks and moves deeper into the room. Every step feels like a threat and it's extremely difficult to hold my ground. The way he walks, the way he carries himself like he owns the world, it used to irritate me. But after seeing him slam Hall into next year, I'm not as irritated as I used to be.

Zane's lips curl up. "Like what you see?"

I glance away. "You shower fast."

"I'll go slow if you're in there with me."

I ignore the sweeping pleasure that lights up my brain. "Viola's not having fun."

"Learning an instrument isn't about fun. It's about discipline."

"You shouldn't pressure kids to learn music. You should *inspire* her to learn."

"Are you schooling me on how to be a teacher?"

"Just some advice."

He gives me a wink and a smile. "My turn."

"To do what?"

He picks up the sticks and holds it out to me. "To teach you something."

I squint at the sticks. I've always wanted to learn an instrument, but I don't know if it's worth learning from him.

"Scared?" He goads me.

I scoff and snap the sticks from his hands. "I'm a quick learner. Don't be surprised if I play better than you."

"I like the confidence." His voice is a purr in my ear as I get situated on the drum stool.

Goosebumps skitter up my arm and it gets ridiculously hot.

"What do I start with first?"

"Pull your skirt up."

"W-what?"

"Your legs need movement." His fingers hook underneath my pencil skirt. The pads of his thumb graze my skin and set a wildfire inside me.

Slowly, he inches my skirt up, and I do my best not to moan when his knuckles brush my inner thigh. A burning ache lights up my belly, electricity whipping through me like a torrent.

Zane's eyes blaze into mine, an arresting shade of blue.

"Enough," I choke out, grabbing his wrist to stop him. I feel too exposed, too vulnerable in this heated moment.

His full lips twist in a cruel smirk.

"Are you teaching me a lesson or not?" I snap.

"Of course." He withdraws.

I let out a quick exhale.

"Ignore all these," he gestures to the smaller drums, "and focus on the basics. He juts a finger down. "The pedal by your foot is the bass drum. Press on the pedal and it pounds the bass."

I ease my foot on the mechanics and hear the satisfying thump.

"Good girl." His fingers sweep over my shoulder as he points to my left hand. "This is for the snare."

He leans over me, his inked arm brushing my side. He smells like fresh leather and sandalwood. My eyes dart in his direction and I find him watching me carefully, probably waiting for me to nod my understanding.

"What's next?" I demand.

He chuckles. "You think it's that easy?"

"If you can do it..." I let the rest of the insult dangle.

He laughs again and there's an edge to it this time. "Have it your way."

My heart thumps hard when he hugs me from behind. His chest presses against my back and sends a violent surge through my body. The zing of electricity between my legs almost has me levitating off the chair.

He grips my wrist, touching the same places Hall did earlier. And yet I have a completely different feeling when Zane holds me.

I want him to touch me more.

Harder.

In other places.

I shouldn't be having such strong reactions, but my defences are down. It's been such a long, rollercoaster of a day and I can't find the strength to put my walls back up.

"This is the easiest drumbeat in the world," he says. Guiding my hand over the snare twice, he murmurs, "Now the bass drum."

I kick, the movement jolting me harder against him.

"Good. Again." He guides me to pound the snare twice. "Bass."

I slam on the pedal.

Heat travels through me when he slides his hand off my wrist, fingers skating over the inside of my arm before drifting away. "By yourself now."

I tap the snare twice and kick.

Tap-tap. Boom.

Tap-tap. Boom.

Zane hums softly in my ear, his breath caressing me.

I stop abruptly. "*We Will Rock You?*"

"A classic." When I turn to glare at him, I find a shimmer of dark satisfaction in his gaze. "Not bad for your first time."

"I can do something more complicated."

"Not so fast, tiger. You need to conquer the basics before you get your own drum solo."

"I hope *I'm* not this irritating when I teach."

"Irritating, no." A teasing smile tugs at his lips. "Distracting? Yes."

My heart skips a beat.

Zane holds my eyes and rakes his thumb roughly over the corner of my lips. Lust screams through me at the tiny touch. He pulls back his thumb and there's a red streak on it. My lipstick must have smudged when Hall put his hand over my mouth.

The reminder of what happened tonight sends an icy shudder down my back.

"What are you going to do if Hall goes to the cops?" I whisper.

"Let him. I'd love an excuse to set my lawyers on his tail."

"Lawyers?"

His grin turns cruel. "We're Jarod Cross's sons. You think we stay out of the press because they care that much about our privacy?"

The words rip through the tension.

Zane is right.

He's not just a student at Redwood.

He's the son of Jarod Cross, musical legend and media darling.

If any hint of our night together gets out, it's not just Jinx and Redwood Prep that I have to worry about.

The entire world will shun me.

Feeling cold, I get up and set the drumsticks on the snare.

Zane straightens too and watches me.

"It's been a long day. Thanks for the lesson," I turn and meet his eyes, "but I think I should go home."

Chapter Twenty-Five

GREY

I can't sleep so I pull my whiteboard out of the closet, set it on an easel and work on Sloane's case beneath the strained light of my lamp.

Over the last eight months, I've been collecting data and piecing scraps of related information together.

The night Sloane was murdered, she got a call from Harris.

She left my place in a hurry.

By the end of the night, she was found in pieces in a bodybag.

I'm trying to pin together what happened after Sloane left my place. It makes no sense that a sixteen year old would disappear without a trace and then suddenly turn up dead at the hands of a psycho. A crime of passion? Since when? Sloane never told me about having a boyfriend and she talked to me about everything.

Well, everything except why Harris was calling her that night.

All the journalists and reporters were happy to swallow the story the police fed them. Despite telling the cops about Harris's call, no mention of it was reported in the news.

What *was* mentioned was Sloane's 'problematic' history. The media blasted the fact that her mother was a stripper. One particular comment said Sloane was 'known to be promiscuous'. It was as if she'd earned what happened to her.

Thinking about it infuriates me and I stare harder at the whiteboard, wishing the pieces would snap together on their own.

"What am I missing, Sloane?" I whisper, tapping my pen against a picture of Redwood.

My last big break in the case was ages ago. I made friends with the officers responsible for Sloane's case and took them out for drinks. Once they were drunk enough, I started questioning them about Sloane.

Someone let a nugget slip. Sloane was seen at Redwood the night of her murder. The higher-ups were told to scratch that out of the files, but it had already made the rounds in the precinct.

Harris.

Redwood.

It's all linked to Sloane's demise.

However, I haven't made any progress since then.

Feeling like my head is about to explode, I push the whiteboard back into its hiding place, throw my clothes on top of it and slip downstairs.

I'm dunking my fork into leftover cobbler when I hear heavy footsteps. I freeze, seeing a tall shadow.

It's Finn.

He comes to an abrupt stop on the stairs. He's entirely naked from the top up, and I'm surprised by how ripped he is. Under his neat Redwood Prep uniform and cold manners, the bassist is shredded.

Finn swings his head around as if he'll move back up the stairs.

"You don't have to run," I say, pushing the plate at him. "Want some?"

He narrows his eyes at me, considers it for a moment and then patters to the kitchen, bare-foot and mysterious.

I bring a fork out of the drawer and hand it to him.

He takes it hesitantly.

I push the plate further in his direction.

Finn scoops out a bite and, the moment the cobbler gets into his mouth, his expression tightens.

"It's good right?"

"Yeah," he mumbles. "Yeah... wow."

I think that's the first thing he's ever said to me.

Mom's cobbler must be made of magic.

We eat in companionable silence for a while.

"I'm sorry about today," I say quietly.

Finn glances up at me, an eyebrow arched.

"I heard you got suspended."

"Only for a day," he responds, his voice vibrating through me.

It always catches me by surprise how deep his voice is. Finn's bassy timbre reminds me of the drums I learned to play tonight. Rolling and dark and powerful enough to rattle the walls. Since he rarely speaks, he must always catch people off guard.

"Zane was the one who got a week-long suspension." Finn pushes his fork around. "Since he threw the first punch."

My shoulders roll with tension. "It's okay to blame me."

"Blame you for what?" Finn balances on his elbows. "He decided to protect you, so we all protect you. That's how it is."

My throat tightens.

He pushes the cobbler away. "That was good. Thanks for sharing."

I nod.

He moves to the fridge, grabs a water bottle and heads to the stairs. I set the plate in the sink and pour water on it so it can soak. As I move, I feel someone staring at me.

I look up.

Finn is paused at the base of the stairs, watching. The light hits his sharp cheekbones and makes his almond-shaped brown eyes glisten.

I wait, sensing that he's about to say something.

"Zane's always been obsessed with doing things people say he shouldn't. If you tell him he can't have something, he'll kill to get his hands on it."

"He's a rebel."

"He's an idiot." Finn's lips soften at the edges. "But he's brave. Way more than me or Dutch. He doesn't hold back. Doesn't overthink. He just goes for it."

"Perfect way to get hurt."

"Or a perfect way to feel alive."

I stare at Zane's brother, feeling a bunch of dark emotions in my chest.

"You're that thing he can't have. You know that, right?"

"I know."

"But it's different with you."

My mouth goes dry. "What do you mean?"

"For the first time in his life, I don't think Zane wanting you has anything to do with it being wrong."

I flinch when I hear the word 'wrong'. "But it is."

"He's eighteen. Legal—"

"He's a *student*. And I'm his teacher. We're not a love story, Finn. We're a scandal. And scandals can only exist in the dark."

"Not if you convince everyone the light is on."

Something shakes loose in my brain.

"Convince everyone..." I mutter excitedly. "Oh my gosh."

Finn looks at me like I'm crazy.

"Finn, you're incredible!" I rush forward, grab his face, and give him a kiss on the cheek. His eyes widen, but I'm already flying past him.

Inside my room, I haul out my whiteboard and fish through the photos I took of the files in the basement.

How do you break the rules in plain sight?

Convince everyone the light is on.

Finn was right. If you tell everyone what's wrong is right, eventually, they'll believe it. Even more, they'll argue with everyone who tries to convince them otherwise.

My fingers whip through the printed files.

My heart is pounding in my ears.

While I was investigating the basement, I found old administration documents that referenced 'The Grateful Project'. They were nothing but long inventories—wine, decorations, cups, food, cleaning services. I took the picture out of principle but didn't expect to get a hit.

"I know I have it. Where, where?" I mutter, thumbing through the pictures I printed out.

The Grateful Project was a school-sanctioned meeting between donors and scholarship students. I attended a couple with Sloane during my years at Redwood and thought it was just another way for the school to humiliate us, but what if it was something more?

"Come on," I hiss.

When I was snooping, I found a ton of invoices for The Grateful Project. Back then, I thought all those documents were just copies of an original, but now...

Finally, I land on one.

The words 'The Grateful Project' are stamped over the top of the page. There's a list of items, presumably used for that particular event.

"Date," I mutter.

There.

I grab my phone and scroll to an old calendar. Official 'Grateful Project' dinners happen in December or early January.

This invoice is dated March.

A foreboding feeling washes over me.

I'm getting close to something big.

"Names, names." I slide my thumb down the paper.

There are no names.

"Damn it."

I start to put the page down.

And then I snap it back up.

My eyes narrow on a series of numbers.

I'd recognize that sequence anywhere.

It's Sloane's student ID.

Chapter Twenty-Six

ZANE

Being suspended isn't so bad.

I wake up as late as I want. Chill in bed. Scroll through my phone. Play a few video games.

Harris thought he was punishing me, but he gave me permission to take a needed vacation. It's been non-stop chaos for weeks, what with Tina dying, dad trying so hard to be a B-rate villain in a slasher film, and Dutch getting married.

It's nice to have the day to myself.

The only thing I regret?

Not being awake when Grey left.

And also, not being there with her at school.

Damn. So make that two things I regret.

I'm worried about her safety. Hall is still a problem.

Last night, I punched the bastard so hard his body made a dent in the ground. I should have buried him there, but I didn't. He might come crawling back to

Redwood like the snake he is and I won't be able to do a thing about it.

I already asked Sol to keep an eye out today. He couldn't afford to get suspended and lose his scholarship, so we told Harris he had nothing to do with the fight. Thankfully, Harris didn't touch him.

At least I can keep tabs on Grey through Jinx's app.

No news means good news.

I slip out of bed around noon because the smells coming from downstairs are driving me crazy.

Marian is in there, humming and stirring a pot on the stove.

I rub my eyes, smiling at her. "Morning."

"Young man, it is one o'clock," she says sassily.

"Afternoon."

Her earrings wiggle and smack her dark cheeks. "Have a seat."

Soberly, I sit.

Does Marian know about my suspension?

I hope not.

I'm supposed to be earning her trust so I can spill the news about dad's true colors. She won't take me seriously if she sees me as the screw-up everyone else does.

I press my hands together. "I'm not feeling well, so I'm taking a sick day."

She gives me a loaded look and I can tell she smells my BS a mile away.

"Before Finn left, he told me about that little fight you started yesterday."

Sheepishly, I rub the back of my neck.

"I heard you punched someone for saying nasty things about Gracie." She gives me a proud little smirk. "How'd you do it?"

"Slammed him across the face with my drumstick."

She sticks out a fist.

Stunned, I punch it lightly.

Marian returns her attention to the stove. "I wasn't sure what you liked, so I played it safe. Baked beans. Barbecued ribs. Slaw. Some mashed potatoes—bland because your palette might not be used to all this flavour."

I laugh and swing into a barstool.

She sets the table and I take a bite of the ribs. An explosion of flavors bursts on my tongue and I moan.

"Damn. No wonder dad married you."

She chortles warmly. "Funnily enough, your dad doesn't like my cooking."

I'm shocked, but not too surprised. Dad's a heartless vampire who drinks blood and doesn't need regular human sustenance.

Marian folds her hands together and peers at me. "I know my marriage to your father was a shock. I also know I didn't make a great impression during our last family dinner..." Her voice trails.

I set my fork down. The last family dinner was when mom came over and told us about our grandmother's inheritance.

"Nobody was in a good mood that day, but it wasn't because of you."

She smiles tightly and pinches at a bread roll. "I guess, what I'm trying to say is that I'm honored to be a part of your family. And I won't let anything jeopardize that."

My fingers tighten on the fork. That's not good. I can't have Marian being too attached to the Cross brand of insanity. She's a key player in my plan to weaken dad's power.

"Is this how you usually spend your day?" I ask, digging into the baked beans.

"I do some shopping, watch TV."

"Dad hasn't been home for a while now," I say, watching her carefully.

Her eyelashes flutter down. "He's on tour."

"Has he called you?"

She launches out of her seat. "Let me pop these rolls back in the oven. They're a little too soft."

I watch as Marian fiddles with the knobs on the stove.

"About dad, there's something I need to—"

"Zane." Her voice sounds tired. "Do you know how Grey grew up?"

I shake my head.

"We lived in a cramped apartment behind a nightclub. The noise was obnoxious. There were fights. Screams. Women sold their bodies on the street near our block. Gangs fought turf wars right in front of our house. Sometimes, the bullets tore through the walls. We could have died in our sleep."

It sounds horrific.

"I swore I'd get her out of there and I did." She turns to face me, a determined set to her chin. "My baby was smart. She got a scholarship to Redwood. She went to college. She made something of herself. That was all I wanted. For her to be better than I was. So I never imagined I'd be here." She throws her hands out to indicate the giant, spacious kitchen. "Living like this. I never allowed myself to dream of it."

The edges of her mouth curve up in a not-quite-there smile. "I don't know why you boys moved in and I don't care. I'm glad to have a family. Me and Jarod, we will *always* be a family."

She gives me a knowing stare, and I realize Marian isn't as clueless as she looks.

"Understood."

Her grin gets more genuine and she pops the rolls out of the oven. When she returns to the table, she sets one in my plate.

"Eat up." The scent of her cocoa butter lotion wafts to me as she pours another glass of sweet tea.

I back off, deciding not to broach the topic of her divorcing dad yet. "This food is really good."

"It's the least I can do for such a sweet little brother."

Calling me 'sweet' and 'little brother' in the same sentence?

Poor Marian.

She has no idea all the filthy things I want to do to her daughter.

Marian folds her hands together and rests her chin on top of it. "You know, I'm so glad Gracie has you boys looking out for her at Redwood."

That makes two of us.

"It shocked me when she said she was moving back and teaching there. She wasn't really treated well in high school. And that horrible tragedy with her friend, well, it traumatized her. Both of us, really. I thought she'd run far away."

"What happened to her friend?"

Marian's lips clamp shut.

I tilt my head, flashing her a charming smile. "It's okay. You can tell me. I won't tell anyone else."

She glances back and forth as if someone bugged the house. Finally, she crooks her finger in my direction.

I drag my chair closer to hers.

"I'm only saying this because you're family. Gracie made me swear not to talk about it with anyone."

I nod, leaning in.

"Her sophomore year, she met this other scholarship student named Sloane. Sloane was a bit of a wild child. Wore lots of short clothes and piercings. She reminded me too much of those ladies in our old neighborhood." Marian makes a face. "But Gracie was lonely and Sloane was the only one who'd talk to her. They got very close."

"What happened to her?"

"She was murdered."

My eyebrow twitches.

"The attacker was Sloane's boyfriend. That's what the police said, but Gracie swears there's more to the story. She thinks there's another reason Sloane got murdered and she thinks she'll find that reason at Redwood."

Chapter Twenty-Seven

ZANE

Finn jumps into Dutch's bed and I swat him off.

He glares at me.

I point down. "We know what happens in here. Get off their bed."

Finn looks unbothered. "If I avoided places because of that, I wouldn't have anywhere to sit."

"Hey, I followed the rules. I never brought a girl home," I say.

Both my brothers give me dull looks.

I clear my throat. "It was one time and I never did it again."

"What's with the emergency meeting?" Dutch strums on his guitar. The strings spell C-A-D-E-Y.

I swear, my twin is embarrassing. No matter how in love I am, I'm never painting some girl's name over my drum set.

"I have an update on dad and Marian."

Dutch looks expectantly at me.

Finn puts his book down.

"It's going to be tougher than I thought," I admit. "Marian thinks dad is her ticket to a new life."

"We knew that already," Dutch says, picking out a complicated riff.

"No, you don't get it. She's *with* him. Rain or shine. She wouldn't dump him if we told her he was banging other women in her bed."

"Did she say that?"

"She might as well have."

"I don't know, Zane," Finn mumbles. "How are you so sure if she didn't say that outright?"

"I'm not an idiot."

Finn gives me a look that says '*that's debatable.*'

I ignore it and sweep my fingers through my hair. "Dad doesn't call her. Barely comes home. Treats her like an afterthought. She's the most single married person I've ever seen and she doesn't care. It'll take more than just telling her about the inheritance to change her mind. We need proof that dad is a maniac."

"If we had proof of that, we would have ended his stupid game a long time ago," Dutch mutters.

"How about we prove he murdered Cadence's mom?"

Finn shakes his head. "I read the police reports. She really did die of an overdose."

"And dad wasn't even in the country when she passed," Dutch said.

"He could have sent someone to do it."

"Sure. I agree with that," Dutch says. "But he's too smart to leave anything that could trace back to him."

"Dad always seems to be one step ahead of us," Finn agrees.

We fall into stiff silence.

"Convincing Miss Jamieson's mom to divorce him is still our best option." Dutch rubs his chin. "Are you sure she's not secretly planning to divorce him anyway?"

"If she is, she has a funny way of showing it."

Finn's jaw works as he thinks.

"It might be different if the warning comes from Grey," I offer. "Marian might not believe me, but she won't ignore her daughter."

I let my brothers stew in that for a beat.

"Speaking of Grey, there's something else."

"Is this about Hall?" Dutch asks. "You scared he might come after you?"

"If he tries to make himself a problem, he'll regret it." My fingers clench around my sticks.

Dutch raises a brow, but he doesn't say anything.

I meet my brother's eyes. "Remember when I told you Harris was being weird that day?"

They nod.

I tell them what Marian confided in me.

"When Harris said that Grey could ruin Redwood, I think this is what he was talking about."

Finn looks intrigued. "No wonder…"

We both turn to him.

"There's this saying that the ghost of the student who was murdered still roams around the school."

Dutch looks grossed out.

I shudder.

"I thought it was just an urban legend." Finn smirks. "I had no idea it was based on a real murder."

My brother is insane. Why is he smiling like that?

"I was thinking…" I murmur, "what if we forge an alliance?"

"With who?" Dutch asks.

"Grey. We'll help her investigate and dish out all the revenge she wants. In return, she convinces her mom to leave dad."

"I like it," Finn says.

Dutch looks at me. "You sure you're doing this for the right reasons?"

"What other reasons could I have?"

He just stares me down.

"It's a work partnership."

Finn snorts. I get the idea that he doesn't believe me.

Dutch's eyes are the same shape as mine yet it's more than just the colors that are different. His is filled with a lot more darkness. The three of us are the same age, but he always acts like the weight of the world is on his shoulders.

"It's one thing if Miss Jamieson is someone you're screwing around with," Dutch warns. "It's different if she gets involved in our business. You blow things up with her, it could ruin everything for us."

"You're acting like I'm radioactive."

Dutch doesn't laugh. He just keeps staring.

I lift my chin. "Grey and I... have an understanding. Besides, she'll need our help more than we need hers."

Dutch relents and finally looks down.

Finn picks up his book again. "What do you think dad is doing right now?"

"Marian said he's on tour." I walk over to the mini-fridge. The moment I open the door, I see a bunch of face masks, sparkling water, and girly crap.

I push past the sparkling water and grab a beer.

"I haven't seen any articles about him," Dutch says.

"I feel uneasy. Whenever dad's too quiet, he comes back with something crazy."

"Like that time he decided to teach at Redwood," I agree.

"Or that time he sent Cadence across Europe and tossed me in jail," Dutch murmurs.

Finn grunts in agreement.

"We can't predict what dad will do next," I tell them. "Right now, we have our own thing. We'll deal with dad when he strikes."

Dutch glances at Finn who nods.

"Alright then," Dutch slips his guitar over his head, "let's do it." My lips inch higher as he says, "Let's strike a deal with Miss Jamieson."

* * *

Jinx: Drumsticks and Stones Can Break My Bones

It's Day One without our resident princes and already, the air feels colder. Redwood just doesn't seem as bright without our three shiny royals. Hurry back, dear princes. There are still so many secrets to be told.

Until the next post, keep your enemies close and your secrets even closer.

- Jinx

Chapter Twenty-Eight

GREY

I yelp when Cadence Cooper appears outside my classroom. She's wearing a powder blue uniform top with a checkered skirt and low black pumps. Her sharp navy jacket falls neatly over her shoulders.

"Cadence, hi. You're here... *again*," I say.

"Hey." She flanks one side of me. Her friend, Serena, presses in on my other side.

"How was class, Miss J?"

"Good." I drag out the word.

"Huh." Serena pops her gum and glances at my books. "You're doing *Othello* with the freshmen?"

"Nice." Cadence smiles.

Something tells me they aren't that interested in Shakespeare's play.

"Where you headed?" Cadence asks.

"Teacher's lounge."

"Oh, we're heading the same way."

I give her a suspicious look. "Actually, I'm going to the cafeteria."

She does a one-eighty. "Come to think of it I was feeling peckish."

I narrow my eyes at her.

"Whoa," Serena mumbles, stumbling behind us.

I glance at the hallway filled with banners declaring 'MASQUERADE BALL TOMORROW'. As the three of us walk in, students part like a riptide, pressing back on either side of the corridor to clear a path.

"You'll get used to it," Cadey says.

"Who can get used to *this?*" Serena hisses. "A few weeks ago, they were pouring yogurt on our freshly mopped floors. Now, they're treating you like a queen?"

Personally, I don't think they're making room because of Cadence's connection to The Kings. I think they're making a show of shunning me. The gossip about my 'relationship' with Zane has spread *everywhere*. If I thought yesterday was bad, today is even worse.

"Ladies," a new voice says.

I glance up, shocked to see Sol join us. The fourth member of The Kings is just as handsome as the other three, but there's something in his eyes that's a little... unhinged. I heard Sol's been struggling with his mental health, and it's been on my mind to check on him.

"You heading to the cafeteria now?" Sol glances down at me, his broad shoulders almost blocking us from view. "Or another class?"

I stop abruptly.

The three of them stop too.

Fingers tightening around my books, I huff. "What's going on?"

"Nothing." The smile on Cadence's pretty face doesn't fool me.

She's a brilliant student and a gifted musician.

But a terrible liar.

"Cadence, you've been escorting me around all day. Do you think I wouldn't notice? And you—" I point a finger at Sol. "You made it so obvious."

Sol lifts both hands. "You'll have to put up with us until Zane comes back to school."

"You can't be serious."

"He's right." Cadence faces me sternly. "We're your bodyguards."

I stare at her slim figure. She couldn't hurt a fly.

"I'm tougher than I look." Cadence lifts her chin as if she can read my thoughts. "Tell her, Sol."

I see his face soften when he looks at Cadence, but it's only for a minute and then it's gone.

Serena grins, pretty red lips stretching over her face. "I'm just here for the free lunch. I heard teachers get an all access pass." She thumbs a finger in Sol and Cadence's direction. "And unlike those two, I am neither married to nor best friends with any member of The Kings, so I have to find other means to get ahead."

I shove my lunch pass at her. "Here. You can have whatever you like. Just... tell them you're buying lunch for me today."

Serena's eyes light up. She's had few things to smile about lately, with her family's financial problems and her mom's chemo. I'm glad to see her excited.

"Off you go." I shove their backs.

Cadence remains in place. "We're supposed to stay with you."

"I'm a big girl. And you three," I point at each of them, "should be worried about studying. The school year is almost over and I know for a *fact* that your grades have been slipping."

Cadence and Serena glance down.

Sol looks amused, as if school is the absolute last thing on his mind.

"Redwood might have its flaws—" *that's an understatement*—"but this place still handed you an opportunity. It's up to you to take that chance and make something of it. Don't get distracted." My eyes slip to Serena. "Even if it's hard." To Cadence. "Even if you feel the real world calling." To Sol. "Even if you feel out of place. You *belong* here. You earned this spot. So fight for it."

Cadence nods.

Serena licks her lips and looks thoughtful.

I start to walk away.

Cadence and Sol move in front of me.

I groan.

Sol smirks. "So... cafeteria or no?"

"I could eat." Cadence shrugs.

Serena slings an arm over Cadence's shoulder and wiggles my lunch card. "I'm buying."

"After you, Miss J," Sol says, jutting his chin in the direction of the cafeteria.

I sigh and follow the three students as they commit the most polite form of kidnapping in Redwood Prep history.

Chapter Twenty-Nine

GREY

With Cadence, Sol and Serena shadowing my every move, I change my mind about heading to the basement after school.

My plan is to come back later tonight when everyone is gone. I want to comb over the boxes I previously searched with 'The Grateful Project' in mind. Now that I have a direction, I can parse through old information with a new perspective.

But the plan goes to crap when I walk outside.

The Kings are parked directly in front of Redwood.

Dutch is sitting on the edge of the hood, blond hair blowing in the breeze like a silent Viking. Finn is planted sideways in the passenger seat, his super-long legs sprawled out and a book perched between his hands.

Zane is the only one who isn't lounging. He's standing up and his stormy blue eyes slice through the crowd like a hawk. When his gaze rams into mine, he smirks like he just found his prey.

A shiver runs down my spine.

"You want to ride with us or with Zane, Miss J?" Cadence asks.

I blink distractedly. "What?"

Serena checks her phone. "Actually, Cadence, could you drop me off at the hospital? It'll take too long by bus."

"Of course." Cadence smiles. "Guess you're riding with Zane. See you there."

"There? Where is..." Before I can get the rest of the words out, Zane approaches me.

"What are you doing here? Aren't you suspended?"

"Semantics."

"You're not supposed to be on Redwood Prep property. Do you want to get expelled?"

"I'm here to pick you up."

My lips form a scowl.

"Get in the car, Grey."

I glance around instead. Students are spilling out of Redwood and they all freeze, staring at us like we're re-enacting the most dramatic scene in *Othello*.

Zane walks right up to me. "Should I carry you there?" He taps his shoulder. "For the hell of it?"

"Don't you dare," I snarl.

"They're going to talk either way. So why don't you give them something to talk about?"

I gasp when his fingers brush my wrist and he tugs me to the car.

Sol gets in the backseat.

Zane slams the door behind me.

A moment later, we're off.

I twist my neck to stare out the window.

Everyone is watching us.

Everyone saw.

"Do you know what you've done?" I whirl on Zane, my eyes darkening. "I'm trying to keep a low profile, and this stunt just ruined everything."

"A low profile. Is that why you're dressed in that oversized curtain today?"

I glance down at my baggy shirt and the shimmery gold skirt that goes down to my ankles. "This is *not* a curtain."

"Sorry to break it to you, sweetheart, but you're wearing my grandmother's drapes. Problem is… you could be wearing a garbage bag and half the guys at Redwood would screw you." He shakes his head with an aggravated twist of his lips. "You're hot as hell either way, so just wear what you want."

The fact that he called me 'hot as hell' doesn't even register in my brain.

I scoff at him. "I wore this because my reputation is totally trashed, and it's the only way to get people to respect me again—"

"You think they respected you before this? You think they cared?" His smirk is all kinds of cold hell. "Take it from me, tiger. They were chomping at the bit to turn on you. And from the way you're caving to them, they're winning."

"I'm not caving. I'm being a responsible adult."

"And that's your problem."

I let out a bitter laugh.

"You can't let public opinion control you. Especially at Redwood. They'll praise you one day, and kill you the next. So why give them that kind of control?"

"You don't understand because the world revolves around you. *You* decide. *You* control. You play with people like toys. The rest of us can't afford to make really stupid decisions and get patted on the back for it. Life isn't a game unless your last name is Cross. Now, where the hell are you taking me?"

Zane suddenly slams on the brakes. His arm shoots out, banding over my stomach and absorbing my forward thrust. I'd have cracked my head on the headboard if not for his fast reflexes.

The car stops completely.

I glare at him. "Are you trying to kill me?"

He undoes his seatbelt and leans over my seat. The heat of my breath and the tension crackling between us gets hotter as his fingers brush my arm.

"You were so busy arguing you never put on your seatbelt."

Our eyes lock, my brown ones on his darkening stormy sea blue.

"Safety first, tiger," he growls, his voice reminding me of the very animal he keeps referring to.

Except this tiger isn't docile.

It's vicious, sly, and on the hunt.

I shiver, even though the air conditioner isn't that cold and the sun is baking the windshield. The click of the belt locking in place snaps through the thick, hot silence.

"Now you can go back to yelling at me," Zane says.

"Uh... did you guys forget I'm in the backseat?" Sol grumbles.

I crane my neck to look in the back of the car.

Sol is glaring at us. "Next time, I'm taking the bus." He hunkers down. "You and Dutch are both so freaking obnoxious."

Zane smirks at the rearview mirror.

I notice we're heading outside of city limits. "Seriously, where are you taking me?"

"Somewhere we can have a private conversation."

That's all the information I get out of Zane.

Rather than continue to argue, I buckle in for the ride. Since Sol is in the backseat, this surprise trip probably won't end up with me naked and on my back. Not that I have any intentions of sleeping with Zane again. Not that I've been thinking about it...

The point is Sol is here and Cadence said she would 'see me later'.

Whatever's going on, it involves the entire crew.

I wonder what they want to tell me?

Zane winds the car through a forest. The trees all look the same and there are no markers, but he doesn't slow down or check for directions. Finally, he stops in front of a giant treehouse and we climb out.

My jaw drops when I stare at the magnificent piece of architecture balanced on thick and sturdy branches.

"What is this place?"

"Dutch bought it for Cadence as a wedding gift," Zane says.

A frown flits over Sol's face. He stomps past us and scales the ladder leading up to the treehouse.

I move forward hesitantly.

"Careful," Zane says, setting a hand on me as I hoist myself up.

I swat at him but releasing my grip on the slats almost sends me flying to the ground. This time, when Zane supports me, I'm grateful for it.

"You okay?" He calls from below. He's so tall that his head is still level with my chest.

I don't respond and climb the rest of the way.

Zane is right behind me.

The view on the deck takes my breath away. I can't stop gawking. The evening sun splays over the tops of thick trees. Birds caw to each other from green foliage.

Inside is even more mind-blowing. I've never seen anything like this.

"Want a beer?" Zane asks.

"Beer tastes like dirt to me. I prefer wine," I answer automatically and then I narrow my eyes at him. "You shouldn't be drinking."

"I shouldn't be doing a lot of things," he says as he walks over to a wine cooler. He pours me a glass.

I hesitate before accepting it.

Drinking with a student. It's not the worst thing on my list of infractions, but it adds to it. I'm pretty sure, at this point, I qualify to have my teacher's license revoked.

My fingers close around my glass and, to my surprise, I notice Zane throwing his beer away and reaching for the scotch.

"You've seen the light?"

He laughs loudly. "No." He pours it into a glass. "I just don't want you complaining about the taste when I kiss you later."

On the outside, my expression remains stern.

Inside, anticipation makes my body throb.

"We are *not* kissing later," I say firmly.

He just smirks at me and downs his scotch.

Sol walks into the room. "When are Dutch and Finn getting here?"

"Should be any minute now." Zane checks his phone.

I hear car doors slamming.

A moment later, Dutch, Finn and Cadence walk into the

treehouse. The seniors grab beer from the fridge and sit in a pile on the ground.

Cadence motions to me. "Sit here, Miss Jamieson."

I want to tell her she can call me Grey, but I think I need the reminder that I'm the teacher and these are still my students. Honestly, it doesn't feel that way. Outside of Redwood and in their regular street clothes, these boys feel like a dangerous gang that I would cross the street to avoid.

"Why exactly did you bring me here?" I ask, my eyes jumping from one Cross brother to the next.

"We're here to make a deal," Zane says, looking at me with those startlingly blue eyes of his. They look more green than blue here in the treehouse, full of threats and dark intentions.

Dutch stares me down, watching every flicker of emotions on my face.

I give nothing away. "What kind of deal?"

"We know why you're at Redwood," Finn says.

"We know about Sloane," Sol adds.

I stiffen.

"Don't worry. We're not going to tell." Zane flashes a smirk at me that feels more dangerous than comforting. "*If* you help us with one thing."

"What?"

"Get your mom to divorce our dad."

I laugh.

No one joins me.

Zane leans forward on his bean bag as if it's a throne made of gold. "We've got a time limit. Two weeks."

My mind churns through this new information. The Cross brothers have wealth, connections, and fame. They own everything, even Redwood—why do they want my mom to leave?

I lift my chin. "Even if you threaten to kill me, I won't do anything that hurts my mother."

"Who said we wanted to hurt your mother?" Zane asks.

Finn frowns as if he's offended I would even say that.

Dutch adds, "Trust me. It's better for her if she's far, far away from him."

"Jarod Cross is a very dangerous man." Cadence touches my arm. "We think he had something to do with my mom's death."

Panic strikes a chord in my heart. "W-why would he do that?"

"Because dad is a sick, twisted psychopath," Zane says bitterly.

"Jarod Cross started teaching at Redwood, married your mother and threw Dutch in jail, all to get his hands on the boys' inheritance. That's the kind of person we're dealing with," Cadence says.

I don't know how to respond to that.

"Like we said, you wouldn't be helping us for free. We'll make sure you get your answers. *And* your revenge." Zane looks at me again and I can feel the dark thread that binds us, that's been drawing us together since that first night, getting a little tighter. It's a hot, sticky sensation. The kind that gets on your fingers and refuses to be washed away.

"Revenge?" I choke.

"We'll make it as dark and as painful as you want," Zane promises.

Dutch nods.

The thirst for justice comes roaring back, eclipsing all the reasons why getting into bed with this crew could destroy me.

I take a moment to weigh the pros and cons.

It all equals out.

Trust them. Don't trust them.

It's really a leap of faith.

I glance at Zane whose stare is level on me. Just like that night when I looked into his gold-flecked blue eyes for the first time, I feel this surge of courage. Of urgency. Like this isn't an opportunity I want to throw to the wind.

Glancing at the other dangerous, brutal, domineering Cross brothers, I realize there's only one answer.

For Sloane's sake.

For my sake.

For revenge.

"Yes."

Chapter Thirty

ZANE

Grey pairs her phone to the projector and an invoice flashes on the sheet hanging from the criss-crossing roof beams. A light breeze flows through the windows. There are no screens, so there's nothing obstructing our view of the stars.

Grey's curls swing back and forth as she turns to face us, wiping a palm against that ridiculous floor-length skirt. A ripple of irritation fills me when I see that thing. I really don't care about her outfit choices. If she wants to dress in an ancient freaking toga, it makes no difference to me.

But the fact that she's changing what she likes to wear because people are talking about her?

Screw that.

Besides it's a total waste of time.

Her curves are still tempting, even if they're hidden. The attempt to cover her body does jack squat. I want to rip all that fabric off her and spread her legs more now than I did when she was wearing her sexy little pencil skirts.

Grey folds her hands together. "Last night, while I was talking to Finn, I had an epiphany."

I spring to attention. "You were with Finn last night?"

My brother smirks knowingly at me.

White-hot jealousy unfurls, curling around my spine.

Dutch sits straighter, hearing the fight in my tone.

Sol rolls his eyes.

Grey pauses. The projector's harsh white light pierces her skin and craters a black circle on her shirt that's buttoned up to the neck.

I keep my scathing gaze on Finn. "What were you doing with her last night?"

"Why should I tell you?"

I'm ready to jump out of my seat and punch him in the face.

"We were just talking," Grey snaps, looking annoyed.

Finn quirks an eyebrow, studying my response.

The freaking snot.

"Close your zippers and have your pissing contest later please." Cadey waves a hand.

"Moving on, something Finn said sparked an idea." Grey points to the document. "Have you ever heard of 'The Grateful Project?'"

I glance around the room. Sol is chewing on popcorn like we're watching a movie. Finn is squinting in concentration. Cadey is perched between Dutch's legs, her arms looped under his knees and resting on his shins. His legs hang over her like he's a human rollercoaster restraint.

Grey explains when no one speaks, "The Grateful Project was an initiative by the administration at Redwood.

It was a way to encourage the rich and influential to donate to the scholarship fund."

"It was for scholarship students?" Cadey clarifies.

"Yes. Every year, we were given these awful waitressing outfits and told to serve at the event. Some of us had to go on stage and read from the teleprompter. The speeches were these exaggerated summaries of our home lives. It was humiliating."

Sol gives the screen a dark look. "I wish they'd try that on me."

"I don't think they would. Not with Jinx on the prowl. But back then, we didn't really have a choice. The Grateful Project was something you agreed to when you accepted the scholarship."

"What does this have to do with Sloane?" Dutch asks, unshakeably calm.

"Up until last night, nothing." She pinches her phone screen and the image on the projector zooms in. "But look at that date."

I peer at the numbers.

Sol leans forward so far he almost drops his popcorn.

"The Grateful Project was a once-a-year event. It usually happens somewhere between Christmas and New Year's, when everyone is in a party and giving mood."

"Makes sense," Finn says.

"But this date says March," I point out.

"Exactly. Why would there be an invoice for an event that had already taken place?"

"They could have been preparing for it in advance," Dutch muses.

"True. But that doesn't explain this." She scrolls down and points to a series of numbers. "This is Sloane's student ID."

I flip my drumsticks, soaking in the information.

"The Grateful Project is the perfect feeding ground for predators. Think about it. If you wanted to match desperate scholarship girls with sick bastards willing to pay for underage sex..." She flinches a little and carefully avoids my gaze, "you do it in a way that won't draw suspicion." Her eyes slip to Finn. "You stay in darkness while telling everyone the light is on."

Finn bobs his head.

"You're saying The Grateful Project was a front," Sol mumbles. "Do you know who was running it?"

"The night Sloane was murdered, she got a call from Harris."

I feel a ripple of surprise tear through the room.

None of us expected a Harris name drop in association with this.

"He was the vice principal at the time. Which makes him calling Sloane that late at night even weirder."

"You think Harris called Sloane to attend one of these..." Cadey waves a hand at the screen, "off-the-books 'Grateful' parties."

"I do. And I think that's where she met the guy who eventually killed her."

A chilling hush fills the room.

We're not dealing with a missing best friend, trying to kick the New Girl out of school, or surviving dad's underhanded power plays anymore.

This is real life.

This is murder.

Sorrow fills Grey's eyes. "She was my best friend. She didn't deserve what happened to her. I want the world to acknowledge that Sloane was a victim of more than just the guy who took her life. She was a victim of the system. She was a victim of Redwood."

Soft golden lamps shimmer in the wetness of her eyes. I hate seeing Grey in pain, so I start to get up, but Cadey beats me to it. She leaves her place between Dutch's legs and wraps an arm around Grey's waist.

"We'll find everyone involved in this project and bring them to justice. I promise."

Dutch meets his wife's eyes and nods.

Sol snarls at the shadows. "Those sick bastards. Back then and now, nothing's different. Nothing's changed."

Finn pushes his hands through his hair. He's the quietest of us, but I can tell he's invested.

"What do we need to do first?" I ask.

Grey looks at me. "There's a basement under the school. Harris put it under lock and key after our talk. I need to get back in there. I can use all the hands I can get."

"Done," Dutch says.

"You said there's a lock?" Finn purses his lips. "If Harris went so far as to put a lock on the door, he'll notice if it's been tampered with."

I consider it. "What if we steal the key?"

Dutch frowns. "We snuck into Redwood to steal something once. It didn't turn out well."

"This is different," I argue.

"Harris has something to lose. He's not going to leave the key somewhere we can find it," Grey points out.

Cadey arches a brow. "She's right. It's too risky. If Harris sees that things have been shuffled around in the basement, he might do something even more drastic." She shakes her head, dark hair spilling around her shoulders. "We need to find another way."

Grey makes a frustrated sound. "I don't care if Harris

finds out, but I can't afford for him to destroy that room before I have a chance to go through everything."

We all fall into thoughtful silence again.

"I have an idea," I murmur.

Everyone turns to look at me.

"It's a little crazy," I add.

"No one assumed that brain of yours could come up with anything sane," Cadence says dryly.

Grey's brown eyes burrow into me, alert and waiting.

"What if there's a way we could take all the boxes out? If we get them into our territory, we can go through them without having to sneak into Redwood's basement every time."

"How would we take them out?" Dutch asks. "There's security twenty-four seven. Even if we go under the cover of night, it would raise a ton of suspicion."

"And how would we keep Harris from knowing it was us?" Sol points out.

"It'll require dressing up." I smirk at Grey.

She narrows her eyes slightly.

I swing around to Sol who stares right back at me with those eyes that used to sparkle and now look dead. "And I'll need something from you."

"What?"

"You still remember how to start a fire?"

* * *

Jinx: You can't banish a king from his own kingdom

Today, our royal percussionist barged into Redwood with a glittering black carriage. His Cinderella didn't seem that happy to see him. Was Snare King sweeping his lady love off her feet or was it a royal kidnapping? They're both on borrowed time. I wonder what happens when that carriage turns into a rotten pumpkin?

Tick-Tock, Sexy Teach.

Let's see if your scandal can really turn into a fairytale.

Until the next post, keep your enemies close and your secrets even closer.

- Jinx

Chapter Thirty-One

GREY

Since we're all going to the same place, Finn rides with us. He's in the backseat, a tablet in his hands. Every so often, he swipes the page.

I peer at him. "What are you reading?"

His eyes shoot to me and then dart back down. "*The Millionaire's Surrogate Lover*," he says dryly. "It's a historical romance."

I can't tell if he's being sarcastic or not.

I glance at Zane for help.

He shrugs. "We don't understand him either."

Finn swipes another page, dismissing me.

Okay then.

"So about *my* end of the deal," I say, staring at the darkness on the dangerously winding mountain road, "before I talk to mom, I need to find out more about Jarod Cross."

"What about him?" Zane drives with one hand. The other he wraps around his cup of coffee.

I watch the way his throat bobs and feel my stomach tighten.

He's so effortlessly attractive. It's annoying.

I drag my eyes away from his wet lips to the railways, which are the only things preventing us from plummeting off the rocky cliffs. "What are his motivations?"

"Easy. He's evil, narcissistic, and gets off on other people's..." Zane glances in the rearview mirror and suddenly clams up.

"What?"

"There's a car..."

Before he can finish, something rams into the back of our vehicle. Metal crashes into metal and I hear the sound of tires squealing on the road. Our vehicle lurches, colliding into the metal railway.

I scream.

Finn's tablet tumbles out of his hands.

Zane shoots an arm out to protect me. It's an almost instinctual act because his eyes are on the rearview mirror and he's fighting to correct the car. "What the hell?"

Our attacker won't let up.

The scream of steel on metal fills the night air.

As our car keeps moving against the railway, metal sparks explode.

There's a black car with heavily-tinted windows ramming us from behind. It's too dark to tell who's in the driver's seat.

"Zane, go faster," Finn barks.

"I'm trying," Zane grits out. He slams his foot on the gas and the car zooms forward.

But that only gives our pursuer another chance to ram into us again.

Boom!

Glass shatters.

Metal crunches.

My body lurches forward and the seatbelt cuts painfully into my chest.

"Zane!" I scream, pointing at a break in the railway up ahead.

The barrier is going to run out.

If we keep going like this, the black car will push us right off the mountain and into the inky darkness below.

"Hold on," Zane growls. Eyes narrowed, he pushes his foot harder on the gas.

I watch the speedometer climb.

We get closer and closer to the edge of the mountain.

"Zane, watch out!" I yell again.

My fingers dig into my seatbelt.

This is it.

We're going to die.

I wince, bracing myself for impact.

At the last possible second, Zane shifts gears, slams the brakes and hauls on the steering wheel. The car drifts to the right, screaming over the highway.

My heart is pounding and I chew so hard on my bottom lip I taste blood. We finally gain some ground and Zane punches it, taking advantage. Our car speeds away, putting distance between us and our tail.

"Grey, you alright?" Zane asks, breathing hard and glancing over at me.

I nod, swallowing the blood in my mouth. If not for Zane's evasive maneuver, I wouldn't just be tasting blood. I'd be drowning in it.

"I snapped a picture," Finn says, his voice so devoid of emotion that it sends a shudder down my spine. "But there was no license plate."

"Dammit," Zane grumbles.

"This is insane," I say breathlessly. "Why would someone try to kill us?"

Finn remains quiet, but his face is hard.

"We've got plenty of takers. Dad, for one."

"Dad isn't this sloppy," Finn says. "And he likes to gloat."

"It could be Hall." Zane arches an eyebrow at me and I feel myself bristling. "I thought he was too quiet after I put him in the hospital."

"Or it could be someone who knows about my investigation."

The car falls silent.

I lift my attention to the woods on either side. Danger is breathing down my neck and it makes me wonder if I made the right choice coming to Redwood.

This is all starting to feel like too much.

I press a hand to my chest, feeling the thumping. Adrenaline is still shooting through my blood and it doesn't stop even when we get closer to home.

It's funny.

No one mentions going to the police.

Neither do I.

This world is so twisted, so dark, that even when my safety is threatened, it feels useless to rely on anyone—even those sworn to protect and uphold the peace. The cops didn't do that for Sloane. Why assume they would for me?

The garage door rises and Zane drives in.

I frown, noticing a shiny convertible. "That car wasn't there before."

Zane's voice holds a hellish chill. "It's him."

"Who?"

Blue eyes drill into mine. "Dad. He's home."

***

Jarod Cross insists we eat out. I kind of wish we'd stayed at home.

Not just because we were almost killed on the mountain tonight.

The atmosphere around this table is so toxic I'm slightly nauseous. It feels like, at any moment, a fight will break out.

It doesn't help that we're in the perfect setting for a black-and-white murder mystery. The Boardroom is a depressing restaurant with heavy velvet chairs, dull lighting and old, outdated furnishings.

Their only claim to fame is a cigar rack that takes up most of one wall.

Whoever thought of putting a cigar shop and a restaurant in the same room needs to get their head checked.

I cough and blow the scent of tobacco smoke away.

"Here," Zane says, handing me a handkerchief, "use this."

"Thanks."

Our fingers graze lightly when I take the cloth from him. Even that simple touch sparks heat through my body.

His eyes burn, and I can tell he felt it as strongly as I did.

"Jarod," mom says, looping her hands around her husband's arm, "you didn't have to take us out. I told you I'd be happy to cook for you."

"No need. Since I'm back in town for a night, I wanted to treat you to a nice meal."

Mom's lips curl up, happy with the crumbs he tosses at her.

"I also wanted to talk to the boys." Jarod's eyes dart between Dutch, Zane, and Finn. "I couldn't believe it when I got the call from Harris saying they'd been suspended."

His accusation is sharp and cold.

I can feel the tension whipping around the table like a storm.

Mom laughs nervously. "Why don't we eat first before discussing anything unpleasant?"

"Yeah, dad," Dutch says, leaning back in his chair, "while we eat, you can tell us all about the tour. When does it start again? I haven't heard anything in the news." Jarod's expression barely shifts, but there's the tiniest clench of a muscle in his jaw when Dutch says, "You need to fire your publicist. They made you look like a liar."

"I didn't know you were so interested in my tour, Dutch."

Mom clears her throat. "Wow, this asparagus is so flavorful. Boys, have you tried the asparagus?"

I want to face-palm. Mom is trying so hard to smooth things over, but there's no stopping this war. If we step in the middle, we're getting skewered.

"You three are old enough to know better." Jarod Cross cuts into his steak with a serrated knife. Blood oozes out of the centre. Carelessly, he sops it up and pops it into his mouth.

Squeamish, I glance away.

Jarod's eyes shift up, two pools of velvety blackness. "I'll be running for the chairman seat. You three should represent me well."

"What do we have to do with your stupid chairman run?" Zane spits.

Jarod Cross chews carefully. "Why would anyone trust me to run Redwood if I can't even show that I can run my own house?"

"Honey, don't be so hard on them. They only fought to defend Gracie. They may have gotten suspended, but it was for a noble reason."

"Noble?" Jarod's eyes cut to me and it feels like an ice cube slithers down my back.

Has he always been that sharp? That dangerous looking? Or is it that I was blind before and the boys ripped the scales from my eyes?

"Is that what you think, Miss Jamieson?"

I lick my lips. "I think things will settle down soon."

"I'm sure you're hoping for that. I heard you've been quite the star at Redwood lately."

Zane's smile is a hard slash across his face, and it frightens me a bit to know there's so much darkness lurking inside him. "Have you been keeping tabs on Miss Jamieson too?"

"I only heard that you almost got her fired."

Zane stiffens.

"What?" Mom's jaw drops. "Gracie, I didn't know it was so serious."

"It isn't, mom," I say nervously.

"What's going on at Redwood?" Mom insists.

"There are some truly abhorrent theories going around, Mar. The kind of torrid things I could never repeat." Our eyes meet over his glass of wine. Jarod Cross smiles and, somehow, it's scarier than Zane's chilling smirk. "Things that could get other, less connected people in a lot of trouble."

I feel Zane going into fight mode beside me and quickly press a hand into his upper thigh.

Dutch laughs darkly. "You pay a lot of attention to gossip, dad. Are you sure you're not Jinx?"

Finn's jaw muscles clench, but he remains quiet.

Zane leans back cockily, but all his muscles are tense. "Dad, you should know better than to listen to rumors. Remember what people were saying about you when you were dating that Peruvian model. What was her name again? Petra? Dishi? I can't remember. You change them so often. But I do remember she could barely talk English. Except for that one word. Sugar... daddy? Was it? Oh, wait, that's two words..."

Jarod slams the butt of his knife into the table.

The china rattles and clinks.

Mom and I are the only ones who shrink back.

Calmly, as if he didn't almost impale the table, Jarod smiles. "You're mistaken." He picks up mom's hand and gives it a squeeze. "I don't need to go looking for anyone else now that I've found her."

Mom looks like her heart is melting to the floor.

Dutch draws his chair back, face darker than a storm. "I think I've been here long enough. Let's not do this again."

"Dutch, wait..." Mom reaches out as if she's thinking of physically restraining him.

Finn draws his chair back too.

When Zane gets up to leave the table, I'm stunned to realize that he's holding my hand and dragging me up too. I quickly shake him off before mom can see.

The brothers drag me across the room.

"This is my last warning," Jarod says to the boys' retreating backs.

They all stop and turn.

"Don't make any more trouble for me." My step-father's voice bristles with a threat. "It would hurt me to have to punish you, but I will." He picks up his knife again and cuts into his steak. "Gladly."

Dutch's nostrils flare.

Finn's expression is carefully neutral.

"And Zane…" Jarod Cross quietly wipes the sides of his mouth. "Think hard and carefully before you act. The more impulsive you are, the more you drag everyone around you down. Especially the people you want to protect."

Zane's fingers curl into fists.

Jarod glances at me. "Miss Jamieson, let me know if you have any more trouble at Redwood. I've heard things are getting dangerous over there, and I would hate for something to happen to you."

Zane flies forward before I can blink. He grabs Jarod Cross by the collar and drags him out of his seat.

Mom shoots to her feet so fast, her chair topples to the ground.

I fly after him, wrenching Zane by the shoulder. "Stop it."

Zane glares into his father's face. "Touch her and I will burn *everything* down, even if I have to light myself on fire first."

Jarod Cross's smile is this wicked sharp thing that sets me on edge.

"Still so reckless, Zane." He tilts his head, unfazed. "How can you ever have what you want?"

"Enough." Dutch drags Zane off.

Jarod Cross smooths his collar back down.

"Jarod, what did you mean by that?" mom cries. "What do you mean something might happen to my daughter?"

"He meant what he said, mom. That was a threat." My eyes narrow in his direction.

Jarod Cross laughs. "A threat? Why would I threaten my own step-daughter?"

When he reaches for me, Finn, Dutch and Zane move quickly between us, blocking me from view.

Jarod Cross smirks. "What is this? A swat team?"

The boys don't say a word.

Jarod Cross cranes his neck past Zane to look me in my eyes. "Are you scared of me, Miss Jamieson?"

"You'd like me to be, wouldn't you?"

He laughs again. "I see the boys have gotten to you. Gracie, you can't believe the words of rebellious and headstrong teenagers. It's easier for them to chase conspiracies than to admit they lack discipline and self-restraint. Of course, that's my fault. I didn't train them well. Not like Marian raised you."

Mom's eyes dart between me and Jarod, still looking shocked and confused.

"We're leaving," Zane growls.

"Mom, let's go," I say.

Her body remains rooted to the ground.

I wait for her.

"Mom," I insist.

Her face tightens and then smooths out. I *see* the moment she chooses him.

"Why don't we all just sit down and talk this through. Jarod can explain exactly what he meant and I—"

"Mom, just *stop* it," I snap.

Her mouth clamps shut and she looks at me like I'm a different person.

Maybe I am.

Maybe Sloane's death was the first step of my transformation.

Maybe my fingers are stained in blood.

Maybe I'm slowly turning into a monster too.

Maybe that's what I have to become to beat a monster that's much bigger than me.

Chapter Thirty-Two

ZANE

Dutch glares into the elevator, his energy that of barely restrained, wild rage.

Finn is emotionless as usual.

And I...

Usually, I'd be pounding my fist into the wall, roaring obscenities, and exploding in every way I possibly can.

But tonight is different.

Because tonight, it's not just me and my brothers in the elevator, spinning out after dad managed to push all our buttons the way he so expertly does.

Tonight...

Grey is here too.

And I'm holding her hand.

Holding it for dear freaking life.

It's the only thing keeping me contained. The only thing keeping me from exploding in a burst of self-destruction.

The anger sizzles under my skin, hot enough to melt the floor with each step.

We almost died tonight, but I'm more pissed that dad threatened Grey openly than I am about our pursuer in the mountains.

The elevator doors open.

We stomp into the lobby.

The girls in the restaurant all stare at us, heads swinging as we pass by. I'm sure we're dragging a black cloud of doom around.

Grey tries to wiggle her hand out of my grip. When I glance back, I see her jutting her chin pointedly at the onlookers. Some of them will probably recognize us—if not as Jarod Cross's kids then as The Kings.

I don't care.

I don't let go of Grey's hand and I don't stop walking.

She's six years older than me.

She's my step-sister.

She's my teacher.

Screw it.

Screw it all.

We get outside and I meet Dutch's eyes.

He frowns, his cell phone raised to his ear. I see his chest cave in relief when he hears Cadey's voice on the other end of the line.

"You okay?" he growls. As he speaks, he gives me and Finn another nod.

I nod back.

Dutch stalks to his car and climbs in.

Finn sticks a hand in his pocket and walks off without a word. His car is totaled and he drove with Dutch, but I don't think my brother wants to go home right now.

I pull Grey along, stopping in front of my bike.

THE FORBIDDEN NOTE

There was no way in hell I was taking dad's car when he drove here. Now, I'm glad I rode separately.

I toss Grey a helmet. She stares at it as if she's never seen such a thing before.

"Goes on your head," I grunt.

"I know how it works," she snaps. "But I'm not... I don't ride motorcycles."

"You do tonight."

Her lips tighten.

I walk over and set the helmet gently on her. Her curls are too voluminous, but I manage to fit it all inside the helmet. Clasping the strap under her chin, I pull her forward. She doesn't protest again.

I climb on top of my bike, my movements rough and impatient.

There's too much noise in my head. A pounding drum solo that's all snare and cymbals.

No cohesion.

No freaking pattern.

Just chaos.

But it quiets a bit when she wraps her arms around me. Her left leg bounces up and down. Incessant. Nervous. She squeezes me tight and squeals before I even turn my bike on.

"Relax, tiger. I won't let anything happen to you."

"That's easy for you to say."

I'm bleeding out from the inside, but she manages to make my lips twist in a wry grin.

I press my hand over her leg to calm it and look back at her. Her soft brown eyes collide with mine and I get this unquestionable feeling of helplessness. It's the weirdest thing, but I suddenly understand why Romeo drank that poison.

This woman... she's my poison and I'm drowning in the most lethal dose.

Ripping my gaze away, I start the bike and take off.

Grey pastes her body to mine. It's impossible to ignore how soft she feels, how fragile. The wind batters my face, but I can still sense the gentle hammer of her breath on the back of my neck and the heat of her hands through my leather jacket.

The streets blur together and the terrain gets much rockier. I take the backroads, pointing my bike away from the flatlands where I usually bring girls and heading toward the ridge.

I stop the bike on top of the cleft jutting out from the mountains. From here, the stars are like shimmering plates on a black velvet table. Close enough I can reach out and touch them.

The night is cold and I notice Grey shivering a bit, so I shrug out of my jacket and wrap it over her shoulders.

"Is this safe?" She glances behind her. "What if whoever attacked us comes back?"

"I can move much faster on my bike than I can in the car."

She seems to turn that over in her mind and then nods.

I sit on the edge of the cliff. Far below are rocky outcroppings. One wrong step and I'll break every bone in my body on the rocks below.

"Aren't you scared?"

"Scared?" I ask.

"Our car almost ran off a mountain just like this."

"Exactly why I'm here." A deep, dark sense of satisfaction fills my chest. "To remind myself I'm not afraid of anything."

Grey's look changes a bit, almost like she's scared of me.

Can't say I blame her.

I'm not sure if I came out of the womb this thirsty for adrenaline or if being in dad's world twisted me, warped me into this version of myself.

"Does it calm you?"

I don't bother looking back. "What?"

"Chasing death."

I snort. "When did I do that?"

"The motorcycle." Her shoes scrape loose rocks as she draws closer. "Sitting on the edge of a scary cliff with no harness or anything."

"I've never gotten hurt."

"That's because you want to." She sighs. "The people who don't want to get hurt are the ones who bruise the most. The ones chasing the hurt... death runs from them."

"Sometimes, it catches up."

"But not tonight." I hear her voice closer now.

Turning, I see her hand extended to me.

I move my gaze from her hand to her face. "You've been touching me a lot tonight."

"You've been worrying me a lot tonight."

I smirk. "It's getting hard to believe you hate me."

Her tongue darts out to wet her lips. "Don't overthink it. Just get away from the edge."

I stare at her, deadly serious. "If I take that hand, I'm not letting it go."

"Zane..."

"I won't let go, Grey. So pull your hand back if you can't handle that."

Her chest heaves and she returns her hand to her side.

I feel a flash of disappointment, but it's not like I didn't expect it.

Behind me, more loose stones start shuffling. To my

surprise, I feel Grey ease herself down beside me. She does it a lot more carefully and clumsily than I would have, but she eventually settles on the ground.

Her eyes peer over the edge and her face blanches. "That's... not terrifying."

I laugh, feeling light as hell. "Don't look if it scares you."

"This isn't like the coffin. Looking or not looking won't stop me from feeling scared."

Rather than answer, I stare at her. The wind picks up her curls and tosses them all over, making them look like sentient fingers beckoning me closer. The smell of her perfume reminds me that she's the worst kind of addiction.

I was wrong.

Earlier.

When I said I wasn't scared.

I think I've found something that terrifies me.

It's her.

The way she makes me feel.

The way she takes over me.

It's like she's drilled into my head, like she's clogging every pore, climbing up my throat, smothering me.

"Don't look. Don't look," she murmurs to herself, closing her eyes. Brown fingers dig into the dirt on either side of her legs. She's trying to anchor herself into the ground.

I sit there, watching her, and I realize that whatever my cure is... it's probably inside her too.

My poison.

My antidote.

Either way, it's out of my hands.

"Zane," she murmurs, "how about we—"

I grab the back of her neck and drive her toward me,

crushing the rest of her words beneath my lips. Her taste is the first thing that pierces my brain.

Soft. Sweet.

Wine.

She was drinking wine during dinner and earlier in the treehouse.

I intend it to be a quick kiss. She didn't take my hand.

She can't even take my hand in the freaking dark with no one around.

But the moment she moves her palm from the ground to fist it around my shirt, there's no stopping the riptide.

Pieces of sand and stone fall from her fingers and skitter down the front of my shirt. I hear it like music. Like a fantasy-inspired drum chime.

I wrap an arm around her waist and gather her to me, feeling like I already jumped off this stupid cliff. Feeling like I'm falling.

She moans and I know she's taking that plunge with me.

I part her lips with my tongue, sweeping into her mouth and staking my claim. Her tongue wars with mine and she twists her head to the side, deepening the kiss and leaving me wanting so much more.

My hands skate under her shirt, burning every inch of skin I can find. I skim over her bra. Heat sears me when I feel lace. She arches into me, almost begging for my touch.

Time suspends until it feels like we're both locked in eternity. But when I start pushing her backward, my hand brushes against a stone and sends it skittering over the edge of the cliff.

I can't hear the shatter.

That's what draws me out of my lust-filled haze.

The stone is so tiny, so inconsequential that it doesn't even make a sound when it hits the rocks.

I pull back sharply, my eyes descending to the rocks below.

It's all dark. All black. All death.

My body buzzes with electricity.

My hands, my mouth, they're full of her.

But I can't help feeling like our kiss tonight sealed our fate. We aren't just falling. We're both a little too close to smashing into pieces at the bottom.

And the worst part?

I don't think anyone will hear us when we shatter.

Chapter Thirty-Three

GREY

My head pounds with the kiss of regret as I wake the next morning.

The sights and smells around me are unfamiliar.

High ceilings. Filmy curtains. Giant balcony. Enormous bed.

This isn't home.

I'm in one of The King's lavish guest rooms.

After Jarod issued his not-so-subtle threat, there was no way I could stay in his house. I accepted the invitation to crash at the boys' place, but it's just a temporary solution. The next step is to get my own apartment and drag mom as far away from this mess as possible.

My body sinks into the bed as I think about my complicated life. Looks like I have to add my step-dad to the growing list of people who want to hurt me.

I close my eyes to hide from the sunlight. In the darkness, last night's kiss explodes in my mind. I see it all. The way Zane's mouth pressed into mine, burning, searing, taking over. The way his hand slipped up my shirt. The way I moaned. The way I never wanted it to stop.

"Last night meant nothing," I mumble to myself, but the words are hollow. It doesn't feel like 'nothing' at all.

Trying to run from my thoughts, I force myself to get up and start preparing for the day.

The masquerade ball is tonight.

There are a ton of details to take care of.

Still, I don't just bound outside. I stop to take off my hair bonnet, run some product through my curls and slap on some lipgloss.

I'm just trying to be presentable, I tell myself.

Carefully, I wrap my fingers around the doorknob.

The hallway is clear.

Breathing a sigh of relief, I tiptoe outside and hasten toward the stairs.

At that moment, the bathroom door bursts open.

Smoke curls from the room and crawls behind Zane who's stepping out wearing nothing but a towel.

I am not prepared.

Not in the slightest.

He's all lean muscle, six-foot-plus of a walking work of art. Tattoos climb over arms and shoulders sculpted to perfection. His whole body is chiseled to the gods.

Large hands run through his hair, throwing tiny sprays of water and making his biceps flex. Cruel blue eyes light on me.

It takes a few seconds for my brain to reboot.

"Hey," he says stoically.

"H-hey." My heart is pounding hard, but I try to keep my tone stern. "Get dressed. We need to talk."

"About what?" He flicks his hair back.

"I'll tell you when you're decent," I say harshly, using my 'teacher' voice.

At the tone, every muscle in his face goes tense all at once.

Rebellion coils in his eyes. "I'd rather be indecent." He stares pointedly at my shorts which are tiny and barely visible beneath my giant college T-shirt. "Come to my room."

"Your room?"

"You can say whatever you want in private."

For a second, my brain misfires, wondering what it would be like to talk with my body instead of my lips. To feel him over me. To wrap my fingers around him and make him moan. To...

"No."

"No?" He arches a brow.

"I..."

"Grey." He moves toward me.

I step back. "Here. Let's talk here."

"Talk about what?"

"Last night."

His lips curl up cruelly. The hewn angles of his jaw hit the light, all rough strength and hard edges. "It looks like you want to do more than talk, tiger."

My nostrils flare.

My heart is about to burst.

Zane has a right to be cocky. With a body like that, I'm sure he's had more than his share of ogling girls.

Folding my arms over my chest, I say, "I'm being serious."

"Mm."

"Yesterday... it was an emotional night. We almost died."

He steps closer to me.

My gaze slides down his broad chest, cut abs and the low-slung towel that teases at a sculpted pelvic bone.

Don't watch.

It's a fruitless ask.

I know what's beneath that towel.

I want what's beneath that towel.

"We also had that run-in with your dad." I swallow hard. Heat throbs under my skin.

Zane looks at me, eyelashes bouncing sleepily, like a lion stretching after a long nap and going hunting for the easiest prey.

I keep walking back, heart skittering, antsy, breathless. "I apologize. It was wrong of me to... to kiss you. As your teacher, I shouldn't have—"

"You shouldn't, but you wanted to."

"No." But it doesn't sound convincing. Not even to my own ears.

Zane takes my wrist and brings my hand to his chest. The contact of skin against skin makes us both inhale sharply.

I'm on edge. Stretched taut.

The fact that any of his brothers, Cadence or Viola can walk out and see us makes this moment feel even more fraught with tension.

"Touch me," he growls.

"Zane." I try to pull away, but he holds my hand captive, slowly dragging it down until it's just above the line of his towel.

Warmth skims the edge of my fingertips.

I glance up and see his eyes lingering on my lips. I swipe my tongue across them unconsciously and his grip on me tightens, almost like he's thinking about that kiss last night and wondering what it would be like if we took it further.

"I'm tired of fighting this," he whispers. "I want to claim that tight little body of yours. Hard and fast. And then slow. So slow you're begging me for more. I want you screaming my name. I want you groaning with need like you did that night in the hotel room when I devoured you against the balcony."

I gasp out, my legs turning to jello and my entire body in flames.

His words are too crass. Too rude.

Too raw.

I need to think of something else to douse that heat.

Bunnies. Sick children. Horrific train accidents.

But it's too late.

This chemistry is powerful.

I can see it. Feel it.

Every sensation of that night. The way he had me gripping the bedsheets. The way our bodies joined over and over and over again.

The wild, rough, forceful brutality to his kisses. To his invasion. Shadows stripped away in the darkness. The thick pulsing need sated by grabbing hands and whipping hips. The freedom of no names, no ages, no responsibilities.

I tasted reckless abandon for the first time in my life and I was hooked.

Then everything turned to chaos.

Student.

Step-brother.

Off-limits.

Zane Cross is the very definition of ruin.

One touch and he could destroy me.

My life.

My investigation.

Everything I've worked so hard for.

His head lowers slowly, his heated blue gaze stealing my breath away.

I turn my face at the last minute.

Shivering, I moan, "Zane... we can't."

His fingers grip my chin and he hauls my face up to his. Those rough hands are strong and almost painful on my jaw.

I squirm, but his body pins me into the wall, harder than granite, lashing up a fiery heat that's nearly violent.

"We can," he says.

"We shouldn't."

"But we will." He leans forward, his lips poised at my ear. The scent of his body wash coils around me, lingering and mixing with the musk of my sweat and desire. "I'm going to have you, Grace Jamieson," Zane says, his warm breath tracing over my tingling lips. His eyes are a dark shadow of seduction. "And no one is going to stop me."

I feel my inhibitions breaking apart. All the desires and wants that have been gathering since our first night together collide in a storm. My body aches, throbbing in time to my errant heartbeat.

My head tilts up.

His sharp mouth curves into a smirk.

At that moment, a door slams open.

Finn steps out.

I push Zane off, horror mixing with the lust that made me powerless to resist him.

Zane's brother gives us a bored look and crosses the hallway to the bathroom without a word.

An exhale skitters out of my lips. Heart screaming and

body as hot as a human bonfire, I rush away from the beast who just made his intentions known.

No one is going to stop me.

Including me.

That's what he meant.

It's a threat.

A promise.

A vile and enticing challenge.

I'm in deep crap.

Because now I see that...

Zane Cross isn't *going to be* my ruin.

The cocky bastard already is.

* * *

Everyone gathers in the kitchen. Dutch is sitting at the head of the table, fingers clenched and eyes glaring a hole into the fancy glass surface.

Cadence is at his right, her eyes full of worry.

Sol is in the chair next to her, his fingers drumming the table. There are dark circles under his eyes. He looks like he hasn't been sleeping well.

Finn is sitting beside me. He hasn't said much. Not that he usually does. If he has any thoughts about what he saw in the hallway earlier—his brother practically naked and pinning me to the wall—he's keeping them to himself.

Zane is leaning against the counter, head cocked to one side, dark hair sliding across his forehead. He's now dressed in an undershirt that shows off arms corded with muscle and ink. Those loose grey sweatpants do nothing to hide his powerful hips and thighs...

Predatory blue eyes meet mine and he smiles that dark,

seductive smile of his that tells me I'm definitely about to be his prey and I might even like it.

I glance away, shaken.

"Tonight is the most important piece of our plan," Dutch says. "We can't afford for any step to go wrong."

"Where are we on the details?" Sol asks, eyes hooded beneath thick lashes.

Zane makes his drumstick dance over his finger. "I already contacted the caterers."

"And I have the camera blockers," Finn adds.

"I'm picking up the van later," Dutch says. "I might be late." His eyes slice through Zane's. "Don't start the party without me."

"Relax, Dutch."

"I am relaxed."

"No, you're wound so tight you're about to pop. Since when were you so anxious?"

Cadence sighs. "It's me. I'm nervous and overthinking."

"This isn't like last summer," Dutch says harshly.

"It better not be," Finn grumbles.

"Cadey reminded me that security will be tighter because of the dance. We might have chosen the wrong night to break into the basement."

"The masquerade ball will cover our tracks. Nothing can go wrong," Zane says.

Dutch's face is still tight. "Don't get too cocky. If anyone spots us and tells Harris, we'll lose our advantage. He already went on a power trip after suspending us. He'll be bolder next time."

"Harris isn't the only one who'll come after us if we get caught," Finn says.

Dutch looks at him.

Sol frowns. "Who else do we have to worry about?"

"Dad."

Zane rolls his eyes. "We always have to watch out for dad."

"Sloane's case." Finn's handsome face tightens with secrets. "I think he knows something. Something he doesn't want us finding out. The way he spoke to Miss Jamieson at the dinner... he tipped his hand. He's worried."

"You think he was a part of The Grateful Project?" Cadey asks.

The boys go deathly silent. They've said nothing but negative things about their father, and yet seem reluctant to admit that he went that far. I guess a controlling man on a perpetual power trip is more palatable than one who was manipulating and exploiting underage girls for... who knows what?

Zane flips his stick around. "If dad was in on it, it's better for us. We can take him down with the evidence. Kill two birds with one stone."

"If dad is involved, it won't be that simple," Finn shoots back.

"Right now, we're focused on getting those boxes out of the basement. If dad was involved or not, we'll find out then," Dutch says.

Cadence clears her throat. "Since Viola is sleeping, I'll make breakfast and then wake her up to help us shop for dresses. Miss Jamieson—I mean, Grey..." Cadence blushes. "Can I call you Grey when we're not at school?"

"Oh... sure..."

"We're thinking of leaving around eleven. Is that okay with you?"

"Um... leaving to go where?"

"Do you have an outfit for tonight?" Cadey asks.

"I'm not going to the dance. I already told admin that I wasn't feeling well, so they're not expecting me."

"I think you should come," Cadence says. "It's too risky if you show up with the caterers. What if someone recognizes you and asks why you're working back there?"

I hesitate.

"At least look at the dresses? It'll be fun," she adds.

I clear my throat and carefully avoid Zane's gaze. "Are the boys coming on our shopping trip?"

"No."

I sigh in relief. An afternoon away from Zane's intense caresses sounds like heaven.

"Then I'm in."

Chapter Thirty-Four

GREY

I'm not expecting Cadence and her friends to shop at a high-end boutique. And I definitely don't expect the VIP treatment when I get there.

"You must be Grey," a woman with platinum blonde hair and a bright smile says to me. Her eyes slide down my frame. "Yes... mm... oh, he gave perfect measurements."

"Excuse me?"

"Zane called ahead. I was admiring his accuracy. I think we picked the perfect dresses for you to try."

"Zane?" My fingers curl into fists.

Cadence gives me a secret grin.

"You younger ladies can't drink wine, but we have some liquor free champagne if you'd like." The clerk gestures to a table. "Miss Jamieson, follow me please."

Breeze and Serena fall into the stuffed chairs near the front of the shop.

Viola goes straight for one of the dress racks.

Cadence heads to the shoe section.

For the first time, I notice no one else besides our group is in the store.

"Grey?" The clerk gestures. "This way..."

"Hold on just one minute," I say a little harshly.

The clerk's got a great poker face and barely blinks. Grin in place, she nods. "No problem."

I stalk over to Dutch's wife. "Did you girls already buy your dresses?"

Cadence looks startled. "Uh... what?"

"You have, haven't you?"

She doesn't bother lying to me. "We've known about the masquerade ball for weeks now. Why would we try to buy dresses the day of?"

The truth clicks in my head.

"This is Zane's idea," I mutter.

"He thought you wouldn't accept a gift from him." Cadey gives me a friendly smile. "I brought Breeze and Serena because the point of tonight is for you to blend in with us." She quickly tacks on, "Not that you don't look as young and pretty as an eighteen year old. But your style tonight can't scream 'teacher'. So I have four different opinions to help you out, since I'm not the fashionista here."

Annoyed, I stomp over to the side and haul my phone out.

Zane answers quickly. His voice curls around me like smoke. "Hey, tiger."

"You shut down a store?"

"I can't have anyone recognizing you tonight. That means even the dress you buy has to be a secret."

"Is that all it is?"

There's a pause. And then, he says calmly, "I want to be

the one to pay for your dress, since I'll be the one tearing it off you later."

I can't control my body or the heat that floods between my legs. "That's never happening."

"It will. Soon." His voice has a dark thread of promise. "Now, why don't you enjoy my little present? Georgia is a friend and my card is already in the system."

I glance back at the perky-looking blonde. She's older, maybe in her forties, but still very pretty. "What kind of friend?"

"Is that jealousy I hear, tiger?"

I dig my teeth into my bottom lip.

"Why does that get me excited?" Zane breathes hard. "I like you jealous."

"You're disgusting."

He laughs, the loud cocky laugh that I've sometimes heard bouncing around the hallway. Whenever I heard it, I'd stop walking and look to see who made him laugh that way.

It would always be a girl. And I'd always grip my books tightly in front of me, ignoring the black, inky fury that threaded through my soul.

"I told you already, tiger. I don't screw women I like."

I open my mouth.

As if he can see me, he says, "You were the only exception."

I almost roll my eyes.

Like I believe that line.

"We don't have a lot of time. You better pick out your dress."

"I'm going to spend all your money," I threaten.

He makes a satisfied little sound. "I think that's going to be my second favorite thing. You spending all my money."

"Second? What's the first?"

"The sound you make when I lick your—"

"I'm hanging up."

His laughter bounces in my ears as I hang up the phone and toss it in my purse like it's on fire. When I turn around, the girls are watching me.

I clear my throat. "I'm leaving."

"But the dress!"

"I'm not buying a dress today."

Cadence pouts. "Grey, wait."

I stalk to the door.

She slides in front of me. "Don't think of it as a gift from Zane. It's for the plan. And the plan is more important than anything else, right?"

My nostrils flare.

The clerk surveys us. "Are you ready?"

I grit my teeth and resist the urge to run out of the shop. Cadence is right. The plan is more important. And I have a feeling that if I don't accept this, Zane will find a bigger, more outrageous way to corner me.

"Fine." I turn. Since Zane is paying... "Show me your most expensive dresses first."

* * *

I lift my face to the mirror, feeling slightly frightened by the way this five-thousand dollar dress hangs off my shoulders and hugs my curves. The material is shimmery and light, even though the skirt is voluminous. It has a low front and a built-in, custom bustier that pushes my chest up and sets my cleavage front and center.

It definitely does *not* look like a teacher's dress.

"This isn't one that Zane picked," the clerk says, zipping me up. "Are you sure you don't want to try those on?"

"No."

She nods. "Actually, this works too. The light tone goes *so* well with your darker complexion."

I slide my hands down my waist as she continues her assessment.

"Your shape is gorgeous. I just knew a strapless would dazzle on you. The pleated skirt is a little avant garde, isn't it? What do you think?"

"I think..." I choke up. "That this dress was made for me."

She gives me a proud little smile and helps to gather up my hair.

When we walk outside, silence falls.

Cadence's jaw drops.

Serena blinks and blinks.

Breeze gulps.

Viola is the first to break the quiet. "You're stunning."

"Do *all* the teachers at Redwood look this sexy or just her?" Cadence's best friend Breeze asks.

Serena slow claps. "If I wasn't such a fan of black and leather, I'd want to borrow that dress."

Cadence rises slowly. "Everyone is going to be looking at you tonight."

"Then I don't think I should—"

"Zane is going to hate it."

I freeze, swept up in a fantasy of Zane grinding his teeth in anger as I dance without him.

"Is that a yes?" the clerk asks, a note of hope ringing in her voice.

I smile villainously, touching the delicate fabric. "We're taking this dress."

***

Jinx: Every Wicked Kingdom Needs A Royal Ball

In just a few short hours, all the Cinderellas will appear in masks, ready to steal the hearts of the royals. Snare King is the rumored favorite now that he's warmed his bed with Redwood's most beautiful governess.

As all the over-worked and underpaid fairy godmothers turn their entitled Cinderellas into princesses for the gala, I wonder who Snare King will steal away with tonight?

Until the next post, keep your enemies close and your secrets even closer.

- Jinx

Chapter Thirty-Five

ZANE

Finn and Sol stand beside me, looking disinterested in the dance floor. Tonight's December Ball is already playing its part. Most of the student body showed up thanks to Jinx hyping up the mystique element of the party. It also helps that students outside of Redwood could attend.

This hellhole is a vicious playground most of the year, but in December, Redwood is known for its epic school dances. Everything is expensive and over-the-top.

Tonight is no exception.

The walls are covered with marble-themed wallpaper. Fake pillars have been dragged in to give the illusion of some kind of palace. Ivy and green foliage drape the pillars and a giant mosaic ceiling dangles above us.

The event planner this year went crazy and added a live orchestra to give the feel of a real Victorian era ball. There are baskets of fresh flowers that I couldn't name even if someone held a gun to my head and servers wearing authentic vests and trousers that look like pirates.

It's not just a dance.

It's an experience.

And the place is absolutely swarming.

"Dutch and Cadence aren't here yet?" Sol asks.

I check my phone and shake my head.

He grips his cup of punch tightly. I can smell the vodka from here.

"You okay with what you have to do later?" I ask, checking his face carefully.

He nods and his lips curl up slightly. That expression promises total hell.

I frown. "It's just a contained fire, Sol. Don't go crazy."

"I already know what I'm going to do."

Unease stabs my gut and I wonder if I should have let him unleash that monster inside him again.

Finn watches the security guards warily, like a wolf might watch a mountain lion. "They're strapped."

I notice the bulges in the guards' pockets.

"Do they normally carry weapons at these things?"

Finn shakes his head 'no'.

"Dad must have tipped Harris off. It's like they expected us to do something tonight." I frown.

Sol curses in Spanish.

Finn wipes a palm against his platoon pants.

We're all wearing similar outfits. Nothing too crazy. Long-sleeved shirts with stupid ruffles at the neck. And long pants tucked into boots.

Finn looks like an actor from those K-dramas Viola likes to watch.

Sol looks like someone from his grandmother's favorite telenovela.

I look like freaking Gaston.

My neck itches.

Damn. I hate these things.

I would have shown up in my motorcycle jacket and jeans, but for the sake of the plan, I wore what Cadey told me to when she stopped by my room this afternoon.

"When is Grey getting here?" I mumble, tugging at the ruffles.

"Maybe she ditched," Sol says.

I wouldn't be surprised if she disappeared just to spite me. Not that it will stop what's coming.

I'm not holding back anymore.

That kiss on the ridge taught me one thing.

I don't mind shattering.

But I'll be *damned* if I shatter quietly.

I'm going to live how I want, have who I want and go out in a blaze of freaking *flames*.

A girl in a voluminous vintage skirt with a sheer top approaches me. I stare at her skin through the shirt and then move my gaze up to her face, trying to place her. It's difficult because of the giant mask she's wearing.

"Zane, right?" she whispers to me. Chewing on her bottom lip, she mumbles, "Or are you, Dutch?"

I say nothing.

She coughs and looks at me again. "Uh... or are you Sol?" I see her eyes darting back and forth behind her face mask. "You're all tall. And standing together like The Kings. But I can't tell which is which..."

Dammit.

Us hanging out makes it obvious who we are.

Finn gets the same revelation because he stalks away without a word.

Sol fades into the shadows, disappearing with his vodka punch and his secrets.

The girl pushes up against me and sniffs. Her mouth opens in a sigh and she whispers, "Definitely, Zane. I'd recognize the smell of leather and exhaust anywhere. You came here on your bike?"

I finally recognize her voice.

She's the girl I screwed in the wilderness a few nights ago.

"I was waiting for you to get here." Her fingers curl into my arm and she starts tugging. "This dance is boring. Want to find a free classroom and have some fun?"

I shake her off.

Her eyebrows hike so far, I can see it above the mask.

"Don't you want to?" she whines.

I do.

But not with her.

I want Miss Jamieson.

In her classroom.

On top of her desk.

I want her choking on my kisses.

I want her hoarse from groaning my name.

I want her legs sprawling open, to an audience of empty chairs and my greedy eyes.

There are so many dirty lessons I want to teach her.

Maybe I'll even give her homework.

Starting with what her punishment will be whenever she uses that teacher voice on me. It's a stern, know-it-all tone and I want to ram her into the nearest wall and drag her skirt down to her ankles each time I hear it.

Would she let me have her tonight?

I bet she would.

Or at least she'll want to.

There is nothing sexier than touching her and watching her fight to maintain a teacher-student distance. Knowing she can't. Knowing she wants me as much as I want her.

I'm lost in thoughts of Grey and I don't even realize I've still got company.

Not until the chick runs her hand down my chest.

"Zane, we've been hooking up for a while now. Don't you think we should—"

A disturbance breaks out near the gym entrance.

Gasps ripple through the room.

People stop dancing and stare.

I swing my gaze around, feeling the energy shift. The double doors are open and someone in a long dress glides in. I blink through the haze of soft white beams and fake ornamental wall lanterns, trying to see who it is.

The woman in the mask steps under a light and the entire room takes a breath.

At the sight of her, a shock of desire punches me in the face. That kind of violent, full-body lust only happens for one person.

Even in a mask and with her hair straight, I recognize her.

It's Grey.

I take a step forward.

"Zane," the girl standing beside me tries to grip my arm.

I press a palm to her shoulder and push her back, stalking past her and aiming for Grey.

I'm too far away.

By the time I arrive, Grey is already surrounded.

"Can I have this dance?" One bozo bows to her, reaching for her hand.

I slam him in the chest. "No you cannot."

"Yes." Grey tilts her head up. Her mask is white and

designed with delicate silver jewels. It covers most of her face leaving only her full, delectable lips and part of her nose free.

Grey smirks at me, walks around my frozen body and takes off with that punk.

My teeth grind together.

I turn and glare at them. I don't recognize the dress she bought, but holy hell it looks incredible. Sexy and elegant all at once. It cuts low at the front and shows enough of her chest to make a guy salivate.

The punk she's dancing with? He's about to slip on his own drool.

Sol appears beside me, his cup newly-filled and the vodka scent stronger. "Who knew *that* was what she looked like outside of pencil skirts?"

"Keep your eyes to yourself," I growl.

Sol laughs and takes another sip.

Anger burning inside me, I prowl over to the guy dancing with Grey. She sees me coming, but she doesn't let go of the joker's hand.

"I'm cutting in."

"No, you're not," Grey says.

"The lady said no, man."

"Beat it," I snarl with enough heat to summon a hurricane. "Now."

The guy gives me an assessing look, sees my fisted hands and backs off.

Grey glares at me through her mask. I can feel her annoyance like a fire on my skin.

"You're drawing more attention to us," she snaps.

"Then let's give them something to watch." I curl my hand over the small of her back and drag her to me so fast she lets out a little cry of surprise. With my other hand, I interlace our fingers and move her back and forth.

"This isn't how you dance the waltz."

My lips skate over her ear. "The waltz is boring. I'd rather have you grind on me."

Her lips purse beneath the mask. "This is exactly why we chose this theme. It forces kids to have some decorum."

"Only in public." I lean closer and her sweet smell poisons my air, making me almost dizzy with need. "But I promise you, most of the guys are crawling under their girlfriend's skirts later."

"Tell me who they are and I'll stop them."

"You'll be too busy later." I meet her eyes and give her a pointed stare.

Her lips part slightly. "Zane, I already told you—"

"Ah-ah." I pull her into me. "You're not a teacher tonight, remember?"

"What am I if I'm not a teacher?" She fires back.

My words whisper across the back of her neck and I see goosebumps rising there. "Until Dutch gives the signal, you're mine."

Chapter Thirty-Six

GREY

I know the students have spiked the punch. I can smell it from a mile away. And, honestly, it feels like I drank my own share of liquor tonight.

Zane Cross is a special kind of drug as he guides my body to the swelling rhythm of the live orchestra. The way his hips pulse into mine with the beat is downright vulgar.

And yet there's something so enticing about it.

Like a tease of what's to come.

A display of unapologetic sensuality.

I can't help feeling like this is the perfect representation of us.

Bodies covered from head to toe in long-sleeves and a voluminous skirt to my ankles. Music that heralds from days when the rules were strict and proper decorum was a must, not a suggestion.

And yet here we are.

THE FORBIDDEN NOTE

In the middle of that cold, unforgiving world.

Bodies pressed together, throbbing with the beat of the music and moving in a way that's neither proper nor decorous.

Zane's hands are on my waist, burning me through the fabric. Each step is deliberate as he takes the lead.

He spins me and, when he wraps his arms around me again, I'm closer to him than I was before.

Zane leans in and puts his mouth near my ear, the soft, tempting curve of his lower lip grazing my lobe.

"It was a mistake to wear this dress, tiger."

"Because it was so expensive?" I smile sharply.

I really hope that hurt his wallet.

His lips curve down my shoulder and move up the side of my neck, drawing out a full-body shiver.

"Because now I want to keep spending all my money on you."

"What money? You act like you have so much, but aren't you just spending daddy's cash?"

His expression becomes a cold, cruel thing. I squeal when I feel him dip me and latch around his neck to stay balanced.

Zane grins behind his dark red mask. It's the color of blood and passion. "Push me again and we're going to postpone the plan as long as it takes to get you naked inside your classroom, do you understand?"

My body hums at the threat. I dig my nails into the fabric of his collar, my breath coming in hard, harsh pants.

Zane sets me upright. His smile this time is touched in victory.

I want to punch it off his face, but I'm too busy shaking.

He's knocking me off balance again, incinerating my

good sense and making wrong feel right. I know it's not. I can feel when the light crawls away and becomes darkness. So why is it so much easier to accept the shadows and wrap myself in a black as thick as night? Why is it starting to feel warm here? Sweet there? Reasonable even, to live a life that most would shun and shame me for?

"I have my own money, tiger. You think we went on tour with Bex Dane and got a thank you note?"

My eyebrows arch.

He chuckles, but the sound is chilling. He runs his fingers down the base of the dress's spine, following the threading of my corset. "Let's not talk about something as boring as money."

"How about we don't talk at all?" I snap.

"Fine with me." He dips his head and flicks his tongue against the base of my throat, right at my thundering pulse. "There are more exciting things you could be doing with your mouth."

"Like praying to save your soul?"

"I'm afraid there's no saving me." He slides his hands up my waist, singeing everywhere he touches. "But you're welcome to try."

I'd fail.

I know that.

In the movies, good always wins.

But in real life...

It's the opposite.

Zane's darkness is the kind that envelops. Traps. Pulls you in before you even realize you've been devoured.

That's why I can't run away from him.

That's why every attempt has failed.

Because that darkness has already become a part of me.

The music changes. The orchestra is playing along with a hip-hop track now, giving the song a modern, sexy take. It reminds me of when Cadence performed at the summer showcase. I attended the show before I got the job here at Redwood. The moment I heard the piano player, I knew it was Mulliez's prodigy.

Just like Cadence was in disguise that day, I'm wearing a mask too. So why aren't I taking advantage of it? When will I ever get to stand in the light with Zane Cross, amongst all the students of Redwood, and be free like this again?

The mental shift makes me bold.

Without warning, I press up and dance against Zane, moving my fingers over the back of his neck and skirting through his hair.

Surprise flashes in his blue eyes, but it only lasts a moment before he growls and moves his body in a way that snaps the breath out of my lungs.

I feel him against me and I gravitate to that heat.

Lips tilting up, I stare into his eyes. Gold and blue. The ocean at night, swirling in shadows. Eyes darkening with lust by the second. Power trips through my veins as I work my hips, showing him exactly what experience and confidence looks like.

Our bodies wrap together, two flames burning as one.

Decorum is out the window.

I'm a wild thing.

And there's no mistaking how much I'm affecting him.

"Are you making love to me?" he growls in my ear.

Laughter spills from my lips.

"This is not making love," I whisper.

He curls his head down and bites my shoulder. Hard.

I cry out in pleasure, hardly believing he has me losing my mind in the middle of a Redwood dance. We're absorbed into the crowd, half-hidden from the eyes on the outer edge of the dance floor, but people are starting to notice.

The way we're dancing, it's not a surprise.

"We need to cool down," I say noticing that teachers are looking our way.

"No."

"No?"

"You don't rile me up like that and tell me to cool down, tiger."

My smile is wicked.

Zane acts so strong, so in control.

But he's not.

Not right now.

Not with me.

Sweat beads on his forehead and a wild sheen turns his eyes to black flames. Before I can speak, he takes my hand and pulls me from the dance floor.

Our steps are loud in the empty hallway.

I have to lift my skirt to run with him.

My heart is pounding and it feels like I'm shedding a ton of weight as I go.

Redwood after dark is a completely different beast.

The lights are low. The hallway freakishly silent.

But I'm not afraid.

Zane's hands are warm and calloused and anticipation buzzes when he pulls me into a classroom.

Not mine.

It's almost like he can't wait long enough to go all the way to my Lit class. Like he can't survive if he's not touching me.

The door slams shut. I hear the click of the lock and, in a blink, Zane is on me. His hands are everywhere and his hot, desperate lips clamp against the side of my neck and down to my chest.

I moan when his lips brush my skin, consuming me with a pleasure that balloons and swells inside me.

Zane drops to his knees, bunches my voluminous skirt and shoves it at me. "Keep that out of my way."

I do.

He rewards me by obliterating every thought from my mind.

I groan, panting hard as he teases me.

The bright, hot thrum of agony tightens.

I dig my fingers into his hair, breathing in desperate, quick spurts.

The depravity of the moment consumes me.

The utter forbidden nature of being here with him... in a classroom like this...

It builds a steady pressure that has me quivering and then breaking into pieces, lights exploding behind my eyes. I don't realize I'm being loud until Zane shoots up and smothers my screams with his kisses, keeping his hands occupied even as he sucks on my lips and pins me against the door.

When he pulls back, my hair is a mess and my body is throbbing.

It's not enough.

I crave him.

All of him.

I don't care about anyone passing by.

I don't care about Harris or Jarod Cross.

Or even the mission.

But Zane's phone rings before we can go any further.

He looks annoyed when he checks the screen.

And then he goes pale.

I lean forward and he turns the phone toward me.

A cold wash of ice runs over my back when I read Dutch's message.

Hall is here. I think there's going to be trouble.

Chapter Thirty-Seven

GREY

Hall's appearance at the dance isn't going to change the plan, but it does make me more anxious. With the increase in security guards as well as their unexpected firepower, we don't need any more unknown variables thrown into the mix.

Still, my mind can't fully process Dutch's warning or what that means for tonight.

I'm still shaking from the after-effects of Zane's wicked caresses. He's standing beside me, his hot breath on my neck and his wicked hand pressing into the door, caging me in on the right side. The warmth of his other hand on my hip is almost liquid-fire.

"I should have kept closer tabs on him," Zane growls.

I shake my head, unable to look into his eyes. He's this all-consuming darkness that scrambles my brain and makes me reckless.

And stupid.

Because following Zane Cross into a classroom and dropping my panties like an eager virgin is the very definition of stupid.

And dropping said panties while all of Redwood Prep is just a floor below is even more foolish.

I know better.

As a teacher.

As an adult.

As the one with the most to lose.

At the very least, I should have told him to wait until later, when we could leave the lion's den.

No.

I shouldn't have let this happen at all.

"Come back to me, tiger." Zane's fingers settle on my cheek and he turns me to face him.

I close my eyes, trying not to think too hard about what we've just done. "We need to focus. Dutch is here. That means they're ready."

I feel Zane's hot gaze drilling into me.

Uneasily, I crack my eyelids apart and find him staring. For a brief flash, I let myself pretend that I'm safe. That it will all be okay. That I can walk out of here, holding Zane's hand and not feel like the world will fall apart.

But the vision only lasts a second.

Even though I love books, I've never been the type who could live in a fantasy.

The closer Zane gets to me and my heart, the more panic I feel.

This won't end well.

There is no universe, no *galaxy*, where this spells out a happy ending.

Zane watches me, watches it all and his face turns hard. He steps back, expression unreadable. I wish I could peer into his mind right now. I wish he didn't feel so untouchable, so unreachable, like a galaxy so far removed from mine it hasn't even been discovered yet.

But I can't be this distracted.

I came here for Sloane.

She's all that matters.

Tonight, I'll be one step closer to the answers I need.

I let the numbness overtake me and step out of my panties clinically.

Zane frowns. "Aren't you going to need those?"

"I brought extra," I grumble, feeling more exposed now than I did when he shoved the front of my skirt at me.

Maybe I knew this would happen. Maybe I was hoping this would happen.

Maybe I deserve to be destroyed.

His lips curl up and there's a flash of understanding, as if he sees my thoughts.

I reach down to pick up the lace, but Zane snaps it from me.

My mouth opens. "What are you doing?"

"Keeping this."

I frown.

My phone rings.

This time, it's Cadence.

"We need to get out of here," I mumble, feeling out-of-sorts. Reaching out a hand, I order, "Give them back."

Zane grips my chin. His fingers are sticky and carry the scent of my musk. "Come and collect them after class."

That is *not* going to happen.

But there's no time to argue.

Neither of us say a word as we slip out of the dark classroom.

I separate from Zane and head toward the bathroom on

the third floor. Cadence is already there. She's wearing elaborate makeup and a bright red wig, fully in Redhead mode.

She gives me a tight nod.

I return it and slip into a stall. Using toilet paper to clean up the mess between my thighs, I slip on a clean pair of underwear and change into the waiting staff outfit.

When I get outside, Cadence hands me a mask.

I slip it over my head.

In the mirror, I see a woman with frizzy, straight hair that took hours to flat-iron, brown skin, and scared eyes hidden behind a creepy theatre mask.

"Finn already blocked the security cameras," Cadence says, her voice low and urgent. "Dutch told me about Hall. With him roaming around..."

"He must be looking for trouble. We need to be faster."

She nods. "At the most, we have twenty minutes."

I cringe.

Her hand settles on my arm. A soft, reassuring touch. "I love plans. And this is a good plan. But you know what's even better than a good plan?"

"What?'

"The Kings."

My chest tightens.

"The boys are in this now. They're crazy and cruel and sometimes frightening, but they're relentless. And they're on your side. No matter what, we're getting what we came for."

I nod, taking comfort in her words.

We scramble out of the bathroom and I stop abruptly because The Kings are there, still and at attention. The shadows creep around them as if even the darkness knows they're too dangerous to touch.

Something is different when I watch them tonight. Usually, the boys move with a kind of languid cockiness, like the world waits for them and time has to bend to their will.

Tonight, there's an urgent energy burning off their skin. Each of them.

Tall. Ruthless. Mysterious.

When I see them standing there, waiting for my signal, adrenaline surges through me.

This is a different kind of power. No wonder Cadence seems so settled, so fearless after coming back from her wedding.

I jut my chin down. "Let's do this."

Finn and Sol break off.

Dutch and Cadey stalk ahead.

"You okay?" Zane narrows his eyes and reaches over, adjusting my mask.

"Yes."

"I'll deal with Hall after this."

I notice the bulge in Zane's pocket and try to pretend that it doesn't excite me. "Don't."

"He hurt you." Zane's jaw clenches beneath his mask. A simmering anger bubbles in his words. "Which means he hurt us. Hall's not stupid. He's got a target on his back. So if he's here tonight, it can't be for anything good."

"Just let him be."

Zane's lips twist into a cruel grin. I've never seen a blood-thirsty expression like that before—raw, vivid, like a coil that spent years being coiled back and is finally springing free.

"Don't engage, Zane," I say again.

He smirks at me.

I know for a *fact* he's not going to listen.

The sound of wheels rolling on the ground interrupts us. I glance behind me and see Cadence, Dutch, Finn and Sol carrying trolleys—the kind hotel waiting staff use to bring up room service. White cloth drapes over the moving table. Stainless steel domes disguise their purpose.

"Great work," I say, motioning to the trolley.

Cadence grins. "Right? They look so authentic."

Dutch smirks a little beneath his mask. He clearly loves that his wife is having fun. Then his smile dims when he checks his watch. "We need to move."

I follow the lead singer down the hallway. Moonlight guides our path, falling through the windows and providing a silver road for us to walk on.

The basement is down this corridor and to the left.

An empty hallway stretches out before us. Tonight's mission is going to be easier than I thought.

I'm feeling good when, suddenly, footsteps pound from up ahead.

A security guard turns the bend and walks in our direction. He hasn't seen us yet, but it's only a matter of time before he notices our suspicious caravan.

We all freeze.

My nails dig into the center of my palm.

Sweat beads on my forehead.

There's nowhere to run or hide.

If this security guard spots us here tonight, our entire plan implodes.

Chapter Thirty-Eight

ZANE

Security is not supposed to be down here, which makes this guy's appearance extremely suspicious. My fingers tighten around the trolley as the tension between my brothers, Sol and me ramps up.

I glance at my best friend, noting the eerie half smile creeping behind his mask. He meets my eyes, an eager tilt to his chin.

Let me handle him.

Knowing Sol, he'll probably set the guy on fire and then shove his body in a closet.

I shake my head slightly.

Glancing over, I meet Dutch's gaze.

His chin juts down at Cadence.

I hear his message loud and clear. He's not going to take the front on this. Above all, his priority is keeping his wife safe, not pulling us out of trouble.

I get it.

Doesn't bother me.

But I'm still on edge.

We made every preparation so the hallways were clear at this specific time. Finn blocked the security cameras. Sol told the watchmen to look the other way and gave them a little something for the trouble.

This bozo in the black 'SECURITY' T-shirt isn't a part of the plan.

The guard gets closer.

I motion to Finn. My brother's blank expression sends a chill down my spine.

I saw what Finn could do the day we got into a fight with those jocks. I want to handle this my way, but if I can't, it's going to get messy. And I want Finn to contain that mess.

I jut a finger at the guard.

Finn nods.

It's decided.

I trust Finn to contain his rage a lot better than Sol.

Pushing my trolley a little faster than the rest, I walk up to the guard.

His eyes narrow when he sees me.

"Hey, man." I smirk. My teeth flashes behind the mask. "Beautiful night, huh?"

In the dark, the guard's massive shoulders tighten and his hand unconsciously drops to his gun.

He's a trigger happy one.

"Who are you? And what are you doing down here?" Bushy eyebrows wrench together. His voice is a deep, over-the-top bass.

"We're just moving some equipment," I say, gesturing to the trolley.

"Moving it where? The dance is in that direction." He points up.

"We're taking the back entrance." My voice has a clip of laughter.

"There's no back entrance that I know of."

I take a step toward him, and his fingers tighten on the butt of his gun.

Smile in place, I stop. "We're not doing anything wrong. I promise. But we're trying to be discreet here. I'll make it worth your while if you look the other way."

"Are you trying to *bribe* me right now?"

Guess that didn't work.

"Enough, kid. You and your friends need to come with me."

I remain in place.

The guard's expression shifts into a dark glower.

I feel my brothers tensing up behind me.

"This is a restricted area," he warns, planting a hand on my shoulder. He starts to steer me around. "We'll take this to the principal. Find out if you really do have permission to be down here."

My mind trips to Plan B.

Screw talking our way out of this.

It's time to take care of the problem.

I meet Finn's gaze and watch for his nod. Without a word, I slam the security guard's hand off my shoulder and throw a fast punch. He barely manages to dodge it.

Finn launches toward him. I'm smiling when I see my brother blur past me. I don't have a doubt in my mind that Finn will do what needs to be done.

Once we take him down, the girls can go ahead with Dutch. I'll stay back and restrain him. The cloth on the trolley will do nicely. I'll use that to tie him up. Maybe lock him in a closet where...

Finn raises his hand to strike, and the guard pulls out his gun.

My brother freezes, every muscle in his body locking up. For the first time in my life, I notice his eyes hold something other than boredom.

The gun changes everything.

And suddenly, we no longer have the upper hand.

In my mind is a revolving chorus of, *'damn, damn, damn'*.

Things just got freaking real.

Behind me, Dutch and Sol step in front of Cadence.

Grey is trembling, her face drained of color. I try to shift away so I'm blocking her from view, but the guard takes my movement as a threat and swings the gun to me.

Spittle flies from his mouth when he hisses, "Don't move!"

Finn grunts and the gun wavers his way.

"Both of you stay where you are or I swear I'm going to shoot!"

Panic spurts through me, but I hide it from my voice. "Relax, man."

The guard grumbles into the walkie at his shoulder. "I have a group of six down here. Dressed like servers with theatre masks on. No clearance."

My fingers clench into fists. It's over now that more guards have been alerted.

We'll have to abandon mission.

I turn my head slightly to the side and meet Dutch's eyes.

"Get them out of here," I hiss.

But my brother doesn't move.

I twist my head urgently, "Dutch, get them—"

In my peripheral, I see the guard's eyes widen at my sudden burst of movement. He pulls the trigger.

Sol springs forward.

So does Finn.

My brother gets in front of me first, covering me with his body and sheltering me from the blast.

It all happens so fast.

The gun.

The guard.

The bullet.

Finn stumbles into me, arms flailing over my shoulders.

Horror screams like ice through my veins.

I grab Finn, holding him up.

Panic rattles my voice. "Finn? Dammit! Finn, are you okay?"

The guard speaks into his walkie again. "Someone was shot. We're going to need a medic."

I hear feedback as if the person with the matching walkie is close to us.

A moment later, Dutch presses a button and I hear his voice coming from the guard's walkie, "Rick, stop messing around."

The hell?

Why is Dutch's voice coming from the security guard's walkie?

Sol gives Dutch a scathing look. "What the hell, man?"

Dutch just looks smug.

Finn groans.

"Finn?" I whisper urgently.

My brother straightens slowly and presses big hands over his chest. I skim my eyes across his white shirt, expecting to see blood stains gushing over the fabric.

There are none. Come to think of it, I didn't hear the *thwip* of a bullet either. I just assumed Finn was hit when he tripped into me.

"I lost my balance when I jumped," Finn explains, looking equally shocked to be alive. "Aren't bullets supposed to hurt?"

Grey steps forward. Her face is hidden behind a mask, but I can feel her confusion because it's a mirror of my own.

"Finn, are you okay?"

"For the last time, what the hell is going on?" Sol yells, his head whipping back and forth.

The security guard does a chin up greeting. "I'm Rick."

"He's my brother," Cadey says, rolling her eyes.

I hear at least three jaws hitting the ground.

"You're..." I point at Dutch. "This is your brother-in-law?"

Dutch shrugs again.

Grey chokes out a laugh. "I can't believe this. I was about to have a heart attack!"

Sol shakes his head slowly.

Finn looks annoyed.

I scowl. "Really, Dutch? You knew all the while that he was one of us?"

My twin smirks. "At least now we know that every member of the band would take a bullet for you."

I've never known my brother to be mischievous. This had to have been Cadey's idea.

My eyes dart to my sister-in-law.

She's grinning wide.

Yup.

Cadey planned this.

Rick motions to his chest. "I'm a security guard by trade, but Cadey asked me to help out. She doesn't ask me for things often." He and Cadey share a loaded look that tells me there's a lot he's leaving unsaid. "And I can't always help. This is the least I could do."

"And the gun?" I frown, giving the weapon a hateful stare.

Rick pulls the trigger again and I flinch.

"It's just for show. Do you think we'd walk around a high school dance with loaded weapons? If someone's kid actually gets shot, that's a PR nightmare and a jail sentence. They don't pay us enough for that."

"I can't believe this," Sol mutters, straightening to his full height.

"I did a good job, didn't I?" Rick gives his sister a meaningful look. "We're square?"

"We're square," Cadey agrees.

"That's enough joking around. We have things to do," Dutch says, pushing his trolley forward.

Cadey and Grey file behind him.

Finn says nothing as he joins us, but there's so much menace in his eyes that I know Dutch is going to hear about this later.

Rick falls in beside me. "Need some help with that?"

"I'm good," I say.

He takes up the rear, glancing around every so often. From the way he's carefully surveilling the area, I can tell he's taking this seriously.

"Why did Dutch ask you to join us?"

"I'm the lookout," he says. "And also an official part of the security crew. If there's a problem," he brings a separate walkie out of his pocket, "I'll hear about it first and alert you guys."

Huh.

I shoot Dutch a look. I should have known my twin

would have a backup plan. He's meticulous in everything, and it seemed weird that he was letting me take the lead.

"Nice set of brothers you got," Rick mumbles to me as we get closer to the basement. "I didn't like your twin at first, but after seeing the way he takes care of Cadey, I accepted it. A lot of punks out here think love is just sex and feeling good, but I know Dutch would die for her."

"He would."

Rick peers at me. "Never seen a group of brothers who'd actually die for each other though. Makes me wish I was a better brother to Cadey."

My eyes shift to Grey then.

She's not looking back. Her steps are determined and she's staring straight ahead like she's going to war.

"No time like the present to be better to someone you care about."

"Yeah," Rick says, "No time like the present."

* * *

Breaking the lock for the door is easy, but no one is eager to walk inside. Redwood's basement is a creepy, dungeon-like room with exposed bricks, a leaking faucet and pipes that rattle.

It's hard to believe Grey spent so much time alone down here.

The woman is either fearless or extremely motivated.

"Leave the heavy lifting to the guys," I tell Cadey and Grey. "You two sort out what needs to be transported."

"Who says we can't lift boxes like you two?" Cadey argues back.

"Listen to him," Dutch glowers.

She glares right back at him, but I don't see her picking up any of the boxes after the instruction.

Grey goes straight toward the back of the room. "I already went through these." She points to a row. "From here to here."

"On it," I say, walking toward her and pushing up my sleeve.

She backs away from me, heading to the other side of the room.

I stand there, confused.

The woman is giving me freaking whiplash. One minute she's grinding on me like we're two animals in heat. The next she's pulling back, acting ice cold and keeping her distance.

But she's not fooling anyone.

Grey already dropped way more than her defenses with me.

The lingerie in my pocket is proof. She might have given up on us before we've even begun, but I'm just getting started.

* * *

We work hard and fast, but there are way too many boxes.

Footsteps thump down the stairs.

I go tense until I see Rick appear.

"I'm hearing some chatter on the feed, guys. They're about to do rounds."

"Of shots?" I ask with a smirk.

Dutch scowls at me, but at least Cadey gives me a pity snort.

This is why she's the more likable half of that couple.

"I think he means something else," Finn says darkly.

Grey sighs. "It's Redwood Prep administrative policy. Teachers and guards do a buddy system team-up. They go around checking every classroom and making sure students aren't doing anything...wrong."

Our eyes meet across the room.

I smirk and pat the side of my pocket. Totally unashamed.

Her eyes dart away.

Dutch frowns at Rick. "So we hide out until the sweep is over?"

Rick scratches his chin nervously. "There's no official ending point. Even if we stay down here until they clear this floor, they'll be paying attention to the exit points. It's going to be hard to explain why you're roaming with these trolleys, even if you're wearing the waiting staff outfits."

"These masks cover most of our faces," Sol says, tapping the plastic he shoved to the top of his head. "They won't recognize us anyway."

"I wouldn't be so sure." Rick's eyes jump from me to Finn, Dutch, and Sol. "You four kind of stand out, even with your faces covered."

"We won't take much longer," I say.

"We're almost finished in here," Cadey agrees.

Behind her, Sol shows a thumbs up. "I'm almost finished too."

"Someone keep the lighter away from him until we've cleared this room," I mumble.

Sol flips me off.

Grey lifts a giant box of documents. Papers fly off the top.

My eyes widen and I rush over to her. Yanking the box away, I shove it on the trolley.

"I told you not to lift the heavy things," I scold.

"I'm fine."

My gaze darkens. "Pick up one of those heavy boxes again and see what happens."

"Is that a threat?"

"Baby, it's whatever you want it to be."

Her lips tighten. "Stop hovering, Zane. I can do this much."

I know she can. That's not the freaking problem. I just can't afford for this woman to break a single fingernail. The protective urge I feel for Grey is as violent as the one I feel for my brothers and Sol. I'd die for them. I'd kill for them. But with Grey, those emotions are... I don't know. More glittery. More pointed. More explosive.

It's almost foreign to have a girl in my head like this.

"Show me another box," I grumble.

Behind me, I feel Dutch, Finn, and Cadey observing us.

"Are those two married as well?" I hear Rick ask Cadey.

"They might as well be," she responds.

A heavy thump of another box hitting the trolley resounds.

Finn grunts. "I'm done."

"Wait." Grey pushes past me and points to a stack of boxes by the wall. "Those too."

"I'm out of space," Finn says.

"Me and Dutch too," Cadey admits.

"Can't we leave those extra boxes?" Sol grumbles.

Grey plants her hands on her hips. "No. They *all* have to go."

"Guys," Rick has his walkie to his ear and he gives us a worried look, "they're about to start sweeping."

"We need to move," Dutch's voice booms.

Sol checks his phone and then glances at us. "Time's up."

"I need those boxes," Grey insists. "We don't know which one has the evidence we're looking for. And there's no coming back after Sol does his part."

Sol grins a little too wide. "She's right."

"I say we cut our losses," Dutch growls.

I purse my lips. There are way too many boxes down here. We underestimated how many trolleys we'd need to get them out discretely.

Cadey places a hand on Dutch's arm, her wedding ring glinting. "Is there really no way?"

Dutch shakes his head 'no'.

Grey wilts.

I get an idea. "No, we'll do this."

Hope fills Grey's eyes and I know I'll do anything to keep her looking at me like that. Like I matter. Like I make her life better. Like I'm not just a screw-up, but someone who can be respected.

"Grey, open the boxes and take out the files inside. Finn, unload the boxes on your trolley."

Finn gives me a confused look.

I stalk to the boxes and help Grey unload the documents. Then I carry them over to Finn's trolley.

"Open up."

"They're full to the brim, Zane," Finn argues.

"Just do it," I snap.

His jaw clenches, but he sticks his knife through the slit and opens the folds. I tape the sides together so the box has a couple more inches of height and then I dump the documents inside. Some of them slip off. I take the ones that do and open up another box, dumping them too.

"That's not going to work," Finn points out.

"It'll have to work for now," I respond.

Cadey hurries over to help with unloading the files

while Dutch, Finn, Sol and I work to top them off on all the other boxes. We secure the overwhelmed mounds with tape. Hopefully, it holds when we're on the move.

"Hey," Rick's face has a fine sheen of sweat, "you need to move out. Now. The sweep's already started."

I exchange a look with my brothers.

Our plan to sneak out of Redwood undetected just got ten times more complicated.

***

Jinx: What Mask Are You Wearing Tonight?

They say there are three things that can't be hidden—coughing, poverty, and love. The Snare King certainly couldn't hide his feelings. Even with a mask on, he was only looking at one person all night.

And his mysterious Cinderella? Well, I have some ideas on who she might be.

Will we get a face reveal before the clock strikes midnight?

I sure hope so.

But be careful, Cinderella. When you peel off that mask, you might take some skin with it.

Until the next post, keep your enemies close and your secrets even closer.

- Jinx

Chapter Thirty-Nine

GREY

"I think it's better if we split up," Zane says, raising a brow in my direction. "We'll be less suspicious that way."

"Good point," Dutch agrees.

Zane and Dutch's eyes look otherworldly in the darkness. Both glowing and sinister. Both predators in their own right.

Zane points. "Dutch and Cadey will go together, obviously. And then me and Grey—"

I open my mouth to protest.

Sol beats me to it. "I need you to stay here and help out."

"No way."

"This is a two man job."

"Let Finn help."

"Finn is no fun."

Dutch narrows his eyes at them. "We don't have time for this. Zane, you help Sol. Finn can take the rear exit alone. Cadey and I will use the elevator. Rick can go with Grey through the front."

"The front is too dangerous." Zane stands off with his brother.

"It's the least dangerous. No one will expect a thief to use the front entrance. Plus Rick will help throw suspicion off."

"The plan is fine. Let's move." I motion to the stairs. There's no time to argue.

Zane leans close to me.

My chest gets tight.

"Be careful, tiger," he whispers.

I wish I didn't feel anything but, when Zane brushes his fingers against my cheek, I feel *everything*.

Turning away without a word, I follow Rick. The music from the dance helps to absorb our steps, but it still feels like we're on the edge of discovery.

He points his flashlight in front of us. "Since we're using the front, we can go a little slower. Moving with urgency draws more attention."

"Okay." I blow out a breath.

His long legged stride throws a shadow on the floor.

I glance up at him. "How come I didn't see you at the funeral?"

"Not really a fan."

"Of funerals?"

"Of my mother."

"Ah."

"Honestly, it's a relief that she's finally dead."

I cringe. That's harsh.

He sees my expression and explains, "She tossed me when I was a baby and then came back years later, asking me to steal money from my foster mom so she could buy drugs. That woman was never much of a mother when she was alive, so I won't treat her like one in death."

"I'm sorry."

"No need." He shakes his head. "Her death taught me one thing. Life is short. I want to be a better brother to Cadey and Viola. I want to be a better boyfriend. You just never know when it's your last time to say 'I love you' to someone."

I think of mom. The last time I saw her, I snapped at her. She hasn't reached out since then.

I should text her tonight...

Up ahead, a shadow skitters by.

I yelp and nearly turn over the trolley.

Rick chuckles. "Relax. It's just a cat on the tree outside."

"Oh." Sheepishly, I lick my lips.

"You're nervous," he observes.

"I'm not much of a risk-taker."

"Really?"

"Can't you tell?"

"To be honest, it's hard to tell anything under that mask."

I give him an assessing look. There's something about the way he watches me. It's not rude or like he's interested. But it's brimming with curiosity, like he's trying to figure me out.

I stare straight ahead. "What did Cadey say about me?"

"Oh nothing. Absolutely nothing." He rubs the back of his neck. "I don't even know your name."

"My name is Grace Jamieson," I say, pushing the trolley. My fingers flex on the handles. "But my friends call me Grey. I teach math—"

"I thought it was Lit?" I stare pointedly at him and his entire face blanches. "You're smart."

"And you're a liar."

He blushes. "Cadey might have mentioned a few things about you. You're her favorite teacher, you know. Apart from the music guy who gave her the scholarship."

"Mulliez," I say. He was my only friend at Redwood before he got on The Kings' bad side, was falsely accused and then left with his reputation in shambles.

Rick coughs. "Are you close with the band?"

"Not really."

"How about one person in the band?"

I stare him down. "No."

"Right. Right." He glances at the trolley that's nearly buckling from the weight of all the boxes. "You want me to push for a bit?"

"If anyone sees us, they'll wonder why you're acting like the wait staff."

The music is louder.

We're getting close to the dance.

I check my watch.

Have Sol and Zane set the fire yet?

Rick's eyes dart around. "So this is Redwood."

"Not that impressive, right?" I say sarcastically.

"Half the time, I don't understand what goes on in this shiny world." He gestures to the marble floors and high ceilings. "It's like the rules don't apply to you people."

"That's not true."

"The rules do apply?"

"I shouldn't be included in 'you people'."

"Come on. You belong here now. Even The Kings respect you."

I almost laugh. He has no idea. "I'm just a cog in the machine. I work for the shiny people. None of their shine rubbed off on me."

And I don't want it to. My dream is to burn Sloane's enemies to the ground and walk away smelling of smoke and revenge.

At that point, I'll have to figure out who or what I'll be next.

He clears his throat. "This place gives me the creeps."

"It's much prettier during the day."

"Pretty things can still be poison."

I can't disagree.

Rick slips a hand into his pocket. "Viola wants to transfer. Did you know that?"

"To Redwood?"

Rick nods. "I'm against it."

"Why?"

"After she moved here, Cadey got married to Jarod Cross's son. *Jarod Cross.* Not just that, she got married to him the *day* she turned eighteen. And a week later, she was burying our mom and moving in with her husband in between going to trig class. Who does that?"

I stare at him with a discerning eye. "You're worried about your sister."

"She grew up too fast." He shakes his head. "And this world is dangerous. Those boys are the masters of it, sure. But that means there's a target on their backs. They'll always draw chaos."

He's not wrong about that either.

My phone chirps.

It's Zane.

Get ready to burn, tiger.

My lips quirk as I imagine Harris's face when he sees what we've done.

Rick notices my expression. "Zane?"

"Huh?" I glance up distractedly. "Oh... yeah. They just set the fire."

"They probably enjoy this. Destroying things."

"Probably."

He eyes me. "You know... it would have made me feel a little better knowing an adult Cadey trusts is part of that psychotic family."

"I'm sorry to disappoint, but I'm not," I say. "I'm just a teacher at Redwood and they're... entitled eighteen year old boys."

"Zane too?"

"Especially him."

He snickers. "The kid was about to take a bullet for you."

"The gun was empty."

He snorts as if I'm being ridiculous.

Maybe I am. I don't want to believe Zane is serious about me.

He can't be.

Neither can I.

What we have is not *serious* material.

I can admit that I'm attracted to him.

I can even admit that I want to sleep with him—although that burns me to confess.

But I have to be realistic.

"If you're not with Zane, then how about I introduce you to someone?" Rick glances hopefully at me. "I have a buddy. Hunter. Great guy. Got his heart broken by some girl he met in Europe recently." Rick tsks. "Poor thing. I've been trying to hook him up—"

Boom!

The floor rattles.

I jolt on my feet.

Rick grabs my arm. "The hell was that?"

Boom! Boom!

Screams break out.

The music stops abruptly. Rick throws the gym door open and it feels like I'm stepping into an alternate reality. Everyone is running back and forth. Kids are ducking in horror. A few are crawling under tables. Someone is puking in the corner. It smells like the spiked punch.

Harris takes the mike on stage. "Alright, everyone! Just calm down! I'm not sure what this is about, but I'm certain there's a perfectly reasonable explanation—"

A high pitched wail cuts him off.

Fire alarms ring suddenly.

Harris yelps into the mike. I watch with a twisted sense of satisfaction as the sprinklers snap to life and spray all over him.

Shrieks erupt from the girls whose dresses are being drenched.

Harris grabs the mike again. "Everyone calm..."

Boom!

Explosions of color crackle outside the windows. Sparks explode in the black night, staining the sky like glittering jewels.

Fireworks.

Immediately, the mood shifts from terrified to awestruck.

Students rush outside in a frenzy.

This is definitely The Kings' doing. I should be angry at them for drawing more attention to us and making a spectacle of tonight's heist, but it's worth it just to see that dumbstruck look on Harris's face.

"Uh-oh. Incoming," Rick says.

I stiffen when I notice Harris bound down the stairs and

gun straight for us. My instinct is to run, so I take a few steps with the trolley.

Rick grabs my hand. "What are you doing? If you run now, you'll only look more suspicious."

"I can't just stay here. What if he recognizes me?"

It's too late.

"Excuse me!" Harris slams his hands on his hips and glares at us.

I stiffen, dropping my head and hiding my gaze from sight. My hair is straight tonight and I'm wearing a mask as well as an ill-fitting waiter outfit, but Harris has seen me everyday for more than six months. What if... he sees through my disguise.

I feel Harris's eyes drilling into my face. My heart climbs to my throat and starts beating as hard as the fireworks exploding outside.

Just as I'm about to choke, Harris turns toward Rick. "You. Find out who's setting those things! And you!" Harris stabs a finger at me. "Caterers use the back entrance. Not the front."

I dip my head and share a quick glance with Rick. He gives me a barely discernible nod and walks off.

I push the trolley toward the kitchen, sure that I'm going to feel a hand clamp on my shoulder and whirl me around. Sure that Harris is going to rip my mask off, throw the cloth from the trolley and point to the documents. Sure that everything is going to be utterly ruined.

But no one pursues me.

I push the trolley through the back entrance and nearly cry in relief when Dutch, Cadey, and Finn meet me at the van.

The boys load the boxes off the trolley.

Dutch slams the door shut. "That's everything."

"We did it." Cadey slings an arm around me, grinning wide.

"We... did it," I breathe in shock.

The Kings are total maniacs, but they fulfilled their end of the deal.

My lips curl up in a smile, but a strange sense of foreboding wafts over me. Why do I get the feeling that it's too early to celebrate?

* * *

Jinx: Where There's Smoke, There's Fire

Things are heating up here at Redwood. And I'm not just talking about the dirty dancing between Snare King and his mystery Cinderella. Although I wouldn't be surprised if that's what triggered the fire alarms.

Screams of terror turned to screams of delight as rain fell from the ceiling and lights shot up from the ground. With the kingdom in utter chaos, I have only one question...

Where are The Kings?

Until the next post, keep your enemies close and your secrets even closer.

- Jinx

Chapter Forty

ZANE

"The hell is wrong with you?" I bark at Sol.

Flames dance in his eyes.

It's insidious.

Ghostly.

For a second, my best friend looks like a creature that climbed out of hell.

"The plan was to set small fires and trigger the smoke alarms. Not blow freaking rockets in the sky."

"They're not rockets. They're timer-set M0-18s—"

My throat tightens. "They're freaking *bombs?*"

"You're just angry because you're missing the show."

"I'm angry because you're going to get us caught."

"What's going on outside is even better than these jokes." Sol eases his way around the metal containers. Inside the buckets, orange and yellow flames crackle, chewing at old newspapers and trash. The smell is atrocious.

I wave at the thick smoke that's already starting to sting my eyes.

Freaking Sol.

Grey wanted these flames contained.

It was a perfect plan.

Until Sol unilaterally decided to kick it up a notch.

"What are you waiting for?" He jerks his chin at the door, orange light reflecting on his creepy mask.

I start to move when I notice a weird crack in the wall.

Am I seeing things?

Sparks hiss from the fire.

Red flames.

Dangerous heat.

But it also provides light.

Something's there.

My body gravitates to the crack, pulled by a curiosity I can't shake. Earlier, we were so focused on getting the boxes out as fast as possible that we weren't looking around for more. Now that there's enough light in here to roast a pig, there's no mistaking the strange groove in the wall.

I change directions and jog over. My hand skates against the seam and I exhale when I press in and feel it give. "Hey, help me move this cabinet. I think something's back here."

Sol goes tense. "What are you doing? We need to move."

"Come on."

He hesitates for only a second and then runs over to me. With his help, I move the shelving aside and swing the door open.

There's a small closet with two boxes stacked on top of each other.

"It's a secret compartment," I mutter, my eyes widening.

"Whoa."

A walkie talkie croaks.

I whirl around, thinking someone is down here with us.

"Your pocket," Sol reminds me.

I lift the walkie to my ear.

Rick's voice crackles in a mix of static and chaos. "Zane, you're clear of the basement, right?"

I glance at Sol. "Not yet."

"What?" Rick curses. "Security just checked the tapes and saw the camera blockers. They're trying to get the cameras back up. My boss is sending a team down there. They're moving in like the freaking SWAT."

Dammit.

I shove one of the boxes at Sol and hug the other one under my arm. "Let's get the hell out of here."

Our sneakers thump on the stairs as we scramble to the landing. Security guards turn the bend and spot us. Their shouts of alarm light a fire inside me.

"Move it!" I yell, shoving Sol in the back.

We take off into a hallway and throw the emergency door open. The lights flicker as we tear down the staircase.

A door above slams open.

"They're down here!" someone yells.

I glance over my shoulder, hissing in annoyance when I see the guards take chase.

"They're splitting up," Sol grunts.

I breathe hard. "They're going to try and cut us off."

"Maybe we should hide out in the practice room?" His voice is breathless and slightly shaking. "They won't have the key."

"But we'll be trapped and they'll know it's us," I answer back.

"We have to do something!" Sol hisses.

I watch him with alarm.

"I can't go back, Zane. I'm never going back."

I meet his eyes and see the distress there. He's thinking about that night when he took the fall for us.

The night everything went to hell.

I won't let that happen a second time.

My mind whirs.

I think fast.

These guards are new to Redwood. They don't know the school like we do.

I tug on Sol's shirt. "This way."

We throw the door open and cut into the fourth floor, right above the science labs. There's an extra room where kids stow away to smoke pot in between classes. It used to be a storage place for dangerous chemicals, but after an accident, they moved the chemical chest to another location.

I crawl into the narrow space.

Sol follows me.

We're breathing hard and nervous as hell. It's pitch black. The boxes dig into my stomach painfully. The smell of dust mixes with the fragrance of pot leaves and a telling chemical burn.

"Where'd they go?"

"Check the cameras!"

"I think it was this way."

Footsteps pound in the opposite direction.

I grab the walkie. "Rick."

He answers. "Where are you guys?"

"We need you to sneak into the security room and disable the cameras."

"What?"

"Just do it! You've got three minutes."

I cut the walkie in the middle of his spray of expletives.

In the darkness, I feel Sol looking at me.

"What?" I grumble.

"You think I'm crazy too, don't you?"

I run a hand over my face. "I think you're even more reckless than I am. And that's saying something."

He snorts out a laugh.

I bristle. "*I* don't go around setting fires."

"No. You just grind on our Lit teacher in front of everyone and then screw her in a classroom."

I stand to attention. "Did you see—"

"No, I didn't." His voice sounds disgusted. "Unlike you, I don't fantasize about my teachers being naked." Sol digs his fingers into the box. "But anyone who saw you two dancing knew what was going to happen next."

I squeeze my eyes shut and let out a breath.

"You like her that much?"

"Screw you, Sol."

"You plan to marry her?"

I stiffen.

"Date her? Ask her to be your girlfriend?" His voice is taunting. "You can't, can you? What do you plan to do with her? Keep dragging her into classrooms after dark and bending her over tables? Then what?"

"Shut up."

"She's going to be your private little whore while you date girls your age?"

"You got a death wish?" I growl.

"Stop treating me like I'm fragile. I'm not the only one with issues."

"Why are you trying to start a fight?"

"Why do you keep looking at me like I'm broken?"

"We're all broken, Sol." I make a sound of annoyance. "Every single one of us. But you cracked in a way we could see."

I feel him glaring at me. "And you're screwing your step-sister."

"You're such a prick," I mutter.

"You're such a bastard," he answers.

For a moment, there's silence.

Then we both chuckle.

"This is freaking insanity," Sol mumbles.

"You think they're still looking for us?"

"Definitely."

My phone buzzes.

I work it out of my pocket and check.

Dutch: Where the hell are you?

Finn: Why aren't you guys out yet?

Sol's phone vibrates too.

He's probably getting the same panic messages.

I text Dutch back.

We're fine. Just making a quick stop. We'll meet you at home. Get Grey and Cadey out of here.

Dutch answers back.

Don't do anything stupid.

The walkie shrieks.

All I hear is the sound of someone screaming at Rick for tripping on a power cord.

"I think that's our cue," I mumble.

Sol nods.

I push the door and it creaks.

There's no one in sight.

We hurry to the exits, racing into the shadows and hiding in classrooms every time we see security.

It feels like forever, but we finally make it outside. Sol and I keep running until we get to the dark, abandoned gas station parking lot. Our catering van was parked here earlier. It's gone now. Dutch must have taken the girls home.

Beneath my mask, I'm drenched in sweat.

Victory tastes like salt and weed.

"I hope these boxes were worth the effort." Sol drops his on the ground. It has two sweaty palm imprints on the side. "That was insane."

I glance up at the sky. "The fireworks are over."

A smirk curls his lips. "I bet someone will upload a few videos to Jinx's app."

"You sound like you're actually excited about that."

He shrugs.

I peer through the trees.

From here, we can spot the school's back steps. My eyes catch on the staircase where I caught Hall trying to drag Grey away.

There aren't any cameras back there.

Which is why he probably thought he could get away with that crap.

"Come on." I wrench my mask off and wipe my sweat with the sleeve of my shirt. "I'll take you home."

"I'm not riding behind you on your bike," Sol grunts.

"Fine. Walk home then."

Sol grumbles under his breath but starts walking with me.

We're halfway to my bike when a black van appears out of nowhere. It screams to a stop on the curb and a bunch of thugs in suits pour out and surround us. My first thought is that dad sent someone to teach us a lesson, but that goes out the window when I see Hall.

He's leading the pack and he's got a murderous glint in his eyes.

"I've been looking all over for you, Cross. Nice of you to finally show."

Chapter Forty-One

ZANE

Hall is holding a sharp, wicked-looking knife with a serrated edge.

I want to laugh in his face.

This guy golfs with the owner of a shopping mall and rides around in his parents' yacht on the weekends. He eats curated cheeses and salami on a charcuterie board that he specially requests from the cafeteria and complains when they don't carry his sparkling water at the right room temp.

He's not a street fighter.

He's nothing but a piece of crap.

And yet, he's standing here with a knife acting like he's tough.

I'm going to enjoy ripping him to shreds.

I shoot a quick glance at Sol.

He peers at me from behind his mask.

I jut my chin at the highway, indicating he should run. My best friend rips his mask off, a crazed smile on his face.

And I understand it as if he spoke out loud.

There's no freaking way he's leaving.

Not because he cares about me.

Although I'm sure there's some of that mixed in.

It's because he's been waiting for an excuse to bash someone's head in.

My crazed expression is a mirror of his.

Damn.

We really are the lunatics of the group.

My eyes return to Hall who's swaggering toward us like he's filming an eighties mobster movie. His finger is on the tip of his knife, flicking it like it's skin and bones. The moon glints against the dangerous edge, dispensing light all over our faces.

"Where's the rest of your stupid crew?" Hall grinds out.

The answer is 'not coming'.

Neither me nor Sol had time to tell anyone we've been ambushed. I really wish there was such a thing as twin telepathy. But there's no way to let my brothers know we've been cornered. They're in the van with the girls, driving far away from this mess.

We're on our own.

"Why?" I smirk at Hall's hired hands. "Did your friends want our autographs?"

Hall throws his head back and laughs. "I forgot you're the funny one."

"Wrong. I'm the one who beat your face to a bloody pulp last week. Remember that?"

Hall snarls, his face twisted and dark. "I'm going to take you down, Cross."

I smirk.

"You Kings think you rule Redwood. But guess what. You don't. Not anymore. I'm taking over now."

I notice his goons closing in around us, forming a circle that we can't break out of.

Sol and I inch together, our backs thumping into each other.

"Scared?" Hall laughs.

"Just wondering how much of your daddy's money went to mobsters."

"Come on, Zane. Did you think you could dislocate my jaw," Hall moves his chin back and forth, "give me six stitches," he indicates the scar beneath his eye, "and just... what? Skip off into the sunset? You don't know who you're messing with."

My smile inches up. "I know exactly who you are. A filthy pig who squealed and wiggled right there on the back steps of Redwood. Remember, Theo? How you begged for mercy? How you peed your—"

"Shut up!"

"The other eye looks a little lonely. Come here. I'll give you a matching scar."

Hall's face turns red and he charges at me. I twist to the side, dodging the knife and grabbing his arm. He's much scrawnier than me and I use his own weight against him, taking advantage of his wild movement.

My shoulder smashes into his chest and I twist his arm painfully. Hall bawls out like a lamb about to get its head chopped off. I try to displace the knife while he's trapped against me, but something heavy smashes into the back of my head.

I lose my grip on Hall and stumble to the side drunkenly. My skull ricochets with agony. White-hot blitzes of pain accordion down my spine all the way to my toes. My legs lose their strength and one bends of its own accord as I struggle to get my bearings.

Through the corner of my eye, I see Sol. He's being cornered by three of the thugs. Arms windmilling, he punches one in the face and gets two blows in return. He's putting up a valiant fight, but there are too many of them. He's going to run out of steam.

We need an advantage, but there's no time to find one.

Hall and the thug that hit me attack me together. I step back and throw a punch at the thug since he presents the bigger threat. I hear the zing of Hall's knife behind me.

I jump away, but the tip slices me in the side. Scrambling around, I block Hall's second attempt and shove my shoulder into his chest, driving him backward.

Hall collides into the thug.

I hear them both grunt in pain.

That's right you ugly twat.

I've been in my share of fights. The girls who jump into my bed aren't always single and there have been a few bar room brawls with jealous gym bros who couldn't keep their anger in check.

I may not know how to fight like Finn does—with whatever secret ninja powers he's been keeping under wraps—but I know how to give as good as I get.

With Hall down and embarrassed about it, I launch at him.

He raises the knife, but he doesn't know how to thrust it. I grab his head, lift my knee up and slam him in the nose.

Blood spurts everywhere.

Gritting my teeth, I grab the hand holding the knife and try to get the weapon away from him.

I hear someone groan in pain behind me.

It's Sol.

Panicked, I glance over at my best friend. His punches are losing steam. The thugs are getting too many hits in.

I need to get over there.

A thug comes charging at me before I can take a step. It's too late to correct my stance. There's no way I can dodge the bat that's coming my way. It crashes into my back. There are nails at the end. I hear the rip of fabric and feel the hot stinging pain as the nails claw into my flesh.

Hall scrambles up again, holding a hand to his broken nose.

Another grunt comes from across the lawn. I turn in time to see Sol swaying back and forth like the ground can't hold him anymore. With one last crushing blow from the thugs, he crumples to the ground. The thugs don't stop. They deliver harsh punches to his stomach and back.

My heartbeat pounds in my ears.

My vision turns red.

I whirl around, noticing the idiot who hit me is cranking his arm back to let the bat loose again.

The world is spinning. I'm pretty sure blood is oozing down my neck, but I'm running on pure adrenaline and fury.

Roaring, I roll to the ground, pick up a rock and slam the thug in the face as hard as I can. He staggers back, but he's so big that my hit didn't knock him out. He regains his balance quickly, but I'm already on the move.

"Sol!" I yell, running over.

I ram into one of the guys who's kicking my best friend. Moving like a wild thing, I kick another one in the knee cap. He goes flying to the ground.

I reach a hand out to Sol.

He grips my fingers, face a bloody mess.

The thugs surround us again.

Hall joins them.

Six against two.

Terrible odds.

I spit blood on the concrete, feeling woozy and fighting to stay in control.

"Round two?" I smirk.

Hall yells and comes at me again. I'm ready for him and brace myself. The moment he's close, I duck and wrap my arms around his waist, tackling him to the ground.

My fist slams into his jaw and chest. Once, twice, three times.

Before I can get another blow in, I'm being hauled off by two thugs. One pounds me in the stomach while the other grabs me by the throat.

I choke, black creeping along the edge of my vision.

Hall jumps on top of me and rains blows on my head and stomach. I let him tire himself out before locking my legs around him and rolling us around. His eyes widen and I know I have the advantage.

Or at least I did.

Until his thugs wrench both of my hands and grab me off him again.

Hall grins, getting up from the grass. His shirt is hanging off his shoulder and he's holding his ribs as if I did some permanent damage.

Good.

I smile when he limps toward me, but the smile turns into a roar of pain when he grabs my wrist and twists it back. "You're a drummer, right?" He sneers in my face. His putrid breath washes over my cheek as he peels my wrist back further.

"Ah!" I scream.

"What will it feel like if you can't drum ever again?"

"Zane!" Sol yells. I see him ram into the guys holding him down, fighting to get to me. He manages to knock one

THE FORBIDDEN NOTE

over, but there are two more to restrain him. They dog-pile on top of his body, squelching his frenzied and desperate attempts to be free.

"Hold him down," Hall commands.

His thugs tighten their grip on me.

Hall twists my hand even further. Desperately, I throw myself to the ground so I can shake him loose and kick my leg to sweep Hall off balance, but his thugs grab me. I'm pinned to the pavement while Hall stomps on my wrist repeatedly.

I hear the bone crack.

My mouth opens in a howl of agony.

I can't help it.

It's the most excruciating pain I've ever felt.

The thugs release me and I sit up, my eyes locked on my hand. My wrist is hanging at an odd angle.

Hall grins evilly.

"What the hell are you doing?" someone yells.

Hall and his thugs freeze.

Rick prowls toward us, swinging something back and forth. "Back off!"

"He's got a gun!" Hall shrieks.

The thugs don't wait around for further instructions. They pile into the black van. Hall chases after them, looking like the pathetic punk that he is. The van is already moving by the time he jumps in.

"Are you guys, okay?" Rick asks as Hall and his thugs drive off.

"You and this gun again," I say breathlessly.

Rick laughs, but it turns into a choking sound when his eyes drop lower.

I won't look at my wrist again.

If I don't look, it won't be broken. It'll be fine.

Rick gently kneels beside me. "The gun is empty, but they didn't know that."

"What if they kept attacking us?"

"Well, they didn't." He swallows hard. "I-it worked."

Sol rushes over to me. His eyes drop to my arm and a look of horror twists his mouth.

The world starts turning black at the edges.

I can't feel my hand.

No, I'm fine.

I'm fine.

I'm going to patch myself up and then hunt Hall down. He's going to pay for what he did tonight.

"I think you should call an ambulance," Rick says softly.

Sol breaks out his cell phone.

Tires squeal in the distance.

I hear a car door slam.

At that moment, my strength gives out. I flop back on the trampled pavement, all the blood rushing out of my head at once.

Dutch and Finn appear over me.

Finn's hands land on my stomach. When he lifts them, the tips are stained red.

"Zane?" Dutch's eyes are wide and gleaming in pain. It's almost like he's the one who got jumped tonight.

Finn's face is also laced in panic. I've never seen my brother look that worried.

I'm fine.

I want to tell them out loud, but I'm tired.

So tired.

There's too much blood.

I can smell it.

Where is it coming from?

Can't be my wrist.

My wrist is fine.

I'm fine.

"Zane!"

Pain strikes my chest. That's the voice that breaks me. That makes me start shaking all over.

I don't want her near this.

She can't see this.

"Zane, no, no." Grey kneels beside me and cradles my face between her hands. "Zane."

"I'm... fine," I manage to choke out.

It's the last thing I say before the world goes black.

Chapter Forty-Two

GREY

"The surgery was successful." The doctor holds up an X-ray to the light. "Thankfully, there's no severe head trauma and only minor lacerations. The bad news is his wrist is badly damaged. He'll need to wear a splint for at least six weeks and then go through physical therapy—"

"But he'll heal," Dutch says, his voice husky and raw. "Right?"

The doctor's face is grim. "Yes. But..."

"But what?" Finn demands.

The doctor goes quiet. "Bones heal, but tendons don't. I haven't seen a fracture this bad in a long time..."

My heart thunders.

I feel sick to my stomach.

"Will he be able to play drums again?" Sol growls.

"It will be hard to know for sure until we get him into physical therapy—"

"Will he. Play. Again?" Sol shrieks.

The room goes quiet.

I glance at Sol. His face is bloody and his eyes are swollen, the left one purple and almost completely shut. There's blood on his shirt and bruises down his arms and neck. He refused to let any of the nurses see him. The moment he got to the hospital, all he did was pace up and down outside Zane's surgical ward.

"I don't know," the doctor admits.

His words slam against us.

I feel my heart shatter.

If Zane hadn't rescued me from Hall, the crazy junior wouldn't have come back for revenge.

Even the fact that we can't call the police is on me. If the authorities start asking questions about Hall, they're going to want to know what we were doing tonight.

I'm responsible for this mess.

I'm responsible for all of it.

The doctor clears his throat. "Mr. Cross is young and healthy. He'll recover well. And in regards to his wrist... I'm sure he can find a new hobby."

Sol grabs the doctor by the collar. "You don't understand. He *needs* to play. It's who he is. It's why he breathes."

"Sol, let him go," Dutch says.

Finn grabs Sol's hand.

Sol looks like he'll start swinging, but one look into Finn's face makes him freeze.

"Stop," Finn says quietly. He's not loud or abrasive at all, but there's enough force in that order to scare a tornado back into hiding.

Sol wrenches his arm away, kicks a chair in the waiting room and stalks off.

"I'll go talk to him," Cadence says, her eyes stained with tears.

"I'll come with you," Dutch says.

Finn juts his chin at me. "I can take you home."

"I'm not going anywhere."

The doctor pinches his lips. "We'll move Mr. Cross to the recovery room and then you can see him."

Silence descends.

It's not broken until a nurse appears to bring me and Finn to Zane's room.

Zane is on the bed, looking pale and helpless. His wrist is in a cast. The doctor's grim prediction that he may never be able to play drums professionally again rips through my head.

My fault.

I turn away, unable to look.

At that moment, Dutch, Sol and Cadence enter the room.

Dutch looks over at Zane, his lips tightening.

Cadence glances down.

Finn stands as still as a statue.

"Dammit!" Sol rams a fist against the wall.

Cadence doesn't stop him this time.

"What are we going to do about Hall?"

The question comes from Finn. His tone sends a black chill down my spine.

"I say we break both his legs," Sol growls.

I lift my attention to the boy with tan skin, wavy brown hair and sharp, chiseled cheekbones.

Sol's eyes are glittering as he adds, "I say we break every bone in his body and bury him alive."

Dutch slides his fingers over his chin, considering it.

"Breaking a few bones isn't enough. We have to make an example out of him," Finn says, almost inhumanely calm.

"And cracking his legs the way he cracked Zane's wrist isn't going to do that?" Sol folds his arms over his chest and scowls.

Dutch rubs his chin, considering it.

I sense their mounting wrath and it frightens me. These dangerous boys would commit murder tonight and be proud of it.

"Guys, we need to regroup here. We can't move on anger. That's how you make stupid decisions," I say earnestly.

Cadey meets my eyes, her worried look reflecting mine.

"Guys," I try again.

But no one is listening to me.

Sol moves toward the door first. "I'm going to find Hall."

Finn marches behind him.

Dutch takes a step and Cadey grabs his arm.

He looks down at her.

"If you leave, I'm coming with you," she says.

"Stay here," Dutch orders.

Cadey narrows her eyes in direct defiance.

"I'm coming with you too." I step forward.

The boys look at me like I just admitted to being a different species.

I glance at Finn, Dutch and Sol in turn. "But if we all leave, Zane will be left at the hospital by himself."

Dutch backs down, probably due to Cadence's pleading look in his direction.

But Sol and Finn still seem determined.

I walk toward them. "I know a little something about revenge, remember? It's so easy to get lost in it. To lose your way and become the same type of animal that you're trying to destroy."

Sol glances away.

Quietly, I add, "Right now, let's focus on Zane. That's all that matters."

Finn leans against the wall, head tilted down.

I breathe a sigh of relief.

They're staying put.

For now.

As the silence stretches, a pained groan filters through the room.

Zane slowly cracks his eyes open. "*My head*."

His brothers and Sol spring forward, crowding the bed.

"Don't try to talk," Cadence says urgently.

Zane struggles to sit up. His face creases in pain.

"Don't move," Finn urges.

He groans again. "Where am I?"

"In the hospital," Sol says.

"The *hell* were you thinking fighting Hall without us?" Dutch growls. "If Rick hadn't heard you on that walkie—"

"Did you get the boxes?" Zane mumbles.

Dutch freezes. "What?"

"The boxes... Grey... secret room..."

His eyes flutter closed.

He's out again.

As one, The Kings turn and look at me.

My heart quivers. I can't stand the weight of their gazes.

"I'm... going to get some water." I stalk outside on wobbly legs. Alone in the hallway, I wilt to the floor and cover my face with my hands.

I was supposed to bring justice to Sloane.

And in the process, I dreamt of bringing Redwood Prep down.

The Kings are the very faces of that despicable school.

They're everything I claimed to hate.

Rich. Powerful. Bullies.

But now that I've made progress with the investigation and humiliated Harris on stage, it doesn't feel like a win. It feels like I'm ruining my life and the lives of everyone around me in my best friend's name.

Chapter Forty-Three

ZANE

I go in and out of consciousness. The meds are strong and knock me out most of the time, but whenever I come to, the room feels more and more tense.

Sol looks like he's about to go on a murder spree.

Finn's face is a cold blank mask, yet I can feel the rage thrumming beneath it.

Dutch hasn't looked this vengeful since we were kids. The twist of his lips, the clench of his jaw—it's all telling. He's normally better at hiding his emotions.

Marriage made him soft.

Or maybe I really look that pathetic.

"You're crowding me," I complain. "What time is it?"

"Time for you to be asleep," Sol says.

Finn slouches in the chair beside Sol and thumbs through a book.

Are so many visitors even allowed in here?

The moment the thought hits, I dispense it. Rules don't

apply to us. Dutch and Finn must have worked it out so that no one questioned why five people are stuffed into my room for the night.

"Go home," I tell them.

"No." Dutch glowers at me from the chair where he's slumped down. Cadey is curled in his lap, her head on his chest and her knees drawn up around her. Dutch dragged a blanket over her body, but she still doesn't look comfortable.

The door opens. I'm surprised when Grey walks in, holding a cup of coffee. Her eyes land on me and widen. For a second, she seems sheepish as if there's a part of her that wonders if I even want her here.

How could she think I wouldn't?

Just looking at her makes it hard to breathe.

"Zane," she says quietly. "You're up."

I keep staring at her, drinking her in. Her hair looks wet and so do her clothes. She must have gotten doused by the sprinklers tonight.

She squirms. "Uh... are you in pain? Should I call a nurse?"

Dutch glances at me.

Finn folds his arms over his chest.

Sol blinks sleepily.

"Everyone out," I say as firmly as I can. Keeping my eyes on Grey, I add, "Except you."

Her eyebrows fly up.

"Don't over-do it, Zane," Sol warns. "You just got out of surgery."

I put a hand on the bed so I can shove myself up. Unfortunately, I'm stopped by a giant cast around my wrist.

My eyes widen at the sight of it.

"How long until I can take this off?" I ask the room.

No one speaks.

"How long?" I grunt.

"We don't know." Sol clears his throat. "The damage is bad, Zane."

I meet his eyes and sense what he *isn't* saying.

A flash of brutally dark emotions overwhelms me.

"What did the doctors say?"

They seem reluctant to tell me.

Finally, Finn breaks the ice. "You might not be able to drum again."

Sol remains quiet.

Dutch glances away.

In the stark and tense silence, I laugh.

Everyone looks at me like I'm crazy.

Maybe I am.

No, I *know* I am.

That's why I don't need any of their damn pity.

"Get the hell out of my room. Dutch, let Cadey sleep in a bed tonight. Finn, Sol's parents are probably freaking out. Send them a text and tell them he's sleeping over after the dance and Sol..."

He goes tense.

"For the love of—let someone clean that ugly mug of yours. There's so much blood you look like an assassin."

"His pain meds must be kicking in," Dutch says.

He's right. The pain is muted, but my head is still pounding and my wrist is still numb. "I'll kick you out myself if I have to."

Dutch lifts his chin stubbornly. "We're staying. Hall might come back. Or—"

"Hall isn't dumb enough to strike twice and you know it."

My twin glares at me.

"I'm fine."

"You're injured. Maybe permanently," Finn says outright.

I smirk. "Have I ever, one day in my life, let anyone besides me decide what I can and cannot do?"

Sol licks his lips. His voice is stern. "You can't make a joke out of everything. This is serious."

I look at each of my brothers. They're so worried about me that they can't even hide it. "I'm going to play the drums again."

Dutch glances down as if he's trying to hide his pity.

"And I'm going to break Hall's legs myself. So don't touch him until I recover."

Sol opens his mouth as if he'll argue.

"Out." I order, more intensely this time. "Go home. All of you."

Finn is the first to walk out.

Sol follows reluctantly.

Dutch cradles Cadey and shares a knowing look with Grey before carrying his wife out of the room.

The door clicks shut.

It's just me and Grey.

"Was that necessary?" She sets the coffee cup down. "They're all worried about you. Cadey just managed to fall asleep after checking on you every three seconds."

"Come here."

Her eyes flicker away. "Zane."

"Come. Here."

She hesitates as if she's considering whether to ignore that instruction.

I bawl out in pain, curling my wrist to my chest. "Ah!"

"Zane!" Grey rushes over, her eyes wide and frightened. When she's close, I grab her hand and pull her to sit on the bed with me. She topples over and narrowly catches her balance.

I use my good hand to keep a hold on her. "Was that so hard?"

Her nostrils flare. "Since you're feeling so much better, I think I should leave too."

I tighten my grip. "I need to talk to you about the extra boxes we found."

"Sol told me about them."

"Have you looked inside?"

"I've been kind of busy."

I smile. The fact that she didn't rush to open those boxes but spent all night by my side tells me a lot of things she'd probably never admit.

"Don't overthink it. I *had* to stay. If I didn't, your brothers and Sol were going to commit murder."

I shrug. "Even if they did, they wouldn't have gotten caught."

"You sound so proud of that."

"I don't make the rules."

"No, you just break them." She sighs. "I'm a teacher. I'm not going to sit back and condone a crime like murder."

"We can't just let him walk, tiger." I grimace as a wave of pain hits my head. "He crossed the line."

"Who said anything about letting him walk?"

I look into her beautiful brown eyes and see a glint of darkness. "What do you think we should do?"

"You're asking me?"

I wait, keeping my gaze steady on her.

She plays with a loose thread in the hospital blanket. "Hall is expecting a violent retaliation. If you give it to him, he'll be ready. Violence for violence is too expected."

"Your solution?"

"The best revenge is tailored to the individual, but it's all the same. You hit them where it hurts."

"And where is that?"

"His pride," she says. Her eyes flash to mine, locking deep and making my skin burn.

I see a glimpse of the Grey she keeps under lock and key.

The one who's fearless and daring and reckless.

Like me.

How did I not see it before?

"What?" She touches the back of her neck self-consciously.

Freaking hell, she's gorgeous.

"I want you so bad right now."

Her eyes widen and she turns her face away.

If I wasn't hooked to an IV, she would be naked.

But since I only have one working hand, I bring hers to my lips and kiss the back of her knuckles. "Okay."

"Okay?"

"We'll do it your way." I glance at Grey and wink. "We'll hit him where it hurts."

"Without breaking the law."

I slide my thumb over her cheek. "Tiger, I *am* the law."

She pouts.

Something weird starts battering around in my stomach. The hell? Are those... butterflies?

It gets worse the more she pushes out her lip.

"Fine," I grumble. "No breaking the law."

Finally, she smiles.

Seeing that lush mouth curl up drives me crazy. How often has Grey smiled at me? I can count the number of times on one hand.

I need that smile aimed in my direction.

Need it like I need air.

A phone rings.

I scowl. Who the hell is calling her this late at night?

"It's Dutch," Grey says, her eyebrows pinched.

I watch her answer the video call.

"How is he?" Dutch's voice sounds guttural.

"What has it been? Ten minutes since I kicked you out? Damn. Give me some room," I mumble.

Grey turns the phone so my scowl is in the shot.

Finn and Sol have also joined the video call.

"I thought those meds would have you knocked out by now," Sol says.

My eyelids are starting to droop, but I'll never admit that I'm tired. "Why did you call?"

"To check if you're dead," Dutch says.

"B.S." I glance up and see a shadow moving outside my room door. Quickly, I drag my eyes back to the phone. "Did you hire someone to watch me?"

Grey shoots a surprised look at the entrance.

"It's just a precaution," Dutch says. "If you don't want us there, fine. But we need to know you're safe."

They're so damn overprotective.

"About Hall," I meet Grey's eyes, "I've decided how to proceed."

They all lean in.

Sol asks eagerly, "What do you want to do with him first? Burn his house down? Drive his car into a river?"

I see when Grey flinches.

"We'll hurt him deeper than that."

Dutch purses his lips. "What do you mean?"

"I want him looking over his shoulder every day and night. I want him to beg for a ticket out of Redwood and never get one. I want him crawling on his hands and knees in front of us." The fingers of my good hand form a fist. "Willing to eat dirt, lick our shoes, do whatever we tell him because he knows the alternative."

"You want him humiliated," Finn says, getting it first. He always does.

"He's going to expect retaliation. He won't expect this. In the meantime, we get our weapons ready. When we bury him, we bury his family, everyone he cares about." My voice goes cold. "We don't start wars." I glance at Grey. "But we end them."

Dutch nods.

Finn gets a little gleam in his eyes. "I'll text Jinx. See what secrets I can buy."

Sol laughs softly. "This is way too refined of a plan for you, Zane. Did that knock in the head switch your personality?"

"Let's just say there's an angel on my shoulder." I smirk at Grey. "A pretty little angel of death."

She clears her throat and pulls the phone back. "All of you. Get some rest."

Her finger taps the 'end' button.

"You too." Grey looks sternly down at me.

Exhaustion is trying to pull me under, but my mind is strikingly clear. And the stern 'teacher' tone of hers really makes me want to get her naked.

"If you want me to sleep..." I pat the bed.

She glances at the space beside me and wavers.

The need to touch her is overwhelming but when I reach for her, she eases back. Her shoulders sink and I know whatever she says and does next will be to draw the line between us.

Her voice is strained. "Zane, about tonight... in the classroom, I—"

"You know what? I *am* tired." I press the button and my bed starts flattening.

Grey's eyes remain on me, cloudy and conflicted.

I close my eyes, but I can hear her soft, labored breathing.

In the darkness, I assure her, "I know what you're scared of, but you don't have to be. Nothing that happened tonight was a mistake and if I have to spend the rest of my life proving that to you, I will."

"I'll take it that the meds are talking and you won't remember a word of this tomorrow."

The meds have me feeling like I'm sinking into the mattress, but my mind is still sharp. In fact, the truth is clearer than ever.

Grey is mine.

She became mine the moment our eyes met in the bar.

She proved she was mine when I kissed her and every time I walked down the hallways and saw her in the distance.

She will always be mine.

But I have a feeling that convincing the world we belong together will be easier than convincing her of that.

Chapter Forty-Four

GREY

I'm not sure when I fell asleep but, somehow, I'm bent over the side of Zane's bed with my head next to his hand. It takes a few blinks to clear my vision and remember why I'm in the hospital.

The moment it all comes back, I jolt up with a startled breath.

I had no intentions of spending the night with Zane. What if someone sees? What if someone took pictures?

Self-preservation demands that I hide.

"Run and I will tear these IV drips out and drag you back," a deep voice says. The darkness inside me paces, head raised in anticipation.

I narrow my eyes at Zane. "Who do you think you're talking to?"

"A tiger that keeps trying to run away."

My shoulders stiffen. The way he speaks is so confident, so full of cockiness. I have no idea how he manages to looks intimidating even with all the bandages, bruises and IV drips.

Zane grabs my chair by the handle and slides me closer to his bed. I jolt forward, my elbows spiking on the mattress.

Zane leans toward me until his face is an inch away. He gives me a long, burning look.

"This is a problem," he breathes.

I blink slowly.

"I like waking up to you in my bed."

My head starts spinning and I steel myself against his dizzying charisma. "I didn't know bad flirting was a side effect of a head wound."

"Morning to you too, sunshine." He smirks. The curl of his lips does nothing to detract from his intense gaze.

I temporarily forget my annoyance when I see Zane's battered face. The bruises on his chin are more apparent now than they were under the cover of darkness. There's a scab on his lip and I'm sure it must hurt to talk, but that doesn't stop him.

"Did you know you drool?"

I quickly drag my fingers to my lips. "You're insufferable."

"Insufferable. I'm assuming that's not a compliment."

"You'd assume correctly."

"Throw the entire dictionary at me, tiger. Come on."

I roll my eyes and stalk around to the dresser to refill his water. "You have such a big ego."

"It's not ego if it's true." He looks pleased. "Keep talking smack. See if I don't steal another one of your panties."

My eyes widen at the reminder and I drop my gaze to his pants. Zane's mischievous smile tells me that he still has possession of it.

I'm about to launch at him and take it back by force when the door opens and the medical team enter. I ease out of the way and let the doctor have room. When they're done, I follow the team into the hallway and listen keenly to the doctor's assessment. The Kings will want a full detailed report and I don't want to leave anything out.

"His wrist *must* remain in that cast until it's safe for physical therapy. And even during PT, he should follow a careful regime. It's pertinent that he not over do it."

"I understand."

The doctor chews on his bottom lip.

"Is something wrong?"

"I sense that he's a headstrong young man and his brothers seem equally... stubborn."

"That's an understatement," I mumble.

"I feel I'll have to rely on you to keep Mr. Cross in line until his PT appointment."

"Me?" My throat tightens.

"Do everything it takes to keep him from taxing that wrist. This is the most tender period of the healing process and the damages could be worsened by overstimulation."

I dip my head.

The doctor walks off.

I return to the hospital room where Zane is with one of the nurses. She's smiling at him as she sets down a tray of food. I stiffen, waiting for the flirtatious exchange that I'm sure will come.

Zane can't help himself. His ability to seduce girls has been made abundantly clear. I see a different girl on his arm every day at Redwood.

But, to my surprise, Zane doesn't even throw the nurse a second glance. Instead, he sees me and juts his chin at the door in a silent order for her to leave.

Zane's attention remains locked on me as she stomps away. "What did the doctors say?"

"That you're terminally annoying."

He laughs.

My lips twitch, but I try to keep my expression severe. "Where are your brothers? I thought they'd be swarming the place by now."

"They must have gotten busy."

I stare suspiciously at him. "Did you tell them not to come?"

"Ow." Zane groans and touches the scab on his lip. "It hurts."

"I'm not buying that again."

He straightens and his blue eyes are dazzling. Their beauty hits me in a different way. It feels like I'm always looking into his eyes in the darkness. And in those moments, they're alluring and magnetic. But there's something about Zane Cross's eyes and sunshine that takes my breath away.

"Like what you see?" Zane says, easing back against his pillows like the hospital cot is a throne. His legs spread out and, for a moment, I imagine myself climbing into his lap and sinking into him.

Genuine horror fills me.

I glare angrily at him to cover it up.

"I'll call Dutch. Only your brothers have the patience to put up with you."

"Leaving so soon?" Zane slips his fingers down and pulls something out of his pocket. My eyes widen when I see the lace in his grip. "Class isn't over."

My eyebrows tighten. "Hand them back."

"Don't worry. I'll give them back to you. But first..." He juts his chin down at the food on his tray.

"What do you want me to do?"

"Feed me."

I scowl at him. "You've got to be kidding."

"Does it look like I'm laughing, Miss Jamieson?"

It would be so good to land one punch. Just one.

"As you can see, I only have one working hand—"

"You're right-handed. I'm sure you can get by."

The very corner of his lips inches up and I can't tear my eyes away. It's as if I'm watching a vampire right before he bites his victim's neck. I want whatever happens after that smile and I know I shouldn't. I know it's the absolute worst thing for me.

I'm still staring at his lips when he speaks again in a low, threatening voice. "You want me to beg, tiger?"

The world goes hazy. I can't even picture a guy as arrogant as Zane begging for anything. "Would you?"

He licks his lips slowly. I keep the moan inside as I watch the desire shadowing his chiseled face. "For you, I'd do something really freaking close."

"Do it." I lift my chin.

He meets my eyes again. "Feed me. Please."

Breath tightening, I walk over to the bed. "That was begging?"

"It was for me."

I clip the edge of the spoon between my fingers. "You better give them back."

He smiles devilishly.

The grin disappears when he tries to drink the soup and it irritates the cut on his lip.

"It hurts?" I ask.

"Not really," he lies through his teeth. This time, his discomfort is clear.

I get up. "I'll call the nurse and ask for a straw."

Zane grabs my hand before I can move. "I'm okay."

I sit back down and feed him the rest of the soup. He tries not to flinch too obviously, but he can't fake it. No matter how strong he appears to be, no matter how influential his last name, he's still human. Still vulnerable.

"Careful," I mutter, noticing the spoon is dripping soup on the bed. I cup my palm under it to catch the soup in my hand and then glance around for a napkin.

"I got it," Zane says. His thumb digs into my palm and he brings my arm up to his face. I gasp when he presses his lips into the center of my hand, tasting the soup with his kiss. Heat flashes through me, pooling at my core and reminding me of exactly why he's such a danger to my plans.

There's a hungry glint in his eyes when he whispers, "That tasted better than anything else on this tray."

I yank my hand away, but he holds fast.

Tension fills the space between us as he stares intently into my face.

Crap. My heart is doing a running leap in my chest.

"Zane..." I warn.

His voice is low, controlled, and commanding. "I know all the reasons we can't do this, but I'm drawn to you and you're drawn to me. No one can deny that. Not even you."

My nostrils flare. "I'm the adult."

"And I'm not a child."

"I'm so close to getting to the truth. I can't afford to make any mistakes."

"You think I'm your weakness, but you're wrong, Grey. Let me be your sword. Your poison. Let me be your revenge. Point me in a direction and I'll destroy whoever you tell me to. Everything you want, everything you don't know you want yet, I'll make it happen for you."

My breath hitches.

"But I won't let you escape me."

"Zane..."

He tips my chin up and leans down to draw our lips close together. The scent of him, his hot skin, his rough hands weave a spell on me.

"Run all you want, tiger, but you're trapped."

The sheer threat crouching in that silken caress of a voice scrambles my brain. Before I can think of a response, the door slams open.

"Zane!" A sharp voice bawls.

I whirl around, my eyes wide and my heart seizing.

It's mom.

Chapter Forty-Five

GREY

Every click of mom's high heels tapping the floor feels like a dagger to the chest. Her eyes are carefully trained away from me, but I can tell it's because she's trying to keep her facade in place.

Yesterday, I wore a mask to the dance and it allowed me to let my true feelings surface.

For just a second, I was free.

But mom?

She wears her mask twenty-four seven to fit into the new lifestyle Jarod Cross has given her. It's obvious, even with all the money and clothes, she's still so confined.

"Are you okay?" Mom rushes over to Zane. "Look at your face! Who did this—"

"I'm fine." Zane pushes himself to sit up.

I instinctually step forward to help him, but mom looks up with a sharp glance. It happens in seconds, but it's enough to drag me to a stop.

"How did you know I was here?" Zane asks, eyes moving to me as if he can sense my discomfort.

I stare at the floor.

"The hospital called Jarod, but he's not in the country right now, so he called me." She frowns. "What happened last night, Zane?"

"It was a motorcycle accident." The lie rolls off his tongue without a hitch.

"This is why I don't trust those machines." Her gaze sweeps to me and lingers. "When you go too fast on a road that's too dangerous, it's only a matter of time before you crash."

I swallow hard. "I should head out. Teachers have clean-up duty at Redwood today. They're probably texting and wondering where I am."

"Postpone the clean up. I need to speak with you."

Mom's eyes are stern. I haven't seen an expression that severe since I snuck out to attend a concert with Sloane and got caught climbing back in through the window.

"Let's talk in the hallway," mom says stiffly.

Zane gives me a long look and I can tell that he's ready to jump into the conversation. I shake my head slightly. He's a wild card. I have no idea if what he'll say will curb mom's ire or worsen it.

In an empty corridor outside, mom whirls on me. "Grace Jamieson, explain what I just saw." She points at the hospital room.

My eyelashes flutter. "What did you see?"

"You're not...?" Mom barks out a pained laugh. "I can't believe I'm even asking this. You're not *sleeping* with your step-brother, are you?"

A sharp stab of guilt slices through me.

Mom scans my face for the truth.

As her eyes drill into me, it gets hard to breathe. My nostrils flare as I take in a big gulp.

She lifts a hand. "Answer me. Are you sleeping with him?"

I lick my lips.

"There's only one right answer to that question."

I keep staring at the ground, trying to avoid her eyes.

She sees right through me. Her fingers on her head, she stumbles back. I try to stable her with a hand, but she shakes me off.

Black eyes filled with accusation, she stammers, "How long have you two been... doing *that?*"

I lick my lips.

"You haven't... it hasn't been since the beginning, right?"

I turn away, feeling the weight of the moment. The guilt is staggering.

Her face blanches. A slow, encompassing panic takes over her expression. "Oh my go—you have got to be kidding me."

Fear and panic swirl like a tornado in my chest.

Mom takes a step back, looking at me as if I'm a monster. "Gracie, how could you... how could you do that?"

I don't have the words to defend myself so I just clench my jaw.

Voice a cold croak, she orders, "Break it off with him. Immediately."

"There's nothing to break off."

That's the truth. Zane and I aren't dating, despite what happened in the classroom last night. He's... a bad habit, but he's not going to be in my life forever. We might be drawn to each other now, but this is a phase that will pass.

"That boy had your face in his hands and you weren't

pulling back either. In fact, you seemed to downright enjoy it."

I glance away.

"No, this won't do." Her eyes lift to mine. "I'll find you a nice boyfriend your own age so you can wake up and stop this nonsense." She pulls out her cell phone with trembling fingers. "Jarod introduced me to a nice young man last week—"

My reaction is instant. "I'm not going on a date, mom."

"Then what? Are you saying you want to be with an eighteen-year-old?"

"I'm saying that I'm not interested in dating anyone right now. And even if I was, I'll find someone myself."

"I can't trust your decisions. You clearly have terrible judgement."

"Maybe I got that from you," I snap.

I regret the words the moment they leave my mouth.

Mom goes completely still.

The stab of guilt in my chest turns into a giant icicle, shooting out of my heart and splintering into a thousand pieces.

Her eyes skate between mine, deeply offended. "What is *that* supposed to mean?"

Our emotions are running high and the tension is about to snap, but I can't let this opportunity go by without warning her.

"Jarod Cross. Something isn't right about him, mom."

Instantly, her lips tighten and it's like watching someone barricading a window for a hurricane. Totally shutting down.

"You told me not to be like those girls who fell for guys because they had money and no character, but what did you do? You fell for someone much worse than any of the guys who used to hit on me."

"Jarod Cross is *nothing* like those low-rate thugs in our old neighborhood," mom snaps.

"Why? Because he's white?"

Mom rolls her eyes. "This has nothing to do with race! Jarod is a respected musician, a philanthropist, and an advocate for the arts. He *happens* to be rich and I'm sure people hate him just because of his money."

"Mom, if you hear what he's done..."

"I will *not* listen to rumors." Her eyes are angry and bulging.

"You've been married to him for almost a year. Love? Commitment? Friendship? Do you have any of those? He barely looks at you. Barely spends time at home. He never calls you or checks on you. He's no better than a ghost."

"He's busy!"

"What about that night?" I hiss. "You saw the way he treated his sons. You heard him threaten me."

Her throat bobs and she glances away. "It wasn't a threat."

"Is that what you think? Truly?"

Mom throws her arm up, getting louder. It's what she does when she can't win an argument. She tries to talk over anyone who disagrees.

"What is this sudden vendetta against Jarod? You were fine with him until you got so close to Zane." She slices a furious look down the corridor. "Those boys are influencing you in the wrong ways, Grey. Since you started hanging out with them, you've become rude and disrespectful to your parents, and you've started a perverse relationship with your step-brother." She stops, collects herself and then says, "If you care about me at all, you'll go on the date."

"I'm sorry, mom. I love you. I will always love you, but you don't control me."

Her look of shock is quickly eclipsed by anger. "From the looks of it, you don't know how to control yourself!" Spittle flies from her mouth and I can see her eyes turning red. "A kid in high school is bad enough. A student is even worse, but your stepbrother? Your brother, Grace. Why? How could you do something so horrific?"

I don't point out that Zane is eighteen.

That I didn't know it at the time.

That he wasn't my stepbrother then.

I don't have any words to defend myself. No armor. No defense. I'm holding my own conscience together with the desperate belief that I truly did my best to resist him.

Mom stares me down. "For years, you were screaming about the injustice that happened to Sloane, but do you even have the right to defend her? You're turning into the very monster that you're trying to hunt down."

Those words crash into me, shattering my heart. I swipe away an angry tear and keep my mouth shut.

"Say something," mom hisses.

I inspect the ground instead.

Mom grabs my arms and shakes me. "Say something, dammit!"

"What can I say? You won't believe me anyway."

Her angry breathing rattles in the hallway.

I stare at her, my chest heaving.

"Do you really have feelings for that boy?" mom hisses.

My heart starts thumping in my throat. I inhale a deep breath as I try to form a sharp and resounding 'no'. But the word gets stuck in my throat, buried under the memory of Zane's touch as he held my hand at the cliff. His kiss as our broken souls found solace under the stars. I see him climbing over Hall and punching him into the ground. I trace the memory of his deep voice when he promised I belonged to him.

The smart thing to do, the *only* thing to do is to deny it.

The word 'no' is so close to my lips, I can taste it.

But my heart thumps faster.

And I can't say it.

I wish I could.

I really do.

Tears crop up in my eyes from the effort, from the pain, from the feeling that I'm being torn in a million pieces.

"Gracie, please—"

"I... don't know."

"You don't know?" Her eyes widen. "You don't... know if you have feelings for an eighteen year old?"

My chin hits my chest.

"Do you know the havoc that would wreak if even a whiff of news got out? Redwood Prep Teacher. Sex Scandal. At minimum, you'll be an outcast. At best, you could go to jail. Do you want your name smeared for all eternity? Do you want your freedom snatched away from you? Because that's what will happen if you keep fooling around."

I inhale a deep breath.

Mom huffs. "I can't look at you. Don't... don't talk to me until you sort this out."

My eyes widen.

Hurt crashes into my chest.

Beyond the pain, I see my chance at talking to mom about Jarod slipping away.

Fists clenched at my side, I struggle to regain control of the conversation, but there's no other way.

"Wait," I blurt.

She stops.

THE FORBIDDEN NOTE

My teeth sink into my bottom lip and I feel like I'm being submerged under water. Like everything is spinning out of my control.

"I'll do it."

Mom turns around. Her eyes fly to me. Surprise shimmer in their depths.

"I'll go on the date," I say tightly.

"Really?" Mom's voice climbs with hope.

"But I want something from you in return."

"You're not in much of a position to negotiate, Gracie."

I know I'm not.

But my deal with The Kings is important. They held up their end by getting me the boxes from Redwood Prep's basement. It's my turn to honor the agreement.

"I'm willing to go on the date... if you agree to have a real conversation about Jarod."

Mom goes completely stiff.

"I'm not asking you to divorce him, mom. I'm asking you to listen to me. The same way you want to save me from myself, that's the way I feel about you."

"I am a married woman. It's completely different," she argues.

"You're not happy and you won't admit it. How is that any different than what you're trying to get me to see?" I step closer to her and she moves back, clenching her teeth. "We both lost our way, but we can find it again. At least hear me out, mom."

Nostrils flaring, she takes a few seconds to think it over.

Finally, she nods. "Deal."

Chapter Forty-Six

ZANE

The door opens and I look up expectantly, but it's not Grey walking into my hospital room.

Dutch scowls when he notices my disappointment. "Nice to see you too, man."

"What the hell are you doing here?"

"You really think one text can keep us away?"

I scowl in his direction.

Dammit.

I know I shouldn't be around my brothers right now. Grey's fearful look when her mother walked into the room is imprinted in my brain. Not being able to protect her, to reassure her, is grating on my nerves.

I can't stand the thought that I'm stuck in this hospital bed with a dud wrist, while she tackles a hard conversation alone.

Marian saw us together. There's a possibility she put the puzzle pieces in place and figured out what's going on between me and Grey. Since it concerns both of us, I don't like that Grey is handling it by herself.

I've decided she's mine.

Whether she likes it or not.

That means protecting her, not hiding behind her.

Finn walks into the room and Sol follows. I'm grateful my best friend doesn't offer any smart-aleck responses as he takes the seat Grey occupied.

"How are you feeling?" Sol asks.

"Like someone bashed the back of my head in with a cement block," I mutter. "You?"

"Like I got jumped by three thugs."

"Where's Miss Jamieson?" Finn asks, glancing over his shoulder.

"Did she finally see the light and leave your crazy butt?" Dutch mumbles, sitting on the edge of my bed.

I kick him off.

He goes flying and whirls around to glare at me with glowering amber eyes.

I know if I keep looking at him, I'll break my other wrist trying to win a fight one-armed.

"Where did you put those extra boxes?" I grunt.

"They're at home," Finn says.

"Are you sure that's the safest place? Martina might clean up and see them."

Finn's expression remains blank. "In my room, they're safe."

I don't ask what he means by that. I just believe him. Finn might have a whole damn cellar in there and I wouldn't be surprised.

"Freaking hell," Dutch whispers.

We all glance up.

"Check your phones."

"What's going on?" I ask nervously.

My twin passes his phone to me. "We got a problem."

Dutch has the school app open and there's a bright red banner at the top of the screen.

Masquerade Ball Burglars Wanted

Beneath it is a write-up of our misdeeds last night—everything from the fireworks to the sprinklers to the way we blazed the basement. I feel a stab of fear when I see a smeary picture of me and Sol running in the hallway.

Finn looks up from his phone, a muscle in his jaw clenched. It's the tiniest of nods to his true feelings. "They're offering a reward."

"Money?" I snort. "Harris thinks anyone at Redwood needs—"

"He's offering bonus points."

I shut up.

"*And* money." Finn thumbs his fingers over the screen. "It's a double deal. Skin in the game for everyone. People are going to be all over this."

I squeeze the phone tightly in my hands, nearly crushing it to bits.

Dutch slips it away from me. "Cadey sent it. She's worried."

"This picture is too grainy. Plus we're wearing masks. There's no way he can tell it's us," I point out.

Sol crosses his arms over his chest. "It's still evidence, and if Harris gets enough students to point us out..."

An unsettling silence falls on the room.

Grey's case makes this threat feel bigger than any we've faced before. Whether or not we can wiggle out of trouble is one thing. Unravelling all of Grey's progress by getting caught is another.

I promised her that I'd exact her revenge.

I meant it.

That means making different moves. This is too grave, too important to act impulsively. Chasing death was fine when it was just me. Now, I can't shatter before giving her what she wants.

For a moment, I close my eyes and breathe.

When I open them again, I'm looking straight at Finn. "Did Jinx say anything?"

He shakes his head slowly. "Nothing yet."

"What does that mean?" Sol wonders out loud. "That she's not interested?"

"No." Finn shrugs. "It means she's probably gathering evidence."

My heart sinks, dragging my mood with it.

Sol starts to fidget. His eyes dart between me and Dutch. "If Jinx starts getting involved, she's going to be a problem."

"What do you want us to do, Sol?" I snap. "Kidnap Jinx? Kill her?"

Finn flinches.

Dutch growls at both of us. "Jinx isn't our problem right now. Principal Harris is."

I open my mouth, but someone at the door catches my attention.

Dutch picks up on my subtle chin-nod and goes quiet.

Finn turns to face the entrance.

Sol sits up straight.

We all stare uneasily at the police officer who rams his knuckles on the door and steps in. He's accompanied by another cop, a stockier guy with beady eyes and a bad haircut.

"Sorry to interrupt. I'm Detective Bradley."

No one answers.

The air turns chilly.

Bradley's gaze snaps between me and Dutch. "I'm looking for a Zane Cross."

My fingers dig into the bedsheets as I try to keep my cool. "And why are you looking for him?"

"I have a few questions."

Dutch steps around my bed and stands in front of me. Finn stretches like a cat waking from sleep and moves over to my side too.

Sol remains by the chair, but he's watching everything with a narrowed gaze.

I push Dutch to the side. Whether this is about Hall or about Principal Harris, it doesn't matter. I won't let anyone take the rap for me.

"I'm Zane," I say.

Dutch flashes me an angry look.

Finn just stays right where he is, arms loose at his side and yet tense, like a panther waiting to spring.

"Ah." Bradley taps his pen against his book. He glances at Dutch. "I need to speak with him in private."

"Is he a person of interest in a case?" Finn asks.

Bradley's eyebrows jump. When he looks at Finn again, it's with a hint of wariness. "No."

"Then we're staying," Dutch declares. "He just got out of surgery and we can't leave him alone."

"Very well." Bradley clears his throat and fastens dark brown eyes on me. I stare right back into them, making calculations of my own.

He's got a hardened face, the kind you'd expect to see on a jaded police officer. His hair is silver along the edges and his mouth is a sharp, slashing line above his chin. There's a no-nonsense air to him, but if he's someone in

THE FORBIDDEN NOTE

Hall or Harris's pocket, I wouldn't be able to tell just by looking anyway.

"Zane, were you at the Redwood dance last night?"

"Yes, so were half the kids in this city."

"And where were you around the hours of eight-forty to nine thirty-two?"

Behind me, Sol holds his breath.

"Me? I was under my girlfriend's skirt, giving her the time of her life." I'm irritated but my tone doesn't show it. A crap-eating smile tugs at the corner of my lips, disguising my true feelings. "She was being pretty damn loud too. Almost got us caught."

Bradley blinks slowly, staring at my face like he can tell I'm full of crap.

But I don't break a sweat. I'm really freaking good at acting like nothing bothers me.

"You were with your girlfriend at that exact time? Are you sure?"

"I wasn't looking at my watch, but yeah. I'm pretty sure."

He nods to his partner who opens up a book. "Can your girlfriend verify this?"

"She can," I say confidently. Dutch's shoulders start tensing. I stare the officer right in the eyes and add, "But before I drag her into this, what exactly are you questioning me for?"

He snaps the book closed. "You're aware of the fire that was set at Redwood Prep yesterday?"

"Yeah, I'd say we all got doused." I lift my wrist. "It was a crappy ending to a crappy night."

"Crappy night? Weren't you enjoying your time with your girlfriend?"

"I said I was doing her, but she never got a chance to

return the favor. As a feminist, I believe in equal opportunity." I finish the statement with a sly grin.

Bradley's face pinches. He jots something in his book and glances at Dutch instead. "And you are?"

"Out of patience," Dutch growls. "If you're done asking your questions, you need to leave."

Bradley stares long and hard at Dutch, taking note of his aggressive stance.

"And where were *you* yesterday around the time of the fire?"

"I didn't go to the dance," Dutch says.

Bradley's forehead bunches and a suspicious look enters his eyes. "I see. Can anyone verify that?"

"My brother."

"Zane?"

"Him." Dutch juts his chin in Finn's direction.

Bradley looks at Finn, looks back at me and Dutch and then eyeballs Finn again.

The stocky one with him snorts. "You three are brothers?"

I hear the sneer in his voice and I nearly swing my legs out of the bed to launch at him. "You have a freaking problem with that?"

Bradley grabs his partner's shoulders. "Thank you for answering our questions."

No one moves until Bradley is gone from the room.

Just as he leaves, Grey enters.

I sit at attention, noticing the way her eyes are red and puffy.

Was she crying?

The panic I feel looking into her face and seeing her upset cuts right through me. This woman is so freaking deep in my head, in my skin, in my soul that I feel her pain like it's my own.

"What was that?" Grey whispers shakily. "Why was the police in your room?"

"Whatever it is, it's nothing good," Sol grunts.

"Harris must already suspect us," Dutch says. "Why else would he send an officer to sniff around?"

Finn nods. "I think Harris already knows who set that fire. He's just looking for the evidence to take us down."

Grey lets out a shuddering breath. Her eyes glint with unease. "Well then… we better open those boxes and take him down first."

Chapter Forty-Seven

GREY

Zane's eyes cut through the room like lasers, hyper-focused on me. I know he's waiting for me to turn and acknowledge him, but I'm not going to do that.

My head is throbbing after that conversation with mom.

I can still feel her censure. Her frustration. Her disappointment.

She was... ashamed.

And there's something inside me that curls up and dies knowing she feels that way.

Zane is eighteen years old.

That's the truth.

That's reality.

Whatever I feel for him...

Whatever he feels for me...

Does it even matter? Is our forbidden story really anything worth fighting for?

I don't think so.

It's time I get my head screwed on straight. I keep snapping back and forth like a plucked rubber band, which is why I'm in this mess. If I'd held firm from the beginning, if I hadn't kissed him on that cliff or lifted my skirt for him in that classroom, we wouldn't have gotten this far.

It's up to me to bring some sanity to this madness.

I glance up and feel everyone watching me. Dutch, Finn and Sol all look mildly uncomfortable with the tension between me and their best friend. It doesn't help that Zane hasn't taken those blue eyes off me since I walked in here.

A wash of awareness hits my body, but I refuse to give into it.

Harris is breathing down my neck.

The police are involved and suspecting Zane.

It's all going to hell.

I need to focus on what's important.

I walk up to Finn. "Can I get a ride with you? I want to start opening those boxes and see what we're working with."

Finn doesn't answer. Instead, he glances behind me at Zane as if he needs his brother's permission before he takes me anywhere.

Annoyance flares in my chest.

"Fine. Dutch?" I arch an eyebrow in his direction.

Dutch lifts both hands. "I don't want to be anywhere near this."

"Near what?" I snap.

"Grey," Zane's tone is soft but firm. I can't tell if he's angry or annoyed by my cold shoulder. Either way it doesn't really matter to me.

I pretend not to have heard. "We need to move."

Zane growls again. There's no hiding the threat this time. "Woman."

I back away from the boys. "If Harris is suspecting you all, then that means he's suspecting me too. We're running out of time."

Still no response from The Kings.

They remain in position like they're posing for some kind of celebrity photoshoot. Finn with his almond-shaped eyes and regal bearing. Sol with his wild, curly brown hair and high cheekbones. Dutch with his amber eyes like an unfeeling psychopath.

And Zane...

Usually he wears an air of frivolity, always with a playful smile tilting his lips. But right now, he's all dark menace.

Even his brothers recognize it. None of them dares to step out of line.

Screw it.

I push the door aside. "Forget it. I'll find my own way."

I take one step into the hallway when I'm suddenly being hauled by the waist and spun against the wall. Zane's uninjured hand smacks inches away from my head.

"Such bad manners," he says into my ear and I jump from the nearness. He pulls back so he can brand me with a disapproving stare. "Didn't you hear me calling you, tiger?"

"Get back to bed."

"Only if you come with me."

I start to shove him and stop when I remember he's injured.

"What do you want?" I snap, my voice shaking.

He leans in a little closer and my heart pounds. The connection between us is undeniable. It would be so easy to fall into that whirlpool of temptation, but I can't.

"What did your mom say?"

"Nothing."

"Grey."

"What?" I put enough attitude in that word to scare off a horse.

Zane doesn't budge. "Are you okay?"

My ribs feel like someone is pinching them closed. My throat turns scratchy. "Of course. Why wouldn't I be?"

"You haven't looked at me once since you came back."

I zip my eyes up to his. "I'm looking at you now."

"Yeah." A smile touches his full lips. He strokes the side of my face with a thumb. "Yeah, you are."

His eyes are an impossible shade of blue. Turquoise waves and bright like the sun, and yet darkness spreads out from the center, swimming flecks of onyx that warn he's not as sunny as he pretends to be. The way he watches me is possessive and I should feel suffocated by it.

But I don't.

The door cracks open.

Sol calls out. "Are you decent?"

"Unfortunately," Zane says, pulling away from me. He turns to greet his brothers and Sol. "Take Grey home and get started on that search first. I'll check myself out of the hospital and meet you there."

I surge forward, nearly knocking into his chest. "Absolutely not. You have a head wound, several bruises, and a broken wrist. You need to stay here for *at least* three more days."

"I'm fine, tiger." He leaks a dazzling smile that would probably send half of Redwood Prep fainting. "But I like that you're worried about me."

I realize I'd spoken too vehemently and inch away from him. "I'm not."

"No?"

I backpedal. "As your teacher—"

"Oh? My teacher?" He prowls toward me.

"It is my responsibility to make sure you don't make stupid decisions." Halting to a stop, I speak intently, "You really shouldn't leave the hospital yet."

Behind us, I hear Sol murmur, "Like he'll listen to that..."

"Okay."

The soft thud of Sol's jaw hitting the floor is all I hear.

Even I'm surprised.

"Let's make a deal. I'll stay another night," Zane leans forward and whispers, "if you spend it with me."

I shove him back.

He laughs softly.

The gremlin.

My phone rings and I latch onto the opportunity to put some space between us.

Walking a few steps with the phone, I call over my shoulder, "Dutch, talk some sense into your brother please."

"Impossible," Dutch answers.

"You think he'd be this way if any one of us could tell him what to do?" Sol grumbles.

Finn just shakes his head.

I turn away from them and put the phone to my ear. "Hello?"

Mom's voice blasts my ears. "Grey, how soon can you shower and put on a nice dress?"

For a moment, her words scramble in my brain and make zero sense to me. "Why do I need to put on a dress?"

At the word 'dress', Zane stands to attention. His eyes

drag over me and I can feel it like a hand skating up my spine.

"I got in contact with a nice young man who made a very good impression last week when we met. He's available to meet you for lunch."

"So soon?" I croak. Sending a guilty look over my shoulder, I mumble, "Mom, we *just* had a conversation about that. Besides, I'm busy today."

Her voice snaps with heat. "If you miss this date, you can forget about our deal."

I chew on my bottom lip. It feels like I'm stuck in an hour glass and the sand is quickly filling to the top with no reprieve in sight. If I don't find a way to break free, I'll be buried.

"Are you going or not?"

I hesitate. Mom is high on emotions right now. I can't afford for our relationship to fracture any more than it already has. Not just for the sake of my deal with The Kings, but for my family.

"Okay," I mumble. "I'll get ready for the date."

Mom heaves a sigh of relief. "Perfect."

Chapter Forty-Eight

GREY

It feels like there's a cosmic push to keep me away from investigating Sloane's case.

First, I had to press pause when Zane got hurt and his brothers were three seconds away from committing murder.

And now, instead of driving to The King's mansion where I can safely sort through the files we stole, I'm heading to a downtown bistro in my nicest blouse and jeans to meet some random guy mom picked out for me.

My phone buzzes.

It's one of the administrators in the Redwood Prep group chat.

Has anyone seen Miss Jamieson today?

No.

Isn't she supposed to be here?

Someone give her a call.

A moment later, my phone starts buzzing.

It's the principal's office.

Hands trembling, I put the phone on silent and inhale a calming breath.

Harris isn't stupid. He'll be waiting for me to make a move against him. And if I don't have a strong net to trap him, he'll find a way to wiggle out and rain hell on me.

There *needs* to be evidence in those boxes against Harris and all the cronies who were involved in The Grateful Project.

If not, it won't only be my head on the block.

The Kings will be a target too.

"I don't like this," Zane growls, sitting at my right. He's wearing a fresh T-shirt, torn jeans and his signature military boots. With those bruises and his hair loose and falling into his eyes, he looks absolutely dangerous.

"You didn't have to come." My eyes drop to the sling cradling his wrist. "You should be in the hospital right now."

"And you should be anywhere but here."

"This is the only way to get my mom to calm down."

"There are other ways."

"Yeah, like what?"

He shakes his head. "She can dislocate my other wrist."

"She'd love to. Trust me. But even after breaking all your bones, she'd still send me on this date."

He runs his uninjured hand through his hair and makes a sound of frustration.

I glance out the window. Quietly, I admit, "Maybe this is a good thing."

The air in the cab shifts.

I know I'm playing with fire but I throw gas on the flames anyway because the only person who can draw a line in the sand is me.

"Maybe me and this guy hit it off. Mom knows me best

after all. It's possible that he's my future husband. Crazier things have happened."

Zane goes deathly quiet.

I glance over my shoulder and my heart lurches in my chest.

A dangerous look is in his eyes. "Try me, tiger. I'll marry you tomorrow."

My heart ricochets and I tell myself not to take it seriously. "What is *with* you brothers and declaring marriage like it solves everything?"

"It solves whether or not we have the right to be together."

"We don't have a right to be together. That's the whole point." I hear the frustration in my tone. "You're the king of Redwood. Sure. Fine. But you don't control the world outside of Redwood. In that world... there is no legal or moral grounds for us to stand on."

"I don't give a damn about laws and morals. I only care about you."

My moral compass is so damaged, so screwed up, that his words send a zip of electricity straight between my legs.

For the briefest moment, I consider throwing off restraint, climbing into his lap and kissing him like nothing else matters.

But I don't move.

"Like I said, you can survive breaking laws and moral codes. I can't. You won't be able to see me if I'm in jail," I snap.

"I'll wait for you to get out." He's half-smiling.

I don't smile back.

Zane is pushing hard on the defenses I have around my heart.

But us together?

It's impossible.

We both need a reality check.

I make my tone intentionally sharp. "What do you expect, Zane? That you and I get to walk into the sunset together? That this..." I gesture between us, "*thing* turns into love? A *real* marriage?"

"Why can't it?"

"That's not happening. That's never happening."

Slowly, he unclips his seatbelt, not breaking eye contact. He slides across the seat. "Should I remind you who this body belongs to? Because it sounds like you need a refresh."

I lift a hand and set it on his chest before he can put his weight on me.

My heart is beating loudly. "As far as I'm aware, I'm single."

"You're mine."

"You're too young for me."

"You're perfect for me."

I scowl. "You should date girls your own age."

"Is that what you tell yourself? That you should date someone your own age?" His fingers slide down the front of my shirt. "Because I don't think that's what you really want."

I twist my head and notice the cab driver staring at us.

Shoving Zane off, I quickly fix my shirt and tuck it back into my pants. My body is aching, desperate for more of his touch. "Control yourself. People are watching."

I'm not just talking to Zane, but to myself.

"Yes, ma'am," Zane says in that deep, mischievous voice that warns me that he'll never listen to instructions.

My skin prickles with heat everywhere his hands brushed and I cross my legs tightly.

Zane stiffens. "We're almost there."

I look out the window and notice the restaurant coming into view. My stomach tightens with nerves. "I hope this doesn't take long."

"Keep in mind that if he touches you, I'll beat his face into the pavement." Zane curls his lips up in a bitter smirk. "Just in case that isn't clear."

"You're going to beat him with one arm?"

"I don't need two arms to fight, tiger." He winks.

"You're that confident?"

"Come to my room tonight. I'll show you what I can do with only one hand."

I swallow hard.

The car stops.

Distractedly, I fluff my curls and take out my lipstick to reapply.

Before I can trace my lips, I suddenly find myself flat on my back with Zane hovering over me. He eyes me hard. "Who are you prettying yourself up for?"

"Zane..."

He frowns, his eyes two stormy pits of blue and gold. "I really don't want to let you go."

My heart is heavy.

Now that I'm here, looking up into the chiseled planes of his face and feeling the heat of his chest, I realize I don't want to go either.

Is that because I have real, sincere feelings for Zane? Or is it just because of the urgency I feel to get back to the investigation?

"I'm only here so my mom can calm down enough to listen to me. I'll take two minutes to apologize for wasting this guy's time and leave."

Zane considers it and then eases off me.

I think he's going to let me go when he leans in and gently brushes my lips with his own. It's only a quick flash of a kiss but I chase his lips down, searching for more.

His hand cups my face. The tender look in his eyes is mesmerizing. And unexpected. This rogue of a drummer with the tattoos, the blue eyes, and the thirst for danger is no longer hiding his affection. It's pouring out of him like a flood and it makes me breathless.

He taps my nose. "Consider that a taste of what will happen later. The sooner you leave, the sooner you can come back for more."

I poke his side, right where he got punched last night.

Zane doubles over. "Ow!"

"Stop messing around and go."

He scrunches his nose and sits straight up. "I'll be watching from here. This guy could be a psycho."

"He can't be worse than you," I mumble.

His finger teases the corner of my shirt. A reluctant smile on his lips, he nods. "At least you know it, tiger."

The cab driver glances at us. "W-we're here."

I ease out of the car on shaky legs. The sun is high in the sky and it beats down on my head. I can feel sweat gathering already.

I lift a hand to shade my eyes from the blaze and enter the restaurant.

I have no idea what mom told this guy about me but, after I break my date's heart I need to figure out a way to break Zane's.

Chapter Forty-Nine

GREY

"Grace Jamieson?" A man in a corner booth waves.

He's tall, wiry and wearing a sharp grey business suit. Small glasses, the kind that most would consider 'spectacles' dangles from the edge of his nose.

He seems nice, if a bit socially awkward. Unlike Zane, whose presence immediately fills up a room until it drowns everyone else out, this guy seems content to be a background character.

It's unfair to compare the two. Knowing mom, she'd pick the opposite of Zane's strong-willed, rebellious, and sensual personality. Plus, this is exactly the type of guy who seems likely to agree to a date the moment it's offered.

I plant my purse in the chair and sit rigidly across from him. "Hi, I'm Grace."

"Steven." He offers his hand and then pulls it back and wipes it against his pants. He offers it to me again.

I shake his hand firmly. "Steven, I—"

"I ordered for you." He jumps in before I can finish my statement. "I hope that's okay. They serve great sliders here And onion rings."

"Thank you, but I won't be staying long." I try to remove my hand from his.

He holds on, his fingers tightening ever so slightly as his voice creaks higher. "Why?"

I slip my hand out of his and watch the disappointment roll over his face. He seems so crushed that I feel a little guilty.

"Steven, what did my mother say to you?"

"She said you're a nice young lady who'd like to date with the intention of marriage." Steven adjusts his tie. His Adam's apple is prominent and I try not to stare at it. "I was so relieved to hear that. Dating these days is so confusing. You never know which way is up." He chuckles nervously.

I lift my lips in what I hope is an understanding smile.

Steven leans forward and says in a shy voice, "Don't take this the wrong way but the picture your mom sent me didn't do you justice. You're way prettier in real life."

Mom sent a picture?

I almost cringe in embarrassment.

"Thank you, Steven. You seem like a very nice man and I'm sure you're going to meet a very nice lady, but I don't think that lady is me." I grab my purse. "If my mother asks, please tell her that I showed up, but we weren't compatible. I wish you the best."

When I start to walk away, Steven jumps to his feet and grabs my hand. "Wait," he calls, "are you going to leave? Just like that? We haven't even had lunch."

"I have somewhere to be."

"Please," he begs. "Stay."

"I'm sorry, but I can't."

Steven's forehead bunches and he gives me another pleading look. "At least give me your phone number. We can set up another date."

"She said no," a voice barges in.

I glance up and see Zane standing at our table, one hand in a sling while the other is fisted at his side. What is he doing? Is he seriously thinking about fighting someone when he barely got out of the hospital?

"You're... you're Zane Cross!" Steven yells, his voice climbing in shock.

Zane pulls me behind him and stands in front of me. He looks Steven dead in the face. "Yeah? And who are you?"

"I'm Steven Winston. I'm a huge fan."

Zane grunts in response. Without wasting a second, he grabs my purse, hands it to me and reclaims my hand. "Grey, let's go."

"Wait."

Zane and I pause.

Steven's eyes are twinkling like stars. "Can I have an autograph?"

"We're in a rush."

"Please? It won't take a second."

Zane glances at me.

I shrug.

He sighs and spins around, extending a hand to Steven.

"I can't believe this is happening." Steven thumbs through his notebook. He no longer seems bothered by the fact that I'm ditching him. "I've been following your band for a while, long before I started working for your dad. I was hoping you'd drop by the campaign office but you never do."

THE FORBIDDEN NOTE

Zane signs with a flourish and hands it back. "Here."

He grabs my hand and tries to lead me away again.

I tug his hand back and glance at Steven. "Did... you just say campaign office?"

Zane turns slowly too.

"I'm not supposed to say," Steven looks askance at me and then back to Zane. "But I guess it's okay, since you're Jarod Cross's son."

I lean forward, something inside me warning that this moment is meaningful.

"Jarod Cross is running for governor," Steven whispers.

My skin starts crawling. Why would someone like Jarod Cross try to grab that much power? What more does he want?

Zane slides his fingers into his pocket and contemplates Steven's words. I notice the way he's still grinning like it's all a joke and I realize how good of a strategy that is.

Steven has no idea he's pumping us with confidential information and he doesn't seem uncomfortable with sharing more.

If it was Dutch, Steven would have clammed up and refused to say anything. But Zane makes everyone feel like a friend. He's open. Inviting. Like a wolf dressing as a sheep to make his lunch feel at ease.

A shudder runs down my spine.

In a way, that's more terrifying than someone who wears their menace on their face. Because you never know when that darkness will come out to bite you.

"Really?" I gasp, taking cues from Zane and putting on a show. "Did you know about this?"

Zane shakes his head.

"You seriously didn't know?" Steven looks shocked.

"I guess dad wanted it to be a surprise."

"Oh no. Did I let the cat out of the bag?"

"Let's sit," Zane says.

Sensing his intentions, I slide into the booth and he falls in next to me. Everywhere from his arm all the way down to his thigh press into me.

With him so close, I struggle to remain engaged in the conversation.

"When did you start working for my dad?"

"Can we eat while we talk? I'm starving," Steven says. He pushes the burger toward me. "Ketchup?"

"She doesn't like ketchup," Zane says, tapping his fingers impatiently on the menu. "Grey, you want me to order something else for you?"

"I'm good."

Steven observes the interaction. An uncomfortable smile cracks his lips. "You two seem really close."

"We're step-siblings," I supply.

Zane stares at me with displeasure, all the light in his blue eyes get sucked into a blackhole of disapproval. He doesn't like me saying that to others, but so what? It's the truth and it'll keep Steven feeling comfortable enough to talk.

Steven lets out a deep breath. "Right. I knew that. I guess... it's good you guys get along so well."

"Yeah." Zane leans toward me. A wicked smile blooms. "You can say we know each other *inside* and out."

Heat blazes over my face. Nostrils flaring, I squeeze Zane's thigh. Hard.

He flinches.

Before I can change the conversation back toward Jarod Cross's campaign, I get a phone call.

It's Cadence.

"Excuse me," I say, slipping past Zane to answer the call near the bathroom. Once I'm in the privacy of an empty corridor, I answer. "Did you find something?"

"We found more than 'something'." Her voice sounds shaky. "Miss Jamieson, you're gonna want to see this."

Chapter Fifty

ZANE

Dad is running for governor.

It's so freaking ridiculous that it actually makes sense.

His play for our inheritance.

The chairman of the board run.

Teaching at Redwood.

Berating us for 'ruining his image'.

It's like someone flicked on a lamp in a dark room, illuminating all the shadows. Scattered puzzle pieces. Magnets snapping into place. Shifting tiles. A master puppeteer. Dad was painting a different kind of picture. One I never would have guessed even if someone shot me in the face with the truth.

Jarod Cross wants to rule more than just the music industry.

"What do you think they found?" Grey asks, pulling me out of my thoughts.

I look at her and try to keep the worry from my face. Her

eyes are bright enough to burn and she's smiling nervously. This is a big moment for her and I don't want to ruin it by freaking out over dad's plan to take over the world.

Or at least this part of the world.

"Zane, you okay?" She arches a brow, her voice going soft with worry.

It's crazy the way she knows me so well.

The way she sees through my facade.

I almost slide over to her and give her another kiss. I know the only thing that would distract me from this nervous energy is unbuttoning her jeans and making her groan in pleasure, but I hold myself back.

Grey's still trying to keep me at bay and if I push too hard, too fast, I'm no different than that creepy Steven who couldn't take a hint.

I'll work her down.

It's just a matter of time until she's mine completely.

I shake my head. "I'm good. What do you think the guys found?"

"Cadey said it was something big," she adds. "That's good, right?"

"All we need is a thread that links Harris to The Grateful Project." I turn so my knee lightly touches hers. She doesn't pull away. "The fact that those boxes were kept hidden means they have ammunition we can use."

"I hope so," she breathes. "Harris knows we were involved in that fire. I've been fielding calls from the administration office all day. The police are involved too. We won't have many more chances after this."

Her knee bounces up and down and I set a hand on it to calm her. "No matter what, we're going to get your revenge."

Troubled brown eyes meet mine and it's a struggle to

stay in my corner of the car. Does she know how badly I want to wrap my arms around her? One look at those luscious lips makes me burn in my pants. With one flash of those deep brown eyes, I'd burn myself and the world to the ground.

Grey inhales a breath, visibly composing herself. "How did you feel hearing your dad is running for office?"

I shift around. "I feel sorry... to all the people who'll be dumb enough to vote for him."

"You think he could win?"

"He's definitely doing all the ground work." I stroke my chin. "It's surprising though. Dad isn't the type to wear suits and ties. I don't understand why he'd suddenly run for office."

"Do you think it's all connected? Him marrying my mom. Your inheritance."

"Probably." I tell myself to smirk, but my lips remain in a flat line. I can't find the energy to smile and pretend that this isn't ten kinds of screwed up.

"You're worried," she notes.

The skin under my cast itches. "I keep feeling like we're always one step behind."

She tilts her head, listening intently.

"What if that's not all? What if, with all this, we're still only seeing a part of the picture?" I mumble.

Every time it seems like we get a leg up over dad, he finds some way to reveal that he was holding the cards all along.

There's got to be a way to end this once and for all. I just don't know if *I* can be the one who makes it happen or if I'll inevitably screw it up like I always do.

A soft hand lands on mine. I glance down and realize I'd

been unconsciously scratching at my cast. Gently, Grey curves dark fingers around my pointer and sets it aside.

"We're going to win."

"You're so sure?"

"In the stories, the good guys always win."

My heart shrinks a bit.

Grey might be considered 'one of the good guys', but me?

I most definitely am not.

And that right there is what I'm most afraid of.

Because the villains... they always get close enough to taste it, but they never really end up with the happily ever after.

I follow Grey up the stairs into the house and note the heavy silence that hits us when we enter the living room. Boxes are scattered all over the rug. Stacks of papers form their own version of white-reamed skyscrapers. Energy drinks are crushed and piled in heaps, evidence of how boring this job was for my crew.

"You're finally here," Dutch says, drawing to his full height.

"Traffic was brutal," I say.

Sol is leaning against the wall, sipping on a beer. His eyes meet mine and then drop to my wrist. His gaze screams murder when he sees my hand in a sling.

"How's the wrist?" Sol asks. "You sure you don't want to go back to the hospital?"

"It's fine."

He purses his lips and takes another sip.

"What did you guys find?" Grey asks, stalking forward.

She lifts her purse over her head and then lets out a yelp of pain.

My eyes shoot straight to her and I realize her purse strap got tangled in her long, curly hair. I destroy the distance between us and stop her as she tries to yank the strap.

"Ease up, tiger," I growl. "You're going to tear your hair out."

"It's so annoying," she mutters.

I brush her hands away and gently unwind her hair from the purse. Easing my lips close to her ear, I whisper, "Be gentle. Even the strands on your head belong to me."

She shivers and twists her neck around. The brown of her eyes is almost completely overtaken by the black.

She wants me as much as I want her.

It's so damn clear.

"Ahem." Cadey coughs to get our attention.

Grey jumps as if she just got caught looking at me naked and whirls back around. If she had fairer skin, she'd probably be blushing. Right now, she's just fluttering her eyelashes and looking like she's suffering from heat stroke.

"W-what... I mean... you... on the phone... you said you found something," she says breathlessly.

"Is it about The Grateful Project?" I ask, moving over to the box that Cadence is standing by. "Does it have dirt on Harris?"

"You can say that," Cadey says.

"Okay..." Grey flips through the files. "What does that mean?"

I peer over her shoulder, pushing her curls aside so I can see into the document. It looks like a bunch of bank statements.

"What am I looking at?" I ask, whipping my gaze up to

meet Finn's. "Was this in the boxes we brought out of the hidden closet?"

My brother nods, his expression tight.

"I don't understand," Grey says. "This has nothing to do with The Grateful Project."

"You could say it's worse," Dutch growls.

"Worse than a group of grown men preying on scholarship girls for their own twisted pleasure?" She shuffles forcefully through the papers. "I don't think so."

"We don't have any evidence that Harris was involved in that," Finn points out.

Grey turns to the side and looks at Finn, frowning. "I know it was Harris who called Sloane that night."

"And that's all the proof you have on him," Finn says, slipping a thumb into his book to hold the page as if he doesn't want this conversation to last long. "But that," he juts his sharp chin at the documents Grey is crushing, "is a real bomb."

"Bomb?" She squeaks and lifts it to the light.

We both look at it again.

"Who's Cassandra Harris?" Grey purses her lips. "Her name is on all these statements."

"*That* is Principal Harris's ex-wife. She changed her last name back to her maiden name after their divorce, so this is basically a dud account. Except it's been getting some giant deposits." Cadey taps her finger against the file. The diamond ring on her hand nearly blinds me. "Guess from who?"

"The Grateful Project's donors?" Grey asks earnestly.

Cadey's smile sinks. "Not exactly..."

"We called around," Sol explains. "And asked a few questions. Turns out those deposits are from the parents of some of the richest bastards at Redwood."

"I cross-referenced with Jinx's app." Finn arches a brow. "The dates coincide with a bunch of major scandals that she wrote about."

"You're saying Harris was taking money from parents to quiet scandals?"

"Not just that. He was also taking money from the building funds account and from a bunch of scholarship programs," Cadey adds. "Which explains why they're so strict with the number of scholarship students that can attend." She exchanges a knowing glance with Sol. "Because someone has to get the money. And it's not a student in need."

Grey closes her eyes and a slow, almost maniacal smile crawls over her face. "It's not what I was hoping for, but..."

"But?" Cadey presses.

Grey smirks at me. "I can work with this."

Chapter Fifty-One

ZANE

Vi comes home from the sleepover at her best friend's house, so we clear up the boxes and try to act as normal as possible for her.

Thankfully, normal for us is leaving the girls to their own devices.

Vi is harassing Grey to feature in her makeup channel again.

I'm glad when I hear Grey agree.

One thing that became clear to me when we were sorting through the boxes is how much this investigation has taken over her life. She needs a break.

I retreat to the kitchen and try to open a bottle of beer. With one arm, it's damn near impossible to unscrew the cap. I'm thinking of getting a knife and hacking a hole into the cover when someone roughly jerks the bottle from me. I meet Dutch's angry eyes and watch as he tosses the beer and replaces it with water.

"You shouldn't be drinking with your meds."

"Whatever," I murmur.

Finn and Sol enter the kitchen next.

Finn is without a book for once and he's not reading on his phone either. Sol stares at me in that unhinged way he started doing after breaking out of the psych ward. It's like he's one traumatic event away from setting the world on fire.

"This is a planned meeting?" I glance from one stern face to the next. "You're not kicking me out of the band, are you?"

No one laughs.

They rarely do.

Well, Sol used to.

Before he went full Joker on me.

"What's up?" I ask nervously, taking a sip.

"Did you notice anything weird about those invoices we found today?" Dutch starts.

"No. Should I have?"

"They were duds," Finn says quietly.

My eyebrows climb.

"None of the numbers line up with the student IDs from six years ago. The receipts check out for real events the school was hosting. In other words, we didn't find anything shady in them."

I set my water on the counter. The smile is gone now.

No one speaks, but the quiet in the kitchen is damning.

I swing my head around to face Dutch. Looking into his dark eyes, I read everything I don't want to know.

"This is a dead end, Zane. It's impossible to take anything from those boxes except for the evidence on Harris's corruption."

My heart sinks and I almost feel dizzy.

"You want to abandon Grey's investigation."

"We have bigger things to worry about," Dutch says. His voice drops low. "Like Hall."

"The guy's about to pack his bags and head outta town," Sol says.

"How do you know that?"

"I followed him," Sol answers brazenly.

My eyes narrow.

He lifts both hands. "I didn't do anything to him. I just watched. Saw him packing his suitcases and driving out to his lake house. The guy knows he screwed up and he's spooked as hell."

"It's not just Hall," Dutch grumbles, setting a hand on the counter and leaning over. "If dad really is running for governor, that means we're in deeper crap than I thought. He's not going to let up when so much power is on the line."

"Dad is never getting that governor seat." I lift my chin, the darkest grin on my face. "And I'm going to make Hall bleed for what he did to me. That's not a question."

"No, *you* aren't going to do anything," Dutch says.

I stand straight and go toe-to-toe with my brother. "Want to bet?"

Finn comes to stand between us. He doesn't have to say anything, but we know he'll kick our butts if he wants to.

We both back down.

Sol laughs. "Nah, let them go at it. They need to get it out of their system."

My nostrils flare and I try hard not to show my disappointment. "Why'd you make that kind of decision without me?"

Finn's expression is carefully blank. "Dutch is concerned about Cadey. He doesn't want to bring a baby into a situation where dad has an even tighter grip on us. We need to focus on what's important."

"And who I want to protect isn't important?" I hiss.

Dutch folds his arms over his chest. "We know you like Miss Jamieson, but..."

"But she's not my wife so she can go to hell?"

"That's not what I said."

"Screw that!"

Dutch's eyes flash. "Are you really serious about her this time, Zane? Because I remember you were messing with other women even after that night you guys hooked up."

"And you weren't banging Christa *and* Paris while you were trying to get with Cadey?" I snap. "So should I assume you weren't serious about her then?"

A muscle in his jaw bunches.

Finn's eyes slice through me and then Dutch. "Enough. We shouldn't be turning on each other."

"No, let them..."

Before Sol can get the rest of his words out, Finn gives him an evil eye.

One corner of Sol's lips arches higher than the other, but he shuts his mouth.

"Something has to give. I'm not saying we don't help Miss Jamieson out if she calls on us," Finn assures me. "And I'm not saying we won't be there for her. She's important to you, so she's important to us. It is what it is. But we can't go any further with her. Diving headfirst into something she hasn't been able to solve in six years is not the best use of our resources."

"We had a *deal*," I whirl on Finn. Nose to nose, I confront him. "We promised we'd help her."

"No, we promised we'd get those boxes for her. And we did." Sol gestures to the living room.

I flip him off. "Shut up, Sol."

"Am I the only one who cares that Hall jumped us and broke. Your. Freaking. Wrist? *That* should be the priority right now. Not this crap."

"Sol is right," Dutch says, his tone firm. "We've got other priorities. Besides, we've paid our price. She's the one who needs to pay hers." I open my mouth but Dutch cuts me off when he says, "Cadey took a pregnancy test this morning."

The world stops spinning for a second.

My throat closes up. "Did it... is she..."

He shakes his head. "She thought she was. Apparently, she took one after our wedding too."

Sol glances away, his focus on anything but Dutch.

"She *was* throwing up that day," Finn mutters.

I remember that day like it's imprinted in my mind. My twin was getting married. How the hell could I forget? And Cadey looked pale as hell thrown over the toilet like that.

Dutch explains, "We went to the hospital. Asked why we're having trouble. The doctor says it could be stress."

My heart jumps to my throat.

"All this crap with dad and Miss Jamieson and The Grateful Project, it's not good for her. We need calm. We need stability."

Two things we've never been afforded.

Money? Fame? Girls throwing their panties at us? We've got a whole lot of that.

But life being incident-less?

Not so much.

I hear what my twin isn't saying.

Cadey comes first.

She always has.

Always will.

That's the price of falling in love with someone.

But the damn problem is that Grey comes first for me too.

"Grey is bleeding for this. She's hurting too." I meet my brothers' eyes. Each of them. Even Sol. "I know Hall is a problem. I know it's dangerous. And I don't give a damn. I'm not walking away until she's had her fill of revenge."

Dutch pulls his lips into his mouth. He looks like he wants to choke me.

Finn's entire face shuts down. He's never been great at choosing sides, which is probably why he prefers to stay out of things.

Sol has on the darkest expression I've ever seen on a human being. If I didn't know him so well, I'd probably be scared.

"Are you saying you're not going after Hall?" Sol asks, teeth gritted.

"I will. Eventually."

He lets out a snort of laughter.

A long silent moment passes where no one moves or says anything.

Finally, I crush the quiet with my words. "I understand. You protect Cadey and Vi. I'll protect Grey. I'll keep you out of it until I really need you."

Sol grimaces, jerking away as if he can't stand to look at me anymore. "He's gone insane over a woman."

Maybe I have.

Maybe I'm making another reckless, impulsive, stupid decision.

But Grace Jamieson is going to be mine even if it dooms me to death.

Which, now that I'm essentially backing her up alone, it just might.

Chapter Fifty-Two

GREY

"Is everything okay with you?" I ask Cadence as Vi skips up the stairs. She's going to research the best foundation for my 'mocha-brown with a hint of red' skin.

Since the boys are in the kitchen having their intense pow-wow, it's just me and her.

"Marriage is a big deal, even for folks much older than you. And to deal with that and school and your mother passing away…"

Cadence's lips start twitching and tears enter her eyes.

The moment I see her about to cry, I jolt out of my seat and cross the lavish room. "What's wrong?"

"I don't know. I'm fine. Really. I am."

I wrap my arms around her and give her a little squeeze. "It's okay."

"I know it is." She lets out an embarrassed laugh. "I have no idea why I'm being like this."

I give her shoulders a rub. "You're carrying a lot."

"Not as much as you." She sniffs and looks up at me with the sweet, innocent gaze that brought Dutch Cross to his knees. "You lost your best friend and had to go undercover at Redwood, dealing with Harris and Hall and all that crap. That must suck."

"Okay, so we're both having a sucky time right now."

She lets out a shaky laugh.

I notice that she's calmer and ease away. "You good now?"

"I am." She purses her lips, looking thoughtful. "These tears aren't what you think. I'm not sad that mom died. I'm just nervous about whether or not someone killed her. If they did, if it was really Jarod Cross like they're all thinking, what does that mean for Vi's safety? If anything happens to my sister..."

"It won't," I say firmly.

She gives me a hopeful look.

"I might not know Dutch that well, but I know one thing. He loves you and he'll protect you and your sister with everything he's got."

"I believe that." A smile warbles on her pink lips. "Honestly, I don't know how I would get through it without Dutch. He's been so amazing to me. Sometimes, I wonder how anyone can be that focused on one person."

"Dutch has tunnel vision," I agree, thinking back to all I've observed of him. From his very first day back at Redwood, the guitarist was following Cadence around.

"I think Zane has tunnel vision too," Cadence says, wiping her eyes and giving me a grin. "It's just that he goes about it in a different way."

And that's my cue to change the subject.

"Why do you think we didn't find any more evidence on The Grateful Project?"

Cadence pops an eyebrow as if she knows exactly what I'm doing.

I stoop down and lift some of the documents, shifting the tone of my voice. "Something doesn't feel right."

"Maybe the numbers you found on that old invoice was a coincidence?" Cadence stoops beside me and brushes her long brown hair over her shoulder.

I stick my tongue into my cheek. "Maybe."

My phone rings.

It's mom.

"How did the date go? Are you still with him?" Excitement rings in her voice and I hate that I'm going to have to crush so many of her dreams.

"No, mom."

"Why didn't you call me as soon as you were done?"

Zane and his brothers enter the living room. I can feel his gaze, this heavy, dark caress that glides down my body and makes me want to do all the things I shouldn't.

It's terrifying that he can make me feel that way when I'm on the phone with my mother.

"I was a little busy. I didn't plan to have a date today, you know. There was a lot to catch up on."

Zane is clearly studying me and listening to my conversation with mom as if he's waiting for me to say something that will give away my true thoughts.

I keep my voice level and give him nothing.

"I'm busy right now. Can we do this later?"

"No."

"Mom."

"Now, Gracie."

"Fine. I'll talk to you at home." I hang up and climb to my feet. "I should go."

Zane lifts his head to look at me and I have to work to control my breathing.

"Thank you, guys." I gesture to the boxes. "I'll have to ask you to keep this here. I don't think they'll be safe anywhere else."

"Of course," Dutch says.

"I know this is where your agreement ends and mine starts." I notice Zane frowning when I say that, but what does he expect? That The Kings will be at my beck and call just because he wants to screw me one more time to get it out of his system? I'm not a high school student. I'm an adult. I'm not that naive. "Is there anything you can give me on Jarod Cross? Any specific evidence?" I arch an eyebrow. "Murder, theft, drugs..."

Dutch flinches. "If you're talking about suspicions, it's yes to all the above. There's nothing he hasn't done."

"I can't convince my mom on theories."

"You'll have to try," Dutch grunts.

I sigh heavily. They're not making my job easy, but I remind myself that it wasn't easy for them either.

"Okay." I lift my phone. "I took pictures of all the evidence against Harris. You guys can keep the originals."

Sol leans against the wall, watching me with this dark, twisted gaze. "What are you going to do with it?"

He's smiling, but it's not a very nice smile. His brown eyes gleam with a kind of maniacal viciousness.

I consider him for a long moment. Sol was the most insistent about attacking Hall, an observation I brushed off that night because he was—technically—bleeding and bruised from being attacked first.

But the way he's gleefully watching me, waiting for me to destroy someone's life, I get the feeling his sentiments about revenge against Hall weren't a reaction to circumstances. They were an outlet for the rage already simmering under his veins.

"These bank statements aren't the evidence I want, so it'll have to be a bargaining chip."

"You could just send Harris off the chess board now," Finn points out. "It's enough ammunition."

"Harris is a pawn. I want the real culprits and he knows who they are." I slip my phone into my pocket and nod. "Thank you, guys for your help. I'll take it from here."

Zane follows me to the door, frowning. Hard. "Harris is scrambling to cover his tracks. Desperate people are the most dangerous and unpredictable. You shouldn't do anything alone. Tell me what your next move is before you make it."

"I can handle myself." I reach for the door.

He closes it tightly. "You can, but you don't have to, tiger." Zane steps in closer, towering over me. I sometimes forget how ridiculously tall he is. Even so, I'm not intimidated by him.

"This is my fight. My war. I already dragged you and your brothers in too deep. It's not your responsibility to clean up my mess."

"What if I want to?" he whispers.

My throat gets tight and I glance away. "And what if I don't want you to? Which one of us will win?"

His fingers close around my chin and he turns my face so I'm looking at him. "That's easy. Me."

I frown.

He smirks at me, cocksure and arrogant. "I always get what I want, tiger." His fingers cup the back of my neck and he pulls me in, his lips a breath away from my face. "You're not going to be an exception."

It's disgusting how tightly my body clenches, in need of his touch.

I don't want to be this way.

I don't want to burn for him the way I do.

Whatever darkness is inside me gravitates to him.

Zane drops his hand without kissing me and I have to throw my hand against the wall to keep from grabbing him by the shirt. I don't trust my own body to stay away from him. It's like he's taken control of my hands, my feet, my heart.

Lifting my gaze to his disturbingly blue eyes, as alluring as the monsters that sang sailors to their deaths, I realize that if I want to win any other fights in my life, I have to get him out of my system.

"One night," I croak.

He looks down at me, understanding snapping through his face almost instantly. A cold sneer chases away the burning passion from only a second ago.

"Just one?"

I dip my chin slowly. "You can have me for one night, but after that, I never want to see you again."

Chapter Fifty-Three

GREY

I stumble woodenly into the large kitchen and set my house keys on the counter. My head is in a daze and I curl my fingers tighter around the keys, accepting the pinch of the metal digging into my palm.

It's a perfect distraction from the stormy thoughts in my head. I shove it in deeper, trying to see how much of the pain I can take before I fold.

Idiot.

Zane coldly shoving me away was *not* the reaction I'd expected to my proposal.

The anger that descended on his face sent a shiver down my spine. And then he laughed and it was this sound that was so frightening, so dark, that I knew I shouldn't have opened my mouth in the first place.

It was already nerve-wracking to make the offer.

Now it feels like I just scratched at a wolf.

What is the monster going to do next?

I don't want to know.

I wish I could walk back the past forty eight hours and avoid him completely.

Pushing my hand over my face, I scrub in frustration.

The air around me shifts.

Silence screams loud, crowding around me, pressing in on all sides.

Something feels... off.

"Mom?" I call, noticing for the first time that the house is completely dark. Shadows crawl along the floor like imps released from hell. The place is cold. Mom likes the thermostat set to 'balmy day on the beach'. She'd never let the house get this morgue-like.

I send mom a text asking where she is.

A noise comes from the kitchen.

"Mom?"

"Your mother's not here," a deep voice says.

I shriek and whirl around.

Jarod Cross stands in the kitchen entrance, looking tall and pale. He's wearing all black, reminding me of a vampire from an old horror film, a supernatural killer come to life with nothing but ice running through its veins.

The light flicks on and Jarod Cross looks at me with exaggerated concern.

I snap my mouth shut, aware of how silly that scream made me appear.

"Sorry, I didn't mean to scare you." He lifts his hands in a placating gesture.

"Well, you did," I snap, noticing the way his eyebrows hike over his perfect forehead. Jarod Cross doesn't have many wrinkles and I can't tell if it's from a killer skincare routine or just spending most of his life not smiling.

"I heard you yelling and hurried downstairs. I'm sorry if

THE FORBIDDEN NOTE

you were frightened." His words are caring. Almost exaggeratedly so.

It reminds me of the way he is with mom when he's trying to calm her down after weeks of not talking to her. As if a few sweet smiles and a little attention can cancel out all the ways he's hurt and neglected her.

"Where's my mother?" I ask, not bothering to hide the accusation in that question. If he harmed her in any way, I'm going to tear him limb from limb.

"She went shopping for groceries. She said there wasn't anything in the kitchen for dinner tomorrow."

Almost as if he summoned it, my phone starts buzzing.

It's a reply text from mom.

Jarod came home tonight so I'm making a quick run to the grocery store.

My fingers tighten over the phone. Mom is like a kid at an amusement park when she visits the store. She can spend *hours* in there. I have no idea what she's doing half the time. How hard is it to grab a couple items and check out?

Jarod's long-legged stride carries him toward me. He moves with the grace of a panther. Light on his feet and yet, somehow, you know it won't take a minute for the claws to come out.

"I'm glad I caught you, Gracie. I've been meaning to have a chat."

"My name is Grace." I lift my chin, scowling. "Don't call me Gracie."

He does a little chuckle, but his eyes are rock hard. "Sorry. Grace."

"What do you want to talk about?" I fold my arms over my chest, keeping my voice carefully neutral. Internally, I'm taking stock of the kitchen for weapons.

Murder.

Drugs.

Who knows what else he's involved with?

Zane and his brothers believe their father is capable of the worst evils.

I can't take any chances.

"Shall we go to the living room?"

I shake my head. There aren't knives in the living room. "I'd rather we stay here."

Jarod studies me like he's trying to find the right words.

"First, I wanted to apologize for what happened that night at dinner."

My shoulders get tight as he glances my way, his mouth forming a thin line. "I let my anger and frustration at the boys get the best of me. I shouldn't have spoken to you like that."

"You threatened me."

His eyes widen and he gives me a look of dazed innocence. "I definitely did not."

"Do you think I'm stupid?"

His eyes narrow. "Grace, I care about you as if you're my own daughter."

I let out a snort of laughter.

"You don't have to believe me, but at least believe your mother. Do you think Marian would continue to stay with me if she truly thought I was a danger to you?"

No, I don't think that mom would do that intentionally. But I know firsthand how easy it is to make stupid decisions in front of the guy you have feelings for.

You can have me for one night.

My insides twist and I feel sick to my stomach.

This is so freaking messed up.

Jarod Cross takes another step forward and stops in the

sliver of moonlight falling through the window. His broad shoulders and lean waist make him look like a star even when he's just breathing. Just existing. It's like he was made to be adored, worshipped by millions.

All the Cross brothers have that effect.

Especially Zane.

An otherworldly charisma that drives women wild.

"You're starting to hurt my feelings." Jarod Cross leans a hip against the counter, his tone slightly coaxing. "As an educator, shouldn't you hear the other side before you form an opinion?"

"You're saying that you have nothing to do with Cadence's mother dying?"

He laughs. "Those boys." As if he's talking about misbehaving toddlers, Jarod says, "I never met the woman. Why would I be involved in a drug addict's overdose? Wouldn't the cops have arrested me, at least questioned me, if I were guilty?"

"The rules don't apply the same to those in power."

His lips crook into an enigmatic little grin, and it reminds me so much of Zane that I temporarily lose my breath. "I can't argue with that, but not even Jarod Cross is above the law. Especially right now."

"Does my mom know you're running for governor?"

His eyes flash to mine. I watch him twist his wedding ring around. "Of course. I don't keep secrets from my wife."

I cringe because I don't believe that for a second.

"Does your mother know the rumors about you and Zane?"

Finally, he's showing his true colors and playing dirty.

I get a little more comfortable. For a minute there, when he was defending himself so earnestly, I almost wavered.

"I've noticed that you don't seem bothered by those

rumors at all. Given you're Zane's father and I'm his teacher, shouldn't you be asking me a different question?"

His lips curl up, almost as if he didn't expect that kind of a comeback. When he glances at me again, it's with a little more respect.

Silence descends as we size each other up.

The rich, powerful rockstar.

The Redwood teacher, born of poverty and grit.

"This is what you wanted, isn't it?" I speak dryly. Absolutely calm. Devoid of all emotion.

I've noticed that Jarod Cross loves it when mom acts on feelings. Snapping at him when she's angry. Forgiving him when she's happy. Fawning over him when she's thankful.

Emotions are his sign posts, akin to an X-ray showing all his opponents' thoughts. He's carefully constructed himself to reveal nothing, while taking in everything around him.

I can't win any of his mind games unless I'm equally in control of my emotions.

Mimicking his posture, I press my elbows on the island. "It didn't have to be her. It could have been anyone, but you chose mom. You sought her out. You observed her. You seduced her and then you married her, but it wasn't for love, was it?"

Jarod Cross smiles and a shiver takes over me. I prefer it when he's frowning or obnoxiously blank. This smile feels too close to his true self and that level of darkness, of evil, goes much deeper than anything I've seen out of his sons.

The tainted smile disappears quickly, as if he let the mask slip out of place by accident and he just remembered to set it back.

"Contrary to your belief, I do love your mother. No amount of ambition can stop love." His lips curl up and his eyes flash knowingly. "You, of all people, should get that, Grace. Having a mission, a purpose you want to protect so badly and yet giving one person the power to destroy everything you've been building towards."

My heart pounds in my chest as he holds me captive, a prisoner to his gaze.

"What do you want?" I whisper tightly.

"What does any parent want from their child? To be respected, to be understood and appreciated." He straightens to his full height and nods. "You took the boys' judgement of me and ran with it, but you missed the truth."

"And what is the truth?"

He walks until he's right in front of me. The custom cologne on his skin swirls around me, making me want to choke.

Eyes darting between mine, he whispers, "I am not a bad guy."

"Good guys don't go around saying that. Only the bad ones do."

He chuckles and puts a hand on my shoulder. The pressure makes me wince. "I love your mom, and I want to be with her. I also love my sons, despite what you—or they—might think."

"You have a funny way of showing it," I say, my voice trembling a bit. Jarod Cross is a walking, talking force of nature. Standing so close to him, I realize how easy it would be for him to turn his hand and snap my neck.

He drops his hold on my shoulder and steps back. The easy grin, the one that doesn't quite reach his eyes, touches his lips. "Do you know where I was before I came here?" He doesn't wait for me to tell him I don't care. "At Redwood, in Harris's office."

"Harris?" I gasp.

"The police concluded their investigation and found evidence that my boys broke into Redwood and stole some things from the basement."

His stare turns hard and I glance away.

"It took a lot of convincing for Harris to not expel them all, but I made it happen. Tomorrow, they'll go to school and it will be like nothing ever happened. I did that... for them. Fully expecting that they won't care or even thank me."

My mind races. If Harris has evidence on Zane, Finn, Cadey, Sol and Dutch, that means he knows about me too.

There's no way I'll last another day at Redwood.

Tomorrow, when I go to school, it'll be the end.

"I need to go," I mumble. My head is already a thousand miles away as I think about what I should do next.

I'm halfway to the door when Jarod Cross calls me back.

"My friend found something."

I freeze.

"About The Grateful Project," he adds.

I turn slowly, my breath coming in sharp bursts.

"He thinks the man who went to jail for murdering your friend wasn't the real killer."

My heart pinches and I stumble forward. "What?"

"I've arranged an interview for you at the prison." He tips his chin up. "If you still want to accept my help."

"How? I've been trying to get an interview for years. Sloane's killer... he never wanted to meet with me."

"He will now."

"What's the catch?" I challenge.

"Believe in me." Jarod Cross smiles. "I'm already on your side, Grace. I just want you to be on mine."

The sound of the garage door lifting interrupts us.

A few moments later, mom enters the room.

"Gracie! You're here."

"Let me help you with those bags," Jarod Cross says, moving over to mom.

As they shuffle around me, I hurry to the bathroom and lock the door. In the stark light, I lift my hands and see that they're trembling. A stain of blood rushes over my skin, covering brown with dark, metallic red.

I know it's not real.

I know.

But it doesn't stop the panic.

Is it true? Is Sloane's real killer still out there?

A shudder runs down my spine when I think about that night we almost got run off the road. What if they weren't targeting The Kings? What if they were targeting me?

That means I have more to worry about than just losing my job.

I could lose my life.

For a second, I let the panic take over, dragging me underneath until it feels like I'm drowning. And then I grip the sink, splash cold water on my face and reach for the unshakeable drive that pushed me to apply to Redwood in the first place.

I died with Sloane.

My body's in that coffin with her and it has been since the moment I decided to bring her to justice.

I'll do whatever it takes to expose the truth.

Even if it means turning my back on Zane, betraying The Kings and making a deal with the devil.

Chapter Fifty-Four

ZANE

Getting ready for school with one arm is freaking torture and I give up on the second button. I hate those corny plaid uniforms anyway. Reaching for a wifebeater and my cut jeans, I shove them on and stalk downstairs.

Cadence is there, making breakfast along with Martina. She's already wearing her school uniform, a light blue blouse with a bow around the neck and a plaid skirt.

I feel a twinge of guilt when I think about her having trouble getting pregnant. We're all counting on them to make a baby before the will expires, so we can keep dad from putting his hands on our inheritance. Cadey is well aware of that.

The pressure to get pregnant could also be the culprit to her stress.

Vi is slurping down orange juice. Her eyes light up when she looks at me. "The bruises are going down. You don't look like a rotten apple anymore."

"Wow. Thanks." I fall into a chair, drag her OJ over to me and drain the rest of it.

"Hey!"

I burp. "Thanks, kid."

Finn emerges from the stairs, his eyes slightly swollen. I notice the puffiness and chuck my chin in his direction. "What happened to you?"

He ignores me and pours himself a bowl of cereal.

Dutch is the last to emerge. He's in a pressed uniform and tie, looking like one of those yuppies we always made fun of. He's been conforming more to the rules since marrying Cadey, but nothing can hide the lawlessness in his eyes or the ink all over his arms that screams 'rule-breaker'.

They say marriage changes a man, but I don't think Dutch is changed. He's just controlling himself better. The monster, the animal, is still prowling around, albeit on a tighter leash.

The married couple meet on opposite ends of the counter.

"Brahms."

"Dutch."

They exchange a heated look filled with sexual tension, and I groan.

"Can you not eye-flirt before eight a.m? It's nauseating."

Dutch flips me off and then drags out the seat next to me. Cadey brings him a plate of eggs. He grabs her hand and pulls her into the seat next to him. "You should be off your feet. Let Martina handle breakfast."

"I'm okay. I wanted to help."

He scowls so hard, I'm sure it'll be a permanent part of

his face soon. The guy's so protective of Cadey she can't even take a piss without him there.

Finn sits across from me. "How did Grey's conversation with her mom go?"

"I haven't checked," I say, reaching for an apple.

"You haven't texted? Or called? Or followed her around like a puppy?" Cadey teases.

I'd flip her off too, but one look at Dutch tells me I'd just as soon lose the finger.

Finn smirks.

Dutch gives me a pointed look. "Did you two have a fight?"

"No."

Vi snorts. "Look at his face. They totally did."

I glare in her direction. This house was a lot more peaceful when there weren't so many girls in it.

Martina slides a plate of eggs toward me.

I thank her with a nod, but I don't pick up my fork. Talking about Grey takes away my appetite.

You can have me for one night, her whispered words echo.

The memory of her body brushing against mine, her sweet perfume filling my senses, her eyes glistening as she dangled that stupid carrot cuts under my ribs. I'd have crushed her against the wall and had her bawling my freaking name in seconds if she hadn't said what she said next.

And then I never want to see you again.

Everything we've been through, everything I've ever done for her went completely over her pretty little head. She thinks I'll be done with one screw? One torrid little affair where I rub her and touch her and sink into her tight body only to what? Never speak to her again?

THE FORBIDDEN NOTE

Hell, I'd get drunk on her for eternity if she wasn't so damn stubborn.

"Who'd have thought that Miss Jamieson is so good at playing hard to get?" Cadey muses, spreading jam on her toast. "It takes a special kind of girl to resist Zane for this long."

"What is that supposed to mean?" Dutch growls.

I run a hand through my hair and flash Cadey a grin that's melted tons of panties. "You think I'm irresistible, Cadey?"

"Rub that stupid grin off your face, Zane." Dutch grips his knife in red-knuckled fists.

Cadey laughs and rubs her husband's chest. "I think you're the hottest guy in this room."

"You better," Dutch says, finally dropping the knife.

"But," Cadey adds, "you have to admit that Zane has a silver tongue and some kind of weird control over girls." Her brown eyes meet mine. "Don't you have, like, a million followers just by lifting your shirt and rolling your abs a bit?"

"Oh, yeah! I love those videos!" Vi exclaims.

I shift in my seat, uneasy with my thirteen-year-old sister-in-law seeing my content. "Someone take away the kid's phone."

Dutch grunts. "You need some tips?"

"From you? No." I drop my fork and rise from the table.

"Where are you going?" Finn asks, peering at me.

"You never answer that question, so why should I?"

Cadey looks concerned. "Zane, we were just teasing you. We know things are complicated with Miss Jamieson. Even if she wanted to like you, it's not like she can come out and say it."

I know that.

And hell, I always thought I'd be fine living my life in the darkness.

But I'm starting to get sick and tired of mud and shadows.

Maybe, for once in my life, I want to taste what it's like to live in the light.

Chapter Fifty-Five

ZANE

I hop on my bike so I can take a quick run around the cliffs. Since drumming is out of the picture and the only girl I want naked and writhing under me is Grey, all I have to work out my restlessness is my bike.

Riding one-handed is going to be tricky, but there's no law that says I can't.

Even if there was, I wouldn't care.

I walk the bike to the front lawn and I'm just about to throw my leg over it when I see a sleek black car slow down in front of the house.

It's dad.

I know by the way my skin curdles.

Hopefully, he's here to screw with Dutch's head and not mine. I'm down a hand, but my twin has two arms to throw sensible punches with.

The window winds down. Dad appears, wearing dark black shades that hide his eyes from the sunshine.

"Get in. We need to talk."

Yeah, I'm not doing that.

I use the back of my foot to flick the stand and try to keep the bike balanced with one hand, but it's so freaking heavy. Maybe I should have kept the stand down so I could balance it better while I hopped on.

By the time I figure myself out, dad's muscleheads are climbing out of the car. One wraps his hands around my bike while the other grabs my shoulder.

"Off." I wrench my arm.

He gives me a blank stare.

I glance at the house. If I shout, my brothers will come running.

I know that like I know my own name.

The problem is that Vi is here. So is Cadey.

What Dutch told me about their pregnancy issues bothers me and dad stirring up another mess with the girls right here doesn't sit well.

I decide not to put up a fight and go quietly.

I'm not as calculative as Finn and I don't have two people to protect like Dutch, but I'll hold my own. Dad's insanity can't be worse than mine.

Swinging my leg off the bike, I stomp over to dad's truck.

Once I slip inside, his meatheads start the car and we take off.

Dad stares straight ahead, wearing a black turtleneck with long sleeves that covers the ink on his body. He's wearing a watch so heavy, I wonder how his wrist can even hold it up.

"Make this quick," I snap. "I've got school."

"Aren't you suspended for a few more days?"

I glare at him. "What do you want?"

He laughs at me, and I hate him a little more than I thought I did.

"Do you know, Zane, that you remind me the most of myself when I was younger?"

I almost shudder. That's not a compliment.

Dad takes off his sunshades and clips it in the collar of his turtleneck. "I'd gotten my first record deal and had my first taste of success. The world loved me and the girls were..." He blows out a breath as if he's recalling every filthy, disgusting thing women were willing to do for him in the bedroom. "I had them eating out of my hand. Anything I wanted, any*one* I wanted, I got them like this." He snaps. "But I was so stupid that I overindulged and almost lost it all. If I didn't have someone straighten me out and show me what was at stake, I would have imploded."

"Thanks for the trip down memory lane, dad, but can you get to the point before I have to puke?"

His eyes narrow on me. "Have you thought about what I said during our last conversation?"

"How I'm stupid, reckless and not worth a crap? Yeah, how could I forget a pep talk like that?"

Dad bares his teeth in a dark chuckle.

"How far are we driving?" I glance out the window. Now that I think about it, dad is heading out of the city.

For a split second, I wonder if he's going to kill me. And then I let the thought go. If he wanted us dead, he wouldn't do it himself.

And it's freaking sad that I know for a fact that dad would kill us if he needed us out of the way.

The car makes a weird noise as we head off the road and bounce over deep potholes. I grab the handle above my window, trying to stay seated.

Dad looks unbothered. "You and Finn moved out of the house. Did you discuss it with Marian first?"

I glare out the window. If I hadn't moved out, Marian would have kicked me out herself. We haven't spoken yet, but I have a feeling she doesn't want me anywhere near Grey.

"She would have been distraught if not for the good news."

I whip my head around. "What good news?"

"Grace went on a date yesterday. She told her mom she had a nice time and she plans to see him again."

I curl my fingers into fists. Dad could be lying but, from that self-satisfied smirk curling his lips, I don't think he is.

The hair on the back of my neck stands on end. Why would Grey tell her mother that she's dating that guy? What the hell is going on?

I want to pull out my phone and text her immediately, but dad is watching every little move I make.

The car stops.

It's right near the cliffs where I kissed Grey that night. The location isn't lost on me. My eyes take in the red clay, large rocks and the dangerous cliff that leads to nowhere but air and then a rocky demise. In the light, this place looks even more desolate and menacing.

Why are we here?

Dad doesn't do anything without an ulterior motive.

This car ride.

The creepy intimidation tactic.

It's all carefully chosen.

As if they'd rehearsed it, dad's goons climb out of the car. The doors slam shut and then a heavy silence drapes over us.

Something crinkles, heightening the tension.

THE FORBIDDEN NOTE

I see dad moving an object from his left side and bringing it to his right. It's a brown envelope.

My uninjured hand remains stiff in my lap.

"Go ahead." Dad offers the envelope. "Open it."

I glare at him.

Dad lifts the envelope and shoves it in my direction, insisting without saying a word.

I drop it in my lap, and peel the tab with my right hand. Dad's eyes never leave me, almost like he's waiting for something.

Once I turn the envelope over, a bunch of pictures come flying out.

My skin starts crawling.

It's me and Grey at the dance. The quality's grainy and whoever took it was probably filming through the glass panel window in the door, but that's definitely Grey.

My lips are on her neck and she's gripping the back of my hair passionately. The next photo is of Grey in the classroom, her head thrown back, mouth open in bliss while I'm disappearing under her skirt.

Someone was spying on us.

My eyes whip up to dad and I give him a look that's pure hell. "You were spying?"

"You really should pay more attention to your surroundings when you're screwing a teacher, Zane. If you can't do the right things, at least do the wrong things well."

I grip the photographs so tight that they crumple.

The leather chair makes a noise as dad leans toward me. "Did you enjoy it, son? Being perverse? Breaking the rules?"

My nostrils flare.

"Now that you had your fun, it's time for the consequences." Dad picks up a picture and shoves it in my chest. "I told you that thing in your pants would get you in trouble someday, but you never listen, Zane. I guess it's my fault for thinking you could do better if you were warned."

His words rake against me, each one like a sharp claw digging into my flesh. My first instinct is to go after dad, but I just keep my fist at my side and glare at him.

One corner of his lips hitches up. He glances down at my clenched fingers and then meets my eyes again. "You wanna hit me?"

Freaking psycho.

I've always wondered—all these years, I've wondered—what it would be like if my father wasn't *the* Jarod Cross. If he worked a regular job at a regular office. If he came home smelling of sweat and hard labor rather than booze and some other woman's perfume. If he taught us guitar because it was once a hobby of his, a dream that he gave up because music rarely pays the bills and he loved his family more than his ambitions.

But that wasn't the cards I was dealt.

And this monster's blood runs through my veins.

Making me a monster too.

Dad lifts one of the pictures, one where I'm kissing Grey on the mouth. "What I had to learn, all those years ago when I was a newbie in the industry, you're going to learn it too. But not in front of the world. No, you're not going to make those mistakes where the cameras can pick them out and laugh at you. At us."

"You went to so much trouble," I snarl, looking at dad in rage. "But what the hell do you get out of it, huh? Just another screwed up way to control us so you can run for governor?"

His brows lift imperceptibly. This time, his eyes fill with amusement.

"Yeah, I know about that," I snap. "You need Gran's

THE FORBIDDEN NOTE

inheritance so you can fund your campaign, don't you? Teaching at Redwood for a semester, running for the chairman of the board seat, it's all to change your image so people are willing to vote for you."

Dad laughs, and the sound sends a black, chilly shadow over the car. He lets out a long sigh, as if his body can't take any more laughter and looks at me with eyes like hell. "Damn, you're an idiot."

I snarl at him.

My phone buzzes and, at the same time, there's a knock on the window.

Dad lowers the glass as I check my phone.

There are a bunch of texts in our group chat.

Cadey: Did anyone know Miss Jamieson was live-streaming?

Sol: What?

Dutch: @Zane You need to see this.

Dad winds the window back up. Whatever his goons told him has him smiling.

I click on the video link that Cadey sent.

It opens up to a video of Grey. She's standing on the front steps of Redwood Prep with a bunch of microphones around her.

My stomach drops.

What the hell is going on?

I whirl around. "Take me back to the city. Now."

Dad peers at my phone and smirks. "Not yet. Let's see what she has to say first."

I notice the blank, almost business-like tone he's using and something snaps into place in my head. I drop my gaze to the pictures and then lift my head, staring at dad with new eyes.

He's right. I *am* an idiot.

"You're not going to use these pictures," I breathe out. It all settles into place in my mind, like a million glass shards reversing in time, each one fitting back into the mirror a moment before it shatters. Whole. New. Reflecting the truth.

My heart starts to race.

"You were *never* going to use those pictures." I lift them. "They're grainy. We're wearing masks that cover our entire faces. The only people who could correctly identify us are me and Grey. No one else would look at these and use them as evidence."

Dad tilts his head to the side, saying nothing.

"Even worse, if people find out, your entire campaign would go up in smoke."

His gaze swings away from me and then ricochets back, stabbing me like a knife.

"You wanted me out here. You wanted me away from her." I think about those boxes. The fact that all the files on The Grateful Project led nowhere and yet we conveniently found out that Harris was stealing from the school. Perfect evidence. A freaking bomb dropped in our laps and wrapped in a pretty bow.

The truth jolts me to the edge of my seat. "You wanted her to do this interview. You want her to be the one who blows the whistle on Harris."

"And why would I do that?" Dad goads.

My mind races.

I dig my fingers into the chairs. "Because..." It hits me. "Because if she's the one who takes Harris down, he won't blame you for his downfall. You take him off the chessboard without any harm to yourself. Or the people behind the Grateful Project." A dark hole opens up in the bottom of my stomach and it sucks the air out of my lungs. "You know something about The Grateful Project."

My nostrils flare when dad smiles.

It's like he's taunting me, daring me to figure out the rest on my own. To admire the full breadth of his schemes. Inviting me to see the bigger picture, the way he played us all along.

"Who are the people involved in that project, dad?"

"I have no idea what you're talking about." He leans forward, his teeth flashing like a wolf's. "But if I did, I'd say they were dangerous and they'd be really, *really* upset with anyone who stirs the pot."

The rest of his words go unsaid, but I hear them like a gunshot.

Those involved in The Grateful Project would be angry enough to silence anyone who threatens to tear their masks off.

Sweat rolls down my back and it gets hard to swallow.

Grey.

No!

At that moment, I hear the most terrifying words.

"Principal Harris was just a cog in the machine that took my best friend's life. But there are others. Guilty perpetrators who were involved in The Grateful Project. Whoever you are, and whatever you've done, I will drag your sins to the light."

I look down at my trembling hand and find Grey on the livestream, eyes fierce and lips pursed in determination.

"Mm." Dad makes a sound deep in his throat. "That's not good."

Frantic, I whirl around and snap the door handle. At that moment, the child locks engaged.

I hear the snap of the door closing.

The handle won't budge.

"Open the door."

Dad just laughs.

I throw my elbow against dad's neck and drive him against the window. He slams into it with a *thunk*.

"Open the damn door!"

Teeth flashing white, dad stares me down. "You behave yourself, Zane. Behave yourself and I'll make sure no one touches this family."

On edge, I grit my teeth. "You won't *ever* get what you want. I'll make sure of it."

Shouts erupt from outside.

Dad's goons see that I have him against the window and rush to unlock the door so they can help him. I pounce on the opportunity, throw my door open and rush through the desert.

I have to stop this.

I have to get to Grey.

Chapter Fifty-Six

GREY

I'm uneasy the entire time I'm giving the speech.

Something's off.

Wrong.

I can feel it in the pit of my stomach.

A bunch of mikes are shoved in front of me, balanced on the podium. Cameras from the news reporters, from the very networks that rejected my story six years ago, hover around me.

Here to pick apart my story.

Vultures on a carcass.

Rats on a dead body.

There's a foreboding feeling gnawing, growing, preparing to explode.

I'm fine.

This is the truth.

Harris is one name I can cross off my list for revenge,

but why does it feel like I'm trading the bass on the hook for a tiny tadpole?

"Miss Jamieson?" One of the reporters squints at me. "Was Principal Harris the only one involved in the Redwood corruption?"

I grip the edges of the podium so tight, my knuckles go from brown to white. The security guards stand at attention. Black sunglasses. Black shirts. Army pants. They're all intimidating and silent, forming a fence around me.

Even with their protection, the lump in my throat grows, and with each word I say, the feeling that I'm making the wrong choice gets worse.

Jarod Cross made this happen.

I should be grateful.

And yet, it feels like I'm waiting for the other shoe to drop.

As the silence lengthens, I remember our conversation last night.

* * *

"You said you want me to believe in you." I approach Jarod while mom is in the shower getting ready for bed. "Prove it."

"I'll help you in any way I can."

The Kings are cutting me loose. It was all over their faces when they came back from their little meeting in the kitchen. I've faced rejection during my six years of investigating Sloane's case enough to know when I'm being dismissed.

Jarod Cross takes my silence for hesitation.

"I've already set up an interview at the prison. With or without me, you can meet the inmate—"

"Those are just words. You can put me off for ages if I wait for that."

"Go on then." *He folds his arms over his chest.*

"I want Harris gone."

He arches an eyebrow.

"I want him out of Redwood. I want all his power stripped. I want all the billionaires and governors and rich folks he was relying on to treat him like a pariah."

"I can make that happen."

"All I want is for you to clear the way for me."

"If it's Harris you want, you can have him." *Jarod Cross frowns. Hard.* *"But I wouldn't advise you to mention anything that you can't back up with evidence. If you do that, then we have a deal."*

* * *

When my step-father agreed to help me blow the whistle on Harris, I accepted his offer thinking I was getting the upper hand. It felt like poetic justice to use Jarod Cross to advance my own crusade.

Last night, I was blinded by my thirst for vengeance.

It was that same feeling that gripped me when I was in that treehouse with The Kings. And yet, when I was taking the help of a gang of teenagers, it felt less insidious than it does now.

A car drives up to my impromptu press conference, tires squealing and spitting rocks.

"What the hell do you think you're doing?" a voice shrieks.

I glance to the side. Harris is jogging toward the security guards. I doubt he'll get far. The scary guys kept the Redwood Prep security guards from kicking me off the sidewalk earlier. And now they'll prevent Harris from getting to me.

The reporters, who all turned out to see a piece of Redwood crumble, smile gleefully as the principal makes a fuss.

I watch it all with a sinking premonition.

Jarod called those reporters.

Everything, the livestream, the security—they were orchestrated by his hand.

It was easy.

Almost... too easy.

The sun glints against the sweat on Harris's bald head and his eyes are two angry slits in his chubby face. It's early in the morning, but already, a few kids are walking to school. Harris shoves them aside, launching toward the sidewalk.

I stiffen, my fingers digging into the wood of the podium.

The moment Harris gets close, the guards step in his way.

Cameras start flashing.

"Mr. Harris, what do you have to say about the allegations of financial fraud?"

"Were you aware that funds were being siphoned into your ex-wife's bank account?"

"How long have you been stealing from Redwood?"

Harris doesn't answer. His eyes, filled with volatile rage, remain on me.

Fear trips down my back. I dig my nails even deeper into the podium, feeling chipped wood come apart. It takes all my effort to seem unfazed.

"You think you won?" Harris laughs bawdily. "You think this is a victory?" As if someone flipped a switch, his smile collapses into a dangerous leer. "You have no idea how powerful they are. They have eyes everywhere, your home, your family, your school—everywhere. You're just a pawn in the game."

A pawn.

It finally clicks.

Too easy.

My eyes widen and I glance down at the papers I'd used to deliver my speech. Harris's bank statements are printed out and stacked neatly underneath it.

Too easy.

For six years, I struggled to get even a shred of evidence against Harris but in one night, it fell into my lap thanks to conveniently hidden boxes locked in the Redwood basement. I was so deliriously happy about gaining some ground, I never stopped to think about an important Lit lesson.

It's a staple of every English class.

What, why and who.

Why would evidence on Harris's misdeeds be stored in the basement?

Who put them there?

What did they have to gain by that?

My eyebrows hike and the truth slams into me, almost knocking me over. If not for my grip on the podium, I'd probably sink to my knees.

I've been played.

Dazed, I watch as police cars arrive, lights flashing red and blue in the bright sunshine. Cops grab Harris, their faces grim and their handcuffs jangling.

I never called them.

I wanted to talk to Harris first before anyone took him away.

But that was my plan.

Not Jarod Cross's.

Cross is the ultimate chess player and I fell right into place like a blind idiot.

The cops start hauling a sweaty, red-faced Harris away. He refuses to cooperate, thrashing and fighting like a cat in water.

"This isn't fair! I didn't do anything wrong!"

They don't listen.

Principal Harris's legs drag in the grass as the police overpower him and pull him toward a police car.

Our eyes meet.

In his, I see a marked hatred. He opens his mouth and yells for the entire crowd to hear. "You're not teaching today, Jamieson. You're fired! Do you hear me? My last act as principal is firing you!"

The cops shove Harris's head into a car and he's off.

As one, the reporters swing back to me.

"Miss Jamieson, do you feel that justice has been served today?"

Eyes blinking. Lips pursed.

They stare at me.

Pawns.

Just like I am.

I lean over the mike.

The sound of my harsh, uneven breaths fill the air.

More students are gathering. They all have their cell phones out. Watching. Waiting. Listening.

Expecting the adults to know better.

Do better.

Be better.

So they can be better too.

What would have happened if one... just *one* teacher at Redwood didn't care about losing their jobs, reputations or lives and stood up for Sloane? What would have happened if they weren't so scared of the powerful and took a stand against the system that broke and then killed her?

Would I still have her with me?

I blink rapidly and adjust the mike. The feedback screams through the crowd and people flinch.

Speaking clearly and intently, I stare at the cameras, "Principal Harris was just a cog in the machine that took my best friend's life. But there are others. Guilty perpetrators who were involved in The Grateful Project." I lift my chin and stare at the Redwood Prep sign. "Whoever you are, and whatever you've done, I will drag your sins to the light."

Chapter Fifty-Seven

GREY

I finish clearing my desk and putting all my things into the box. My co-workers stare at me like I'm infectious, saying nothing.

They're glad to see me go.

I walk out without a goodbye.

Students clear a path when I walk out. I'm sure they have questions, but no one asks me anything. It's almost like I'm a virus. Contagious.

Redwood is finally getting rid of the poison.

"Miss Jamieson!" One of my best students chases after me. "Is it true? Are you really leaving?"

I nod. "Don't let this distract you. Keep studying, okay? You're almost at the finish line."

Her bottom lip trembles and she steps back so I can pass.

Once I get to my car, my limbs feel heavy and my head is pounding. The adrenaline I felt from being on TV and giving Harris his due is gone, replaced by a strange emptiness.

No, worse than that.

It's like I'm naked.

I stripped myself of something—some armor, some protection—when I put myself in front of the world and unmasked a villain. Now, I'm left with the shambles of a life I'd built here at Redwood. It's gone. The students. The memories. Someone else will have to protect them now.

I climb into my car and grip the steering wheel.

Up ahead, the parking lot is filling up with fancy cars, all belonging to the rich and privileged students of Redwood Prep.

For a moment, I don't move.

It feels like I'm staring into a strange, yawning abyss.

My phone buzzes in my purse.

It has been for a while now, but I ignore it.

Whether it's more reporters, Harris's lawyers, mom or Zane, I don't want to talk to anyone. My thoughts are sloshing around in my head. Liquid chaos. I just want to get away. Take a breath. Feel more like myself.

The car starts with a rumble.

I'm so glad I got it out of the shop. I would have hated to catch a bus with the way I'm feeling.

Rather than heading home, I take the open road. Somehow, I find myself heading in the direction of the cliff where Zane took me the night we kissed.

When I realize where I'm going, I jolt and glance around guiltily as if someone's going to jump out of the bushes and accuse me of finding consolation in that forbidden moment.

There's no one there.

I laugh softly to myself. "You're being ridiculous, Grey."

Shaking my head, I slam on the brakes so I can make a right turn and go home.

My heels pump the brakes all the way to the ground, but nothing happens. The pedal's lack of resistance takes me completely by surprise and, at first, I wonder if I imagined the sensation.

Weird.

My brakes don't feel like that.

The world outside the car blurs as the vehicle keeps moving, speeding up on pure momentum.

I slam on the brakes again sure that the first time, I made some kind of mistake and that *this* time, the car will slow as it's supposed to.

But it doesn't.

The first trickle of panic steps in. It's like venom dripping on my face.

My eyes widen and I grip the steering wheel, pumping the brakes pedal furiously. The sound of the metal gears creaking fills my ears. It merges with the howl of the wind outside, battering my window.

Panic consumes me.

Fight or flight kicks in.

Should I jump out of the car? One quick glance at the speedometer tells me that would be incredibly foolish. There's no way I could survive.

Up ahead, I see another car coming my way.

I honk like crazy and wave my arms.

"Help!"

They keep driving, probably wondering why some crazy person is making noise on the road.

My heart is slamming into my ribs, clamoring all the way up to my throat.

What do I do? What do I do?

Zane's face pops into mind.

I reach over my purse and the car swerves wildly. Screaming at the top of my lungs, I wrench the car back so it's flying straight and pick around my purse until I get my phone.

There are a ton of missed phone calls on my notification bar.

Fingers trembling, I swipe past them and call Zane's number.

He picks up on the first ring.

"Tiger, where—"

"Zane!" I shriek louder than I ever have before. "Zane, my brakes aren't working! I can't control the car and any minute now it's going to crash." The last words are barely understandable. Something about saying my predicament out loud makes me blubber like a baby. "Zane!"

"Sweetheart, listen to me." He sounds breathless. Has he been running? "I need you to stay calm and answer two questions, okay?"

"No, I can't..."

"Okay?" He sounds more firm.

I pant sporadically. "Yes."

"Are there any cars on the road?"

"No." I lick my lips nervously.

"Where are you?"

"Close to the cliffs. The one where we k..."

His silence is pointed, as if the significance of that isn't lost on him.

The car roars.

"Zane!"

"Are your park brakes working?" he asks urgently.

"I don't know." I start to reach for it.

"Don't yank it yet," he growls. "Or you might go sideways."

The world is a blur outside my window.

The panic is biting.

"Should I turn off the ignition?"

My fingers go for the keys when I hear him yell, "No! You'll lose power and steering and you might lock the steering column."

"I have to do *something!*"

"Just take a deep breath."

I inhale even though the very last thing I want to do is breathe when my world is spinning out of control and it's very possible I might die if I don't get control of this car.

"Now, I need you to downshift and *very gently* pull the park brakes to slow your speed." He coaches me in a calm voice. "Are you doing that, tiger?"

"Yes." I follow his instructions to a tee.

The speedometer starts to dial back.

"If no one is around, you can swerve back and forth on the road. But. Be. Careful. And keep an eye out in case you're in the wrong lane."

I start to turn the steering wheel. My fingers are slick with sweat and they almost slip off the leather case.

"Don't get carried away," Zane warns. I can hear wind rushing in the background and the sound of stones shifting under his feet.

"Are you... running?"

The sounds continue. "Focus."

I keep doing what he instructed.

"It's working." Near maniacal laughter pours from my lips. "Zane, I'm slowing down!"

"Good, tiger. We're almost there. Now, I need you off the road. A rough surface will create resistance on the tires.

Can you pull over to the side? Preferably somewhere grassy?"

"I don't see grass." I peer over the steering wheel, "but I do see a sort of off-road path."

"Go there." He sounds even more breathless than before.

"Zane, are you okay?"

"I'll be okay when I hear that you're okay."

My heart skips a beat.

"Tiger."

"Mm?"

"Are you focusing?"

I drag my gaze back to the road and steer the car into the rough path. The sand and rocks help slow the car even more and I eventually roll to a stop.

"I did it!" I scream. Throwing my head back in relief, I squeeze the phone to my ear. "Zane, I stopped."

"And I'm almost there."

"What?" My eyes bug and I glance around. There's no one on the road. "How did you drive here so fast?"

"It's a long story and I'm on foot, unfortunately." His pants get even louder.

I unzip my seatbelt and glance over my shoulder, trying to see the direction he's coming from. At that moment, I hear the roar of an engine.

The sound is familiar.

I whip around.

A tinted black car speeds toward me.

For a split second, my memory takes over and I realize it's the same vehicle that tailed us that night after our meeting at the treehouse.

My fingers clamp around my phone and I let out a breathless, "Zane…"

Before I can get any other words out, the black car crashes into me. I fly to the roof and then slam back down on the steering wheel.

Pain flashes through my body, searing my skull.

And then it all goes black.

Chapter Fifty-Eight

ZANE

I…
    See…
    It…
    Happen…
    The truck that appears out of nowhere.
    The way it rams into Grey's car.
    The way her head slams on the steering wheel.
    I hear the crunch of metal.
    I feel the roar of pain that tears out of my chest and rattles through the mountains. And it's even a little louder than the squeal of the attacker's car as he backs away and speeds in the other direction.
    I want to chase him, but I can't leave Grey behind.
    I'm running and then full on sprinting toward the wreck.
    I don't feel anything.
    The wrist in a cast.

The exhaustion from hiking all the way down the mountain and then turning and heading back up to reach her.

Inside, my heart is pounding.

No, no, no.

Grey.

Please, God.

No.

With each step I take, the pain increases.

A shedding.

A trial by fire.

Somewhere, something—the little kid I was before I met her, the boy I was before I fell in love with her, the person I was before fate gave me something as precious as a person I could cherish...

It seeped away like the blood staining her leather steering wheel.

I died.

There is nothing, *nothing* worse than watching someone you love get hurt and not being able to stop it. As I cradle her face and watch her limp body, it all becomes crystal clear.

I am *nothing* without her. Damn. She's my everything.

"Grey!" I'm trembling so much I can barely move. "Grey!"

She's not responding.

There's so much blood.

So much...

The horror is paralyzing.

I want her to open her eyes. Those beautiful, intelligent, kind brown eyes.

I want her to snap at me.

Call me arrogant and obnoxious with those big vocabulary words she earned from years of reading and teaching.

"Grey!" My hands, stained with her blood, rush into her hair. She's limp in my arms. "Grey, please."

My first call is to my brothers.

My second is to the ambulance.

Everything outside of that is a blur. I don't remember the medics setting Grey on a cot and wheeling her to the ambulance. I don't remember climbing into the back of the truck. I don't remember the ride, the full-on sprint inside the hospital, the time that ticked by in the waiting room.

I don't remember when Dutch, Finn and Sol appear.

Or when Cadey shoves a bottle of water into my hands and Dutch tells me to wash the blood off.

I don't think I remember how to breathe.

Not until I hear that she's okay. That she's bruised but there's nothing broken. That she's lucky to have come out unscathed. That if the car had rammed into her just a little more to the left, she would be dead.

But she's not.

She's alive.

And I am too.

Life pours into me, my veins, my muscles, my heart.

I have a reason to keep going, to keep breathing.

I'm by her side through the night, cleaning her hands, making sure she's warm, watching over her when my brothers—one by one—leave the hospital room.

And, when she finally opens those eyes I know so well, I grab her hand.

Grey groans in pain. "Where am I?"

"The hospital." I help her to sit up.

She peers at me, her dark skin making it seem like there

are no bruises on her face. But there are and they'll throb like hell in the next few days.

"Zane," her eyes widen and she flinches, "there was a car. It was the same one that—"

"I know."

"Someone's trying to kill me," she whispers fearfully, as if the words are live snakes that'll bite her.

My fingers curl into fists. "I know that too."

Her gaze lifts to mine and what I need to do next drops into my mind with such clarity that it feels like I'm not even in control. Like it was all pre-destined. Written out in the stars.

"Marry me," I say firmly.

Her eyebrows hike. She sets a hand on her head. "Am I the one with the head injury or is it you?"

"From now on, things are only going to get more dangerous." I take her hand and rub my thumb over her knuckles. "The best way to protect you is as your husband."

The blood drains from her face as she realizes I'm serious.

I bring her hand to my lips and kiss the back of it. "Grace Elizabeth Jamieson, will you be my wife?"

* * *

Jinx: A Snare Queen Rises

Loyalties are shifting at Redwood Prep. Who decides what's right and wrong? The ones who hold all the power, of course. But some sins are more unforgivable than others.

There's a reason dirty deeds are better done in the dark.

When you drag the forbidden into the light, it wreaks one thing: chaos.

Until the next post, keep your enemies close and your secrets even closer.

- Jinx

TO BE CONTINUED...

* * *

Thank you so much for reading *The Forbidden Note*! Part 2 of Zane and Grey's story is coming soon. Visit neliaalarcon.com to learn more.

Join the mailing list at neliaalarcon.com for an exclusive deleted ending from **The Forbidden Note**.

The Darkest Note
Excerpt

The Darkest Note
Chapter One

CADENCE

The saddest key in music is Dmajor.

It's the key that rings through my head whenever I think of my mother, fingers trembling, arms dotted with pucker marks, body stretching far beyond the empty cupboard to the stash she keeps in the jar.

Some mothers store cookies in those potted tubs shaped like bears or seashells or flowers.

My mother stored weed.

She'd puff it in my face and laugh, low and haunting. It was always that tone.

D#major.

Like a vampire coughing up blood.

I love you and Vi more than anything in the world.

The line from her suicide letter plays on a loop in my mind.

I thought if I burned the words they'd disappear, but the ashes rose from the dead and started haunting me.

I love you and Vi more than anything.

Mom had nothing but audacity.

Love? Her twisted version of love was a descent straight into the darkest chords, full of brokenness and black keys.

I always saw the chaos in her, but I never let it stain me. I created a space inside my head where the music would die. Because if I couldn't hear music at all, then I wouldn't hear her notes either.

But now that she's gone, music has tiptoed its way back into my life. Or more like it slammed into me at a hundred miles an hour and now I find myself on a ride with no idea how I got there and no clue how to get off.

"Like a wreeeecking ball!" A soulless, upbeat version of Miley Cyrus's hit blasts from the speakers on the stage.

I'd descended into my thoughts to escape the noisy cover, but it seems like the music's gotten even louder.

Three girls wearing dressed-up versions of bras and booty shorts gyrate to the rhythm.

The girl in the center suddenly rises in the air, propelled by a thin harness. Her legs spread wide as she flies over the crowd, flashing everyone in attendance.

Heads tip back in adoration. Roars erupt from the audience like they're all her worshipers and this is some kind of cultish mating ritual.

I wonder if it's too late for me to rip my wig off and run.

"I thought you'd dipped, you skank!"

A hand grabs me before I can make my escape.

I force a smile on my face and ease around.

"Me? Run from this," I gesture to the blonde performer who's soaking in the 'woof, woof, woof' erupting from the guys in attendance, "lavish display of musical prowess?" I blink innocently at my best friend. "Never."

"You're such a music snob, Cadey. Now bend down so I

can unbutton your shirt. You're not showing enough cleavage."

I swat her hands away. Breeze tilts her head up and gives me a scolding look.

"Don't you dare undress me," I murmur.

"Do you see the act you're following?" she whisper-shouts. "More of your clothes need to come off. Stat."

I look down at the leather jacket, white shirt and unreasonably short skater skirt that Breeze forced on me. Black heels, giant hoop earrings, green eye contacts and heavy makeup complete the look. It's all a part of my best friend's fool proof plan to rid me of stage fright—a plan we came up with when I scored the role of Mary in our school's Christmas play.

Six years later, I still need the wig to perform in front of crowds, but at least I'm performing. I guess you can call it a rousing success.

"Maybe this is proof that I don't belong at Redwood Prep," I murmur.

"It's too late. You already accepted the scholarship." She fixes the red bob that's covering my long, brunette hair from view. Blue eyes focused, she fusses until the strands meet her approval. "And you know why you can't turn this down."

She's right. My entire future is at stake, but is it worth spending senior year as the 'new girl' at Redwood Prep, home to the elite and stupidly wealthy? Girls from the wrong side of the tracks get eaten up and spit out here.

As if summoned, the trio who just performed glide off the stage in their sparkles and glamor. They look left, catch sight of me and then laugh rudely as they walk away.

Breeze whirls around, nostrils flaring. She's already on the defensive. "What's so funny?"

"Breeze." I grab her arm to keep her at my side. The only thing shorter than my pint-sized best friend is her fuse. "Don't engage. I don't want to get on their radar."

"You can't spend your entire year being invisible," she argues, eyebrows tightening to punctuate her point.

Actually, that's my sole plan. Starting next week, I'll be a ghost floating through the halls of Redwood Prep. On the weekends, I'll trade the sprawling lawns and elegant fountains for chain-link fences, graffiti and garbage. Once I'm on my turf, I'll come alive long enough to get my bearings and do it all again the next week.

The curtains on stage wheel closed and the backstage crew frantically sweep all the glitter and confetti from the floor. There's dedicated staff for the task. I've never seen a high school production this size and it just goes to show how seriously Redwood Prep takes their music program.

"Focus. It's almost time," I tell Breeze when I see she's still evil-eyeing the Mean Girls trio.

Breeze huffs and adjusts the collar of her funky quilted shirt. "At least *you* have actual talent!" she yells loud enough for the entire backstage to hear.

"That's yet to be determined," I murmur.

She flicks me with her French-tipped nails. "Shut up. We are not allowing self-doubt to have a seat at the table."

"Self-doubt is the only one at the table," I grumble.

"What was that?" Breeze frowns and leans in. Then she quickly jumps back. "In fact, I don't want to know. It was probably something self-deprecating and not true." She flaps her hands. "Let me repeat myself, Cadence Cooper. You are going to kill it out there."

Even with my stomach twisted into knots, her words lure a smile from me.

A member of the crew approaches at that moment.

"Hey, are you Sonata Jones?"

He squints at the clipboard as if he's not sure he's saying that right.

Breeze snorts and covers her mouth with one hand. I pretend not to notice. Creating new stage names for every performance is a thing I do. It helps me pretend that I'm someone else while I'm playing.

I nod. "Yes, that's me."

He gives me another weird look before saying, "Our final act isn't here yet, so we're going to intermission. You'll be up as soon as they arrive."

"Are you kidding me?"

He gives me a blank look.

"What act is so important that you'd go into intermission rather than cut them from the lineup?" I demand. "Isn't this supposed to be a student showcase?"

It's not that I *want* to perform for the students at Redwood Prep tonight, but I'm halfway through my next-on-stage jitters. The thought of prolonging the torture makes me physically ill.

Clipboard Guy purses his lips. "Look, it's already unprecedented to have an act we've never heard of open for The Kings." His stare turns icy. "Feel free to bow out if you have an issue."

"You'd kick *me* out rather than the ones who couldn't be bothered to show up on—"

The rest of my words die a flailing death as my best friend bumps me out of the way with her hip and shrieks, "The Kings are playing tonight?"

I give Breeze a bewildered look. "You know them?"

"Of course I know them. How do *you* not know them?" she accuses.

Clipboard Guy stalks away as if he can't be bothered.

My phone chirps, drawing both our eyes to the device in my hand.

Breeze leans forward nosily. "Your brother?"

There's a painful scratch against my heart when I shake my head. Trying not to let Breeze see how much it affects me, I shrug it off. "As if he would care enough to call me before I performed."

If he did call, it probably wouldn't be to say anything encouraging.

Her eyes turn wide. "It says 'unknown number'. Maybe it's a scammer." She flicks her wrist. "Hand it over. I'll deal with it for you."

"It's not a scammer." I shut the phone off because I don't want to think about anything other than the performance.

"Who is it then?" Breeze insists.

"I don't know."

"If you don't know, how are you so sure it's not a scammer?" She plants her hands on her hips, causing her bangles to dance.

Yup. *Definitely* not a conversation I want to have right now.

I lift my head and point to the stage. "Look, they're bringing out the piano."

Breeze looks that way and her eyes brighten. "I'm going to check it out. You stay here and try not to hyperventilate."

I eye her suspiciously as she crosses the stage. When I see her chatting it up with one of the guys in the crew, I realize why she was so eager to leave my side.

Typical.

I've known her since we were in diapers. Breeze will never give up an opportunity to flirt.

With her effusive presence gone, I'm back to being

stuck in my own head.

I glance towards the exits one last time, wondering if I should back out now rather than step into this new and frightening chapter.

But those thoughts skitter away when the door bursts open. The air backstage shifts and something deep inside, some primal part of me, warns me not to look directly at whatever caused the disturbance.

I force my gaze up anyway because I never listen to that voice.

Three deities stalk backstage, all broad shoulders and brooding eyes. They move as one, like a pride of lions about to close in for the kill, bodies knifing effortlessly through the crowd that parts for them.

Predators. And proud of it. Their presence sets off a chorus of squealing from the people backstage.

They ignore the noise. Unbothered. As if this clamoring, this worship, is only right.

I can't look away even if I want to. A steady thrumming fills my head. The perfect background music to their gait. A diminished chord progression.

A# D# G

Wild and dramatic. The sound of a hurricane at its peak, winds strong enough to uproot a tree and send it lashing into a building.

They draw closer. The music in my head swells as I notice the finer details of their faces. Hard jaws and cheekbones chiseled by the gods. Straight noses. Full, pursed lips.

The two at the front look exactly alike although one is blonde and the other is raven-haired. The third has thick brown hair and almond-shaped eyes.

They're all wearing faded shirts that stretch across their large, barrel chests and taper down to narrow hips. Blue jeans cling to long legs that go on forever. Their incredible height sets them above everyone else and their gait is better than any model on any catwalk. Ever.

I've never seen people who look as hauntingly beautiful and effortlessly intimidating in real life.

Are these The Kings? The boys who were powerful enough to shut down the entire show?

The two brunettes at the ends break off. One is twirling drumsticks while the other clutches a guitar bag. The blond in the middle gets flocked by two girls who edge up under his armpits for a selfie.

Clipboard Guy huffs toward me.

I rip my eyes away from the three guys, realizing that I'm flushed and a little breathless.

"Okay, Soprana," Clipboard Guy says.

"Uh, it's Sonata."

He waves away the correction. His eyes jump from the three newcomers and back to my pale face. "Curtains go up in three."

I nod my understanding.

He turns and yells in his headset loud enough for everyone to hear. "Surano's opening for The Kings in three! Get the lights ready!"

The three forces of nature—there's no other word to describe the way they suck the air out of the room—notice me at the same time. The two on either end smirk and glance away, but the blond keeps his killer eyes on me.

Dear *Bach,* he's beautiful.

The lights burn an orange glow across his tan skin so it seems like he's bathing in fire. He raises a muscular arm—that looks like it lifts more than the guitar on his back—and squeezes the strap. I swear my soul presses in right along with it.

He smirks and my breath is ripped away by a charisma that doesn't ask but demands my attention. Everyone disappears. All I can see is him. His dark eyes trap me in place. Violent and merciless.

I feel every step he takes in my direction. The rhythm of his stride ricochets down to my toes.

It's frightening, the chokehold he has on me. I don't know where it's coming from. I only know that—if bad news had a face—it would be this guy.

Tattoos climb under his braided leather bracelet with the gold beads and disappear into the worn sleeve of his shirt. From the shaggy blond hair to the easy way the tight T-shirt wraps around his pecs, it all screams danger. Damage. Destruction restrained to the body of a Greek sculpture.

My heart starts racing at an unhealthy speed. The music in my head screeches to a halt. I don't have a chord progression for him. I don't even have a melody. He's too much. He pushes out every sound, every thought until he's all that's left.

I want to look away, but I can't take my eyes off him.

"What are you doing?" Clipboard Guy is back. And he sounds annoyed.

Breeze is beside him. Her smile is dreamy and I wonder if she hit it off with the guy she targeted on stage.

"You ready for this?" my best friend asks.

I drag my eyes away from The Kings and am eternally grateful that Breeze catches sight of them when I'm already enroute to the piano.

I hear her excited squeals and figure Clipboard Guy is getting attacked by her swatting. My best friend's arm turns into a paddle board when she's overjoyed.

The piano falls into my line of sight and I feel the draw

the way I always do. An undercurrent, similar to the one I felt when I spotted that guy backstage, vibrates the air around me. Except this tug isn't violent. It's gentle. Warm water on naked skin. Sunlight kissing my palm. Enveloping. Whispering that I could drown and like it.

I tried my hardest to resist the call, especially when mom found out that I could make money playing music. She turned something beautiful and precious and stained it with her junkie fingers.

Even so, even when music felt dirty, it still sang to me. Dug under my skin and told me that I could never run away.

I feel my skirt flare around my hips as I take my seat behind the piano. It's a Steinman and I'd be confused, dazzled even, if I didn't know that this is Redwood Prep. Of course they have one of the most expensive acoustic pianos lying around for random students to use in their end-of-summer showcase.

I lift the lid and run my fingers over the gleaming keys. The weight of it takes my breath away. I've been practicing on the keyboard I lugged out of a thrift store. Those keys sounded like a dying toy and the key bed was so cheap that it sprang like a jack-in-the-box whenever I touched it.

Just outside the curtain, an announcer yells my name to the crowd. No one claps. Not even out of politeness.

They don't know me.

They don't welcome me.

I take a deep breath and settle my nerves. It doesn't matter. They will never know me. The real me.

And there's safety in that.

I'm not Cadence Cooper.

In this red wig and heavy makeup, I'm braver than her.

Cooler. And this audience doesn't have to like me, but they will respect me. They'll listen to what I have to say.

The curtains roll back and a spotlight bursts to life, aiming right at my head. I feel the warmth of the light and hear the shuffle of bodies packed close together in front of the stage.

I keep my eyes on the piano.

The first few notes are a haunting melody. Dark. Oily. They flow through the auditorium like imps set loose from the darkest depths.

I shift octaves, taking the crowd on a journey. Faster. Faster. I pound the keys with all my heart, throwing myself into the moment because that's the only way I know how to play.

And then I pause.

The lights go dim.

A new, heavy beat pours from the speakers. It's the track I gave to the sound guys. The music is heavy on the bass and kick. Hip-hop to the max. I layer my melody on top of it. The threads intertwine like lovers who are opposites in every way yet helplessly drawn to each other.

The crowd starts to come alive. I hear their distant cheers and astonished gasps from somewhere outside of myself.

I knew that would happen. I chose this piece based on data. It's the song that raked in the most cash when I bussed in the park.

My fingers dance above two black keys as I hold out the crescendo, building to a climax along with the backing track. My back is bent over the keyboard. My hair's all in my face.

Adrenaline pounds in my veins. My soul moves right

across the keys, dancing in the flames and blowing heat all over my face.

At last, I strike the keys once. Twice. Three times.

The note suspends and then bursts like a bubble, leaving nothing but silence. I push the red strands out of my face and stand.

Someone starts a slow applause.

It catches on like a flame.

Then it sweeps through the auditorium, building to a roar.

The rich folks of Redwood approve.

Whistles follow. The roar strips me of my joy and leaves something nasty in its place. The shame comes swiftly, drenching my skin. It doesn't matter how many layers of clothing I have on. I feel naked and vulnerable.

Breeze is to my right, in the wings. She's gesturing for me to come her way. Clipboard Guy is standing behind her, clapping. An impressed look is on his face.

I struggle to breathe.

Out.

I need to get out of here.

I rush to the opposite side of the wings where the sound booth is set up. Skating past the crew who give me wide-eyed stares, I tear through a long, concrete hallway and crash through the exits.

It's only when I'm outside and far from the crowd's prying eyes that I feel the oxygen hit my lungs. A second later, the door bursts open and spits out Breeze.

She stumbles toward me. "Damn, Cadence. You were... that was... holy crap. You were incredible. Even the Kings stopped and took notice. I saw Dutch staring you down like he wanted to pick you up and," she curls her tongue, "lick your face."

"Dutch?" I don't know why, but the name sends a tingle down my spine.

"The lead singer of The Kings. The blond one. His brother's Zane." She fans her face. "Hotness personified. He's the drummer and the social media king. Finn, he's their adopted brother but he's just as sexy with his eyes and his mouth... *oh.*" She chews on her bottom lip. "I've been listening to their music for months." Breeze clutches her hands and does a little hop. "I can't believe I got to stand so close to them tonight."

"They're professionals?" I wonder. It would explain why they got preferential treatment. Although they seem a little young to be famous rockstars.

Her jaw drops. "Do you really not know?"

I shrug. Between taking care of Viola, working, and keeping up with school, I don't have time to keep up with the latest trends.

"They're *amazing*. Their singles have, legit, gone viral. Plus they're Jarod Cross's kids."

"Who—"

"If you don't know who Jarod Cross is I will literally smack you across the face," my best friend threatens.

I frown at her. "Of course I know who Jarod Cross is. What I was *going* to say is who cares? They're a bunch of rich, entitled musicians with a famous dad. Does that give them a right to show up late and hold up the entire show?"

Yeah, I'm still not over that.

"Their dad practically owns this school." She blinks. "Out of everyone at Redwood Prep, they're the only ones who have the right to do whatever they want."

A rolling electric guitar riff screams from the building. Breeze whips around, her eyes bright. "Oh my gosh! They're starting!"

"You go ahead. I'll take off now."

"What?" Her jaw falls in disappointment. "You're not going to stay? I guarantee you're going to love their set. They're amazing."

"Viola's home alone," I tell her. My little sister is thirteen going on thirty-five, but I still don't like it when she's alone with no supervision.

Her bottom lip trembles. "Okay. I'll come with you."

There's not a bone in her body that means that.

I let her off the hook. "It's okay. You stay."

"Really?" She squeals.

I nod.

Breeze jumps on me and hooks her arm around my neck. "Best best friend *ever!*"

I watch her scurry inside and turn to face Redwood Prep's sprawling courtyard. The school is as big as a college campus and twice as distinguished.

I rip my wig off and turn back into the Cinderella with rags.

* * *

Unknown Number: Nice wig, New Girl. But friendly advice, you might want to leave that on until you clear the campus. If not, I won't be the only one who knows your secrets.

Unknown Number: Call me Jinx, by the way. Welcome to Redwood Prep. And good luck. You're gonna need it.

* * *

Visit neliaalarcon.com to read THE DARKEST NOTE now

Also By Nelia Alarcon

<u>The Redwood Kings Series</u>

The Darkest Note

The Ruthless Note

The Broken Note

<u>The Plutonian Warrior's Series</u>

The Alien Warrior's Mate

The Alien Warrior's Woman

<u>The Alien Warrior's Heart</u>

<u>The Alien Warrior's Vow</u>

<u>Mates Of The Plutonians</u>

Made For The Alien Warrior

Printed in Great Britain
by Amazon